ALSO BY NICK TRIPLOW

Getting Carter

Praise for Nick Triplow

A richly researched, brilliantly crafted recounting
... of ... tion's most influential
... Jason Linskey on *Getting Carter*

NICK
TRIPLOW

NEVER
WALK
AWAY

NO EXIT PRESS

First published in the UK in 2023 by No Exit Press,
an imprint of Bedford Square Publishers Ltd,
London, UK

noexit.co.uk
@noexitpress

A CIP catalogue record for this book is available from the British Library.

This is a work of fiction. Names, characters, places, and incidents either
are the product of the author's imagination or are used fictitiously,
and any resemblance to actual persons, living or dead, businesses,
companies, events or locales is entirely coincidental.

ISBN
978-0-85730-562-6 (Paperback)
978-0-85730-563-3 (eBook)

2 4 6 8 10 9 7 5 3 1

Typeset in 11.25 on 13.9pt Times New Roman
by Avocet Typeset, Bideford, Devon, EX39 2BP
Printed and bound in Great Britain by
CPI Group (UK) Ltd, Croydon CR0 4YY

Look into my eyes
See the descent of a nation

James Varda – *Just a Beginning*

NEVER WALK AWAY

Part One: February 2006

1

Max

EVERYONE TOLD MAX HE was wasting his time. Andre Connor wasn't coming back to Tottenham. Two weeks surveillance in a dank flat on Mount Pleasant Road paid for out of his own pocket and Max was ready to concede the point. One more night, he told himself. He shut out the cold, narrowing his focus until there was only him and the terraced house across the street.

Street detail blurred into shadow as minutes and hours passed. He came away long enough to rub the tiredness from his eyes and was back in time to see a group of kids amble into view, patrolling the postcode. A tight little crew, this lot. They dressed well, which meant someone was paying. Max reckoned it had to be Connor. They made their way towards Lordship Lane like they owned every inch of pavement, which effectively they did. A lad on a bike Max hadn't seen before rode alongside for a time, pulling stops and wheelies, then jumping the kerb and heading north, leaving the others to turn back towards the estate.

A shouting match broke out between the sisters from the flatshare three doors down. Sounded like it had been brewing indoors before they brought it to the street: Sister One claiming Sister Two had ripped off her phone and racked up a bill neither could pay. Sister Two said Sister One was a tight bitch and she'd paid for the phone in the first place. Sister One said Sister Two never paid for a thing in her life. The spat grew louder, more vicious. A police patrol car came by. A second car and van pulled in behind. It took half a dozen uniforms to calm the girls down and persuade them back inside.

Max noted the time, 2.43am.

Twenty minutes later, the uniforms drove away and the neighbourhood locked itself down for the night. A black dog loped from an alleyway into the arc of a streetlight, cocked its leg and sauntered back to the shadows.

After that came a lull. Max lost track of time; his thoughts drifted as boredom set in. His mind wandered into dark places, dipping in a well of what-ifs and if-onlys, pulling out every lie he'd told, every time he should have stayed quiet, every time he'd screwed up. He saw the faces of people he'd lied to, people he'd hurt, settling on a line from the song he'd listened to last, *walk away – in silence.* He repeated the words like a mantra until they lost their meaning and slipped away.

The drizzle that had fallen since early evening turned to rain. Rain from the cracked gutter dripped against the outside wall. Some nights it was so loud he could barely think. Tonight, it gave him something to listen to that wasn't that nagging inner voice revisiting the chain of events that brought him here. DI Redding maintained the guns Connor was known to have stockpiled somewhere in north London were at his girlfriend's flat in Bounds Green, because that's what Tanesha Dorgan had told him. Tanesha was a player in her own right; she was also Connor's cousin and her story of a petty rift between them over money hardly justified selling out Connor, who'd raised her when her mum died, bringing her through the ranks of his crew as soon as she was old enough. But Redding had invested in Tanesha and wanted what he'd paid for.

Max disagreed.

Redding said nothing at the time, summoning Max back later and telling him he didn't like being called out in front of his own team. If he was so sure, go his own way and run his own damn surveillance. Redding was serious. Max was to provide daily written reports, accounting hour by hour, sharing every scrap of intelligence. He couldn't help thinking he'd dug himself a hole and Redding had walked him in. For weeks, he made those few square miles of north London his ground, walking the streets, tea and toast in the cafés, making himself a regular in the pubs. He'd blagged games of darts with locals in The Ship on the High Road, bought pints and had them bought for him. What they knew, he knew. All Redding had to do was trust him, but he wasn't about to do that. So he'd taken on the flat, paying up front out of his own pocket. Fourteen nights being Billy No-Mates and he had nothing to show for it other than creeping self-doubt and a stiff back.

He took a break, rubbing warmth into the backs of his legs. He pulled his coat around him. It gave off stale cigarette smoke and something of the flat's fustiness. That smell had got into every scrap of fabric in the place – the curtains, the rug, the sofa where he slept in daytime. He reached in his pocket for the last cigarette, the one he'd been keeping for morning. What the fuck, he'd toss for it. He balanced a ten pence piece on his thumbnail. Make your choice, he thought. He flipped. As he grabbed for the catch, there was a flicker of light in Connor's house. The coin hit the carpet and rolled onto bare boards.

Max refocused the night scope as a shape passed left to right across Connor's upstairs window. When the second pass came, he was certain and reported the contact. He heard static. He sent DI Redding a text: *Connor came home.*

A dark SUV cruised by and turned into Adams Road. When it came back the other way moments later, brake lights glowed red and it pulled to the kerb. Its occupants sat tight, waiting.

Max couldn't say for sure who was in the car with the rain and net curtains between them. His earpiece crackled. Redding demanded a call sign and code word.

Max got to the point. 'I've got movement here. Three IC3 males in an Audi Q7 and one other in the target address.'

Silence.

'You get that?'

'Do you have a confirmed ID on the target?' Redding wanting Max to be wrong.

'It has to be him.'

'That's not what I asked.' A longer silence. Thinking time. 'We're about ready to go at the Bounds Green address. I'll get some people to you once we've secured this place. Stay put.'

The men stepped out of the Audi and went inside the house. A light came on in the upstairs room. The curtains closed. Shortly afterwards, the driver came out of the front door. Max hadn't seen him before. He'd have remembered; the guy was like fat fucking Larry. Larry checked the street then stuffed himself behind the wheel. A second man followed, carrying two large holdalls that he lifted into the car's open boot.

Max updated Redding.

'Enough. Backup's on its way, just wait and hold your position.'

Max cut the link.

The Audi stayed parked, engine idling, Fat Larry smoking. There was no other movement. Max sensed the entire neighbourhood knew the score. Ten minutes since he'd called in. He whispered to himself, 'C'mon, what are you waiting for?'

The answer came with a rattle of the downstairs door handle and the crack of a bolt being forced. Evidently, not backup. A low murmur of voices in the hall. Two at least. Max slipped his coat over the chair, adding a body-shaped shadow in the darkened room, knowing it wouldn't fool anyone. He crouched out of direct sight-line of the door and listened to footfall, heel to toe on the stairs. Stair seven gave a hollow groan.

He shouted, 'Police, drop your weapon.'

The first shot split the door panel and sent a thick splinter into Max's cheek, knocking him off his feet. A second thudded in the plasterwork behind him. A third, presumably aimed at the coat, shattered the window. He held his breath, frozen, waiting. Couldn't have been more than seconds. He heard them go downstairs and followed, vaulting the last half-dozen stairs. Twenty feet behind, walking on broken glass in the kitchen and gaining through the backyard. They saw he was following and fired two shots blindly behind. Max's feet slipped from under him on the wet path, palms stinging as he broke the fall. He picked himself up and gave chase through the alley between the houses into Mount Pleasant Road, then into the estate. They ran without looking back and split by the community centre. Max followed the slower of the two towards Willan Road. He turned the corner and almost ran into the parked Audi, doors open, occupants waiting: four masked, hooded figures; four handguns aimed at him.

Max stopped dead, his chest heaving. Rain soaking through his sweater. He kept his arms away from his body and caught his breath. 'I'm a police officer. I'm unarmed. You want to see some ID?'

'I know who you are.' The voice muffled behind a red scarf. 'I know where you eat, where you drink, where you shit.'

One by one the gunmen retreated to the safety of the Audi until only the last was left. Andre Connor pulled the scarf from his face. He lifted his gun high, walked up to Max and pressed the business end firmly against his forehead. 'Down on your knees.'

Max felt blood run warm down his face. His teeth bit on splintered wood and he spat.

Connor pushed the gun harder. 'On your fucking knees.'

Max made eye contact. 'Not in this life.'

'You know what this is gonna look like?' said Connor.

Max imagined news footage zeroing in on the moment of impact. His body dropping. Cold, grey silence. It would look like what it was, a police officer killed in the line of duty. For the mute witnesses in the glow of phone screens in Stapleford House, it would look like a settled score. Another line in Andre Connor's legend. For every fucker with an opinion to sell, it would be content.

Connor said, 'That's my mum's house you're snooping on.'

'She's not there now, though, is she?'

Max felt Connor's grip tighten. This was the moment.

Connor looked up at the windows. 'My streets. My neighbourhood. My estate. I own it like I own you right now. I see you again...' Connor dragged the barrel across Max's forehead, twisting it into his eye. 'I will shoot your fucking eyes out.'

Connor gave a nod and the Audi reversed slowly. Fat Larry behind the wheel, Tanesha Dorgan in the back, phone pressed to the window filming one for the family album.

'My estate, remember that.' Connor climbed in and they were gone.

The sun dragged itself over the houses on Mount Pleasant Road as Max sat on the arm of the chair by the broken window. He held a wad of gauze to the wound on his cheek. The paramedic said he'd need stitches and a tetanus shot. DI Redding wanted to see him first – just arrived, now hunched in the rain in conversation with a uniformed sergeant in the street below. Max was distracted by the bullet buried in the plaster just above head height. Closer than he'd realised. Waiting gave him time to think through the night's events: changes in the street's rhythms he'd failed to connect; the foot soldiers calling it a night too soon; the messenger on the bike; even the sisters' screaming match distracting the community police team. Connor had known he was there. The rest had been a show for his benefit.

Redding's tread was heavy on the stairs. He threw a cursory glance at the door panel shot to matchwood and ran his fingers through thinning hair – he hated getting his hair wet. 'You got a towel?'

'Bathroom. Second left.' Max nodded towards the corridor. His tongue felt fat in his mouth.

Redding came back, gently rubbing his hair with Max's ragged blue hand-towel. 'So, you want to tell me why you couldn't wait ten minutes?'

'You didn't have ten minutes.'

'I told you to stay put. Your brief was to observe and report.'

'Did you find anything?'

'What?'

'Bounds Green, Connor's girlfriend. Did you find anything?'

'Not as yet.'

Redding turned to leave, then changed his mind. 'I took you on because you were an experienced officer. I was told my people would benefit from your knowledge, your influence. It's not working, is it?'

It wasn't true. Redding had accepted Max under sufferance because he'd shown himself incapable of handling organised operators like Andre Connor.

'Yeah,' said Max, 'which part of being your *asset* did I get wrong exactly?'

Redding picked his words precisely, as if he'd drafted his statement on the way over. 'The part about being a lone police officer pursuing armed suspects into Broadwater Farm Estate without due consideration for yourself or my operation, and against my explicit orders. That part.'

'And what about Tanesha? Sends her love, by the way.'

Redding ignored the comment. He scanned the room. 'I don't know how you live like this. This place is disgusting, a bloody tip.' He tossed the soggy towel on a chair.

'You want me to get a cleaner?' Max fished the flattened pack of Marlboro Lights from his coat pocket and lit his last, slightly bent, cigarette.

2

Tyler

MICHAEL TYLER CAME OUT of Oakwood Station and took his bearings. The fog had barely lifted. Traffic was slow and exhaust fumes caught the back of his throat. He pulled off his gloves and reread the directions he'd written down. He took his place in the bus queue. Unfamiliar route numbers and names of places he'd never been made him feel a long way from home. He wrapped his arms around himself against the cold. Even with the extra thick socks Emily insisted he wear, his toes were numb within minutes. He fumbled through layers of clothes for his watch. By the time the bus sailed through the murk and pulled to a stop, he was late.

He sat downstairs on the bus and watched tree-lined suburban streets pass, looking for the church he'd noted as a landmark and wishing he was in the spare room at home, quietly researching the Tyler family tree as he did most Saturdays. But this was important, he assured himself. The previous evening he'd had a call from Patrick Theobold, senior consultant in the director's executive team, asking if he'd retrieve a file from the director's home address and return it to the department on Monday morning. He didn't go into the specifics over the phone, but there was, he said, the issue of a 'classified data breach' – something on the file that ought not to have been there. He rattled on about 'documents sent in error' and needing to 'avoid embarrassment'. After thirty years as a civil servant, the last fifteen in the Home Office, Tyler had said yes without thinking.

As he approached Derek Labrosse's home on the outskirts of Enfield Town, the porch light came on, but it wasn't the director who opened the door before he'd had a chance to ring the bell. The woman looping a pale grey silk scarf around her neck was clearly irritated at being made to wait. 'About time,' she said. 'I'm supposed to be meeting my daughter in town at four.' She spoke over his apology, waving away the ID badge he presented for her to check that he was who he said he was. A clutch of thin wooden bangles slid down her wrist. 'Christ knows why this couldn't wait until Monday. You'd better come in. And wipe your feet, will you, I've just had the floors polished.'

Tyler did as he was told.

She softened a little. 'Jesus, you're freezing. Do you want a hot drink, I could heat up some coffee from this morning, if you don't mind it nuked?'

He must have looked confused.

'Microwaved.'

'Please, that would be lovely.' Tyler pocketed his gloves and warmed his backside against the hall radiator. A series of muted modern paintings hung on the walls. Thick oil-textured rusts and browns; spindly wind-bent trees edging unploughed fields. He looked up at a wide open-plan staircase which opened out on a galleried landing and a series of wooden panelled doors. The air was thick with the smell of furniture polish.

'It's a touch on the grand side. I always feel I ought to wear a ball gown when I come down for breakfast.' The woman smiled and handed him a mug. 'We'd better get on with it. I'll take you up to Derek's study.'

Tyler followed up the stairs. He stood aside while she unlocked a door at the far end of the upstairs gallery. A monumental desk filled a third of the room, its leather top littered with not-so-neat piles of paperwork. 'Presumably you know what you're looking for.'

Patrick Theobold's direction had been unambiguous: the file would be in a green cardboard jacket, stamped *Confidential*, and have a unique reference number. The way he described it, Tyler assumed it would be ready to collect. He showed the woman the reference.

'That means nothing to me.'

Tyler scanned the loose papers, shelves crowded with books and management journals, battalions of box and lever arch files, and a squat oak filing cabinet. 'It's difficult to know where to start.'

'I really don't have time for this.' She keyed some numbers into her phone and waited. 'Bugger, he's not answering... Derek, look it's me. I just wanted to let you know Mr...?'

'Tyler.'

'Mr Taylor is here to pick up this file your people called about. I'm supposed to be meeting Ruth from the train at four. God knows what time I'll get there. I'll leave my car at Oakwood and give Mr Taylor the keys to lock up. We'll see you later for supper.'

She ended the call and issued instructions about which keys fitted which locks, which he should leave unlocked and to post the keys back through the letterbox. Her boot heels sounded hard on the wooden staircase. When she slammed the front door, the house shook.

Tyler unzipped his jacket. He told himself that, by working systematically, he'd be done and home sooner. On the way he'd buy flowers for Emmy and a bottle of Merlot to go with the lasagne she was cooking for their dinner. He had told her only that he was going into work and given an excuse about preparing for a meeting that had been brought forward unexpectedly. Mr Theobold insisted the task remain confidential between the two of them. She'd given his hand a sympathetic squeeze before he left and asked that he call when he was on his way home.

He pulled box files from the shelves one at a time, leafing through the contents until only the desk remained to be searched.

The desk drawer opened part way, then stuck. He tugged sharply and it opened fully, sending a muddle of notes, receipts and paper-clipped theatre tickets fluttering to the carpet. Beneath a stack of correspondence was an A4 manila envelope, sealed and addressed to Mr Jonathon Coles at an address in St Albans. Most of one corner had been torn – the result, he assumed, of his wrenching the drawer open. A green cardboard cover was visible through the tear. Tyler slit the envelope seam from its ripped corner, pulled out the file and checked the reference, 62A/47/09.

He stared at the file for a few seconds, trying to make sense of how it had been in the possession of anyone from his office, let alone how it was mistakenly sent to the director or was being forwarded to what appeared to be a private address in St Albans. Mr Theobold said that, if he returned the file, its absence would be overlooked. Any problems, contact him and only him. Tyler flicked through the first few pages, absorbed by what he was reading. It was inconceivable that such privileged information had ever been allowed to leave the building. Correspondence between directors and ministers was subject to strict protocols. He'd seen enough to realise 62A's confidential designation was woefully underpowered. Tyler told himself he didn't need to know. All that mattered was that he'd accomplished the task. He closed the file. As he stood up, something made him look behind. Derek Labrosse filled the doorway, red-faced, running his gaze over the chaos of his office. 'Who the fuck are you?'

Tyler's heart thumped. He slid the file back into its envelope. 'I'm sorry. I was sent to pick this up and bring it back to the office.'

Labrosse motioned for him to put the file on the desk.

'Is there a problem?'

Labrosse raised an eyebrow. 'Other than you breaking into my house, ransacking my office and reading classified material? No, no problem at all.'

'Your wife let me in. She left you a message. Please, check your phone. My name is Michael Tyler. I work in the third floor registry.'

'It comes to something when they send an amateur from my own department. What's your end of this, you getting paid? Or you doing someone a favour?'

'Neither. Please, you need to ring Mr Theobold.'

Labrosse snorted. '*Theobold*. That makes a kind of sense. Him and the Americans. What about Lillico, is he a part of this? Of course, he is. Who else?'

Tyler tried to remember, had Theobold mentioned other names? 'I don't –'

'*Don't* tell me you don't know.' Labrosse slapped his hand down hard on the desktop. The keys dropped from the drawer. 'Who else?'

Frightened to say he didn't know a second time, Tyler shook his head.

'Bugger this, we'll let the police deal with it. You can explain to them. Stay here.'

As Tyler remembered it, what he did next was the result of fear; it paralysed his thinking in a way that made the irrational seem perfectly sensible. All that mattered was removing himself from the situation, the wrongness of it suddenly blindingly obvious. Others would have to explain. He put on his coat and picked up the envelope containing the file. As he started down the stairs, Labrosse was coming to meet him. 'I told you to stay.'

'I'm sorry, I have to go.'

Labrosse snatched at the file. It slipped from the torn-open envelope. Off balance, Labrosse lurched backwards, his free arm flailing for a non-existent banister, striking Tyler in the mouth, then clutching air. In almost comical slow motion he struggled to regain his footing, trying to correct the bizarre backwards stride he'd taken. He twisted, stumbled and fell. His face hit the stairs, wrenching his neck. He slumped on his side to the bottom stair and was still. Blood spilled from his nose across the newly polished floor.

Tyler was in the bathroom for a long time. Labrosse's backhand had split his lip and he let it bleed into the sink. He rinsed his mouth and washed his face in cold water, letting the tap run until the blood disappeared. He dried his face and refolded the towel, placing it on a pile of fresh laundry in the airing cupboard. A week's worth of crisply ironed white Van Heusen shirts hung on identical padded hangers.

The house was in darkness. The porch light's orange glow shone into the hall across Labrosse's body. Tyler made his way down the stairs, stepping carefully over the dead man. His eyes were partially open, the neck twisted, bulging oddly. Until that moment Tyler had known death only as a controlled experience, hospice-clean and in the hands of those for whom it carried a quiet certainty. This was not like that at all: it had blood, the crack of broken bone, and a dead weight fall. It carried culpability. He should call people, he realised that. Tyler dialled Patrick Theobold's number.

An hour later, he stood at the end of the platform at Oakwood with the file and its bloodstained pages in a Sainsbury's 'Bag for Life'. Thinking but not thinking, unable to see more than ten feet ahead as the fog grew denser, muffling the slow beat behind his eyes.

On Saturday evening he thought through what would happen when the police came, running the sequence in his imagination: dark figures crowding the hall, their uniforms and their bulk. An invitation to answer questions as they sat on the edge of the sofa. *Where were you this afternoon between the hours of two and five o'clock?* And he would have no answers, only the truth. He imagined Emily's expression when he came clean and brought out the bloody pages from the file.

The police didn't come on Saturday night. On Sunday, they visited Morden Hall, Emmy's favourite place for a browse among the gardens and a skinny latte overlooking the wintry pond. Snowdrops were in flower; the daffodils and crocuses wouldn't be far behind. Back at home, she brought out her sketch pad and pencils. Morden had inspired her, she said. Plans for their own garden. It needed freshening up.

Tyler waited for the knock at the door.

On Monday, he phoned in sick. After breakfast, he locked himself in the spare room, trying to pick up the thread of family history he'd left on Saturday morning. The names and dates held no interest. All the project had confirmed was that he was the latest in a succession of middling achievers: tradespeople, shopkeepers, conscripts and clerks. He closed down the PC and stared at the blank screen. Later in the afternoon, he slept on the sofa in front of *The Third Man*, waking up to Anton Karas's zither and Joseph Cotten's long, long wait for the girl who walks by.

That night they were in bed when the house phone rang once and stopped. He was halfway into his dressing gown, heart pounding. He rested his head on the pillow, wondering if he'd heard the phone or dreamed it. Emmy's breathing had kept its familiar sleep rhythm. He listened to footsteps in the street outside, envisioning the front door off its hinges, the lock smashed in one blow. His imagining had boots on the stairs, torches shining in their eyes. Hard men with harsh voices.

Accusations as they hauled him from bed in his pyjamas. Emmy crying. They were at the front gate, waiting. He was afraid to move, then the voices and laughter grew distant, footsteps echoing in the silence long after they'd gone.

When the children were small, Tyler had developed the ability to rest in a semi-awake state, sensing the slightest noise – those little coughs and cries the kids had – almost before they happened. Sometimes they would want to be held; a few quiet words could bring them back from their bad dreams to a place where daddy would make everything safe. That night he prayed. *Our Father, who art in Heaven.* Words of comfort, doing for him what he'd done for his children. He slept, but only for seconds. *Give us this day our daily bread.* Then another noise outside. Then sleep. Then awake. *Lead us not into temptation. Temptation*, the word repeated. But he hadn't said the part about *Forgive us our trespasses.* Or had he? *Amen. Amen. Amen. Amen. Please God, don't let them come.*

On Tuesday morning the phone rang three times and stopped.

'Probably a call centre.' Emmy kissed him. A friend was giving her a lift.

When she'd gone the phone rang again. Tyler picked up.

It was Theobold. 'Your mobile is switched off and I haven't seen you in the office. I was wondering whether you were dead. Apparently not.'

'I was expecting a call,' said Tyler.

'And now you've got one.'

'From the police.'

'It's been dealt with.'

'But I didn't report what happened to the police.'

Theobold paused as if conferring with someone else. 'That won't be necessary.'

'They'll want a statement, and Mrs Labrosse –'

Theobold said, 'I've given the police the statement you gave me over the phone. Mrs Labrosse is being supported by us and by her family. Everything else is taken care of. I can clarify any other issues when you come into work. Tomorrow would be good, if that's okay with you. Don't forget the paperwork.' He hung up.

That evening when Emily came home, she tossed the *Evening Standard* on the table open at a photograph of Derek Labrosse. 'One of the girls at work showed me this. Didn't you know him?'

Tyler shrugged. 'I met him once or twice in passing.'

He changed the subject, talking about booking a weekend away at the coast, but Emmy wasn't deterred. 'You must have known *of* him, people always know things about people.' Her smile grew thinner.

Tyler forked through the leftovers on the edge of his plate. 'Please can we let it go? I'm not going to gossip about someone I hardly knew.'

Emmy cleared the dinner things, crockery and cutlery clattering in the dishwasher. When she left for her evening class, Tyler retrieved his old brown briefcase from the cupboard under the stairs. He worked the combination and clicked the catches. He spread File 62A's contents across the kitchen table. Some loose pages were stuck together with blood. Those that were difficult to separate, he steamed over a boiling kettle. He moved everything upstairs to the office, turned on the computer and scanned a Home Office letterhead. He retyped the content of the spoiled pages using the same corporate font, then printed and filed the copies in date order, marking their file number identically to the originals, destroying each bloodstained page as he went. It wasn't perfect, but it would do.

Just after ten o'clock, he heard Emmy's key in the door. There were, he counted, six pages stained to varying degrees that he hadn't had time to retype. He locked them back in the case with the doctored file and left it under the desk. He came downstairs and kissed Emmy on the cheek. While the kettle boiled for tea, he polished his shoes ready for the morning.

Second carriage from the front on the 07.12 to Victoria Station. He opened the biography of Francis Walsingham he'd been reading. Sunlight flickered between city buildings across the passengers' faces. As the train movement rocked him to sleep, his grip on the book loosened and it fell through his fingers. Jerked to consciousness, he reached down to pick it up and touched the hand of the woman sitting next to him. He sensed the other passengers measuring the mishap and his reaction to it. He straightened the book's creased corners, thinking how closely they watched.

In the office, he placed the file in a new envelope, resealing and taping the seams and placing it inside another envelope as Theobold instructed. He addressed the outer envelope and took it upstairs to the Director's office. The atmosphere was subdued, the Director's PA had been crying. He handed over the envelope. 'It's for Mr Theobold.'

'I'll see he gets it when he comes out of his meeting.'

As he walked down the back stairs to his office, it struck him how easy it was for people like Patrick Theobold to construct their morality in a way that allowed rule-breaking without consequence. He'd never been one of those people. For him, without honesty there was no release.

Theobold found him later as the afternoon team meeting broke up. His appearance hurried Tyler's colleagues from the conference room. When they were alone, he closed the door and sat next to Tyler, clasping his hands in front of him. Tyler stared ahead.

'What did you make of it?' said Theobold.

'I didn't read it.'

Theobold smiled. 'Of course not.'

Tyler turned in his seat. 'You knew full well that no one in my office could have had hands on that file. Why did you send me?'

'Think of yourself as a courier.'

'*He* thought I was stealing. And he was right wasn't he? And his wife – oh my God, his poor wife. She needs to understand what happened.' Tyler took off his glasses, rubbing his eyes.

'Give me those.' Theobold took the glasses, removed a cream silk handkerchief from his breast pocket and polished the lenses. 'Do you think she has a right to know her husband came home half-pissed and fell down his own stairs – surely you realised he'd been drinking. Or perhaps we could tell her that instead of delivering government policy, he'd been working to undermine it and contravened the Official Secrets Act in the process. Do you think that would be a comfort to her right now?'

'Can I have those?'

Theobold lifted the glasses to the light. 'What I'm doing is supporting you, Michael. Just as I'm supporting Mrs Labrosse.'

'I should go to the police.'

He laughed. 'For what reason?'

'To *explain* for Christ's sake.'

Theobold refolded the handkerchief, picking it off the table like a cabaret conjurer, fussing until it was perfect with three peaks visible in his breast pocket. 'I can see why you'd think that might be the right thing to do, but ask yourself, who gains? Certainly not you.'

Tyler said, 'I think the police –'

'Your conscience. Is that what this is all about? You feel bad?'

'Of course, I do. Bloody terrible. Please may I have my glasses?'

'But the police aren't interested in you, are they? They're satisfied there's no case to answer. The coroner will deliver a verdict of accidental death, which according to you is what happened. Am I right?'

Tyler nodded.

'So, if you present yourself now, you'd just be muddying things and making the police appear incompetent. Though I do admire your honesty.' He placed the glasses back on Tyler's face, settling them gently on the bridge of his nose. 'Better?'

'Yes. Thank you.'

'Just be aware of the pressure you'd put yourself and your family under. It would be far worse than you imagine. You'd lose your job for a start. There'd be a court case. You don't strike me as the sort of person who'd keep up a principled stand in the dock for very long. That's aside from the cost. Legal representation does not come cheap. Go cheap and risk a custodial sentence. Are you ready to tough that one out? What if the CPS decided somehow that it was manslaughter? It's not impossible.' He patted Tyler on the back and went to the corner table, tilted one of the flasks and poured a coffee. 'Some left, you want one?'

Tyler's hands were shaking. 'It doesn't alter the fact that you sent me to the Director's house and before then I'd never touched that file.' His voice dropped. 'I should tell the police I was there. I've made up my mind.'

Theobold emptied a carton of creamer in the cup. He walked towards Tyler and slapped him hard across the cheek. His glasses flew across the table and over the edge. Instinctively, his hands rose to protect his face. When he dropped them a few seconds later, Theobold hit him again, harder than the first time. 'You want this? Is this what you want? What it'll take for you to understand?'

He flinched again when Theobold sat next to him. As the ringing in his ear subsided, Theobold's voice took on a note of concern. 'Please Michael, take my advice, you really don't have a choice, so put the thought out of your mind. No one wants it. And you wouldn't be able to handle the consequences. Understand?'

He swallowed hard. 'Yes.'

'Do. You. Understand?'

'Yes.'

'Say it.'

He looked up, tears pricking. 'I understand.'

3

Max

MAX SLEPT A LOT in the first week of his suspension. After that, barely at all. He stayed close to home around Swiss Cottage. He'd paid cash for his second-floor, one-bedroom flat in Goldhurst Terrace after a windfall some years ago. It had been legal, if not entirely above board. Either way he'd taken advantage of the last, brief window of affordability for someone like him in a neighbourhood like this. It wasn't an especially affluent part of London compared with others nearby, but it still priced out most Londoners. Max was content here. His corner of NW6 was home and sanctuary. A world away from the noise of the job. It had his books and records, and a framed *Down By Law* film poster on the wall.

On Friday morning, he received the call he'd expected, inviting him to a session with an HR welfare officer. Certain this was DI Redding looking to force him out, he said he couldn't talk and hung up. But somewhere along the chain of command the decision was made for him. A second call later that day made it plain, he was to make the appointment. Damned if he did, damned sooner if he didn't. He said he needed the weekend to think about it; he'd get back to them on Monday morning.

There was something he needed to do first.

The morning of the appointment was clear, bright and cold. Max dared to think the worst of the winter had passed as he walked the short distance from Victoria to a Georgian townhouse on the corner of Ebury Street.

The receptionist buzzed him in, leading him through to Sally Meehan's consulting room: a neutral space decorated with the kind of artless prints sent as freebies from your friendly office stationery supplier. Max dropped into one of the two easy chairs, recognising the counsellor's voice – soft, posh Geordie – somewhere in another room. In their phone conversation she'd assured him she had a track record of tidying up the lives of men who lied for a living. It had sounded like a threat.

She breezed in on the dot at ten-thirty and set her laptop on the table. As she leaned over, a small gold crucifix dropped out from her sweater. She replaced it quickly, ordering her notes, resting them in her lap. 'So, Mark, it's good that we can meet finally. Before we start, I want to explain what I'd like to get from the session and we can take it from there.'

'People call me Max. From my surname, Lomax.'

She didn't ask why. If she had, he wouldn't have told her. Covert operations meant creating an identity close to your own. In his previous job he'd been Max for so long he answered to no other name. It was who he was.

'As you know, *Max*, we should have been having this conversation last week, but you didn't want to do that, which makes it doubly important that we make headway today. Otherwise I'll need to submit a report which says you've decided not to cooperate and, based on the statement of your senior officer and several colleagues, you're unfit for work and unlikely to return for the foreseeable future, if at all.' She twisted a biro between her fingers. 'Inspector Redding has accepted you were working under extreme pressure and that your reaction was –'

'Justified.' He sat back in the chair.

'Not exactly, but we can start there. Pursuing suspects into

Broadwater Farm without support from colleagues and against DI Redding's orders, you feel that's justified?'

'In context, yes. Andre Connor was an important target. Still is as far as I know. I was attempting to arrest one of his crew. That makes a difference. Shows he's fallible, gives us a chance to learn more about his intentions and who knows, maybe persuade a young kid there's a better life possible, one that doesn't end with him dead on the street.'

'The suspects were armed.'

'I'm aware of that.'

She flicked a page from her notes and quoted, 'In 2003, you were a member of the Special Demonstration Squad under command of the then Detective Chief Superintendent, now Assistant Commissioner, Kilby. On that occasion you also made choices that endangered an ongoing operation.'

Kilby. Out of nowhere, Max sensed the hand of his former mentor, otherwise how had she had access to Special Operations details? 'That was different, personal. I had a relationship with a woman who was involved with the organisation I'd infiltrated. I'd lived under an assumed identity for an extended period. That kind of thing happens.'

'Often?'

'Once was enough.'

'It says here you were withdrawn because there were doubts regarding your reliability, that you were "politically and personally compromised".' She turned another page. 'According to the file, an independent security services assessment considered you a security risk. You placed yourself and other officers in danger as well as jeopardising the integrity of an operation into a known subversive organisation. You allowed this woman to influence your actions. I'm quoting here, *"the officer was manipulated into making decisions that were not in his best interests or those of the operation, suggesting, at best, that his loyalties were split."'* Ms Meehan looked up. 'She suspected you of being a serving police officer. You maintained your cover was intact, when you knew it wasn't.'

Max counted off. 'One, there were no other officers involved other than my handler, who had no issues at the time and certainly wasn't in danger. Secondly, the threat within the group, so far as it had been a threat, was nullified. It broke up, a natural process. People move on, they have disagreements, whatever. Lastly, I came out when Kilby ordered me to, because we'd achieved all we set out to achieve. At which time the relationship ended. I moved on.'

'But you placed yourself at risk. Just as in Tottenham.'

'That's not how I see it.'

Ms Meehan closed her notes, folded her hands in her lap. 'Even if we accept that and even if we back your judgement that you had cause to go after the armed suspects, as reckless as that was, it doesn't explain this...' She turned the laptop, lifted the screen and pressed play. Max recognised the raw image of Mount Pleasant Road in CCTV monochrome. 'We've got a man in a hoody with a scarf around his face. Timeline says 03:24, Monday before last. The man walks towards a parked four-by-four. He takes out the headlights with a hammer, then empties a can of liquid over the roof and the bonnet, judging by the effect on the paintwork, some kind of corrosive. A second man appears and confronts him. The second man is assaulted and left on the pavement. The assailant walks out of frame and we pick him up further along the street at which point he drops his hood and is caught cold by a second camera. She paused the footage with Max's image frozen on screen. 'So?'

He said nothing.

Ms Meehan persisted. 'Come on, Max. It deserves a response, doesn't it? What do you *think* about that person? Because I think he looks out of control.'

She was wrong. He'd known exactly what he was doing. That night was a parting shot, the sum of his frustrations after months of work, gathering intelligence and setting the operation up. There was no chance of Connor's arrest now. The guns would have gone, stashed across north London and beyond. He glanced at the screen again, then looked straight at Sally Meehan. 'Andre Connor thought by shoving a gun in my face he'd owned me. That was my considered answer and it made me feel better.'

'*Considered*. I'll say. This is two weeks later.'

Max sat up. 'Do you really want to know what it makes me think? It makes me question why there are CCTV cameras covering Connor's place that weren't there before, given that I asked Redding for covert cameras in exactly those locations on three separate occasions. It makes me *think* that a senior officer is covering himself because he knows he's not very good at his job.' He reached forward and closed the laptop. 'Redding shoved me into that hole with zero support because I challenged his authority. He paid lip service to wanting my know-how, then dumped on me when it wasn't what he wanted to hear. But what do I think? That it really doesn't bother me.'

She lowered her voice. 'The footage alone is enough to have you convicted of a dozen offences. It could get you sent to prison. This…' she motioned to the closed laptop, 'it's a form of surrender. A failure of reason, of training, of common-sense, of *instinct*. I think when you ran into the estate, you knew Connor would be waiting. I think you wanted him to be. You wanted the confrontation and that worries me.'

She waited for a reaction and when none came, she said, 'You need to give Assistant Commissioner Kilby a call. If you're serious about finding a way back, I suggest that would be the route.'

Max shook his head. 'You've read my file. He buried me.'

'Let me put it another way, you might want to ask yourself how this has been kept quiet. DI Redding was all for asking Connor to make a formal complaint. You'll need to make another appointment to see me. Come back in a couple of weeks and we'll talk again. In the meantime, speak to Kilby. Make your decision and I'll rewrite my report.'

As she wound the session to its close, Max felt a slow release of intensity. His world had become diminished in recent weeks, preoccupied by the thought he'd be forced to resign. But that wasn't going to happen. Not today and not on DI Redding's say-so. They drifted into conversation, feeding off generalities until the end of the allotted time. Afterwards, he walked through the streets of Belgravia, past embassies and gated gardens in tree-lined squares. A bright day and Kilby wanted him back. That was worth something.

Part Two: June 2006

4

Max

A HOT SATURDAY AFTERNOON in mid-June and Turnpike Lane was a collision of colours, rhythms, transactions and smells, not all of them legal. Max passed doorways reeking with dope smoke. His first weekend off since he'd rejoined Kilby's staff, he had no trouble turning a blind eye, slowing his pace to match the afternoon crowd. Sally Meehan had been as good as her word, signing him off on the condition that his work was restricted to back office functions. Since then he'd functioned as Kilby's proxy in routine meetings, taking on policy research and strategic analysis, if not with relish, at least appreciating the favourable odds of not being shot at. Today was about something else, a conversation with an old friend. Something he'd been meaning to do since that morning in Sally Meehan's office.

He was drawn by the gaze of a dark-skinned young woman leaning against the open door of a convenience store. In the window a handwritten sign claimed: *We Sell Everthing*. He returned her smile. She asked if he was thirsty.

'I'm fine, thanks.'

'You are tired, buy a cold drink.' She walked a few steps alongside. 'I have cold beer in the fridge.'

In the shop it was cooler and darker. Max lifted his sunglasses. A group of older men played dominoes behind a hooked-back bead curtain, the air around them heavy with cigarette smoke. One of the players glanced over his glasses, slamming down a tile to a riot of protest. Max watched the next hand transfixed. The old boys played with the aggression of prizefighters. One guy waved him through. They wanted him to play. The girl was at his shoulder. 'No, no, no, time for games is later, maybe.' He got it, by the time they'd finished with him, he'd have nothing left to spend. She drew him into the shop, sweet-talking him through a tour of the crowded shelves, pulling out arbitrary food items – groceries without which, she insisted, his life would forever be incomplete. He came out after ten minutes with Spanish red wine, bread, cheese, apple tea, and chilled Evian. She waved him on his way towards Wood Green High Road. When he looked back, she was reeling in someone else. His shirt smelled faintly of her perfume.

He stopped at an anonymous green front door. A white-on-black embossed nameplate read DELANEY AND COLES SOLICITORS above a faded Legal Aid logo. Max looked up and saw movement at the blinds. He took a chance that it was Delaney not Coles and pressed the intercom: three short rings, one long.

A woman's voice. 'Who is it?'

'It's Max.' A silence, the sun beat the back of his neck.

The intercom crackled. 'I'm working.'

'Can I come up?'

'No.'

The intercom went dead.

Max waited a few moments, then pressed again. A pimped BMW slid into the kerb, bass-bins pounding. Three Asian lads gave him the once-over, gunning the engine. After a few seconds, the door buzzed open. He took the stairs two at a time. 'I think I've upset the locals.'

Liz waited on the landing, dress-down Saturday in dark jeans and a pale blue collarless shirt. She lifted her glasses to hold back her hair. She looked tired, the lines at her eyes heavier than he remembered. It had to be three years since they'd last met. There hadn't been a week go by that Max hadn't wanted to see her again.

They'd first met soon after he began to infiltrate the activist groups that came together around Green Lanes in the early 2000s. Liz was a notable and vocal presence in meetings at Tottenham Green Centre on Tuesday evenings. Their first proper conversation was at an impromptu post-pub gathering in a flat just off Bruce Grove. In the back room, away from heartfelt discussions of student activists, charity workers, teachers, and a handful of refugees chewing over injustice and real-world suffering, Liz and Max talked mostly about music and books. They'd both been at a Television gig at the Town and Country Club in 1993. On the night, Max had found himself standing next to Robert Plant. Liz ragged him about white boys appropriating the blues. Going their separate ways at dawn, he'd known he was in trouble. His cover as a mature student on an English course at Middlesex University, with little life experience, kept him at the periphery of political debate. As the weeks went by, he discovered that Liz had a watching brief over the groups that used Delaney and Coles' office as a holding address. It didn't take Max long to work out that her heart and soul were set on where the real work was. Quietly authoritative, thoroughly professional, Liz was committed to legal activism, making her name by taking on hard-to-win immigration cases against the Home Office. Max had done his research and gradually they were drawn together. Falling in love was the last thing either of them needed. But it had happened and it was real. For Max, it'd never gone away.

Liz said, 'You know the only white faces that knock at this door are lawyers and police.'

'It's not like I'm in uniform.'

'Might as well be.'

On the landing there were crooked pillars of books, piles of law journals, Amnesty International magazines and stacks of string-bundled files. 'You moving house?' Max picked up a loose folder and flicked open the cover.

'Some of it's for the shredder, some for archiving and a load of it just needs to be kept out of harm's way. Since last summer your people have raided once a month.' She snatched the file. 'Anyone'd think you had a pain in the arse quota to hit.'

Max held his hands up. 'Not my people. I'm strictly deskbound. I just do the boss's legwork.'

'New boss same as the old boss?'

'Same boss, as it goes.'

'You're still undercover pig for Kilby?'

'Less pig, more gopher. Strictly above board.'

This wasn't the conversation Max wanted. It had the hallmarks of their last fretful and increasingly resentful meetings. 'I'm back with him in the administrative sense. I've spent the last month in meetings, in-between organising his archive. The dark and dirty doings of a career in covert policing. You'd love it.'

'So, he wasn't purged last year.'

Max gave a little. 'The consensus is that no one could have – or did – see it coming.'

She nodded. 'So no one read the papers, saw what two lads from Bradford could do in Tel Aviv and thought maybe it could happen here?'

'Like I said, whatever loop there was, I'm out of it. Can I come in?'

Liz fingered the faint outline of an old chicken pox scar at her temple. 'Leave your shopping here,' she said.

'It's a picnic.' He opened the bag. 'No hidden cameras, no wire.'

She turned her back. 'I'll check it when you leave.'

Delaney and Coles' legal practice occupied most of what had once been a residential flat over a sari shop. They paid the owners a peppercorn rent as part repayment for a favour. Downstairs, the shop was thriving. From the look of the place, you couldn't say the same for Delaney and Coles. Max followed Liz through the warren of individual rooms that functioned as offices.

'These were full a few months ago. Now we can't get tenants for love nor money. People are frightened to do their work here.'

'What does Mr Coles say? Congratulations on the partnership, by the way.'

'Jonathon is semi-retired. He works from home mostly. He lectures, writes academic articles for the Law Society Gazette, and preaches to the *Guardian* faithful. He does some casework, but not much. Mainly stuff that gets him face time on *Newsnight* or *Channel 4 News*. I manage the office and deal with everything that doesn't.'

'He trusts you then, first name on the plate?'

'Everybody trusts me, Max. I'm a lawyer.' She risked a smile.

Max knew of at least three campaign groups for whom the Turnpike Lane address was still a registered office, a front for extremists – maybe not. But the usual mix of crackpot leftists who rarely, if ever, set foot in the place these days. She kept a small staff. Nikki had been Liz's longstanding legal exec and Jamie handled admin and bookkeeping two days a week. Most of the rooms were locked or empty, but someone could be heard in animated conversation in one of them. Liz knocked and opened the door. A young man in a sweaty peppermint green shirt, sleeves rolled up almost to the shoulders, moved into view on an office chair. His hand covered a phone mouthpiece. 'What?'

'Phil, this is Max.'

'Alright, mate.'

'Detective Sergeant Lomax.'

He uncovered the receiver. 'I have to go. Call you later.' He wheeled himself backwards, kicking the door closed.

Liz sat in behind her desk. She unearthed a packet of Silk Cut from the overlapping columns of papers and lit up. 'So, what do you want?'

Max cleared a coat and bag off another chair and sat down. 'It's a peace mission. I thought – actually, I'd hoped – the dust might have settled enough so we could go for a drink. Not trying to rekindle anything or atone for anything, just a drink.'

'Well, aren't you the cockeyed optimist?' She chipped the cigarette. 'I don't think so. Too tired, too busy. And there are people who'd doubt my integrity if I was seen with you.'

'We could go somewhere out the way.'

She pulled herself forward. 'On my desk I've got the papers for a 79-year-old Syrian woman due to be deported next Thursday – all her extended family are here. If she goes, she's on her own in a place you wouldn't send your worst enemy to. Needless to say, the Home Office are their usual obstructive selves. In about ten minutes time I'll get a call from Mrs Hassan – she calls me same time every day, desperate to know if I've been able to trace her eighteen-year-old son, last seen by his mates after Friday prayers three weeks ago. He's somewhere in the system, some shitty detention centre, but I can't find out. Do you get my drift here, Max? These people are not fanatics and you're not on my side.' She glowered, took a long drag from the cigarette.

Phil appeared around the door and said to Liz, 'What time are you leaving?'

She checked her watch. 'At this rate, not until midnight. Go if you want, I'll lock up.'

'What about…?' Phil cocked a thumb at Max.

'DS Lomax and I have known each other for a long time. He's carving out a new career as the Met's tart with a heart.'

'I'm flattered,' said Max.

'What he doesn't realise…' she stubbed out the cigarette with a flourish, 'is that these days you have to do a bit more than go home and listen to your old Clash albums to make a difference. We deal with a very different kind of politics, Max. We lose more than we win and the territory we operate in is chipped away year after year. Like threading needles by candlelight, but we keep going.'

Max felt the burn of old antipathies and wondered if this had been a rotten idea from the off.

'I'll leave you to it, then.' Phil closed the door.

Max took the wine out of the bag. 'How about it? One slug of this highly recommended Rioja and I'll leave you to save your lost souls.'

She took the bottle, weighed it in her hand and read the label. Her nose wrinkled, 'Recommended by who?'

'The girl in the shop down the road.'

She laughed. 'Phil calls her The Siren.' Liz put the bottle back on the desk. 'No thanks.' She stood, moved past him and opened the door. 'I really have got a ton of stuff on and one glass is never enough, is it? And I don't want to spend an evening arguing the toss about who said what, or what did or didn't happen, which we inevitably would. It's past, which is where I want it.' She touched his arm. 'I appreciate you giving it a go.'

Max made his way towards Hornsey past shuttered shops on Turnpike Lane. Some would stay open all night. This part of town never truly slept. Instinctively he wanted to stay where there was life and he didn't feel like being alone. *We Sell Everthing* was open, but the girl had gone and the domino players cleared out. His mobile bleeped. A text. Kilby: *call on 12*. Paranoid about phone taps, the boss changed numbers and phones at random intervals. Max speed-dialled *12*.

Kilby answered immediately. 'Are you alone?'

'It's my weekend off.'

Kilby said, 'I need a pick-up, it'll be on your way home.'

'I wasn't going home.'

47

'The Cock Tavern in Kilburn High Road. You know it?'

'Johnny Doyle, the Republican publican.'

'You do know it. Ask for Mr Wallace, he'll have a package for me. Drop him fifty quid and I'll sort it out on expenses.'

Dusk was settling in by the time he got to Kilburn, the evening still balmy. He withdrew fifty quid from the cashpoint in the High Road, conscious of two lads in the shadows. He stared them straight as he passed, holding tight to the bottle in the bag. In the Cock Tavern, a string of faded Irish tricolours linked the dusty bottles behind the bar. In the back, a pool game was reaching a noisy conclusion.

Max said, 'I'm looking for Wallace.'

The barman nodded to the pool players. A red-faced bloke in a yellow polo shirt smacked the black ball towards the pocket, missed by a mile. 'Ah ya cunt.' He threw the cue down. Max sensed the nervousness in his mates' laughter.

The barman called him over. 'Mr Wallace, bloke here wants to see you.'

Wallace called Max through. 'What's the code word?'

Max sized up the bloke, short-arse, half-pissed. Max felt eyes burning the back of his neck. 'How the fuck should I know? Let's say there isn't one.'

Wallace laughed, reached into his back pocket and pulled out a sweat-dampened brown envelope. 'There you go. That's for Senor big bollocks.'

'That's it?'

'What did you expect, messenger boy, a fucking bow on it?'

Max parted with the fifty. Wallace said he'd been promised a ton.

Max shrugged, 'He told me fifty, you've got fifty.'

Wallace's opponent rolled the pool cue across the fag-pocked blue baize.

Max glanced behind him, the two lads he'd seen at the cashpoint stood in the doorway. One had to be Wallace's own boy, something about the dead-eyed expression and three-quid haircut spoke volumes. Max kept his voice down, 'It's not like the old days, Mr Wallace. I don't put money in the box.'

Wallace's threats followed him into the night. The envelope stayed sealed. It was still his weekend off and more than anything he wanted several drinks. He took off north along Kilburn High Road in search of a pub and the noise of a live band.

Sunday morning, Max was pouring Rioja dregs down the sink when his mobile rang. He ignored it, black-bagging foil trays and clearing takeaway clutter. He scrubbed unsuccessfully at turmeric stains on the worktop. He needed breakfast and coffee. The three eggs in the fridge were a week past their use-by date and the bacon had a mottled greenish tinge. He tossed them in the rubbish bag. Just toast then.

It took a while thumbing through the paper before he found the sports section. He reached for his glasses, ignoring the missed call message on the mobile. In the shambles of his living room, books and records spilled from their shelf space. His Telecaster leaned against the amp. Last night he'd lost an hour trying to get some dirty old blues thing down before the wine took over and his fingers ceased to function. On a low table covered with magazines, he'd cleared a space for his records, the corners lifted on half a dozen 12-inch singles. *Song to the Siren* was still on the turntable in the corner.

Max slipped the record back into its sleeve. He polished butter smears off his glasses on a handful of t-shirt and listened to his master's voicemail. Kilby required his attention. He'd call back after the hour he'd promised himself with the papers. He sat up straight and felt a sharp pain in his lower back, his body's revenge for a night on the sofa. He'd finished a mouthful of toast when the phone rang again. Kilby's persistence won over. He answered.

'About time. How did you get on with Mr Wallace?'

Max's memory muddled for a moment. 'I've got it. I'll bring it tomorrow.' Kilby left a space that Max was obliged to fill. 'Unless you need it sooner.'

'Do you want me to come to you?'

'I'd rather not.' He surveyed the state of the room.

'What do you suggest?'

'I'll see you in an hour, usual place. We'll have a beer or something.'

Max shaved and changed into clothes he was prepared to be seen in beyond the boundaries of his own street. The Sunday papers would have to wait. He left the second slice of toast, its corners curling on the plate.

5

Max

THE CLARENCE WAS ONE of Max's least favourite pubs. Squeezed in at the northern end of Whitehall opposite the Old Admiralty Building, it had once been the haunt of Soviet agents sniffing for the drunk and disillusioned. These days the Russians invited their marks to drinks parties in Mayfair. The narrow bar felt like an old station waiting room. Pre-lunch on a bright Sunday, the only other drinkers were a pair of elderly Dutch tourists fussing over a guidebook. A bleary-eyed barman scratched his arse. As Max arrived, the cleaner finished mopping the dark boards, leaving a disinfectant vapour trail in her wake. Max bought a pint and sat at the table furthest away, one which gave the best view of the door. He was early and sat quietly, enjoying the beer.

He could never describe his relationship with Kilby as comfortable. True, they'd set aside many of the formalities of rank, but Kilby was brass. You did well to remember that. After a 20-year career in counter-insurgency, he'd been appointed Assistant Commissioner of Special Operations from a shortlist of one. The post gave him resources and unprecedented autonomy. Kilby had recruited a different kind of policeman for his new team: independent, intelligent and, above all, loyal. You made your oath to the Crown at Hendon, but Kilby's word was law.

Max was in mid-drink when the boss strode in, pseudo-preppy in blazer and chinos. They met at the bar. Max bought

Kilby's iced tonic water and slotted Wallace's envelope into his folded newspaper. They moved back to Max's table.

'I've spent the morning with the Commissioner in Lewisham. It's an interesting place, some good grassroots work going on.'

Max nodded. Interesting was one way of looking at it.

'Business, then,' said Kilby. 'A piece of work has come up at short notice and it needs attending to.' He topped up his tonic from the bottle. 'What do you know about a man called Derek Labrosse?'

Max shrugged. 'Next to nothing. Senior Home Office official, took a tumble down the stairs a few months back.'

Kilby pushed a plain white envelope across the table. 'Tell me what you make of this. Delivered by hand last week, addressed to me personally. We traced the courier to a firm near Seven Dials. No trace on the source.'

Max turned the envelope in his hands. Typed address label, standard font, no postmark. They could identify the paper and printer type for what it was worth, but not much more. Inside the envelope were six photocopied pages from the police investigation into Labrosse's death, partial witness statements and an incomplete forensic report. Kilby opened the envelope Max had retrieved from Wallace. It contained an original page from the file, this one signed by the senior investigating officer.

'From the same source,' said Kilby.

The real thing, Max thought, presumably to authenticate the photocopies. After a couple of minutes reading, he looked up. 'And you've no idea who sent this?'

Kilby shook his head. 'As I said, anonymous. Wallace is a postbox. Knows a man who knows a man.'

That, in itself, was odd. Max gestured with the papers. 'This isn't for real though, is it? If it is, they went through the motions and no more.'

'Officer in charge was called Bailey.'

Max nodded. 'I know him.'

'He works or I should say worked, for Chief Superintendent Rothwell in Homicide, based in Enfield, who you also know. Bailey has since taken early retirement and is now employed as a Community Safety Officer at Hackney Council.'

Not an uncommon career move. Cash in your pension and take a part-time job to keep out of trouble. 'And your interest, aside from curiosity?'

Kilby lowered his voice. 'Last August, the Commissioner asked me to sit on a Home Office implementation group, chaired by Labrosse. Terms of reference were to compile an operational brief for a national identity card system. What would we need and what was best practice in terms of delivery? Given the Home Office track record when it comes to pissing billions up the wall on failed IT, and our budget taking the hit as a result, I pushed for a full operational impact assessment. Consultation at all stages. Let's just say, mine was not a popular perspective. It slowed things down, which they didn't like. The others on the group were equally sceptical, but they didn't say so. We met fortnightly. I thought we were making progress. Then, at the back end of November, nothing. All further meetings cancelled. No reason. Dealing with these Home Office and Treasury procurement people is murky at the best of times. But killing the project entirely with no explanation? Especially when the PM's making public noises about public safety, national security, compulsory carrying of ID, enforcing travel restrictions. More to the point, they'd wasted my bloody time.' He leaned forward. 'Just after Christmas, I managed to get hold of Labrosse. He told me my views had not been welcome. In his words, *there's a ready-made solution waiting in the wings and delivery agents with the expertise to make it work.*'

Max picked up his beer, cleaned the drips off the bottom of the glass.

'Two months later he was dead.' Kilby waited until Max's glass was back on the table. 'I looked into it and was warned off. Under no circumstances was I to approach the Home Office or Derek Labrosse's family. I had a quiet word with Chief Superintendent Rothwell.'

'And?'

'He assured me his team had conducted a thorough investigation. Labrosse's death had been an accident, no question. Then last week, this arrives.' Kilby checked his phone as he spoke. 'That's why I want you to go through Derek Labrosse's case file. Find a reason I can use to persuade the Commissioner there's a case to answer. Make it detailed, substantive, and unequivocal.'

Max caught the vacant gaze of the barman who looked away.

'Straightforward enough, I'd have thought.' Kilby finished his drink.

'So, now I'm doing your casework?'

Kilby leaned in. 'For heaven's sake, it's a paper exercise. Examine the file. Detective Constable Denny has an eye for detail if you can't summon the enthusiasm. Trust me, I wouldn't ask if there was anyone else.' He put the papers back in the envelope and stood up to leave. 'Just work the file and see where it takes us. It'll be on your desk tomorrow morning. Enjoy the rest of your weekend.'

6

Max

ON MONDAY MORNING, MAX arrived at Carteret Street early.
He made his way upstairs to the first floor office he shared
with Detective Constable Maggie Denny. Denny had arrived
at the end of April. A complex career path that had taken her
from Lisburn, Country Antrim, in uniform with the Police
Service of Northern Ireland, to England, the Met and Special
Operations. She'd told him that much, precious little else.
What he knew had been gathered from scraps of overheard
phone conversations. Mainly that her partner was a needy twat
who resented her commitment to the job. Now they occupied
an office barely big enough for their desks, filing cabinets and
a spare chair. Rumour had it that Kilby once ran clandestine
ops out of the place. It had a nicotine-stained plotters' charm,
but you couldn't help feeling you'd messed up somewhere
down the line to have landed there. An anteroom contained
the half-dozen double-locked cabinets of yellowed papers and
classified files Kilby referred to as his 'memoir in waiting', an
unredacted archive of infiltrations dating back to the early 90s.
Max's name was in there. He punched in the door combination.

Sunlight fell across his desk in shafts between the bomb-
blast curtains. The Labrosse case file was waiting. He tossed
it onto Denny's desk. She wasn't far behind. She hung her suit
jacket on the back of the door, neatly folded up her shirtsleeves
and scanned the file cover. 'Labrosse?' A file request slip in

Max's name fell out. *For your signature* scrawled on a post-it note. 'You need to sign this.' She slid it across.

Max pushed it back.

Denny signed and put the slip in the internal post. 'Not a good weekend then?'

He told her about Saturday's phone call, the trip to Kilburn, and Sunday's meeting.

She shrugged. 'It's a paper exercise, let's get it done.'

Denny started reading while the kettle boiled. It clicked off and the coffee stayed unmade. 'Mr Kilby doesn't need us to give him a reason to look at this again. It's garbage.' She turned pages, dismissively. 'The notes are illegible, most of the statements are handwritten scraps. No one's bothered to type it up. Hardly any dates or times, the evidence reports are incomplete, no witness transcripts. I can't find a single statement that's countersigned. Whoever did this wasn't taking it seriously.'

As the morning wore on, they worked to piece the file back together. Everything dated in order, then the undated papers fitted into a timeline by deduction or guesswork. Max numbered each page, pencilling his comments on post-it notes while Denny compiled an index. The morning sunlight disappeared and Max flicked on the desk lamp. There were pages of press cuttings, one or two broadsheet reports. A local hack had sniffed a story and syndication rights. Preoccupied with what he called *sinister causes*, he'd cited Labrosse's work with the Home Office as motive for something darker than an accident, but there were no details to back it up. Denny raised an eyebrow.

'He's fishing,' said Max.

'We'll talk to him though, right?'

'We would if we were investigating the case, which we're not.'

'But if we were.'

Max took his wallet from his jacket. 'I'm getting a sandwich, you want anything?'

Denny worked through Labrosse's obituaries. Those not on the file she found online. There was a photograph of the funeral and memorial service, high profile attendees at Enfield Crematorium. She had the Coroner's report emailed over. Accidental Death. Signed, sealed and delivered. She printed out the last of the paperwork, adding it to the file. In Max's absence, she worked freely. Something wasn't right here and she was interested.

Max tossed over the carton of chicken pasta salad. Denny pulled at a corner of the plastic covering, reading between forkfuls. 'Derek Labrosse was the kind of man *uniquely capable of bringing those with opposing views together in common interest... a skilful negotiator with a track record of successfully delivered programmes. In adversity, Derek earned a reputation as a man who got things done.*'

Max leaned against the door.

'That glowing tribute was from Gavin Lillico, recently appointed Labrosse's Assistant Director.' Denny continued. 'This is better: *a man of intellect, vision and ambition within the often stifling confines of a Whitehall reluctant to embrace modernisation. Derek Labrosse was a visionary. His ideas would have helped shape our nation in years to come. First and last, he was a gifted public servant, dedicated to serving his country. A tragic loss. We send our prayers and condolences to his family.* Overtime in Downing Street Press Office, that last quote was attributed to the PM.'

'Almost like he meant it,' said Max.

'You want me to give them a ring and see who actually wrote the thing? I could find out who gave them the brief.'

Max held up his hands. 'Just get Kilby what he needs.'

'We have that already.' She shuffled in her seat. 'C'mon, Max, this is making me itch.'

'Yeah, well don't scratch.' Max finished his sandwich. 'I tell you what you can do, Kilby wants a briefing this evening. Ring his private office and see if you can find out who he's meeting with tomorrow morning. Speak to Janice. If she's there, tell her we need to know for the distribution list.'

Max sat back, trying to ignore the warning song that was beginning to play in his head. He went back through the refiled papers as Denny talked diaries with Janice, she wrote names on a pad and pushed it towards him. *Commissioner, Minister for Security – J Creedy, Home Office – G Lillico.*

Max let out a low whistle and the warning song played a little louder.

As the afternoon dragged on, the office turned into a sweatbox. It was nearly seven by the time Kilby bustled in and took a seat. 'What have you got?'

Max opened his notes. 'We'll start with the timeline, as far as we can gather. Derek Labrosse takes a fall down the stairs at his home sometime during the afternoon of the 18th of February. The fall results in multiple injuries. Crucially, breaks to the third and fourth cervical vertebrae and a fatal injury to the spinal cord.'

'And we're assuming this was an accident,' said Kilby.

'No reason to think it wasn't,' said Max. 'What's less clear is what happens next. Labrosse is discovered later that evening but we don't know by whom. The first uniformed officers at the house seal it, presuming the Scenes of Crime Team will want a clean sweep of the place. Detective Sergeant Bailey is the duty homicide officer that evening. He receives the call at Enfield and arrives ten minutes or so after the Scenes of Crime Officer.'

Denny cut in, 'SOCO is Kaye Wells. Relatively new to the job, still officially on probation.'

Max picked up. 'It's Saturday night, the rest of her team are working a multiple shooting at a party in Edmonton. She's sent to prep the ground on her own, because everything points to this being an accident. Bailey assists in an initial search of the premises, presumably to save time. There's no evidence of forced entry and no apparent disturbance in any of the rooms. Uniformed officers carry out cursory chats with neighbours, but not everyone. According to the file, Bailey instructs one of them to go back later to speak with those they missed, but there are no records of other visits taking place. Or of Bailey checking to ensure they do.'

Kilby made a note. 'Continue.'

'Bailey's initial assessment is accidental death. He doesn't seem to have considered any other option.'

Denny cut in, 'Kaye Wells mentions there being blood spatters around the taps at the bathroom sink. So not related to the fall.'

Another note made, with a slow nod this time. 'Anything else?'

Max continued, 'One of the neighbours thinks she heard doors slamming, a couple of cars coming and going at some point during the Saturday afternoon, but no specific time, no make or registration and no description of a driver. More to the point, no one follows up. As far as we can tell, no one else is questioned to corroborate any of these points. And Kaye Wells' lab reports are not on the file.'

Kilby closed his notebook. He turned to Denny, 'Say it's your case, what's your opening?'

'Then or now?'

'Let's say now.'

She glanced at Max and wished she hadn't. 'DS Bailey has questions to answer. I'd go back to Kaye Wells and the Scenes of Crime Team, find out who sent such an inexperienced officer and why did she process the scene solo? This local reporter seems to have an angle and I'd like to know what that's based on, see if there's anything worth following up. And I'd see if we couldn't trace the lab work. There must be a record somewhere.

There's no reference here to the family, no background checks. Did anyone interview his wife or daughter, his colleagues, friends? We don't know and we should.'

Kilby stood. 'Agreed. Someone at least needs to trace the forensics if nothing else. I need to clear this with one or two people in the morning, I'll get back to you.' All this to Denny, then to Max. 'You okay with this?'

'Of course.'

When Kilby had gone, Denny spoke first. 'I'm sorry. That wasn't what it looked like.'

Max walked to the window, looked into the street. 'Don't apologise, not on my account. The boss asks, you answer. Just be careful what you wish for, that's all.'

'I'm not wishing. I just want to do the job. Isn't that what they pay us for?'

7

Max

THE CALL CAME THROUGH mid-morning. Twenty minutes later Max and Denny sat in Kilby's office. They had conditional consent to look into Labrosse's death. Labrosse's former deputy, now acting director, Gavin Lillico, and James Creedy, Minister for Security, had raised objections on the grounds that a reinvestigation would cause undue stress for Labrosse's family, upset his colleagues and risk unwanted press attention. Kilby looked to Max. 'I reassured them that wouldn't happen. To précis what was a very long, very boring meeting, they don't believe taking a second look is in anyone's best interests.'

'For which, read *their* best interests,' said Max.

'Quite. What we've agreed is a focused reinvestigation, targeting the specific areas of concern we've identified.' Here he nodded to Denny. 'This takes place over a limited period and with the cooperation of Lillico's department. We consult with them and, if there are new developments, they're kept informed. If anything looks like it might have wider public implications, or be referred to the CPS, we'll handle it jointly.'

Max's aversion was physical. He sensed the colour draining from his face as Kilby offered him the file. Denny had seen it, too. She watched him like someone waking from an anxiety dream, convinced he was about to reject the opportunity that could buy her out of career purgatory.

'There are better people than me to handle cold cases.'

Kilby stiffened. 'Hardly cold, Max. As I see it, we have a straightforward, time-limited investigation with clear parameters. If there's nothing there and it's just bad admin by an officer with one eye on the door, that's fine. We'll deal with it. I'm just asking you to join the dots.'

'Yesterday it was a paper exercise. Now it's a case.'

'And if I had the resources to assign it elsewhere, I would. A man died. If the original investigation is lacking, I want to know why.' He offered the file again. 'Convalescence is over, Max. I'm not paying you to shuffle papers indefinitely. It damages your credibility and mine.'

Max looked up. 'Since when did you give a shit about my credibility?'

'Take it on or go. Denny can go back to Dover and you…'

From the way Denny's head dropped, Max guessed he'd not been the only one to take a call from Kilby at the weekend. He'd sounded her out and, so far, it was going exactly as she'd told Kilby it would. Not that it mattered. He had no bargaining position. 'With you, there's never a choice, is there?'

'Oh, there's always a choice. Let me know if there's anything else you need. Regular updates please. Tread carefully with the Home Office. This man Lillico is as twitchy as hell.'

Max pushed his tongue tight to the back of his teeth. This had been Kilby's intention from the off. His reasons for taking the scenic route to get it done were not yet apparent, though Max suspected they'd become so once he and Denny shredded the credibility of the initial investigation. And it was no surprise that Kilby would play him. If anything, what pissed him off was Kilby knowing he'd stay to be played. But there was, as they both knew, the small matter of some CCTV footage of an unwanted paint job on Andre Connor's car, unmentioned but underlying.

Max took the file. He'd work the case with one eye on Kilby and take care of himself at the same time. Denny as well if she'd let him. On the way back to Carteret Street Denny said, 'You were going to turn him down.'

'I was.'

'But you didn't.'

'No, I didn't. What was the Dover thing?'

'I was seconded there. Part of an investigation I'd been working on back home, breaking up trafficking routes. Girls mostly. Still kids. It brought me to England, then this came up.'

'You didn't say.'

'You didn't ask.'

Before they could say more, a police car came screaming down the street followed by two unmarked Range Rovers, their windows up tight. A cyclist pulled her bike onto the pavement just in time as the convoy turned towards Victoria Street. Max loosened his tie. He needed to walk.

8

Tyler

THE ONLY SOUNDS IN the hotel's breakfast room were self-contained murmurs of conversation and the clink of spoons on cereal bowls. Being there made Tyler feel like an old man. A cardboard name plate had been placed centrally on the table: *To Michael and Emily Tyler, Cynthia and Alan's guests at The Ashbury, the best little family hotel in Bournemouth – please remember to settle all bills on departure.* A waitress brought a pale egg, a sausage and a couple of rashers to the table. Emmy buttered a slice of granary toast. 'It's cold,' she said.

'I know.' Tyler shivered for effect.

'The toast.' She tutted.

'So's the egg.'

She pushed the plate aside. 'Do you mind if I go up and finish packing?'

'Of course not.'

She left Tyler to his bacon.

This had been their promised few days away. A chance to spend some time together. They'd kept busy on garden visits, eating out and making the best of the June weather on walks along the front. Then, on Sunday evening at dinner, Emily said she wanted to go home. Tyler protested and persuaded her that, having booked until Friday, they should stay. They'd finished their bland pub meal barely speaking and were in bed by ten.

They spent most of Monday in the hotel lounge reading. Then the call came.

Tyler was in the hotel bar, waiting for Emmy to come down for a pre-dinner drink. He hadn't recognised the number, but then he hadn't expected to hear from Theobold again, so hadn't saved his contact details. Theobold skipped the pleasantries. There was, he said, the possibility of a second investigation into Derek Labrosse's death. Nothing certain and nothing to worry about, even if it did happen. He'd just rather Tyler heard it from him.

Tyler sipped his half of bitter. When Emmy appeared, he said he'd been thinking about what she said. Maybe they should go home. The hotel wasn't up to much and if she wasn't happy – he didn't want her to be unhappy.

'Thank you, Michael.' She smiled for the first time in days.

Tuesday morning they were on their way immediately after breakfast. Dispensing with the usual pub lunch in Tunbridge Wells, Tyler had them home by midday.

'I'll put the kettle on.' He made tea.

'I'm going upstairs to unpack, then I think I'll have a nap.'

He dropped into his chair and put the television on. He heard a low murmur of conversation – Emmy would have called Fiona, their eldest and only daughter, grown-up, married. Once he might have envied their shared confidences, called up a 'say hello from me'. Now it was simply another thing that happened outside of his sphere of influence. He preferred not to think about it.

Lulled into a shallow sleep by the test match commentary, he woke and changed channels to hear the afternoon news. Home Office minister, James Creedy, with oily soundbites about how it was his responsibility *to support the police, ensure a service fit for purpose, to keep the citizens of Britain safe*. The phrases rolling off Creedy's tongue took on a familiar note, defending the recruitment drive for new police community support officers who would be given powers to stop, search and arrest; and the creation of community action zones to isolate and lock down anti-social neighbourhoods. There would be enhanced training for tactical police units and deployment of special task groups. Tyler could have written the speech from Derek Labrosse's papers. For Labrosse, the policy had been flawed, short-sighted, and even dangerous. Creedy was making it his personal manifesto.

After dinner that evening, Emmy moved the plates aside. 'Can we talk, Michael?' She held both his hands across the table. 'Michael, I'm too fond of you to let it carry on like this. I really didn't enjoy our time away.'

Fond. It seemed such a sad word.

'We used to be honest,' she said, 'about everything.'

'We still are.'

She fiddled with the enamel oval of her pendant, a souvenir of another, more warmly remembered weekend away. 'I can only ask what's wrong so many times. If I'm not clever enough or trustworthy enough, or whatever it is that's stopping you from being honest, or even talking about it.'

'It's nothing, I promise. If there was, I'd tell you.'

'But there is *something.* There just is, please tell me you can feel it. Is it work? Are you ill, is that it?'

'Just a little out of sorts, maybe. I do love you.'

'Then tell me.' She settled the pendant against the black of her blouse.

'There's nothing to tell, I promise.'

She sighed and gently pulled her hands away. The lie burned him deeply, tightening inside him. His phone buzzed. A text from Theobold. *New investigation confirmed. Meet soon.*

'Do you want coffee?' said Emmy.

'Sorry?'

'*Coffee.*'

'Please.' He pulled out his chair to follow her to the kitchen.

9

Max

CLOUD HUNG OVER THE streets. Crossing Birdcage Walk, Max felt a sharp pain under his heel. He sat down on a bench in St James's Park next to a woman feeding the birds from the crusts of a sandwich. She smiled as he slipped off his shoe, shook out a stone and straightened his sock. His foot still hurt, but he needed to walk off the growing sense of unease.

He kept moving and thinking, barely registering the afternoon passing. A kid pestered a parent for an overpriced ice cream from a van parked at the top of the steps at Carlton House Terrace. Max headed towards Piccadilly, picked up a paper outside Green Park Tube station. He felt drunk, the city's hot breath on his neck and darkening skies that threatened to unload. A despatch bike belted up a rat-run side street as he crossed between lines of black cabs.

He found himself outside the Leicester Arms on the corner of Glasshouse Street. Its buttoned seats and heavy curtains reminded him of the photo he kept on the wall in his office. The sort of anonymous West End boozer they'd have ended up after work in the old days. It was no coincidence that most of that first team Kilby put together had either burned out, left the job, or lost their way. Two months ago, word reached him that Matt Lloyd, the only other colleague from those days still working, had been found dead in the toilets of a private club in Holborn. A place Max knew as a home from home for

Eastern European businessmen and the kinds of Englishmen who brokered deals on their behalf. Cocaine was from source, cheap if you knew people. Lloyd had been buying under the odds and marking up to sell himself, walking both sides of the line. Kilby cut him adrift with no remorse. Max knew he'd do the same to him without a second thought.

He bought a drink, thumbing through the loose change in his pocket to make sure there'd be another. His conscience pricked. He called in, told Denny he'd see her in the morning and they'd make a start on the case. She said she'd already spoken to the journalist who'd written the Labrosse article in the local paper. He'd admitted juicing up the story to keep his editor happy. The suspicious death angle was speculation. Max was silent. Denny asked, was he all right?

'Just working things through.' He hung up.

He felt at home in the Leicester Arms. You could be alone there without feeling lonely. He had a view of the street. He scribbled in the crossword on the back page of the paper and had turned to the sports pages when a fight started outside. An American tourist caught the hand that dipped his wife's purse. The big guy was slapping this kid and giving a homespun morality sermon, threatening in the name of all that's holy to take him down the alley and bury him in a trashcan. The kid was fighting back, shouting 'I'll fucking cut you up,' over and over, a big fearless smile on his face. All this time the American's wife was getting to her feet, dusting herself down and picking up the scattered contents from her handbag, stopping every now and again to dab a tissue at a graze on her knee. When the kid's shirt tore, he made a move and was away dancing into the crowd. The big guy was left with a fistful of shirt, the lecture sticking in his throat.

Max shook his head. He thought of Denny. Bad luck for her to be in a backyard like Carteret Street. Bad luck to live with her wanker boyfriend and his weekly *me or the job* ultimatums.

Good for her that, so far, she'd chosen her career. Max had a sense she'd been underplaying her hand. He wondered how good she was. She was Kilby's next protégé, that much he knew – the boss always needed one and Denny made no secret of her desire to make the position permanent.

He counted his change one more time, slid off his seat and went into the street. He thought for a moment of calling Liz, but didn't fancy another knock-back. He made his way to Bond Street station looking in the Regent Street shop windows. Past Austin Reed with new suits and boots he couldn't afford, but looked terrible on the dummies anyway. Past the locked fronts of Savile Row tailors with faded awnings and a *By Royal Appointment* over the door. Past the celebrity spotters in New Bond Street and South Molton Street. Arty window dressing and tanned skin on show. Beautiful people on display with even more money than sense. You could bomb this place to shit, he thought, and people would still shop.

Max dropped the newspaper in a waste bin, bracing himself for the airless press of the short tube journey to Swiss Cottage. He didn't see the woman fifty paces behind, the one in the summer dress. She might have been window shopping, just taking that route as a coincidence. Same as she may have been feeding birds in St James's Park at lunchtime. Or watching him watch people from a dusty boozer at the corner of Glasshouse Street.

10

Theobold

PATRICK THEOBOLD WAS FIRST to arrive for the scheduled meeting. It was late in the afternoon. He stood at the window of the Home Office fifth-floor boardroom, watching heat haze shimmer over the city. He placed the palm of his hand against the glass and let his mind play out a strange fantasy, that if he pushed and the window gave way, he'd surf across the rooftops on the intact pane. A blast of cold air from the overhead air-con vent sent a chill against his cheek. He took his suit jacket off the back of the chair and hung it over his shoulders.

Hannah Rees shouldered open the door. 'You look like a gangster.' She parked a wheeled suitcase and shoulder bag in the corner of the room. 'Where's Lillico?'

'On his way,' said Theobold. 'He had a couple of things to clear up.'

Rees circled Lillico's newly acquired boardroom table, running her finger across the backs of the chairs – Lillico had them reupholstered in cream leather. 'Does he know I have a seven-thirty Heathrow to Dallas?'

She was heading home and, as far as Theobold was concerned, not before time. Much as they were a working partnership, Rees brought her own brand of intensity and that needed careful handling. 'He knows.' Theobold pulled out two chairs, sat on one and patted the seat of the other. 'How was Selfridges this afternoon? What did you buy – something expensive I hope?'

70

'I didn't make it as far as Oxford Street.' She smiled. 'Too damn hot.'

Theobold knew this. Lillico had returned from that morning's meeting at Scotland Yard having failed to stop the Labrosse reinvestigation in its tracks. He claimed they'd given him no choice. Rees had not been impressed, interrogating Lillico about what'd he'd said or failed to say before returning to her hotel to call head office in Oklahoma City. Theobold followed her, first to the hotel, then to St James's Park. From a distance, he watched her feed the birds. She seemed relaxed, aimlessly strolling, taking tourist photos and window-shopping. Just another pretty girl in a summer dress.

Now she was all business. Her white shirt crumpled as she sat down. She smoothed her skirt. Her hair was tied back and a light touch of foundation covered a blemish on her forehead. 'Actually, I followed the cop,' she said. 'I just wanted to get a feel, satisfy myself he's who his file says he is. Judging by the beer he was throwing down his neck this afternoon, the man's a drinker. Cute, but a drinker. You want to take that lemon-sucking expression off your face, Patrick, you know exactly where I was. You think I didn't see you?'

'You didn't need to take the risk. I could have checked him out.'

'And how long would that have taken?' She checked her watch. 'If I'm going back with a report for the board, I'd better be sure of what I tell them. Bittman will want to know.' She paused. 'Although, I'm really not sure Detective Sergeant Lomax gives much of a damn about anything beyond the glass in his hand. I saw a woman have her purse snatched outside the pub he was in this afternoon. He didn't lift a finger.' She checked her watch again.

'Want me to call Lillico?'

'Better had.'

Theobold dialled. Lillico's internal number went straight to an out-of-office voicemail. 'He must be on his way.'

She persisted. 'Try his cell.'

She'd been this way since their paths crossed during bi-lateral intelligence briefings in the early 2000s. At the time, the talk was transatlantic partnership and reciprocity. Theobold's hands were tied by Whitehall. He'd come across like a bureaucrat, which he resented. When he criticised his masters' lack of commitment in a private conversation, it was fed back and they withdrew him from the remaining meetings. Later that evening, Hannah Rees invited him to dinner. The business they conducted that night was off the record, concluded over two large brandies and indulgent petit-fours. A quiet alliance that stood them both in good stead. Theirs was a proven association in an unpredictable world.

Some months later Theobold introduced Rees to a former colleague, David Bittman, newly appointed Chief Executive Officer of IDI, a private sector security corporation based in Oklahoma City. It was no surprise that Bittman liked her. Within weeks she'd joined his management team. A year later IDI landed its first US Government security contract. Hannah Rees's intervention had been crucial. IDI's non-hostile research and development work programme shifted focus to data farming and domestic surveillance technologies – Rees's area of expertise. She had a fat contacts book, friends in secure technologies, and a clutch of favours owed that propelled IDI into the Forbes 500.

When the UK government dispensed with Theobold's services, Hannah Rees was the first person he called. She repaid the favour. Now he was brokering the deal between IDI and the government that had considered him surplus to requirements. It felt good to be taking their money.

Gavin Lillico burst into the boardroom balancing coffee and files. He took off his jacket and sat at the head of the table. 'Right, do we have an agenda?'

Hannah Rees brought her chair up to the table. 'Gavin, there are three points I need you to clarify before I bring David back here in two weeks' time.'

'No agenda then.'

Theobold caught the sideways glance from Hannah Rees. She took a breath, inhaling for a count of five before continuing. 'Security. Has to be better. I do not want another Derek Labrosse undermining our work here, we've come too far. You have to make a better job of keeping your people in check. Keep monitoring them. Keep feeding back. And you have to *manage*.'

'Of course.'

'And please, support Patrick to maintain the integrity of our work. By which I mean, if there are breaches or leaks or whatever, he handles them without you on his tail. He knows what he's doing. You employ him because we trust him. That okay?' She opened her hands, inviting Lillico's acknowledgement.

'Absolutely.'

'Well, can we agree, then, that Patrick will work without your interference?'

Lillico blanched. 'I just said so. You want me to say it again?'

'That'll be fine.' Her tone was brisk. 'As for the police investigation, Patrick will take you through it, step by step. You take his advice on board and we'll have no problems.'

Theobold slipped his arms into his jacket sleeves. The meeting was going to be over sooner than he'd expected.

'Next point, who are to be the signatories for the contract documents?'

'It'll be the Home Secretary, myself, James Creedy, Minister for Security, and a representative from the Treasury, we don't know who as yet.'

'Okay, so not the Prime Minister as we requested?'

'I have tried. It's a matter of diary commitments.'

'Which are?'

'Number Ten doesn't discuss the Prime Minister's appointments.'

'But we do still have his support, right?'

'Absolutely.' Lillico swallowed. 'It's a simple clash of diaries. These things are agreed months in advance. When it comes to the final sign-off, he'll make himself available.'

'You're saying you can't push a little harder for us now, Gavin? This is a big investment we're making. David would appreciate five minutes with the senior man, face to face.'

'I have tried, Hannah.'

She checked her watch a final time. 'Last point then, are you going to be able to handle this, you and your people, your politicians?'

Lillico's pen rolled across the table top. He stopped it dead. There was frustration in his voice. 'We have consulted with key ministers at all points. You have in-principle Cabinet support. Clearly it can't be allowed to enter the public realm at this stage, so we're keeping it tight. When it's time to brief the press, we will do so together. As for me personally, my commitment is absolute. I think I've demonstrated that.'

'That's good, Gavin, because once I bring Bittman here in two weeks, your government will be committed to this. No more lost asylum seekers or foreign students on walkabout visas; no more freed suspects, no stretched police resources. We're looking to create a momentum here. Once it starts I want to see our objectives hit on time. No delays.'

Lillico had had enough. 'Patrick, please would you see Hannah downstairs. I wouldn't want her to miss her flight.'

'Absolutely,' said Theobold.

As they waited for the lift, Theobold said, 'You get such a kick out of giving him a hard time.'

'He wouldn't be in that position if we hadn't put him there. He'd certainly never have got past Labrosse.' She rooted through her bag. 'You know how this goes, Bittman depends on me to keep little details from becoming big ones. Two per cent smarter than the rest – all the time. Is there a place I can buy some cigarettes?'

Theobold produced a pack of Marlboro Lights.

'You don't smoke.'

'I keep a pack handy when you're in town.' The lift arrived empty and they stepped in. 'What do you want me to do?'

She rocked back on her heels. 'When I get back, I'll set up a video conference. It'll be late tomorrow, maybe the day after. Talk to Bittman, tell him what you've told me. Convince him you have the security situation under control.'

'This reinvestigation, if it becomes problematic?'

'Do what you do and keep us out of it. Let's hope it doesn't come to that. I want to give you some practical support for a few weeks, one of our people based over here, officially he's a driver. Use him to take the load off. He'll make sure you get to where you need to be. I suggest you make one of his first jobs to drive you to Caroline Labrosse before the police get around to speaking to her. And talk to this Home Office man, James Creedy. He's been hassling my staff for updates.' There was a jolt as they reached the ground floor. 'While you're at it, see if he has sway with the PM. They probably go to the same fucking club.'

11

Max

MAX WALKED KAYE WELLS up the Carteret Street stairs. She
told him she had nothing to say. Wasn't interested in raking
over old cases for no good reason that she could see, whatever
they were. They had no right to take her from her work
and she certainly did not appreciate being reminded about
professionalism by 'that Irish girl'.

'That would be Detective Constable Denny who you spoke
to on the phone when you agreed to this meeting.'

'Otherwise you'd have come crashing into my office for the
whole world to see. That's what she implied.'

Max said nothing. Denny warned him they'd not exactly
hit it off. She'd leaned on the accountability angle, maybe too
heavily. Stonewalling Kaye Wells' questions about the exact
nature of the interview had frustrated her even more. Denny
was leaving the interview to Max while she tried to set up the
next round of meetings.

Kaye spent ten minutes in the first floor lavatory. Afterwards
she was more composed. He showed her to the small meeting
room they'd borrowed for the afternoon. Unshouldering her
bag, she took the seat, declining Max's offer of coffee. She
folded then unfolded her arms. 'I should be at work,' she said.

'You are.' Max put the Labrosse case file on the table.

'Your colleague said this was about discrepancies in one of
my cases.'

76

'This one.'

She ignored the file. 'So why didn't the request come through my supervisor?'

'You were the lead Scenes of Crime Officer on this case earlier in the year. I'd like you to look through the file, then tell me what you think.'

She glanced down, but gave no sign that she recognised the name on the cover.

'I have a right to know what this is about. I should have representation.'

One protest too many. She was beginning to piss him off.

'Kaye, this isn't a formal interview. You're not under investigation and we're not from Professional Standards. I have no authority to hold you to account, but I do have authority to look into this man's death. I didn't come through your supervisor because that's for you to decide once we've had our conversation. Tell him if you want, that's fine.' He rested his fingertips on the file. 'So please just have a look at the file and tell me what you see.'

She sighed and opened the cover.

'Thank you.'

She read with her finger running down the outer margin of each page, turning slowly and deliberately. After the first few pages she looked up and caught Max's eye. She took off her jacket and produced an A4 note pad. 'Do you mind?'

'Fine by me.'

She wrote down numbers, annotated comments in tight little bullet points, leaving a line between each. She chewed the pen as if dragging back recollections. She asked if they could have the door open. Max obliged, stealing a glance at her notes. The handwriting was small, neat and well enough formed for him to read. She asked for water, sipping as if to minimise the contact between her lips and the plastic cup. Eventually, she said, 'Okay, here's what I see. Most of my lab reports are missing and some of the timings in here aren't right. I've written those down as best as I can remember. Maybe a little off, but closer than it says here. Also, Detective Sergeant Bailey's report...' She tapped the pen on the file and shook her head. 'Let's just say he's mistaken in a number of key areas. You want a copy of these?' To his surprise, she offered the notebook.

He was impressed. To write so much and say so little. The notes were conditional, academic, littered with ifs, buts, and maybes. Enough to claim she'd cooperated and no more. There was little in her recollection that he and Denny hadn't gathered from their reading of the file the first time around. He said, 'You're still not telling me what happened.'

She shrugged. 'That's all I can say. You want my notes or not?'

'You *were* there, right?'

A defiant silence.

'I'm trying to work this out, you say here that you took blood samples from the skirting board and a towel you found in the bathroom. Whose blood was that?'

'I can't say, we don't have the test results.'

'Unlikely that it was Labrosse's, though?'

'Speculate all you like. I can't confirm anything without lab reports.'

'The file talks about a coffee cup found in the upstairs office, presumably you took a swab, prints, that kind of thing, they could be re-examined?'

'I don't remember. It's possible that Detective Sergeant Bailey did that.'

Max thought for a moment. 'Did Bailey pressure you to amend the notes you made at the scene?'

No response.

'If he did, now would be a good time to say. If you refused and they were changed later or removed from the file altogether, you're better off making a formal statement. To cover yourself.'

She shook her head. For the first time, she seemed to be weighing the options.

Max said, 'I think there are signs the file has been doctored. Any thoughts about that?'

'I like my job and I'd rather keep it, thanks. I won't go on the record and I won't provide you with a statement. Really, that's all I can say. There's a stack of things I should be doing.'

His voice was calm, the words measured carefully. 'Kaye, I've been asked to look at this case because Assistant Commissioner Kilby has concerns that it was mishandled. I'm open-minded on the whole thing. But if I find evidence that it wasn't done right, either negligently or for a reason, I guarantee it will be someone's fault.'

'Not mine.'

'You seem very sure.'

'I did nothing wrong.'

'You're an Assistant Forensics Officer. In February, you were six months into your probation, right? You didn't wait for the rest of your team, instead you worked unsupervised. You allowed DS Bailey to influence your actions. That makes you culpable.'

Her shoulders sagged. She held his gaze. 'I'd been on duty for seventeen hours without relief. DS Bailey was at the house when I arrived, wandering around as if he was looking for something. I didn't ask, he didn't say. There were no uniformed officers, no incident tape, just him and Derek Labrosse at the bottom of the stairs. I told him we needed to wait for the rest of the team, then we'd follow the appropriate procedures, but he said it couldn't wait, that we needed to get on. I wanted photographs of the body, the stairs, the blood spatter. He said I should just *get on and do my fucking job.*'

'And?'

'What do you think? A senior officer with Christ knows how many years' experience. A dead man with a high-ranking government position, and me driving halfway across London in the bloody fog to deal with it on my own. I did what I was told. Anything else you want to know, ask the Senior Forensics Officer.'

There was nothing more to be said. Max escorted Kaye Wells down the stairs. He thanked her for her time and would have offered more in the way of support, but she was already striding towards Tothill Street, the bag over her shoulder.

When he got back to the office, Denny was wearing out the carpet.

'That man Bailey is impossible.'

'You spoke to him?'

'Yes, but he won't see us.' She dropped into her chair. 'I've been on the phone non-stop for two hours tracking him down. I get through and you know what he says? He says, "No thanks, love. Think I'll pass." And hangs up. Maybe it's a bloke thing, maybe he'll talk to you.'

Max knew making the call wasn't likely to get them what they wanted, if anything the opposite. If Andy Bailey was the man he remembered, something for nothing would help. 'Try and get hold of him again. Tell him you'll buy him breakfast tomorrow morning.'

She muttered something he didn't catch and hit last number redial. An automated answering system took the call. She put it on speaker: *Thank you for calling Hackney Council. Press one for environmental services, two for Council Tax enquiries...* 'I have to do this every single time. Can't we just go to Hackney and knock on his door?'

In the street below, the evening exodus to St James's Park Underground was in full swing. Max felt uneasy. He couldn't help thinking he should have got more from Kaye Wells. He'd rushed her at the end, sensing maybe that he was pushing too hard. But if she was being straight with him – and he thought she was – they were closer to verifying the order of events on the night Labrosse died. And that meant there were more questions for Bailey.

Denny threw the phone down triumphantly. 'Praise the Lord and pass the whisky, he'll see us tomorrow before work. Nino's café in Mare Street. He says, on no account are we to visit him at his office. I've agreed.'

Max nodded. Tomorrow promised a trip down bad memory lane.

12

Theobold

THE GAY HUSSAR WAS at the northern end of Greek Street. Once a run-through to Soho Square, these days the area bore the scars of land grab and gentrification. The restaurant had been a haunt for politicians and Fleet Street reporters for decades, its walls a gallery of framed political caricatures dating back over half a century. Theobold had been summoned by James Creedy. The Minister's PA had been persuaded to share her boss's lunch arrangements, but he wasn't among the downstairs diners. The maitre d' approached, smiling behind his moustache. 'Sir, you have a table booked?'

'I was told James Creedy was here.'

'Mr Creedy has a private booth. It is not –'

'Thank you.' Theobold pushed past and followed a waiter upstairs.

Creedy was recognisable from the back, dining with another man Theobold knew, but couldn't place. A white-jacketed waiter was clearing the debris from their recently finished lunch. Theobold stood aside and was noticed by Creedy's companion. 'Someone for you I think, James. Looks like a man on a mission.'

Creedy looked up, a half glass of Bull's Blood midway to his lips.

'I got your message,' said Theobold.

The smile fixed, transparently so. 'Not *here*, though, Patrick, I'm at lunch.'

'Looks like you've finished.' He fixed on the companion. The man produced his credit card.

Creedy waved him away. 'Absolutely not, Oliver, this one's on my expenses. A pleasure, as always. We'll do it again soon, very soon.' They shook hands across the table.

The companion eased out. 'He's all yours.'

Theobold slid into the vacant seat.

Creedy looked around, making sure they were alone before letting rip. 'What the hell do you think you are doing, chucking your weight around? I'm at lunch. It's not good for us to be seen together, especially not by a shite hawk like Oliver Watts.'

'I thought I recognised him. Does he still rehash *Telegraph* stories for the *Mail*?' Theobold pushed aside a dessert plate, found some sticky substance on his hand and wiped it on the tablecloth. The waiter finished clearing. 'Can I have a large Remy Martin?'

The waiter looked to Creedy who nodded. 'Two.'

'So where's the fire, Minister?'

'I need to know where we stand for the next few weeks, the timetable for negotiations. You've gone bloody feral since that woman's been in town and her people won't talk to me.'

'That's because they don't like you.'

Creedy quartered the napkin in his lap, eased forward. 'Then they join an extremely long list. Given the scale of our ambitions, whether IDI's people like me or not is immaterial. This time next year they'll be delivering Europe's largest domestic surveillance contract. For us. And if that works out, I want them tendering for new PCSO contracts.'

'Under the noses of the Met.'

'Achieving that takes a degree of consensus among colleagues which must be built and serviced. To say nothing of managing the public messaging. If you don't feed them, they bite. Hence...' He waved in the direction Oliver Watts had departed. 'Keeping one's friends well-fed. I must be provided with up-to-date information as a matter of course. The Metropolitan Police is a cherished institution and making a pig's ear of it is not a good look.'

'A rather inappropriate choice of words, don't you think?'

'I have the greatest respect for the Commissioner and his people.'

'Of course, you do. Our policemen are wonderful.'

Creedy's eyes flashed. 'Don't be a cunt, Patrick.' The waiter brought their drinks. 'It's sensitive, the Met is the best in the world at what it does. But there are new specialisms required. They are expensive and our American colleagues' proposals are compelling. At least, they are to me. Others may need to be reassured. You know what Oliver just told me, apparently regular police officers refer to PCSOs as *Chimps*.'

Theobold killed the punchline. '*Completely Hopeless In Most Policing Situations*. It's as old as the hills. It doesn't mean the Commissioner and his senior management team will sit by and watch you contract out the service. They're not fools.'

'The Commissioner will be persuaded to move on along with certain others of his management team, which is why I need to be certain you've dealt with the detail. Labrosse, for example. Are we clean? I want no flies in the ointment once Bittman arrives.'

'Why in God's name you didn't replace Labrosse when I told you…'

'It's an irrelevance.' Creedy sipped his brandy.

Theobold didn't like these people, never had. Didn't matter what colour tie they wore, come polling day, in his experience, those who climbed this far and stayed there were shits. Creedy was not a stupid man, he had that over most of his contemporaries. And he seemed to have staying power. He'd give him his briefing. 'Hannah Rees is satisfied for the most part. Not happy that the Prime Minister will not be attending in person, or signing heads of terms. They think he ought to be making a more public endorsement, but they'll live with it for now. As for flies in ointment, it's down to me to deal with any matters arising. Rest assured, Labrosse will not be one of them, so you don't need to fret.' He gave Creedy's hand a gentle pat.

Creedy pulled away. 'You work both sides because we allow it. *I* allow it. I made this deal and I want it in place by October.'

'Your deal? You'd better tell Gavin Lillico, he thinks it's his.'

'It isn't. Nor was it Labrosse's. He didn't have the vision or the balls.'

Theobold adjusted his tiepin. Creedy hadn't been so dismissive when Labrosse was alive.

Creedy finger-clicked the waiter for the bill. He signed a slip of paper and left a folded ten pound note on the salver. The waiter gone, he turned to Theobold. 'This has to happen quickly and smoothly or it may not happen at all. I'm asking, can you guarantee that?'

Theobold nodded.

'Good. Now fuck off. In future we meet when and where I say so.'

Theobold stood on the Soho pavement in blazing sunshine. A rumble of masonry down a rubble shoot sent a cloud of dust in the air. As he watched it settle, it occurred to him that it didn't matter how they tarted it up, an air of the dissolute would always hang over Greek Street. Its history of villainy and dirty squad collusion, of tarts and pornographers rubbing shoulders with politicians and peers of the realm, made sure of it. Whatever Creedy thought, no man came away without dirt under his fingernails.

13

Max

FROM SOMEWHERE, NINO'S CAFF had produced two sets of cheap garden furniture and planted umbrellas on the pavement. Max and Denny joined Andy Bailey at the table, Mare Street faking a downmarket Mediterranean thoroughfare in the morning sunshine. Bailey being Bailey, he played it like his own corner at the Savoy. A blob of red and brown sauce from a fully loaded bacon sandwich found its way down his tie. He still behaved as though bullshit was the new rock 'n' roll. Max knew from the off they'd do well to get anything useful. 'You've been elusive.'

'I'm busy, mate.'

'I was going to stick an ad in the Gazette: *wanted, one cardiac case DS to explain monumental cock-up.*' Max put a hand on his arm. 'You've got sauce on your tie.'

Bailey smeared the sauce with a napkin. 'I don't mind helping out, I just don't need all the aggravation that comes with it.'

'So, Derek Labrosse?'

He shrugged. 'Yeah, she said on the phone. I don't remember much about it.'

'It was four months ago, give or take.' Denny's voice had an edge to it. She had Bailey's attention.

'Yeah, well I've slept since then. I'm doing three, four meetings a day. I never stop. It's complicated stuff, Max. Political. Racial. Not easy to remember every detail from four

86

months ago. You know what it's like, once you're out, you're out. That's all I'm saying. This is a different world.'

'It's a few questions, Andy. Piece of piss for a man like yourself. Loose ends, that's all.' The conversation halted while a young waitress brought Bailey's coffee. The Arsenal mug it came in was Bailey's own. 'Looks like you're well-in here,' said Max.

'Best move I've ever made. It's got its aggravations, but I don't miss the job. Got my pension and doing very well.' He leaned in confidentially. 'And I get to straighten out the odd moody councillor once in a while, know what I mean? I don't buy my suits from British Home Stores anymore.' He laughed and a morsel of chewed pink meat flew the short distance from his mouth to the handle of the cup. He picked it off and flicked it away. 'People respect my opinions. And if they don't, I've always got the professional high-ground. Self-respect, it's important.' He sat back, wiped his mouth. 'So, you're back working for Kilby.'

'For now.' Max ignored the dig. 'You must miss your mates, though. Mr Rothwell ran a pretty tight bunch as I remember, or do you lot still manage to fit in the odd night out in the King's Head?'

'Yeah, I have a few pints now and again with the Enfield lads.'

The claim rang hollow. Bailey hadn't been back and, from what Max had heard, he wouldn't be welcome if he did show his face. He'd coasted his last year, dumping the bulk of his caseload on those good mates of his.

Max gave Denny the nod.

'So, Mr Bailey what can you tell us about the Labrosse case? As I explained on the phone, we've come across some discrepancies between what's on the file and what should be there. Anything you remember would be helpful.'

'Such as?'

Denny took a deep breath, opened up her notebook. 'Such as who made the initial call to the emergency services?'

He shrugged. 'You'd have to check the tapes.'

'Who assigned you to deal with the incident?'

I got the nod straight from Chief Superintendent Rothwell.'

'What time was that?'

'Late afternoon. Evening maybe. Can't remember exactly.'

'When you first got to Labrosse's house, did anything strike you as odd?'

'What, apart from the dead bloke?'

'What I'm asking is, with the benefit of hindsight, could you say what it was you found in the Labrosse house that made you decide not to formally treat it as a crime scene?'

'Whoa there, hold on, love. I'm doing you a favour. Play nicely.' The smile had gone. He rolled his bread crusts into the napkin. Sauce seeped through the waxy tissue. He tossed it on the plate and looked to Max.

Max opened his hands. 'It's a legitimate question.'

Denny continued. 'You were the first to arrive at Labrosse's place.'

Bailey directed his answer to Max. 'Not true. The SOCO girl was there before me. A bit green around the gills. I assumed she'd been inside. One of the neighbours had given her a key.'

Denny persisted. 'You're certain of that. She was first to the scene, there when you got there?'

'Why, does she say different? If she does, she's wrong. Two things, Max. Firstly, don't believe everything you read. Secondly, I didn't do the bloody filing. Know what I'm saying?'

'Andy, I've been on this three days. I've already got enough to tell me there was more to Labrosse's death than your investigation uncovered and I'm not even trying. The case is a mess.'

'It's not my responsibility, not anymore.'

'And I don't want to be the one to make it. But I do need to know what you found and who told you to disregard crime scene protocols.'

As Bailey sat up, he jogged the table, knocking coffee from his mug. 'I did my job, Max. I did it for twenty-three fucking years. I was on my way out. I did what was necessary. The bloke fell down the stairs. The scene said so. The evidence said so. My experience told me so. There was no banister, for Christ's sake. If that doesn't compute, find someone or something that proves me a liar. Otherwise keep your circumstantial bollocks for the files. I'm not being lectured, not by you.'

'You won't have seen this.' Max handed Bailey a copy of a statement and gave him a moment to take it in. 'The SOCO says you took control of the scene from minute one. She was grateful to have an experienced hand to guide her. She's also quite clear that you were there when she arrived and that she came across blood spots in the bathroom where you said you'd already looked and which you hadn't told her about, same for the towel in the airing cupboard. Signs of blood, the lab analysis of which is also absent from the file.'

Bailey finished reading the statement. He wiped his nose with a grubby handkerchief. 'Look, Max, I didn't want to drop her in it. The kid was nervous, flapping a bit, and we agreed between us how best to handle it. I had no idea this bloke was a big fucking name.'

'And that makes a difference?' said Denny.

'In terms of the shit you're in if you get it wrong, course it does.'

'And did you get it wrong?'

He looked to Denny. 'We followed the rules as they needed to be followed. We assessed the case on its merits and got the job done to the best of our ability. Understand, we got the job done. That's enough.'

Max took back the statement. Bailey had left his greasy

thumbprint on the corner. 'When did you say you'd last spoken with Chief Superintendent Rothwell?'

'I didn't. But if you're asking, it was at my leaving do. He's the same with everyone. It's not personal, he just doesn't keep in touch.'

Or couldn't wait to see the back of you, thought Max.

As Bailey stood up to leave, the waitress dived in with a J-cloth to wipe away sauce spots and coffee puddles from the plastic tablecloth. 'Here y'are, love.' Bailey put a pound coin on the table. She dropped it in her apron pocket and said 'thanks' without looking up.

For a moment they stood awkwardly on the pavement. 'Appreciate you meeting with us,' said Max, 'I'll be in touch if we need anything else. I'm sure you've got things to do, reports to write, councillors to upset.'

'No need to take the piss.'

'Seriously, I'm glad things have worked out. Good to see somewhere an ex-policeman is appreciated.' Bailey wandered off towards the Town Hall as if he wasn't sure where he was going. He glanced back over his shoulder before turning the corner. 'Even one as bent as you,' said Max.

They walked back to the car in silence, lost in thought. Denny got in and launched her bag at the back seat with enough force to spill half its contents. 'You didn't tell me Kaye Wells had given a statement.'

'She didn't. I gave him the notes she gave us.' He pulled into the traffic.

'Typed and signed on a statement sheet?'

'I know what he's like, he'd have given us nothing otherwise.'

'Did you not think you might have told me that before we started?' Denny fished for her mobile. She picked up a voicemail from Chief Superintendent Rothwell's office. 'Rothwell's cancelled. Sends his apologies and says we'll have to reschedule later this week, early next.'

And so the game continued. One after the other, making it harder than it needed to be. Max kept the car heading across Clapton Common. 'What time was Rothwell's message?'

'Nine-twenty-three.'

Bailey hadn't lost any time. As they slowed for the lights at the junction with Stamford Hill, Max thought it through. Either he turned left, down through Stoke Newington and back into central London, or take a right towards Enfield and Chief Superintendent Rothwell. Max checked the mirror, then eased into the right hand lane.

14

Tyler

TYLER SPOKE TO NO ONE about Labrosse. He occupied evenings and weekends on his research, writing notes he knew no one would ever read, all the time fooling himself into thinking Labrosse didn't matter, that it was something he'd learn to live with. As the weeks passed, the lie he'd expected to plague his conscience had taken his voice as well. Days went by. He and Emily barely spoke.

After the Bournemouth weekend, they'd grown more distant until one evening he came home and found her furiously rubbing at a patch on the sideboard where wax from a candle had spilled and stained the wood. As he looked more closely, he saw the pad she was using to polish had almost stripped the veneer away. She seemed not to have noticed. 'You let it burn down,' she said, without looking up. 'It's bloody ruined.'

He loosened his tie. The sideboard had been a gift from her parents, both now dead. It had taken pride of place in the living room. Their first and, in the early years of their marriage, only piece of quality furniture. He hadn't realised at the time the wax had dripped and burned. It was a genuine accident that he'd forgotten to mention.

She was shouting now. 'You were last up. You're always last up. You let it burn down. You ruined it and you couldn't even tell me. And then you covered it up with – with this. I wondered why it had been moved.' She knocked aside the clock the kids had given them for their twentieth anniversary. He eased it away from the edge of the sideboard.

'I'm sorry. I should have said something.'

'Saying *something* would be a start.'

'We can get it restored, it'll be fine.' He put an arm around her shoulder. She drew back, shaking him off.

'I won't cry for you, I won't. I know you want me to.'

'Don't be ridiculous, of course, I don't.' And he thought he didn't, but by then he was shouting too, wanting her to stop.

She said, 'Just let me clean it. Let me do what I want. You do, upstairs in that bloody little room. For once, just let me do what I want. I didn't ask for your help or your advice. You just push me and push me to see how far I'll go. Well, now you know.'

'Emmy, that's crazy.'

'Now are you satisfied?'

He went upstairs, kicked off his shoes and lay on the bed. Half an hour later he heard her footfall on the landing. She came in and sat on the edge of the bed with her back to him. He stared at the shapes in the artex ceiling, imagining them into objects. Maps, old men's faces that looked a bit like Greek gods.

He broke the ice. 'I'm sorry we argued.'

'I don't think you have the first idea. Do you know how much you've cut yourself off?'

'What about you?'

'Me?' Slowly she shook her head. 'Please don't blame me, Michael. It's been like this for months. You're irritable and miserable, permanently preoccupied.'

He sat up. 'I'm surprised you noticed. You're hardly ever here. If you're not working late, you're at some pointless evening class. What is it this week, paint a pot? Chinese cookery? And then at weekends you're over at your sister's.'

'And did you stop to think why?'

He didn't answer. A collection of artex swirls formed an abstract likeness of the outline of England.

Emmy said, 'You take us, take *me* for granted.'

'I know I'm not perfect.'

'That's so typical of you.' She punched the pillow. 'I'm not asking for perfect. Heaven knows we've all got our flaws, but you won't even hold a conversation.'

He shrugged, tired. The ceiling shapes danced and were still dancing when he closed his eyes. The desire for peace was overwhelming. 'Can we get a drink?'

He followed her downstairs into the kitchen and clattered in the drawer for a corkscrew.

'Sometimes, I want flowers,' she said.

'I'll bring them. And chocolates if you want.'

'And we *have* to spend more time together going out, doing things.'

'Maybe we should book a holiday.' He regretted saying it instantly. He levered the cork, grateful for busy hands.

Emmy said, 'The way I feel right now I don't think I could bear a week in your company. Small steps are fine.' She paused. 'This is hard for me to say, but once in a while, I want you to want me. For you to show me you want me. Do you know what I'm saying? I need that, even if you don't.'

He looked away.

'You don't understand, do you? I haven't given up like you have.' She took the glass of wine he offered. 'Sometimes, I do still want...' She left the sentence unfinished and sipped her wine. 'I sometimes wonder if you know what it is to be happy. Pleasure, Michael. Doing things you like to do, because they make you feel good. Do you *feel* good? Are you enjoying your life?' She topped his glass up, took the rest of the bottle and went to bed alone.

In the unlit living room, darkness closed in. He didn't feel comforted by their home. Their cushions, furniture, television, the books, the DVDs, the sofa were components. Like parts of a kit that you bought and glued together to make a family home. He put the anniversary clock back in its place with the photographs either side. He picked up one of the family, a holiday on a beach. He remembered the day at the seaside with the kids, the sun tingling on their backs, shining off rock pools. Had he been happy? He looked happy in the photo. But in truth, he couldn't remember. It felt like someone else's life.

Emmy was moving around upstairs. She came down and he stood to meet her, lifting his arms to hold her. She remained in the doorway, the light from the hall behind her. She said, 'I'm not being fair to you.'

'I'm so sorry,' said Tyler. 'I shouldn't have let things get to me like this, it's idiotic.'

She backed away, 'Michael, listen.' His name sounded foreign on her lips. Something in her tone, like a doctor with test results you don't want to hear. His hands dropped.

'There was a man I got talking to at my cooking class a month or so ago. We went for a drink afterwards, a group of us. I thought nothing of it, but the next week he asked me again. None of the others were able to go. I think he already knew that. Actually, I think he might have planned it. But I went anyway. We chatted about the food we'd been making, music, things we liked, things that made us laugh. Then he invited me back to his flat for coffee and I went. I took it so far, then I stopped it.'

'You had sex.'

'No. Nothing happened. It's over. It's done and I didn't sleep with him.'

'But you wanted to.'

She hesitated. 'He was the sort of man I could become friends with. But what I knew absolutely was that to have slept with him, even to have kissed him, would have meant leaving

95

you. I'll never be unfaithful and I'm not ready to leave. So, it couldn't happen.'

'You say that as if you will be ready at some point.'

She looked at him then, her eyes filled. 'Only if you keep me out. Make a space for me, please.' She took his hand. 'Come to bed with me.'

Emmy turned dismissively, wordlessly, to face the wall. Tyler was still for a while, a weight on his chest. Crushed. Impotent. 'I was hoping you'd understand.'

'I do,' she said.

'Well, be more understanding.' A silence. 'Hold me, please.'

'I can't.'

There was nothing more to be said.

15

Max

CHIEF SUPERINTENDENT ROTHWELL HAD been Max's final handler in a decade of undercover work. Before Kilby ended the Green Lanes operation, they'd got to know each other well. Not exactly a friendship – status weighed too heavily against Max for that, but working undercover meant he looked to the senior man for guidance and reassurance. There was something protective in Rothwell's overseeing that earned Max's respect. Rothwell had never let him down, nor did he rubbish the relationship with Liz, not to Max's face at least. And he'd benefited from the work – Max's main task for Special Operations opened up sidelines of investigation that put fresh impetus into two other cases, both homicides on Rothwell's ground. It counted for nothing now. Max knew his reappearance would not be welcome and he was right. Rothwell was pissed off at the intrusion. Denny made the mistake of defending it. 'Sir, with respect –'

'If you respected me, you wouldn't have come after I'd cancelled our meeting.'

'We didn't get the message,' said Denny and wished she hadn't.

Rothwell gave a slow shake of the head. 'Just... don't.' He turned a cigarette end over end on the desk. 'I've got a fifteen-year-old kid downstairs. He's suspected of murdering a fourteen-year-old on his way to school this morning. We think an argument over a girl, so he waits for the lad off the bus and stabs him. I should have been leading his interview ten minutes ago, so now, because of you, someone else has to do it. If we're lucky, we'll get enough to hold him. But it's my job. I should be making sure. You come with Assistant Commissioner Kilby's mandate, which means I have to stop what I'm doing.' He turned to Max. 'If you have something to say, just say it.'

Max set out the list of procedural glitches that littered the Labrosse case. With each telling, they felt less like coincidence or even negligence, and more a premeditated attempt to confound. 'There's no way of knowing whether Derek Labrosse was murdered because neither DS Bailey or yourself seemed to consider it a possibility. The SOCO –'

He interrupted, 'Kaye Wells was a rookie as I remember.'

'She was,' said Max.

Denny said, 'The problem we have is that, whatever decisions were made by you or DS Bailey, they can't be substantiated by the paperwork. We don't even have Mrs Labrosse's statement on record. Assuming there was one.'

Rothwell leaned back in his seat and clasped his hands behind his head. 'You trying to make me look bad, Max?'

'That's not my intention.'

'Must be Kilby's, then. What do you want?'

'We need you to answer some questions.' Denny had the notebook out again.

Rothwell laughed. 'Are you interviewing me, Detective Constable Denny?'

'If you don't mind.'

'Come on, Max, play the game. You can't just turn up and conduct an interview with a senior officer. I wouldn't cough for Kilby without someone from my team in the room. And I'd want it on tape, you know that.'

Denny said, 'We're trying to keep this informal.'

He sniffed. 'It's just possible you might be naïve enough to think that, I know damn well he isn't.' He raised a finger in Max's direction.

'Our brief is clear,' said Max. 'Was everything done that should have been done for Derek Labrosse? DS Bailey was a month off his pension, so perhaps he was careless, tossed it off. If that's the case, I need to fill in the gaps, work out what did happen and provide some explanation as to why it wasn't picked up sooner.'

Rothwell swung in his chair. The arc of cool air from a desk fan rustled his papers. He placed his palms flat on the desk and stood. 'You have my attention. Get everything you want down and email it across to me here. I'll give you what I can. But I want it all in writing.' He fixed Max with his very blue eyes. 'Take my advice, Max, draw your conclusions from *all* the evidence, not just what you've been fed. Now, if there's nothing else…'

Rothwell escorted them along the corridor. 'Don't be a stranger, Max, but make an appointment next time, eh? And you DC Denny, I've heard good things. Come and spend a little time with us if Mr Kilby lets you off the leash.'

Back in the car Denny fumed. 'What was that shit about *all* the evidence? No one's telling us bloody anything. And you gave him Bailey as a get-out on a plate. If I'd known we were just looking for a scapegoat –'

Max loosened his tie, 'Chief Superintendent Rothwell is not someone either of us want to get on the wrong side of. He's not who we're up against.'

'And you'd know that because?'

'I've worked with him before.' Max started the engine. 'I want to meet Mrs Labrosse today if we can. The house isn't far from here.'

'I can't get hold of her. It's like she's permanently on duty.'

'So?'

'I'm saying she never answers, never gets back when I leave messages, not once.'

The barrier lifted and Max drove out of the car park.

Caroline Labrosse wasn't at home. They parked on the Ridgeway, the main road a short distance from the entrance to Farorna Walk, and watched people come and go. Curtains twitched in one of the houses. There wasn't a car parked in a drive more than a year old. 'No way could you get in or out of here without someone seeing,' said Max.

'Apparently it was foggy.'

'Where did you say she works?'

'I didn't, but as you ask, Northwick Park Hospital, out near Harrow.' She checked her notes. 'Senior assistant pathologist.'

They hit the North Circular and made it as far as the Great North Way junction before traffic slowed to a crawl, then came to a standstill. Max switched off the engine. An armed police officer made his way down the line of cars, leaning into each on the driver's side.

'What's the hold up?' said Max.

'Vehicle checkpoint. We're operating a stop and search on all vehicles. You're to stay in your vehicle until instructed to move on. Failure to do so may result in a charge of obstruction for which we will prosecute under emergency powers.'

Max showed his ID and got out of the car. He walked down the line of stationary vehicles as armed officers persuaded hot and irritated drivers to remain in their cars. Dog section had arrived and were now patrolling the first hundred metres of stopped cars. A bevy of complaints and protests fell on deaf ears. A woman and child were escorted to the roadside. The woman pulled down the crying kid's pants to piss in full view. At the head of the jam, police vehicles blocked the road. A stinger team were stationed twenty metres further on alongside another armed unit. Boiler-suited teams of three searched each car, at the end of which, the drivers were given a leaflet and directed to U-turn. Max picked up a crumpled leaflet from the roadside. It thanked the recipient for their cooperation in enabling Counter Terrorism Command to carry out their duties. It gave the Home Office website and a phone number for complaints.

'I need to get through,' said Max, once more pulling out his ID.

'You'll have to go back the way you came.' The sergeant waved a blue delivery van forward and the three men went to work. 'Nothing's coming through here. Nothing goes west or north. Those are my instructions and I don't give a shit who you are.'

'You been doing this long?'

'All my working life, mate. Belfast to Basra.' The sergeant moved back. Max noticed the absence of a number on his epaulette.

They were waved out of line. Max was in the process of U-turning when one of the officers tapped on the window. 'Sir, can you hang on a minute, I've just been told there's a problem with the car. Is it yours?'

'Last time I looked.'

'Apparently, it's not insured.'

'What?'

'We've just run a check. ANPR database says you don't have valid insurance for this vehicle. Can you pull over, we'll need to confirm your ID.'

'You're fucking joking.'

The sergeant approached.

'You've seen my ID.'

'We need to be certain.' The sergeant's hand tightened on the weapon across his chest. Max turned the engine off and handed over his ID. The sergeant made his way back to the command vehicle at the head of the queue. He brought back a printout. No mistake. 'Your ID checks out, but the car doesn't seem to be insured. You need to sort it with your insurance company. Legally, you shouldn't be driving.'

'I've got personal cover,' said Denny. 'That okay with you?'

The sergeant shrugged. Max and Denny switched places.

Whatever else the sergeant said was lost as Denny pulled away from the kerb. As she drove back towards Enfield, Max negotiated insurance company call centre security checks. Finally, with a voice at the other end of the line, he received an explanation: the insurance had been cancelled a week ago – the call centre rep checked – by Mr Mark Lomax. Max asked to be transferred to the fraud team. They ran a match between his voice and the Mark Lomax who'd cancelled the insurance. Patently not the same person. Denny turned off the North Circular and pulled in near Bounds Green Underground Station.

Max finished the call and hung up. 'Someone cancelled the insurance for this car and insured me for a top of the range Audi I don't own. Unbelievable. The customer service bloke said they'd written to me to say the premium had gone up.'

'And did they?'

'I've no idea, I haven't checked the post.'

'Do you want me to find another route to Harrow?'

'No, it can wait. We'll go back to the office.' Most likely Caroline Labrosse would be stuck in the same traffic they'd left behind.

As Denny drove into town, they worked through the points Rothwell needed to explain. Based on the information from Bailey and Kaye Wells, there was still a question of the first call, had Rothwell assigned Bailey, the straight-up assumption of Labrosse's death being accidental, and why the follow-ups had been ignored. Denny wanted to go further. Like it or not, Rothwell was responsible for the standards of case files produced by his officers. Something had broken down and it needed to be asked. Bailey might have been lazy, but this bordered on negligence.

Max disagreed. 'You're not wrong, but don't ask it on paper. He won't answer it.'

They argued about that for a while, but narrowed the rest down, compromising on a clean half-dozen questions.

'Do you want me to email him when we get back?' said Denny.

'I'll do it later.' Max let his head fall back on the headrest and closed his eyes. As they tracked down Holloway Road, he thought about Rothwell saying *don't be a stranger*. It was easily dismissed as a throwaway. Max didn't think so.

16

Theobold

FROM THE OUTSIDE, NOT much about the Labrosse house was different from his last visit. A few more weeds in the borders, a front door untreated this year and showing signs of fading in the early evening sun. Caroline Labrosse answered the door in an old blue button-down shirt, presumably one of Derek's, and bleach-marked track bottoms. Her hair was tied in a scarf. He asked if she'd been decorating.

'Of course not,' she said blankly. 'What brings you here, social or the other thing?'

'Bit of both.'

'You'd better come in.'

He followed her into the kitchen. The cupboards had been emptied, their contents covering all available workspace. Crockery at one end, tins, bottles, jars and nondescript pots at the other. He picked up a tub of baking powder.

'I was going to do some cooking,' she said, 'but one thing led to another and, well, it's all hopelessly out of date.' She picked up a tin. 'That one's a souvenir from before the war.'

'Which one?'

'The one just finished or the one you're about to start. Are you coming through?'

Theobold edged last night's dinner tray aside with the toe of his shoe and sat on the sofa. There were new photographs mounted on the mantelpiece. Derek and the family, Derek with foreign dignitaries, Derek shaking hands with the Prime Minister. None of Caroline and Derek together. 'So how have you been keeping?'

Caroline sat back, lit a cigarette and exhaled. 'Mrs Andreas finally left.' She began as if picking up a conversation momentarily interrupted. The fact that he neither knew nor cared who Mrs Andreas was had no bearing. 'She said she couldn't carry on working in the house where Derek died, said it made her feel *sad*. I think she just missed the extra twenty quid he used to slip her for ironing his shirts. He used to say I never quite got the creases out – he was right of course, I hate ironing. Mrs Andreas got through a can of spray-starch every week. But to answer your question, Patrick, I've been *keeping* like shit. I've had no one to help me with this place. Ruth is back at university trying to catch up on the work she missed when Derek died so I hardly see her. I'm still waiting for probate to be sorted. Until then I can't own the house, or benefit from Derek's will, or receive my widow's pension, which leaves me getting by on my frankly shitty salary from the hospital.'

'You should have called, I can help.'

'Yourself.'

Theobold did not defend himself. A month or so after Derek died, he'd lent a hand going through the paperwork in the upstairs office and set aside a series of Derek's files to be returned to the Home Office. Caroline took exception to some of the files being taken. These were Derek's personal files, she said, not official documents. At the time Theobold conceded. Later she discovered the files were missing and called him. He denied taking them, but said he'd check to see if they'd found their way into the crate they'd taken away. He told her they weren't there. She didn't believe him.

Caroline looked out into the garden. A cat was using the cover of the overgrown grass for a low crawl to the bird table. 'What is it you want, Patrick?'

'I heard you went to see the local police.'

'You shit, I knew this was no bloody social call. So what, are you here to tear me off a strip, tell me I'm casting shame on the Department?'

Caroline's am-dram widow performance was beginning to irritate him. 'I was concerned and I wanted to know if you were okay. Clearly, you're not.' He leaned forward, his fingers interlocked. 'Caroline, if you need information from the police, ask me. I can get it.'

'Yes Patrick, but you'll only get me what *you* want me to know.'

He pulled a magazine from the seat behind him, sat back and crossed his legs, arranging the creases in his trousers. Plainly this was a different Caroline. What concerned him wasn't so much that she no longer deferred to him as she'd done in the weeks after Derek's death, but that her animosity seemed planted, as if someone had been whispering, telling tales. 'What did the police say?'

'Not much. I wanted to know about the man who was here the day Derek died. Remember, I asked you months ago and you did bugger all about it.'

'That isn't fair. I told you, he was interviewed and eliminated from the police enquiries.'

'I don't believe you. What did he say? Where's the statement? I want to see it.' She stubbed out the cigarette and went to the kitchen. He heard a bottle top unscrewed and the slosh of liquid in a glass. She came back and handed him a glass of red wine. Her own glass was at least twice as full. After the first few sips she seemed to relax, her eye drawn to the garden again. 'I can live without Mrs Andreas, but I'll have to get a gardener. I can't do the lawn by myself. Acres of the bloody stuff. I told Derek we should have got it decked, some of it at least, but he liked the green. Wanted to put a hole in the middle so he could practise putting. Which was odd as he'd never played golf.

The one time he went to the club he hated it, said it was like being at work. Too many arseholes loving the sounds of their own voices.' She sighed. 'Anyway, you'll be pleased to know the police told me nothing. Detective Sergeant Bailey doesn't work for them anymore and Chief Superintendent Rothwell is a charming man who covers his immaculate arse. He told me the same as you: the man was interviewed, cleared and allowed to go. Only he's a more convincing liar.'

Theobold finished his drink and gestured for a refill. Caroline waved towards the kitchen. He brought the bottle back and left it on the table within her reach. She waited a few seconds and topped herself up. He took a deep breath, 'I am sorry you've been left to cope on your own. I ought to have given you more time, but it's difficult when you're not sure if you're intruding. And I'm sorry about the misunderstanding with those files. To be honest, Derek's loss has been difficult to cope with at work and we've struggled. If I took them, it was a genuine mistake.'

She waved the apology away. 'Just bad timing. I didn't want to let more of Derek go than I already had. I doubt there was anything we actually need. Can we change the subject, what's the gossip? How's the boy wonder handling my husband's job?'

He laughed. 'Gavin? He's capable. He doesn't have Derek's gravitas.'

'Or his principles.'

Someone had been talking. He smiled. 'You and he didn't get on, did you?'

'It was a bit undignified, don't you think, jumping behind Derek's desk that quickly? Maybe he didn't have a choice. Either way, it seemed almost planned.' She drank again, this time emptying the glass.

'Caroline, I'd like to help you sort things out. Give me a couple of weeks and I promise to see if I can't get to the bottom of this business with the police, and I'll give these idiots the hurry-up about the money matters. We need that settled, don't we?'

'I know I bloody do.'

Her lack of gratitude made him spiteful. Time, he thought, to make the puppet dance a little. 'There is something I want you to hear first from me, though. The police are carrying out an internal enquiry into the conduct of the investigation of Derek's death. They're saying Detective Sergeant Bailey wasn't as thorough as he might have been.'

Her eyes lit up. 'So, they do acknowledge they got it wrong?'

'Not exactly. I'll be honest, we think they're using it as a cover to investigate the Department's activities towards the back end of last year.'

Her fingers trembled. 'What activities?'

He hesitated.

'For Christ's sake, Patrick, what?'

'There were financial irregularities. Monies transferred to unspecified accounts with Derek's authority, classified papers missing. It's bullshit, an oversight I'm sure, but it might explain why it's been difficult for you to be awarded probate.'

'I don't believe it.' She shook her head. 'Why didn't anyone tell *me?* This on top of everything else.'

'That's why it's important for you to be careful with what you say if the police speak to you. Just give everything a dead bat.'

'What does that even mean?'

'That you and I need to be clear about what you're going to say.'

He heated a pasta ready-meal in the microwave and persuaded her she should eat something. She insisted he share. He managed a couple of forkfuls of soggy tortellini while schooling her in what she should tell the police. It crossed his mind to ask whether she'd discussed her concerns with Derek's other colleagues, but left it for another time. He put the kettle on and was making coffee when he received a text from Hannah Rees telling him she wanted to send this damn driver to his home. Theobold arranged a neutral venue and made his excuses. As he was leaving, he rested his fingertips on Caroline Labrosse's arm, 'Caroline, let me be a friend to you. And don't worry, I promise you there's nothing we can't sort out.' He kissed her lightly on the cheek and felt her recoil.

17

Max

MAX PARKED CLOSE TO Northwick Park Hospital. He found the place visually forbidding and deeply unsettling, its square blocks of cold concrete and glass leaving him in no doubt this was somewhere he didn't want to be. As they walked towards the entrance, a succession of HGVs rumbled past. He was keeping his expectations in check, although anything Caroline Labrosse told them would be an improvement on what they had already.

Denny had to raise her voice to be heard above the traffic noise. 'Is there a plan?'

'I thought I'd leave that to you. Maybe keep your notebook in the bag this time.'

They found the laboratory complex with the help of a hollow-eyed woman in a mauve dressing gown who insisted on acting as tour guide. The woman walked impossibly slowly, pointing out those areas of the hospital with which she'd had personal experience, recalling the names of her doctors and their specialisms. She looked quizzically when Denny asked her own name. 'I think it's Joyce.'

The pathology receptionist told them to wait. After a few minutes, Caroline Labrosse, in pale blue scrubs and lab coat, strode through the double doors to the front desk. 'This needs to take no more than five minutes.'

Denny made the introductions. 'We'll be as quick as we can.

Thank you for agreeing to see us. Is there somewhere we can go? Some of what we're asking may be a little sensitive.'

'Here's fine.' She checked her watch.

Denny kept her voice low. 'We're looking into the conduct of the investigation around your husband's death. I did try to contact you a number of times yesterday and the day before and left messages. Obviously, you've been busy.'

'I put in the hours. It's what one does, so my daughter tells me, keep oneself occupied.' Her gaze flitted, not meeting Denny's.

'Mrs Labrosse –'

'It's Caroline.'

'Caroline, if you wouldn't mind, we need to ask you what you remember of events on the day your husband died.'

The receptionist looked up. 'If you want to use Jill's office, she's out most of the day.' She ushered them into a cramped side office and closed the door behind them.

Caroline sat behind the desk. 'I was here that afternoon. On call for the whole weekend. Derek was absolutely fine when I left him in the morning. He was going to work, which he did often on Saturday mornings. Sometimes we met for dinner – there's a Thai restaurant in Winchmore Hill that we both liked. Other times I might not see him until Sunday. I had the call from Detective Sergeant Bailey sometime around seven in the evening. He told me there'd been an accident. Look, this isn't something one wants to discuss endlessly. Surely, it's all a matter of record.'

Max said, 'Can you remember which phone you took the call on?'

She hesitated. 'My mobile's in my locker while I'm on duty, so the one at reception I think. All calls come through there.'

'Even at weekends?'

'If not, they're redirected either to the switchboard or to the senior on call, which would have been me. We are extraordinarily pushed, so I'm sorry if I don't remember precise details.'

Denny nodded sympathetically. 'It's okay, we can check. Please, carry on.'

'That's it. My husband had an accident. We'd taken the handrail from the stairs to make it more open. Bloody stupid idea, as it turned out. Anyway, we disagreed about it, argued in fact, because I felt it was unsafe whatever it did aesthetically. We were planning to have it put back. My sister was coming to stay – she has young children and I had visions of one of my nieces taking a fall. I had thought Derek would be more careful.'

'Would you say your husband was a careful person?' asked Denny.

Caroline's eyes flashed, 'What does that mean?'

'Just generally, was he accident-prone, preoccupied with his work, perhaps?'

'No, he was not.'

Through the glass panel in the door, Max could see the receptionist filing patient notes. He wondered how soundproof the partition walls might be and guessed not very. She caught his eye and moved away.

Denny changed tack. 'Can you remember what time you got home that evening?'

'A friend gave me a lift. I was in no fit state to drive. It must have been about a quarter to nine.'

'Who was the friend?'

'Leanne, she was an agency nurse here, but she's moved on now.' The receptionist knocked and entered. 'Sorry to interrupt, Caroline. Doctor Caulfield needs you to look at Mrs Dean's results. Her daughter's here and he'd like to update her.'

'I'll be there shortly.'

'He's asking for you now.'

Caroline stood. 'I have to go.'

Denny touched her arm. 'Perhaps we could arrange a time when it's more convenient.'

'Look, this is your business. It has nothing to do with me. My husband died because he fell down the stairs. He wasn't drunk, he wasn't accident-prone. He was a good man and he loved his family. And he worked hard. Probably too hard, but which of us doesn't? He was the most principled man I ever knew. So, please leave it alone. Christ knows this has been awful enough without dragging it all out again.'

As they filed out, Max said, 'Caroline, I was looking at some press cuttings of your husband's memorial service. I didn't see you in any of the photos.'

She stalled. 'I didn't go to the official one. I couldn't bear the thought of them all queueing up to offer their vacuous bloody condolences.'

'Did someone advise you to stay away?'

She looked straight at him. 'Do you think I'd have paid any attention if they had? No, we had a quiet committal ceremony. Just family and a few old friends. Our marriage might not have had much in the way of springtime and roses, but please don't insult me by suggesting I didn't care. We were good together. We loved each other.'

'I promise you, no one's doubting it. Or him.'

'Look, if you want to finish this, I can meet you in the canteen in half an hour. Right now I have work. People need me, living people.'

Max and Denny waited in the canteen, an unwelcoming sterile space, walls lined with self-service snack machines and drinks dispensers. A woman sat alone at a table, red-eyed, struggling to hold back tears. *God help us all*, thought Max. He swilled the last of his coffee, grimaced at the grit in the bottom of the cup. He paced the room, ill-at-ease with the functionality of the place. 'Doesn't make it any less like a hospital, does it?'

'What?'

'It's like a departure lounge.' He caught Denny's expression. 'Don't say it.'

Patients and staff came and went, so did the half-hour. Caroline Labrosse didn't show and when Max went back to Pathology reception, he was informed that she'd had a migraine and left for the day. He handed his card to the nurse and said to tell Mrs Labrosse he'd be in touch.

They walked out from Northwick Park's shadow into bright sunshine. Max was certain that Caroline Labrosse hadn't been at work on the Saturday her husband died. He had the distinct impression that she, like Kaye Wells, like Bailey, had been briefed what to say. None of them afraid to be caught in the lie.

18

Tyler

AT LUNCHBREAK ON FRIDAY, Tyler bought flowers for Emmy. Heavenly-scented lilies with pale satin blooms that cost a fortune. In the office they joked, was he on a promise? He cut a plastic bottle in half, filled it with water and propped the flowers in the corner.

That afternoon an all-users email flashed up simultaneously on every screen in the building informing staff that the police would be conducting interviews in the coming week in connection with the death of the former director, Derek Labrosse. His heart palpitated. He printed the email and left his desk. He locked himself in the toilet cubicle and sat with his head between his knees.

The police would be making routine enquiries. There had, ran the email, been a thorough investigation at the time. However, there were outstanding issues and points of fact that had come to light recently which required clarification. Staff were expected to cooperate fully. But should any staff member feel the need for trade union, management or colleague support during the interviews, this would be positively encouraged. Anyone who wished to opt out or to make their own arrangements had the right to do so, but was advised to speak with the Human Resources department in the first instance. The email was signed by the new director, Gavin S Lillico.

Routine enquiries. Tyler's first thought was that Theobold had decided to turn him in and this was delivery of his punishment in-waiting. He lost himself in a muddle of self-explanation. Justification for his actions and inactions turned over and over until a stray helpful thought emerged: here was a chance to do the right thing. The opportunity he needed to be at peace with himself, with Emily and the rest of their lives.

He made his way back to the office. The afternoon passed lazily in expectation of the hot weekend. It had an end of term feel. Around three o'clock, the girls went down to the kiosk to buy ice creams. They looked idiotic, he thought, licking Cornettos and grinning like children. He used the time to tidy up, throw out some old papers and declutter his desk. Eager to be home, he managed to catch an earlier train, carefully laying the lilies in the overhead luggage rack. As he stood in the overcrowded carriage, he thought it all through, re-establishing the details as he remembered them. He would explain to Emmy, then write everything down if necessary to get it all straight in his own mind before he spoke to the police. He would say what he needed to say and there would be release. And consequences, of course. But he would have done the right thing. Someone would know what he knew. Then things would change and their lives would be back to normal.

The carriages pulled slowly into the station and, as he followed the Friday night crowds down the steps, he was overwhelmed by a sinking feeling in the pit of his stomach. He'd left Emmy's flowers on the train.

19

Max

LATE IN THE AFTERNOON of the Home Office interviews, Max left the room he and Denny had been allocated. He walked through the building, sensing the atmosphere. He spoke to people randomly, until a chance conversation took him to three former members of Derek Labrosse's private office. Kate, Richard, and Alan sat with their workstations screened from others in the open-plan area on the third floor. Max introduced himself and took a spare seat. 'Do you mind? I take it you've been told what I'm here for.'

Kate kept her focus fixed on her PC monitor. 'We know you shouldn't be talking to us.'

'Which is a bit odd, given that you must have known Derek better than anyone.'

Alan looked up, but said nothing.

'I'm trying to build a picture of the man and, so far, I've got half a story at best. Lots of people giving me the corporate line. I just wondered if you'd tell me what he was like to work with.'

An exchange of glances.

'One word, just give me one word.'

A silence.

'Alan?'

'I'd say uncompromising.'

'Richard?'

117

Richard threw Kate a nervous look, which she ignored. 'Demanding, I guess.'

'Kate?'

'What they said.'

'Did you like him?'

Alan sat back from his keyboard. 'I don't know about *like*. He pushed hard and expected us to deliver, which we usually did. If you were struggling, he'd help you work out a way through step by step. We did what we did, because he made us feel it was important.'

Max sensed something unsaid. 'Can I borrow this?' He took a post-it notepad from Kate's desk, speaking as he wrote. 'Before today, has anyone else asked you about Derek or his work?'

Kate tilted her head and smiled. 'What do you think?'

'How long did you work for him?'

'Too long.'

'Now, we're high and dry,' said Alan.

'It isn't just that,' Kate said sharply. She sighed and looked at the other two. 'Near the end, say in the six months before he died, Derek demanded a lot from us. We put in the hours – I'm not saying anyone minded, but he used to call us in on Saturday and he'd keep us working late most nights. You knew the work would have his name on it, but he used to acknowledge the effort we'd put in. We were a tight team, but since he died they act like we were never there. It's the way it goes, we understand that, but it doesn't make it right.' She gave a shrug and pushed away from her desk. 'I'm getting a cold drink, anyone want one?'

As she left, Kate stood aside for Lillico who marched towards them, waving a sheet of paper. 'You were supposed to stick to the list.'

Max sat back. 'We have.'

'This list, the one you agreed to this morning. These people aren't on it.'

'My colleague is working through your list.'

'We had an agreement. Look, can we take this discussion somewhere a bit less public?'

Max followed Lillico through the maze of workstations to a glass-walled meeting room screened from the main office. Max dropped the blinds. Lillico made deliberate eye contact, but couldn't hold it. 'I told you there would be boundaries. Clear boundaries. Boundaries beyond which it would be wholly inappropriate for you to conduct your investigation. We cannot operate without –'

'Boundaries. I get it.' Max sat down.

Lillico paced. 'I will be speaking to Assistant Commissioner Kilby about this.'

A silence ballooned and filled the room. They sat, not as they had that morning in the air-conditioned boardroom, Lillico surrounded by stone-faced acolytes. Now it was just the two of them and his bluster was short-lived. 'You've exceeded your brief and undermined my authority, strolling around the place, upsetting the staff. You've disrupted the working of this department, which is not acceptable.'

'Because I asked a few questions?'

'Hardly. Your presence here is a professional courtesy offered by the Home Secretary and I will not stand by and see you abuse it.'

'This is a police investigation. It's my job to engage with as many people as have relevant information. Maybe I didn't explain it clearly enough, but this being, as you rightly point out, the Home Office, I thought you'd have a basic understanding of how these things work.' Max pulled the sheet of paper towards him and straightened out some of the creases. 'Tell me, how many staff are you responsible for in this building?'

'I can't give you an exact figure.'

'Roughly.'

'In the region of a few hundred at any one time.'

'And how many are there on this list of yours – a dozen?'

'These are the people who it is relevant for you to see. Further than that, its contents are not open for discussion. I don't want staff interrogated. We've been through this. Assistant Commissioner Kilby gave me his word.'

'Some of those people I've just been speaking to were moved down from the fifth floor.'

'If you say so.'

'Derek Labrosse's team, is that right?'

'Possibly, yes.'

'And they're not on the list. Would you say that's *relevant?*'

A trickle of perspiration followed the line of Lillico's cheekbone. Fair dues, he was sticking to his guns. 'What's relevant is that you give me your undertaking to restrict your interviews to those on the list.'

'They were transferred immediately after Labrosse's death and your appointment, so presumably it was your decision. No explanation, just kicked downstairs and marginalised.'

'After Derek's death, we reorganised. It happens all the time. If this is about how I run my department, you're straying out of bounds again.'

'You put a screen between them and everyone else. They are physically separated from their colleagues. I don't see that on any other floor.'

'I don't oversee the office plan.'

'Who picked up Labrosse's work, was that you?'

'The majority, yes.'

'Hard man to follow.'

Lillico sat up a little. 'We'd worked together closely on most things before Derek died. It was a challenge, but we managed.'

'You moved his *team* down here.'

'I told you, reorganised'

'Say that often enough, you'll believe it.'

'It means what it says.'

Max gently tapped the table, playing a silent melody with the fingers of one hand. 'In that case, perhaps you can shed some light on this. People have commented on the American delegation occupying the suite of offices next to yours on the fifth floor –'

Lillico cut in, 'They are representatives of an extremely important US Government-sponsored exchange programme. Here as our guests to develop transatlantic links with UK security industries. I suggest you'd waste less time if you paid less attention to office gossip and stuck to the task as agreed.' He stood up, tipping the chair over behind him. 'I'll ring Kilby, you'll be finished here today.'

Max kept his seat. 'One of the people we interviewed this morning – one from your list – seemed to think we were suggesting you had something to do with Labrosse's death. He became quite defensive on your behalf.'

'I'm not surprised, it's a ridiculous allegation.'

'Detective Constable Denny reassured him that wasn't what we were investigating. I just mentioned it so you'd know. Also, we've had to make it plain a few times today we're not interested in professional jealousies that existed between you and Labrosse.'

Lillico paced again. 'Absolutely right, my professional relationship with Derek was never an issue.'

'But you were poaching areas of his work before he died?'

He hesitated, then picked the chair up. 'I had been allocated some work he'd been responsible for. I'd hardly call it *poaching*. The work was delegated directly by the Minister.'

'Did he have a problem with that?'

'I don't think so. I'm sure he'd have told me.'

Max beat a two-finger drum roll and got to his feet. 'Thanks for your time, Mr Lillico. I'll be in touch.'

Lillico walked out. Max followed. He saw Kate across the office. She headed him off as he waited for the lift. 'What did he say, are we in trouble?'

'I think your boss is taking his frustrations out on someone else today. Is he always this uptight?'

'He's not my boss.'

'No?'

'Well, kind of, but these days we work through Patrick Theobold.' She looked at the floor. 'The HR Director came down when you were in there. We were told not to speak to you.'

'Yet here you are.'

'I've told you I can't tell you anything.' She bit at the corner of her thumb.

'If you want to talk to me privately, I can arrange it.'

She shook her head. 'No thanks, I've a mortgage to pay.'

He guided her to a blind spot by the lift, out of sight of the main office. 'Kate, tell me, what exactly was your job with Labrosse?'

'We were his project team. You know that.'

'What was the project? Between you and me.'

She hesitated, her neck reddening, and took a deep breath. 'We were carrying out a feasibility study for a networked surveillance system. The highest possible specification. I know he looks like he's just out of college, but Alan's got a greater technical insight into that stuff than anyone in this building. The system would have brought every existing CCTV system in the UK under a single central control, fed into software matched to image recognition systems, passports, driving licence details, everything from your Nectar card to social media and bank details. All singing, all dancing. We'd costed it, completed all the impact assessments, made recommendations, drafted the final report. Then Derek killed it.'

'The report or the whole thing?'

'All of it. One day we're sorting out a distribution list, next morning, project terminated. He refused to pursue it. I can't say more than that, we weren't involved in the negotiations, but there were formal ministerial objections.'

'What now? Come on Kate, don't tease.'

She lowered her voice. 'Same project, different management, higher cost. Private contract, single tender with a corporation providing the technology, implementing and managing it. Our government leases it back.' Her voice dropped until it was barely a whisper. 'This is the biggest single contract the Home Office has ever awarded and the government never owns it, IDI does.'

'Who's IDI?'

'*They* are ID International. Google them, you'll get the picture.' She called the lift. 'We're non-people here. They don't want us, but they can't afford to let us go.'

The lift arrived. A woman stepped out. Kate sheepishly acknowledged her greeting. Max stepped in and held his hand against the lift doors. 'Kate, were you working on the Saturday Labrosse died?'

'We all were. The atmosphere was horrible. Derek left about three, I think.'

'When you say all?'

'Derek, Gavin Lillico, James Creedy, Patrick Theobold, and the three of us.'

Max took his hand away. The doors closed.

He worked on at home that evening, digesting information gained from the day's formal interviews. He checked out IDI online, trawling through news articles and references. Most related to the company's Chief Operating Officer, a self-made man called David Bittman. Otherwise, the company website was slickly corporate and wholly unmemorable. He flicked through Denny's notes. Lillico's briefed functionaries had stuck dutifully to the party line. *Non-people*, Kate said. Max rubbed his eyes and switched on a reading lamp. He was ready to call it a day when Rothwell called. He had the answers to the questions Max had sent, suggesting they would be better discussed one-to-one, if Max could face a second trip to Enfield in a week. They agreed to meet the following morning.

Max slumped back in his chair. He poured another glass of Rioja and went to the window. He opened it and leaned out, feeling the warmth of the evening on his face. Down in the street he watched a Vauxhall Astra inching into an impossible parking space. A resident's permit gave you the right to park on Goldhurst Terrace, but it didn't guarantee the room to carry out the manoeuvre.

There was a time when, as a professional watcher of people, Max maintained you could keep any suspect under covert surveillance indefinitely. It was a matter of knowing your subject, having a clear objective and a plan to achieve it. After that, patience, practice, technique, training and numbers. Especially the numbers. Those were the principles DI Redding allowed him to put into practice in his first year in Tottenham. Max had schooled the team from scratch. Some were recently out of uniform and all of them new to the game. Within months, they'd collected a cache of information on a dozen serious and organised criminals. All involved with drug dealing, violence, and intimidation. All of them working on recruiting kids to make the next generation in their own image. Thanks to Max, DI Redding's team knew patterns of behaviour, networks of associates, personal profiles. They tracked shifts in status and allegiances. Where were the pinch points? Who'd be vulnerable to the feel of the law closing in? Until Andre Connor, the tactics were producing positive results. It didn't matter how many times Max reran the events of those last weeks, Connor hadn't beaten them. Redding had lost his nerve. They beat themselves.

The Astra driver abandoned his attempt to rewrite the laws of geometry and gave up the parking space. Max watched the taillights head up towards the Finchley Road. Something drew his attention to the space left behind. As he looked down, a lone figure hurried from the shadows of the steps leading up to the front door as if he, too, had been observing. The way he was moving, keeping close to the wall, Max had the impression this time he was the subject.

20

Max

CHIEF SUPERINTENDENT ROTHWELL WAITED in the shade opposite Enfield police station. He tapped his watch as Max jogged across the road. 'Can we walk? I've been in a budget meeting for most of the morning and I could do with the air. God knows why they insist on doing these things on a Saturday.' He donned a pair of expensive-looking sunglasses. Max kept his Camden Market Wayfarers in his pocket.

They made their way along the crowded High Street. Max caught a whiff of a Chinese restaurant opening for midday trade. He stopped to look at the menu. Rothwell kept walking. Max caught up and they strode through the gates of the Town park.

'My exercise yard.' Rothwell led them into the open spaces away from mums and kids picnicking and playing games in the Saturday sunshine. He picked an empty bench that offered a 360-degree view. They sat either side of a polished brass plaque that read *In memoriam Edith and Alfred Foster 1986*.

There was a familiarity in the tone of their meeting.

Rothwell said, 'I'd appreciate it if this conversation stayed between us.'

'Of course,' said Max. 'If that's what you want.'

'Are you making progress?'

Max smiled. 'Slowly.'

'What does Kilby think to that?'

'Until now, he's left us to get on with it. Get the job done and done right, that's the brief.'

Rothwell straightened the creases in his trousers. 'Who's covering your back?'

'Working for Kilby tends to deter most people looking to screw us over.'

'You know what I'm getting at.'

Max stared at his scuffed black Doc Martens next to Rothwell's polished oxblood, wing-tip brogues. 'I'm not sure I do. The case was poorly handled, but so far there's no hard evidence. Even if there was, I don't think anyone really wants it. It's a paint job to cover the cracks.'

'So drop it. Tell him you've taken it as far as you can and there's nothing doing.'

Max looked up and found himself squinting into the sun. 'And why would I do that?'

Rothwell stiffened. 'I'm telling you, Max, you don't want this investigation. There's nothing in it for you. In fact, it's bad for you.'

Max shook his head. 'Can't do it.'

'At least let it drift a while. He'll get bored and take the hint.' Rothwell checked his phone, scrolling as he spoke. 'I was disappointed when I heard you'd gone back to work for him. You know better than anyone he can't be trusted. Then I thought about it and wondered if maybe this is your play to make a name for yourself. Balls to integrity and screw me in the process.'

'Absolutely not. Even if I wanted to come after you –'

'You couldn't if you tried, Max. Certainly not over this.' He straightened the clip on his tie. 'Your anonymous source – the pages from the file Kilby used to justify the reinvestigation – I know where they came from.'

Max was silent.

'Look a little closer to home.' He took a slim brown envelope from his inside pocket. 'My written response to your questions.

There's some additional information. It gives you Bailey's timelines for the night Labrosse was found. You'll find there are still gaps, but these are from my own records.' He slapped the envelope across Max's legs. 'You'd do better to look through the files yourself. I'll put the registry at your disposal if that would help. Should be quiet, Saturday afternoon.'

'Thanks, I'll do that.'

Rothwell patted Max on the back as he stood up. 'Remember what I said. I'll be around later if you want to talk.'

'Cheers for this.' Max waved the envelope.

Rothwell called back, 'Don't thank me, you don't know where it leads yet.'

Ken Dwyer was waiting in the registry with a mug of tea you could stand a spoon in. 'Mr Rothwell said I'm to give you the run of the place. Just let me know what you need. Kettle's in the corner if you want a top up and there's a packet of Bourbons open in the tin. You can have two.'

Max asked about the Labrosse file. Dwyer had obviously been briefed. He shrugged apologetically. 'I've been through virtually every file in this place. I've checked everything that was booked out at the same time. Nothing else was in that kind of state.' He shook his head. 'We had no temps, no virgins, no interns, and no obvious morons. And it never went to the CPS. Someone pulled it apart and didn't care how they put it back.'

Max looked down the list Rothwell had given him and pulled half a dozen of Bailey's case files going back six months before his retirement. Two were ongoing, still logged out and unavailable. Three of the other four confirmed what he already knew, that Bailey's casework was sloppy at best in the months leading up to his departure. Luckily for him, those cases hadn't gone to court. As functioning records of an investigation, they were as useless as the Labrosse file. The difference being that, as slapdash as the paperwork turned out to be, some effort had been made to put a case together and nothing was missing.

Max sipped the tea. Rothwell hadn't opened the doors to his records for him to find what he already knew. He returned the files to their cabinets. A thought occurred. 'Ken, what reasons might there be for a file to be taken from the building?'

'Doesn't happen as a rule. Anybody wants anything, they come down here and take a look. I'll take copies of odd documents. Rarely more than one or two and there's always a record of what was copied, who for, and where it's held.'

'But you log all movements from here?'

'I keep my own database. Anyone can access it, but I'm the only one with the password to update it. I can print out a record if you want.'

'Please.' He handed over the Labrosse file reference. 'From the beginning of the year.'

The printer spat rhythmically twice.

What at first appeared indecipherable, a mess of part-words and numbers crammed into each tight line, needed translation. Dwyer pulled up a chair and talked Max through the system. 'This is its initial registration – 19 February, the day after Labrosse died. Each investigating officer has a login code. 218 AB is Bailey, 129 KR is Chief Superintendent Rothwell.' Dwyer highlighted the last line in fluorescent green. 'And this is the file coming down to you, booked out to Special Ops Support Team. You'll have signed a receipt for it.'

Max traced the entries back up. The file had been withdrawn once in mid-May, once in April, but more frequently in February and March. The May entry caught his attention. 'Who's this?'

Dwyer leaned over his shoulder. 'Occasionally we'll get requests for file reviews, could be for a case audit – maybe the CPS did request something and I missed it, only that never happens. Or sometimes we'll archive dead files. They need to be appraised and signed off before archiving. This one's too recent to be archived. Looks like it's been upstairs to be checked.'

'Who by?'

'Could be the investigating officer, possibly it's Chief Superintendent Rothwell, or could be anti-corruption branch, they occasionally spot-check files. These look like they're central references, from Scotland Yard, but I'd have to look up the codes.'

'If you would.'

Dwyer busied at the keyboard for a few minutes while Max went back over the list. For a case that was never considered a crime, it had proved a popular read. Aside from helping with context, nothing so far explained Rothwell's keenness for him to check the file's lineage.

'Janice Locke from the Commissioner's private office.' Dwyer read from another sheet. 'She had the file couriered to her in April and again on the May date.'

'I know Janice.'

'You want me to check, see who authorised the release?'

'That'd be helpful.' He looked at his watch. If he went back now, he might just catch Janice before she left for the evening.

Dwyer came off the phone. He grinned. 'You want to know who had these files twice, once on April the 17th and then again, May the 21st?'

'Go on.'

'Assistant Commissioner Kilby.'

Max found Rothwell still at his desk. He knocked at the open door. 'You got a minute?'

'Find what you wanted?'

Max pulled up a chair and sat down. 'You knew.'

'If I was you, I'd think carefully about what you do with

this. Ask yourself how far back this goes. He transferred you back home for a reason.'

'For this investigation?'

'You were doing good work with Redding. He told me that himself. Something shifted to make things turn out the way they did. What do you think?'

'I don't buy it, not like this.'

'Max, you were his boy. The chosen one. The way he saw it, you let him down. I can't tell you what his motivation is, his *grand plan*. But he will have one and you're part of it.'

Max sat in his car for a long time, filtering through what had changed. Fundamentally, the situation was no different. Labrosse had died naturally, accidentally or been killed. The investigation into his death wasn't worth a light. Botched or bent out of shape intentionally. But behind it all, Kilby was pulling the strings and that had everyone worried, including him.

21

Kilby

THE HEAT IN CENTRAL London had become more oppressive as the afternoon wore on. Kilby walked back from Tavistock Square. There were fresh bunches of flowers laid close to the scene of the bomb attack that had torn the city apart. That morning, a year ago, he'd been at a meeting nearby, close enough to feel the blast, the noise as if the fabric of the streets was being ripped apart. What struck him in the aftermath was how the first minutes of chaos had been confronted, dealt with and then overcome. His officers, the rescue services, the paramedics, doctors, nurses and medical teams had imposed order. He'd never been prouder to wear the same uniform as those people.

Then the inquest. Any semblance of peace he'd known before that day was history. What followed was wholesale review and realignment. The positive picture given to the world outside was one thing; the recrimination and challenge to his team and others meant a change in priorities. They were on notice. In some people's eyes they bore a share of the responsibility for not seeing the attack coming.

Since that day, Kilby made a point of walking through Tavistock Square if he had business in Holborn. It constituted a small act of defiance. Something for his sanity.

A tide of human traffic moved against him as he crossed

Southampton Row. All these people were safe only as long as he and others did their work. Even so, there would be other attacks. More young men and women would be radicalised. He walked back across town. Rather than go back to his own office, he took a turn into Carteret Street.

Denny buzzed him in at the door. 'Is he here?'

'No, sir.'

'Have you got five minutes?'

He made himself at home at Max's desk. 'It's been a while. Is he holding up?'

'As far as I can tell.' She made him a coffee and fished a sugar sachet from her desk drawer.

An incoming email message pinged on Max's PC, distracting Kilby briefly. 'So, what happened at the Home Office?'

'They've been in touch?'

'They have.'

'Gavin Lillico stage-managed the process. Everyone reading from the same script, briefed within an inch of their lives. Versions of the same tosh about what a wonderful man Derek Labrosse had been, how they all missed his contribution, insight, leadership. How his work was continuing. We finished the interviews yesterday and came away with nothing of any real worth.'

'And in a hurry, so I hear.'

She anticipated his next question. 'Max didn't tell me why that happened. I was in the middle of an interview and he came in and told me we were leaving. I called a halt and we left.'

Kilby shook his head, blew ripples across the surface of the coffee. 'That isn't enough. When I asked you to keep an eye on him, I said you'd have to be smart about it. I need him on task and on message, not crusading.'

'I don't think he is crusading.' She looked over her shoulder as if expecting Max to be there. 'If anything, he's too careful. But I haven't had a chance to talk to him since yesterday. We went our separate ways as soon as we left.'

Kilby lowered his voice. 'This is your secondment, your opportunity. You need to make it work for you.'

22

Max

'WHERE HAVE YOU BEEN? Your phone's been off all day. I needed to talk to you.' Denny stood at the door to their office, the light behind her.

It had taken Max longer than expected to get back from Enfield. Kilby's private office was locked by the time he called in. The day had caught up with him. He walked past Denny and sat at his desk, exhausted. On the way back into town he'd been processing Rothwell's disclosure and the likelihood he'd known for some time that Kilby was taking a particular interest in the case. More to the point, Kilby must have realised Max would find out sooner or later.

'Max, I need to speak to you.'

'I heard you the first time.' He looked at his watch. 'D'you want to go for a drink?'

'No. Actually, yes. I'll say it straighter with a glass of wine.'

Max winced.

The Grapes Wine Bar entrance led down a narrow staircase into a windowless cellar, close enough to the District and Circle Lines at St James's Park to feel the vibrations. The only other customers were a party of four whose collection of empty bottles suggested they'd been on the go since lunchtime. Max and Denny took an alcove table. It was too quiet for an argument, but Max sensed one heading his way. The waitress brought a menu and lit the candle in the wax-dripped bottle.

Denny said, 'This is cosy. Or seedy. It's too dark to tell.'

'I used to come in here a lot.' Max affected a those-were-the-days smile.

'Ah, he's getting all nostalgic. *Bless*.'

'So, come on then.'

She took a deep breath. 'Firstly, I want to know what happened yesterday. Why did Gavin Lillico have us kicked out of the Home Office?'

'Like it matters.'

'It matters if I'm supposed to know how to deal with it. I don't mind working to a plan, Max, even an unorthodox one, as long as I'm included.'

Max's gaze wandered.

Denny pulled him back. 'Right, here it is: I spent the best part of last week setting yesterday up. We sit through a meeting to discuss their interminable conditions, which you don't challenge, not once. Then halfway through you leave me to manage a procession of sweaty yes men who might as well have been reading off a cue card for all the good it did. To top it all, you crash the only interview I'd had all day with anyone that came forward of their own volition and tell me we have to leave.' She paused. 'We got nothing. Nothing. And you were off as soon as we got out the building. No debrief, no *call you later.*'

'Tell me about him, the last one.'

'I'd seen this guy hanging around on and off all day. When their HR minder took a break, I ran into him outside the interview room. I asked for his name and was he on the list? He said he didn't know there was a list, but he had information. He wouldn't say what about. I brought him in and was talking him round when you called me out. So, if I knew why we were suddenly in the shit, maybe... Max, are you listening to me?'

Max had been looking for a waitress. 'I am. I'd just like a drink while I'm being lectured.'

'When I went back in after you told me we were leaving, he hadn't moved a hair. This bloke's in his forties. I swear, he looked like a kid in the headmaster's office. When I told him we'd been asked to wrap up for the day and said I'd get in touch and we'd reschedule the interview early next week, he just sat there. So, I asked him again, what did he know? But he wouldn't say. I gave him a card and told him to call if he was serious about giving us information.'

'Did you get his name?'

'Michael Tyler. Max, this guy was vulnerable. Frightened.'

'You checked him out?'

'Of course not, I've been waiting to speak to you first.'

Max ordered the wine, asked the waitress to bring it straight over. They waited while she levered the cork and went through the process of offering him a taste.

Denny picked up, 'I needed to run this by you and I needed to do it today, which I couldn't because your phone was off and I didn't know where you were.'

Max fingered the stem of the glass. 'You're right, we need to check him out. Thank you.'

Denny slugged back half the glass. 'And, while we're about it, I want to know why you don't trust me. I realise you didn't want to take this on in the first place. But I've been trotting round after you all week. You knew Bailey, but didn't tell me. You knew Rothwell and he clearly knows you, but you didn't tell me. You took us into the Home Office yesterday with some agenda of your own that got us thrown out. So what exactly are *we* doing?'

Max shook his head. As of this afternoon, he wasn't sure.

Denny said, 'Max, we've worked together for what, three months? I know nothing about you other than whispers I get from people who knew you before.'

'Really.'

'They say that you can't be trusted. An inspector I knew in

Maidstone warned me off working with you. Told me you're in Kilby's pocket and that you have a shady past.' Max met her gaze and she rowed back, 'Although I imagine we've both got one of those or we wouldn't be here.'

'Maybe.' He picked a line of hard wax from the bottle, softened pieces between his fingers. He topped up their glasses, spilling a little. 'I go back a long way with Kilby. Most of it *is* shady. But I'm not in his pocket, far from it. When I joined Special Operations, we discovered that I had the ability to live two lives and be equally committed to each. It meant I could work covertly, live a lie and believe it until it ceased to be a lie. It makes you guarded.'

'I get that.'

He looked up. 'Do you?'

'You don't grow up where I did and not know people whose secrets would've got them killed.'

Of course, she knew. Max thought for a moment and made a judgement call. If he was going to share with anyone, it might as well be Denny. 'Three years ago I was operating undercover in a group of not very well connected activists, a rough collective of small anti-globalisation and oddball leftist groups. SWP offshoots, former Class War anarchist hard-cases. Senior officers at Counter Terrorism Command and MI5 considered them subversives, but they weren't a threat, not even close. Certainly, there was no one with the ambition, the imagination, or the funding to do anything dangerous. There was a lawyer on the group's fringes. Her name is Liz Delaney. She's a very committed, quite prominent human rights solicitor. We became very close. When Kilby found out, he used me to use her, which I did for about a year. We were based in a flat just off Turnpike Lane and I'd do routine drops at Ally Pally and debriefs with a handler at Lea Valley Park, a café on the Hertford Road, Crouch End Library – those kinds of places. Detective Chief

Superintendent Rothwell was my handler.' He paused for a drink.

Denny sat forward, elbows on the table.

'As far as I was concerned, the group was on the verge of fizzling out. Which was when MI5 dropped the news that they'd had their own source inside. Their source was coming back with hard intelligence that the group were planning an *event*. It was laughable. Apparently, someone'd got hold of, or was getting hold of, explosives. MI5 had reasoned it was to sell on to an Islamist terrorist cell. Kilby got twitchy. I traced the lead back to this kid, Jim McIlroy. He was in his first year at Middlesex Uni, which was where I got to know him. He used to hang around with us, selling papers outside Wood Green tube, turning up at the flat when he was hungry. He was this skinny kid with his arse out of his jeans. Committed, but totally misguided. Young, earnest, a teenage Trot spouting crap he'd got from some website. I think he genuinely believed that we could change the world. I passed the intelligence back through Rothwell to Kilby, and told them to back off.'

'And?'

'They came after him anyway.' Max drained his glass and was silent for a long time.

None of his ghosts stirred the deep-rooted sense of regret the way Jim McIlroy did. 'It was their way of backing me off and it worked. I blew my cover trying to get the kid out of harm's way. It was a mistake. Too little, too late. He was killed.'

Max took his time refilling their glasses. Denny drank and listened.

'Jim used to sit on this old sofa we'd bought, skinning up and smoking half the night, but it never seemed to chill him out. He'd still be talking a hundred miles an hour. Every few seconds he'd stop for breath, sweeping this blond fringe he had from off his face. Putting CDs on, listening to one track, then changing the album. Loving everything like he was hearing it for the first time. He might well have been. I don't know where he grew up or what kind of upbringing he'd had, but you just knew he was having the time of his life being there in that conversation.'

Denny drew back from the table. 'I'm crossing my legs here, Max. You okay for a minute?' She touched his shoulder as she passed.

Max ordered another bottle. In the time it took for Denny to go to the toilet and slip back into her seat, he kept his train of thought. 'Liz went to pieces after Jim died. She felt responsible. I *was* responsible. I'd never had a problem doing the work, but this was someone I cared about and I had no control. I'd given Kilby, Rothwell, CTC, and the security services all this information with no control. No filter. I look back and I was fucking naïve.'

'Isn't that the job, though, what we do?'

'It's not what I do. That boy was harmless and I was too slow to read the signs. Afterwards, things got sticky.'

'You were compromised.'

'Only with Liz.' He paused. 'In truth, she'd known for a while. She didn't tell anyone else.'

Denny shook her head. 'Jesus, Max, why take the risk?'

'Love. Politics. It's all politics. I didn't have what it took to keep them and us separate in my own mind. Lillico was right about one thing: you have to have boundaries. Things you absolutely will not do. Well, here's the news. I had my rules and I broke most of them. I was ready to jack it in, but Kilby wouldn't have it. After the chaos I left behind, I was looking at time inside. Kilby had me transferred to Tottenham, which is where I stayed until four months ago. So, now you know, that's my shady past. Anything else you've heard is bullshit. Probably.'

'Rothwell was your handler. That makes so much more sense.'

'We were on his ground. He was astute, he kept me safe, and he tried to look after me when it went tits up.'

Denny blew hard, taking it in. 'Can we eat something?' She ordered a cheese plate, bread, olives and fizzy water.

Max took another candle from an empty table and lit it from the dying flame of the first, but the light seemed to dim further. More people had come in, couples mostly. Married couples didn't come to places like this. These were the kinds of bars and restaurants he and Liz had often found themselves in. Out of the way in unfashionable corners where they were less likely to be known. The thrill of the illicit, or at least its memory, cheered him.

Denny was speaking, trying to disguise a slur. 'I can do more if you let me in. I'm not completely useless.' A woman at the next table looked sympathetically in Denny's direction.

'No one said you were,' said Max.

'They don't have to. Try getting people like Rothwell and Bailey to take you seriously. I watched Rothwell talk to the top of your head rather than look at me straight.'

'Because he knows me.'

Denny was undeterred. 'Yeah, but when *you* don't even tell me what you're doing, why should they take me seriously?'

'Until I find out what this is really about, I have to be careful.'

'So you trust me, but not enough to tell me what you're doing because you're being all *risk averse*. That's such a lot of shit.'

Another long silence. The bar was packed and getting hotter. Max sensed the wine about to call a halt to serious discussion. He leaned forward to make himself heard. 'Rothwell called me at home last night. That's where I was today, in Enfield. He warned me to drop the investigation, said it was no good for me, for us.'

'No good for him. What did you say?'

'I said I would do, only you wouldn't let me.'

'That's not funny.'

Max looked around him. The place was too crowded. 'Can we go for a walk?'

'Are you okay?'

He poured himself a glass of water and drank it down. 'One other thing you should know, the anonymous info, the pages from Labrosse's file, Kilby set it up.'

If Denny was surprised, she made a good job of not showing it. Max wasn't even sure it had registered.

It was difficult to tell who was walking who to Victoria Station. The warm Saturday night brought the city into the streets and sent the wine to their heads. Max felt good about being part of the great social swell. They walked on to the concourse and Denny checked the indicator board.

'It's between us, what I said,' said Max.

'Of course,' said Denny. She kissed him on the cheek. 'That's my train. G'night, Max.'

As the train rolled and jerked across the points at Clapham Junction, Denny found a seat. She opened a magazine and spread it across her knees. She stared out at the backs of street after street of terraced houses and found herself thinking about Kilby, all he knew about her and all he must be keeping from her. She thought about her own boundaries and wondered whether lying to Max was one of those things you simply did not do.

For Max, the hot night went on.

He showed his ID to the armed officers at the Broadway checkpoint. They waved him through and watched him weave a path as far as the entrance to Carteret Street. If he'd looked back, he'd have seen them shaking their heads.

Inside, he let the filtered light from the street guide him. His intention was to pick up his things, make the last tube then let the homing instinct carry him the rest of the way. He needed to think. He took off his watch and rubbed the sweaty strip around his wrist. He went to the bathroom and washed his face. Suddenly, he felt as though his legs wouldn't carry him as far as the Underground station. He leaned back in his chair, ran his hand around his face, feeling the prickle of a midnight shadow. Kilby was playing out a strategy, he'd taken that much for granted. But Rothwell offering to cover his back and warning him off, that bothered him.

He put his feet up on the desk and fell into a disturbed sleep. As he slept, he was aware of a pain through to the bones of his arse. His consciousness kept a foothold in his dreams. Rothwell's warning and the wine bar conversation repeated with the nagging addition of his subconscious telling him he'd given too much away. He went deeper. Then for the first time in a long time, he woke with a sense of dread. His sleep troubled by the face of a dead eighteen-year-old boy.

23

Tyler

SUNDAY AFTERNOON AND THE news that Fiona was pregnant meant everyone speaking at once. Emmy was fussing over due dates and decorating schedules, offering babysitting in perpetuity. She stroked her daughter's hair and managed a hug for her son-in-law who, for once, didn't bristle at the display of affection. They'd been married for just over a year. As they sat side by side on the sofa, Keith's hand rested on Fiona's knee.

Tyler tried to say the right things. He opened a bottle of Prosecco they'd been keeping in the fridge. He suggested they go outside and Keith, flushed with the achievement of having impregnated his daughter, spilled half a glass of wine which fizzed on the hot patio. Tyler tried to help.

'I can manage,' said Keith sharply. There was a darting eye contact.

'Sorry,' said Tyler. He looked to Emmy for support, but she had eyes only for Fiona.

Tyler angled the parasol to ensure Fiona and Emmy had full advantage of the shade. They settled, but as the conversation swam around him, Tyler found himself irritated by the way Keith charmed Emmy and Fiona with bad taste jokes he'd heard circulating in the office.

Tyler said, 'What d'you think, Fi, you want a boy or a girl?'

Emmy shot him a look as if he had physically drawn all pleasure from the occasion. He might have argued that an announcement like this one couldn't be devalued, even by the odd fatherly platitude, but thought better of it.

'I don't mind, Dad. As long as he or she is healthy. That's all that matters.'

'Remember, Fi, when we still had the lawn and we used to play cricket?'

'A tin bucket for a wicket and if you hit the ball over Mrs Acourt's fence it was six and out.'

'Of course, we had the patio laid, must be five years now.'

'Really,' said Keith, 'that's interesting.'

Before Fiona's wedding the previous year, they'd held a surprise party. Keith had been away on some unspecified business trip in Jersey and couldn't make it, but Emmy's brother Miles and his wife Lauren came up from Lewes and, at the last minute, they'd contacted some of Fiona's old schoolfriends. Emmy had 'friended' her daughter on Facebook and invited those she knew well enough from their photos and whom she remembered from hockey matches and teenage sleepovers. Tyler had put tea lights in glass jars and lit them around the garden as it grew dark. It had been a warm night and, as they sat reminiscing into the early hours, he had drunk more than he had in years, listening to their voices, his hands clasped around a whisky glass as one by one the candles burned down and went out. He recalled that night, but didn't finish telling the story as Fiona needed to move her chair further into the shade.

Keith spoke over him. 'You didn't hang around at the hotel after our reception, did you?'

'No, we had to get back.'

'*That* was the party to end all parties. We drank the bastards dry. Half of my lot slept in a bunker on the sixteenth. Martin said he was still getting sand out of his crack a week later.' Emmy laughed. Fiona laughed. They sipped their wine in unison.

There in the garden he had tended for the best part of 25 years, with the flowers in full bloom, in the surroundings of the home which he worked every day to make a place of comfort and safety, with people he had loved and cared for most of his adult life, Tyler realised that he no longer had a place. He could think of nothing more to say.

The afternoon wore on. Intoxicated by the wine and the perfume from the climbing roses on the trellis, the baby conversation and Keith's anecdotes became more remote to him. His contributions stuck in his throat. Later, when they were eating, it became an almost physical sensation and he found himself making excuses for a quick exit back into the house.

He went upstairs and tried to read, but his concentration wandered. He stretched out on the bed. A breeze through the open window kept the curtain moving. Downstairs, the voices rose and fell, Keith's highhandedness darkening Tyler's mood. He ought to have been there, but couldn't bring himself to rejoin them.

He came down as they were leaving and shook hands with Keith. There were more congratulations. Fiona kissed him on the cheek. He stood by Emmy at the door and waved them off. When they'd watched the car turn the corner at the end of the road, she said, 'You feeling better, then?' in a voice that suggested she wished the opposite. 'I made your excuses. Heaven knows why.'

'Thank you.'

'I've cleared up the tea things. You can bring the chairs in. I'm off for a bath.'

He heard the taps running as he folded the chairs and put them in the cupboard under the stairs. The old briefcase was there. For the first time in months, he worked the combination and removed the half-dozen bloodstained pages. He sat down at the dining table and reread them. He thought of Keith, tanned, trim, the collar of his pink Crew polo shirt turned up, his career trajectory apparently stratospheric. What would he think if he could read these pages, if he knew how the blood came to have stained them? And Fiona, pregnant with his first grandchild. He was her dad, but he had no thousand pound cheque in an envelope to give her – Keith's mum and dad's little celebratory gift.

He got a pad and wrote *THEOBOLD* almost without thinking. Then dates, times and names, starting with the initial phone call that February Friday evening, the misplaced file and his journey to Farorna Walk.

Emmy came downstairs in her dressing gown. 'I meant to tell you, I've got that Thai cookery class starting up again tomorrow evening. I'm going straight from work so you'll have to sort yourself out for dinner.'

'Okay,' he said, covering the papers.

'Can you not use the office tonight, I'd like some peace and quiet and your keyboard tapping is more than I can stand.'

'Of course.'

As the evening passed, he was aware of the bathwater coursing the downpipe, Emmy's hairdryer and her steps across the landing. He heard their bedroom door close and the creak of bedsprings as she climbed in. He worked at the dining table, writing down each detail of the day Labrosse died and the months since, as he remembered them. When he'd finished, he locked the front and back doors, filled the kettle for the morning, and made his way to bed. The heat from Emmy's body crept across the cool sheets. There was a time he'd have lightly kissed her shoulder to let her know he was there, but he knew that touching her now would upset them both.

24

Max

MAX HAD INTENDED TO walk to Regent's Park to meet Liz that Sunday evening, but his shirt was damp against his skin inside the five minutes it took to reach Finchley Road. He caught a cab to the north gate of the park. Liz greeted him coolly and they began walking around the Outer Circle, past the false facades of those grand Edwardian mansions.

'What do you want to do?' she asked. 'See a film? Go get a drink? We could eat, I'll take you to Appeninos, my treat.'

'Maybe.'

Her hair brushed her shoulders, longer and darker than he remembered. The loose folds of her silver-white skirt swished around her bare legs. She helped it with a couple of flamenco swirls. 'D'you like it?'

Max smiled briefly.

There was a lightness to her step in spite of the airless evening. 'I bought it especially for you. Actually, that's a lie, I got it from Kensington Market years ago, been waiting for a chance to show off, thought you'd like it.'

As they walked into Regent's Park through Sunday evening crowds, he still hadn't spoken.

'Max, it was you who called me, remember. I could be at home now doing, I dunno, *something* that isn't being ignored by you.'

They were distracted by the giggles of kids chasing each

other around the scrubby flower beds. Liz said, 'Come on, let's sit down.' They left the path and walked across the grass until they came to a space. 'So, why the silent treatment?'

He brushed his palm across the brown grass. 'I'm into something, a work thing. And last night, I had a drink with a colleague.' He paused.

'You shagged her.'

'No, I didn't. Anyway, how did you know it was a she?'

'You wouldn't have shagged him if she was a he.'

'There's a case we're working on and she was giving me grief for keeping things to myself. I told her more than I should and it brought a lot of things back.'

She nodded. 'Thought you said you were desk jockeying these days.'

'I was. Kilby had other ideas.'

'Surely not.'

'I'm investigating the death of a senior civil servant. Or, to be accurate, reinvestigating. The original case was botched. They said it was an accident, that he fell down the stairs, which might well be the case, but...' He stopped himself and looked across the park towards the Post Office Tower. 'It's just that the more I scratch away at this man's background, the dirtier it feels. No one wants to talk about him. It's like doing a jigsaw, only each piece makes the picture more obscure. And there's a fear around his family and the people close to him. It bothers me.'

'You need to trust your instincts. I mean it. We doubt ourselves too much.'

'You know why I'm telling you?'

She sat round, pulled her knees up to her chest and rearranged the folds of the skirt. 'I've thought about what happened to Jim McIlroy a lot. I suppose I'm more honest with myself these days. More pragmatic.' She stared across the park. 'I think it comes from spending time with Jonathon. We worked together

149

for most last year when I took over my part of the practice. It clarified things for me: you're either part of the conspiracy or you're conspired against.' She flicked a tiny insect off a cherry-painted toenail. 'If you stand with one foot in either camp or neither, you get caught. Like you did, like I did. Jim was innocent, we knew it. But once the State decided it wanted him, for whatever twisted reason they'd chosen to justify it, there was nothing you or I could have done. You can't protect people.'

'I don't know how you reconcile that. I can't.'

'Complicate it if you want. Or move on and do something about it.'

'Not if you've got my job.'

'You make your own choices.' Now the cherry toenails scrunched. 'Look Max, I really didn't meet up with you to talk about this. For one evening, it would be good to forget we're on different sides of the fence. I came ready to try. I thought that's what you wanted.'

As they walked across the park, what looked at first like a remote-controlled helicopter hovered high over the trees. Max looked for the earthbound pilot, expecting an enthusiast, but could see no one.

'What's up?' said Liz.

'The helicopter.'

'Some rich kid's payoff for a term at boarding school.'

'It flew towards the Baker Street side of the park, then back.' Max thought it seemed to be running a pattern. 'It's a surveillance drone. It's covering the park. Watch, it'll come back this way, bank towards the mosque, then back towards Baker Street. It's like it's programmed.'

They stood and watched. The plane's tiny rotors whined into earshot as it took the route he'd predicted. No one else seemed to have noticed.

She took his arm. 'Can we just go?'

Later, after a film, the food and the wine, they walked down Haverstock Hill to find a cab. Max had held the question back since they left the wine bar. He said, 'Do you want to come back to my place?'

She stifled a yawn. 'No. I don't think I do.'

'It's been all right.'

She was silent. They walked on.

'You never asked me his name or anything, my notorious civil servant. I thought you'd be curious.'

'To tell you the truth, I don't care. I come up against his sort every day. They're all raging careerists. Just some better at it than others. Although that could be the wine talking.' She let out a small belch. 'No, sorry, *that* was the wine talking. Anyway, you wouldn't have told me if I'd asked. You'd have got all suspicious and quiet.' She tapped her nose. 'Let's keep it on a strictly need-to-know basis.' They reached the junction with Chalk Farm Road and stopped. 'It was good to see you, Max.'

'Really good.'

She hailed a cab. It pulled into the kerb. They kissed awkwardly, lips missing lips. As he began the slow walk home, the cab passed him and he willed her to look out of the back window, but at the last moment he dropped his head. It was better not knowing.

25

Tyler

TYLER SAT AT HIS desk and switched on his PC. He clicked past the Home Office home page into his own files and created a document, giving it a name corresponding to an authentic admin file. He began to copy out last night's notes, this time entirely conscious of the process and its implications. He'd planned to get into work early over a few days, but once started felt compelled to keep writing. He kept going when his colleagues drifted in around eight-thirty, recalling each detail of his part in Labrosse's death and all that haunted him since. At one point, he thought Mrs Richards had read over his shoulder. He opened up a work-related file, keeping it on screen for a few minutes. She made no comment. He phoned in apologies for a ten-thirty meeting and, for the rest of the morning, snatched time to write as often as it was safe. By the time his colleagues disappeared for their midday shopping rendezvous or lunch dates, he had completed the full confession.

He'd ignored hunger pangs all morning. With the job done he felt the onset of a headache. He'd take a break, eat and then take painkillers. He closed the document, giving it a password.

'I'm just going out for a sandwich.'

Mrs Richards called across, 'Team meeting at one. I want you there. On time please.'

He walked down the back stairs, grateful for the less intense light and coolness of the stairwell. His head throbbed.

Outside, the sun beat down and people pressed against people in Strutton Ground. The glare forced him to squint as he threaded through the crowds. He cut left and joined the queue at the sandwich bar. There were three people in front of him. He looked up at the menu board hanging above the counter. Its words misted and doubled. Shadows formed in his peripheral vision, a migraine early warning.

The girl behind the counter wiped her hands on her apron and smiled expectantly at the next customer. Tyler watched the sandwich handed over to a woman in a dark suit. There was a flicker of acknowledgement. At first, he couldn't place her, then he realised she was the detective constable, the one who'd come to the office and given him her card. She brushed past him on her way out. Tyler hesitated, three seconds… four… five… six, then excused himself from the queue. 'I'll be back later,' he said.

'You want to leave an order?' The girl's voice yelled behind him.

He caught up and tapped Denny on the shoulder. She took a step back and sized him up. If Friday's attempt at an explanation had been tongue-tied, the stream of half-cocked fragments he strung together barely connected at all. Frustrated, he took out the card. 'You gave me this.'

She put her hand on his arm. 'I remember, Mr Tyler. Just take it easy, say what you need to say.'

He felt the sun burn the back of his neck. 'I'm sorry, I have a splitting headache. I have information about the case. I thought about it over the weekend. I want to make a statement. On the record.'

'My office is around the corner, we shouldn't talk here.' She made a move away.

'I know I'm in trouble. The thing is, this is all wrong.'

'Mr Tyler, I want this conversation off the street. Come back to my office now, or we can meet when it's convenient and you can tell me whatever it is that's on your mind.'

His stomach churned. 'Please, there's no one else I can talk to. I've written a statement of everything. Names, dates, places. I'll print it out now and bring it to you. Will you be there?'

Tyler walked back towards the office, the card in his pocket. His headache came on strongly. He went into a kiosk and bought a cold drink, held the bottle against his forehead as he queued. When he came out, Patrick Theobold was waiting. 'Nice little performance, Michael. I thought it was you.' They stopped at the pavement edge. 'Who's the lunch date?'

'No one.'

Theobold shook his head. 'Surely, someone.'

'So, how are things?' Tyler asked, desperate to change the subject.

'*Things* are fine. Busy as always, big week this one. Actually, I'm glad we bumped into each other. There are some *things* I'd like to discuss with you. Why don't you come up to my office now? You're already late for your one o'clock meeting.'

'I've got a headache.'

Tyler felt Theobold's hand on his arm. As he went to move away, Theobold's grip tightened. Going with him seemed the sensible thing to do.

While Theobold fussed in his desk drawer for a pack of paracetamol tablets, he explained to Tyler that his office computer was being monitored and had been for some weeks. Software had been installed that read every keystroke. He put the pack of tablets on the desk in front of him. 'You have your water, don't you? So, this morning when you came in especially early and beavered away on an odd little file you'd just created, we checked. You know what we found? Of course you do, you wrote the bloody thing. Idiot. Anyway, you should know your hard drive is being destroyed and that bizarre confession has been erased.' He waved Tyler's handwritten notes in his face. 'What in Christ's name were you thinking?'

Tyler swallowed, unsure if it was the migraine or being found out that made him feel sick. 'I wanted what was best, to do the right thing.'

'I want that too. The difference is I know what the right thing is.' Theobold took two pills from the pack, which he placed in Tyler's open palm. 'Take those, for Heaven's sake, you look terrible. Drink.'

Tyler complied.

'What did you say to the police, Michael? Did you tell them about us, about our agreement?'

'I didn't mention your name if that's what you're worried about.'

He sniffed. 'I'm the least worried of anyone connected with this. I know you, they don't. I know how to take your life apart piece by piece. So no, I'm not worried. What have you told the police?'

'Nothing.'

He shook his head. 'I warned you, didn't I? I told you what the consequences would be. I dealt with your problems and kept my promise to keep you out of trouble.' He shook his head.

Tyler could hardly hear him above the pounding in his head. 'I *need* to tell the truth.'

'No, Michael. I don't think so.'

26

Theobold

THEOBOLD SAT AT LILLICO'S desk, watching family snapshots dissolve in and out of each other on his screensaver: his wife, Sara, in a straw hat; his two girls with ice cream smiles; an elderly couple – presumably parents – well turned out with a family party around them; Lillico on a Mediterranean quayside at sunset, pressed blue chinos and loose collarless shirt. As the sequence ran again it was this last image that Theobold found most disagreeable, something about its smug complacency. This man would never carry the weight he carried, or take the risks he took. He'd sent Tyler off with a reprimand and the knowledge that his career was in the balance, their discussion to be continued. Right now, there were more pressing things to attend to. The IDI delegation had arrived that morning. Hannah Rees had called three times on the flight over and again as soon as they'd landed.

David wants an up-to-date report on security issues.

David wants to know if there are any potential obstructions.

David wants to know why we can't get five minutes with the Prime Minister.

David wants James Creedy's home telephone number

David wants...

Theobold watched the photomontage once more and satisfied himself with the thought that, for Lillico, these were reminders of a loving family. For him they were leverage. He had calls to make. Time some people were reminded of their obligations.

Caroline Labrosse picked up quickly, as if she'd been waiting.

'It's Patrick. How are you?'

'I'm on my way out.'

'I shan't keep you long then.'

'You've phoned me three times this week. You know what I want to hear, either you found this man Tyler or you have his interview statement. Which is it?'

She had Tyler's name right this time. 'Caroline, is there anyone with you?'

'None of your bloody business.'

He sensed she was recording the conversation, that she was not alone. The last time they'd spoken, she'd gone out of her way to convince him she was sticking to their agreed plan. She'd told him how she fobbed off the police at the hospital as directed, how she'd followed his instructions to the letter, not taking calls on the landline, giving updates to the agency laboratory assistant he'd placed to support her.

Theobold said, 'I just want you to know, I've spoken to our solicitor on your behalf. He thinks we can sort out the probate issue. In fact, I'm hoping I'll have some good news towards the middle of next week.'

'Good.'

'And once this police investigation is over, we'll clear Derek's pension payments pretty quickly.'

'That's good of you. Then I'll be able to pay my mortgage and my daughter's overdraft.' A pause. 'Actually, Patrick, I've spoken to one of Derek's friends, he's also a solicitor. Quite a good one. He seems to think there are no grounds for the money to be withheld even if Derek is under investigation. He's offered to look into it for me.'

Theobold sat forward, jogging the desk. The screensaver

was replaced by a still photograph of Lillico's too-perfect family. 'Don't mess things up, Caroline. I've worked bloody hard to try and sort this out. If some joker sniffs a fee and interferes –'

'Actually, he's doing it pro bono as a personal favour.'

'But that could take us back to square one. Let me pop round with the paperwork and I can explain in person.'

'That isn't necessary.'

'I'm asking you, don't go behind my back. It would be bad for you.'

'Goodbye, Patrick.' She killed the call.

When the driver pulled up outside Gavin Lillico's home later that evening, Theobold said nothing for a full minute. In spite of the heat, he'd insisted they keep the windows closed and the air-conditioning off on the way over. He said he preferred not to breathe exhaust fumes. The driver made some crack about mad dogs and Englishmen, which he'd ignored. The man had the self-assurance of a professional soldier. Theobold suspected Special Forces, but had no intention of opening that conversation. He told the driver not to wait. Someone had to keep an eye on Caroline Labrosse. He needed to be informed immediately if anyone came or went.

Theobold kept his thumb pressed on Lillico's doorbell for a full five seconds, casting an eye over the neat lawn and well-kept borders. Lillico came to the door, wiping his mouth on a gingham napkin. 'What are you doing here?' He looked at his watch. 'It's after bloody nine.'

'I take it you weren't in bed.'

'I'm in the middle of dinner with my family, what's going on?'

Theobold pushed past him into the hall. In the dining room, Sara Lillico was losing the battle to stay calm with Amy and Melissa, something to do with finishing dinner before dessert.

A glass of blackcurrant squash went over. Mummy said a naughty word. Lillico pulled the door closed. 'Not one for the screensaver,' Theobold said.

'Patrick, what do you want?'

'Isn't it a bit late for the kids to be having dinner?'

'Sara let them stay up as a treat seeing as I'm staying in town from tomorrow. Not that it's any of your business.'

Raised voices could be heard from the dining room. 'Well, I am sorry to have spoiled it, Gavin, but I have been trying to get hold of you all day and you weren't returning calls.'

'I've been away from my office.'

'I waited for you to come back.'

Lillico shrugged. 'Did we arrange a meeting?'

'I shouldn't have to make an appointment to see you this week of all weeks. I waited in your bloody office for an hour. You should make yourself available.'

The absurdity of the argument dawned on Lillico. His eyes flashed anger. 'Well, whatever is so urgent, either tell me or piss off and let me eat my dinner.'

The spark of temper satisfied him. 'If you're not going to extend the courtesy of a seat at the family table, you could at least offer me a drink. Gin and tonic for a colleague, that's what one does isn't it, out here in the suburbs?' He followed Lillico into the kitchen, rubbing his hands together. 'I've earned this.'

Lillico splashed a couple of fingers of Bombay Sapphire over ice and lemon slices in two glasses. 'How much?' he said, pouring the tonic.

'Make it a long one.'

Lillico led them into the garden through a lemon-scented conservatory full of plants. Theobold pulled a leaf from the tree and rolled it between his fingers then sniffed. 'I love that smell.'

'You're in my house, you've got your drink. What is it you want?'

'David Bittman and Hannah Rees arrived at Heathrow this afternoon. I'm told the IDI team is seven in total.'

'I know this, my PA made the reservations.'

'Plus they've brought two specialist contract lawyers over and above their usual legal team, and the finance director, a chap called Warden, and their top tech, Goodwin, used to head up BAE Electronics division in Nashua.'

'Not a problem.'

'You and I will be staying in the hotel with them to burn the midnight oil if needs be, is that still the plan?'

Lillico nodded. 'You know it is.'

Theobold took a slug of the gin. The ice sent a pain shooting through to a nerve in his temple. 'Bearing in mind Miss Rees's predilection for focusing on the detail, I want to make sure you're as up to speed as I know she'd want you to be.'

Lillico walked a few paces to a neatly presented border and deadheaded a rose. 'So?'

'I spoke with Caroline Labrosse earlier this evening while I was waiting in your office.'

'You called from my office?'

'From your desk on your phone to be precise.'

'You make that sort of call from my phone. *Jesus*.'

'You should have been there.' He swirled ice cubes around the glass. The drink came close to spilling. 'I've told her she'll have to wait a little longer for Derek's pension issues to be cleared. She seems to be adamant about seeing Michael Tyler's non-existent police statement, so we'll see if Mr Rothwell can be persuaded to provide one. You'll have to do that.'

'There's no way he'll do it for me.'

'In that case, you need to find someone he will do it for.'

'Why don't I just sign the release papers for Derek's money? Caroline might be more inclined to be flexible over the other things if we give her that.'

'Once this week's over, give it a few days for the ink to dry, then you can do what you want. While she's broke, it's not in her interests to piss me off.' He drained the glass.

'Is she pissing you off?' A plastic sandpit had spilled its contents on the patio. Lillico kicked the sand into the lawn.

'If she does, I'll deal with it.'

Lillico shook his head. 'And Tyler?'

'Mr Tyler has been told in no uncertain terms to do what I fucking tell him. Although I suspect his priorities are elsewhere at the moment.'

'What about Lomax?'

'Last seen going round in circles. Hannah agrees, he doesn't have the stomach for it.'

'I'll consider myself briefed. Thank you.' Lillico turned his back.

Theobold was close at his shoulder. 'Gavin, you compartmentalise your life and keep Sara and the kids in one box, your work in another, you may even place yourself above the more sobering aspects of what I do for you, but please do not try to act as though they do not concern you.'

Lillico said, 'I've worked hard for this, as hard as anyone. It's my deal, my career and, in case you'd forgotten, it's me who signs your invoices.'

Theobold grinned. 'Stay focused, that's all I'm saying.' He sloshed a few slivers of ice around the glass. 'Prove them wrong, show them you're not too weak to see it through.'

Lillico gripped the glass. 'Is there a threat buried in there somewhere? I'm not fluent in your coded bullshit.'

He leaned in and whispered in Lillico's ear, 'I'm doing what you pay me for.'

'Maybe don't make it so obvious you get a kick out of it, putting the fear of God into people.'

Sara stood at the patio doors, barefoot, arms folded. 'Gavin, your dinner is cold and Melissa wants to know if you're coming for ice cream? They're getting tired and I could do with some help.' Lillico didn't answer. 'Gavin?'

'I'll be a minute.'

'We're just discussing our American colleagues. Does Sara know you've got a crush on Miss Rees? Don't be bashful, she brings out the submissive in the best of us.'

'Oh, piss off.'

Theobold's mobile bleeped. It was the driver. He read the text and the smile fell from his face. 'Caroline Labrosse is having another visit from the police.' He put his empty glass into Lillico's hand. 'Go easy on the ice cream.' He slapped Lillico's stomach with the back of his hand. A little too hard to be playful.

27

Max

MAX SHOULDN'T HAVE BEEN at Caroline Labrosse's house on
his own, but what he had to say wouldn't wait. The forensics
laboratory had called to confirm they no longer held any
samples collected in connection with Derek Labrosse's death.
He'd pressed for an explanation: *if they weren't there, where
were they?* The best they could come up with was that the
samples had been 'disposed of' because, as far as they were
concerned, there was no ongoing criminal investigation. He'd
asked to speak with Kaye Wells. She'd been unavailable.

Max pushed the bell a second time. The last of the evening
light was fading as Caroline Labrosse came to the door. 'What
do you want?'

'To know why no one's telling the truth about your husband.'

She studied Max for a moment, then turned and went into the
house leaving the door open. He followed. On the way through
the kitchen, she flicked her cigarette in the direction of the
ashtray and picked up a half-empty bottle of wine and a clean
glass, which she offered to Max. 'You might as well join me.
I was supposed to be going to dinner with an old friend. But,
frankly, I couldn't face it. I'd rather keep my own company.'
She poured unsteadily. 'You don't count.'

He raised his glass.

'These days self-medication is supposed to be more
sophisticated. I don't think that applies to us lowly pathologists.'

163

She picked a framed photo from the bookshelf, dusted it on a shirtsleeve. 'My daughter, taken last year when we went to the lakes for her birthday.'

Max saw a younger version of the mother. A fresh complexion, the glimmer of a smile on her lips.

'She's stronger than me,' said Caroline. 'Schooled by her father in the ways of gods and men.' She dropped into an armchair, pulled her legs up beneath her. 'Sit down there.' She flapped a hand at the sofa.

'I have some questions,' said Max.

She sighed. 'Not another one.'

'Another what?'

'Doesn't matter.'

He pushed a slim folder of documents across the small table between them. 'Detective Constable Denny did some background checks and dug these up, have a look.' Her arm swept clumsily across the table to pick up the folder. 'I wanted to discuss it with you first. You see, when we spoke before, you seemed pretty certain that you were at work the day your husband died. Hospital records differ. You were due in, but you swapped shifts.' Max put his glass on the table. 'You were at home, is that right?'

Without looking up, she said, 'I can't tell you anything.'

'But you weren't at work that weekend.'

She was silent.

'I'm asking you, were you at home on the day your husband died?'

She pulled a navy-blue sweater from the back of the chair and over her head. 'Do you find it chilly in here? Only the bedroom and the kitchen get any direct sunlight. I get cold once the sun goes down.' The sleeves of what was clearly a man's sweater hung down over her hands and she balled up the excess in her fists. 'Things about my husband were complicated. *Are* complicated.'

'Why didn't you tell us?'

'And spoil the surprise?' She caught herself. 'I'm not helping you to destroy his reputation. Faithful to the last.' She picked up the bottle. Max declined a refill.

'Destroying Derek's reputation couldn't be further from what this is about,' said Max. 'What Derek did during his life is not the focus of my enquiries. All I'm interested in are the circumstances around how he died. Caroline, please listen to me, I don't think we did right by Derek. We didn't look after him. He deserves better.'

She swallowed hard and hugged herself. Her hair fell across her face and when she threw her head back, she put her fists in her eyes. 'Oh God, I promised myself I wasn't going to do this again.'

'Caroline, do you know who put the call in to the police? I can find no record of a 999 call. Was it you?'

'You'd better ask Bailey. I haven't got a bloody clue who called it in.'

Her fingers fumbled in the packet for another cigarette. 'I wish I didn't bloody do this. Not exactly a good example, is it? Still, at least I'll be able to do my own biopsy when the time comes.' She held up her hand, examining the cigarette between her fingers.

Max waited until she'd lit up. 'Why aren't you telling the truth about your husband?'

She looked at him straight. 'Why do you give a shit?'

Max's voice was quiet, persuasive. 'Your husband dies and you say you weren't there. I think you were. When we saw you at the hospital, you went out of your way to convince us you were untouched by the whole thing, but you wear Derek's sweater like a kid with a comfort blanket.' He shook his head. 'It's all wrong.'

She bit at the skin on her lip. She looked up and straight into Max's eyes. 'Please don't keep asking. Please.' The jumper-covered fists came up across her mouth and Max watched her slip away from him.

'Was Derek under pressure at work?'

'Always,' she said, muffled into her fists.

'What about in the weeks before he died?'

Her hands dropped. 'I had nothing to do with his work, nothing at all.'

'So, after he died?'

'I did as I was told. Exactly as I was told. I accepted their support, their advice and their *people*. I made no public statements, gave no interviews. I agreed not to discuss Derek or his work and stayed out of any political bullshit. Never had a minute's peace. *How are things, Caroline? Anything we can do, Caroline, you must say.* They did nothing.'

'What about now, don't you deserve some peace?'

Her voice became a hoarse whisper. 'I don't even know what that is.'

She slipped her backside off the chair, knelt in front of him and shared the remainder of the wine between the two glasses. She stared into her glass, rubbed her thumb across a lipstick smear. When she spoke, she didn't look at him. 'There was a man who came here on the afternoon Derek died. He said he had been sent to pick up some papers, some file that was needed urgently at the office and that Derek had brought home in error.'

'A courier?'

'Someone from work, so he said. Gavin Lillico phoned that morning to tell me he was coming, but when I tried to call Derek, there was no answer on his office number or his mobile. I stayed as long as I could, but I was meeting Ruth at Waterloo and I didn't want her to wait. We had tickets for the theatre and she was adamant we should go, to show we weren't afraid after the bombs last year. But I was nervous about it. I didn't want her waiting, so I left the man here. He seemed reasonable enough, quite inoffensive.'

Max watched her drift, reading the emotions as they played across her face. Suddenly, she got up, put her hand to her mouth, made it to the kitchen and was sick in the washing-up bowl. Max was beside her, lifting her hair out of the way as she heaved again. He pulled off a dozen sheets of kitchen roll. She spat, got her breath back, splashed cold water in her face. 'I'm sorry, I'm usually a bit more together than this.'

'It's fine.'

'What an idiot, look at me. I'm so sorry. I'd got myself so worked up about going out, then I bottled it. Oh God!' She was sick again. Her head hung over the sink for some time, then came up suddenly. 'The man's name was Tyler. Apparently, he's Mr Invisible. I've asked to see his statement God knows how many times. I know he was here. But they tell me I'm being a nuisance.'

'Who are they?'

She laughed, wagged a finger. 'Drunk but not incapable, down but not out. That's me. No names, no pack drill.' She ran the hot tap until it steamed and glugged some Dettol in the washing up bowl. 'I'll be a minute, please sit down.'

She eased herself on the sofa beside Max and lit another cigarette. She had a pint glass of water in front of her. 'The man who tells me Mr Tyler is invisible is the same man who tells me you're investigating Derek because of criminal activity he's supposed to have been involved in and that I need to be wary of what you'll do to me, to our family and Derek's legacy, whatever that is.'

'Do you believe that?'

'I did. Now not so much. He called tonight. He'll have known you were coming.'

Max pressed Caroline for the name. There was a long silence. She blew out a stream of cigarette smoke. 'Patrick Theobold.'

It was an hour later when Max closed the door behind him, grateful to be back out in the fresh air. Caroline was asleep.

The smell of her cigarette smoke clung to his jacket. He was troubled at the way she'd held him, how hurt she'd been, hanging onto him, making him promise to call her. He walked into Enfield Town. The King's Head was quiet. He sat at the bar with a pint of Marstons. *Trust your instincts*, Liz had said. But Caroline had given him more. Now there was a name and a reason to keep going.

28

Theobold

WAITING WAS MAKING THEOBOLD restless. It niggled him that he'd risen to Lillico; who did he think he was? *His* project, *his* deal. And the crack about enjoying making people fear him. Didn't it have to be that way? People like Creedy, Lillico, Hannah Rees, even Derek Labrosse, they all expected him to do their bidding. That came with the kind of pressure you had to find a way to handle. The driver changed radio stations for the umpteenth time.

'For Pete's sake, stop doing that.'

The driver smiled, 'Take it easy, Pat, we're in no hurry.'

'It's Patrick.'

They'd been sitting within view of Farorna Walk since shortly after dark. Lomax was still inside and that bothered him. He turned the radio off and opened the window a few centimetres. The only sound was traffic on The Ridgeway. Still, better that than the driver's burger-breath yawns and that bloody awful music. A gang of kids came away from the petrol station, their conversation punctuated by screamed expletives and laughter. As they walked past, one deliberately clipped the wing mirror. The boy peered in. Theobold and the driver stared ahead. Another thirty minutes passed in silence. Then there was movement. The door opened. 'That's him,' said Theobold.

Max stood at the edge of the main road as if uncertain which way to go. He checked his watch, then followed the kids' route towards Enfield Town Centre. They waited to see if he'd come back.

'I'll be back soon.' Theobold already had the car door open.

The driver twisted in his seat. 'Just to be clear, we can have her out of the way and looked after until this is over. I can make the call and it will happen.'

'I want to satisfy myself she's done nothing stupid.'

'Thirty minutes, Patrick, no more. Keep it together, okay?'

Theobold crossed without looking, barely conscious of the traffic. He made his way up the drive and let himself into Caroline Labrosse's house. She was out for the count on the sofa, breathing heavily in the half-lit room. Lomax must have put the blanket over her. He pulled the curtains, put the kitchen light on and rescued an unwashed mug from the sink. He rinsed it, dropped a spoonful of coffee in and put the kettle on.

He shook her. 'Caroline, wake up. I want to talk.'

'Go away.' She turned her back, pulled the blanket over her shoulders.

Theobold left the coffee. He went to the kitchen and half-filled the washing-up bowl with cold water. 'Get up, Caroline.' He stood over her and steadily emptied the bowl. She sat up. Water dripped off her chin. Wet hair stuck to her cheek. She looked up, trying to make sense. He stood back and smiled. 'What did he want?'

'Sorry?' She wiped her sodden sleeve across her face.

'Your visitor. He trotted out of here like a dog with two dicks about ten minutes ago. Did you fuck him?'

'Don't be ridiculous.'

'So, what did you tell him?'

She took a sip of the coffee and winced. 'He told me there is no Tyler statement on Derek's case file.'

'Tell me what *you* said.'

'Absolutely nothing.'

'Did he ask you about Derek?'

'Not really.'

'About me?'

'No.'

'He was here for over two hours. He must have said something.'

'Patrick, I'm going to speak to a solicitor.'

'So you said. I advise against it.'

'Derek's friend says there's no reason why I shouldn't see the police files and he's willing to take me on as a client.'

He stared at her cradling the cup, working to keep her hands from shaking between sips. The dry part of her hair was matted, she must have laid in something unpleasant. Or perhaps she just hadn't washed it for a while. 'Caroline, do you know you're beginning to acquire a quite distinctive smell?'

'Piss off, Patrick.'

'No, seriously. It's actually quite rank, a kind of combination of vomit, stale cigarette smoke and alcohol.' He sniffed. 'And your unwashed body – actually, I can't tell if it's you or this place. You're blending with your surroundings.' He sat down on the arm of the chair, took the empty cup from her. She was drowsy now. He kept her talking. 'It's a shame you've let yourself go so quickly. I honestly thought you'd keep it together a little longer than this. Poor show really.'

'Oh, I can't do this anymore.' She tried to get up, but fell back in the chair, barely coherent.

'I know.' He rolled a pair of latex gloves onto his hands, flexed his fingers. 'What did you tell the policeman, Caroline?' Her head dropped forwards. He lifted her chin, slapped her cheek. 'Come on, there's a girl.'

'Told him Patrick Theobold's a thieving, manipulative bastard.'

He moved around in front of her, slapped again. Harder. 'What else?'

'Fuck off.'

'Again, what else?'

'That Derek never trusted you.' Her eyes opened a fraction wider. 'Derek always knew you were a whore for power, you with your shitty deal, selling yourself. He felt sorry for you. *That old whore, Pat Theobold*, he used to say, *selling his arse for ten bob.*' The words slurred and her head lolled to one side. 'S'why we had a little something put away... rainy days.' Her head dropped.

Theobold cleared a path between wine bottles, used tissues, wads of kitchen roll, the dropped damp blanket, the empty washing-up bowl. In the kitchen, he scrubbed the coffee cup thoroughly and put it back in the cupboard. He wiped every surface he'd touched and braced himself against the work top, then pushed away. Caroline was slumped in a Rohypnol stupor. Lillico was right, there was pleasure in instilling fear. But what did you do when they stopped being scared?

29

Tyler

WHEN EMMY DIDN'T COME home from work on Monday evening, Tyler had assumed she'd been delayed and gone straight to her cookery class. He'd occupied himself, reading around his forbears' transition from Sussex shopkeeping to the Western Front in 1915. When he looked up from his computer, it was midnight and he'd heard nothing. He thought about calling the police, but what would he say? The conversation they'd had about the man she met nagged in the back of his mind. Perhaps this time she let him kiss her.

Tuesday morning came with no word. Tyler called Fiona. She told him that her mother had been there on Monday night and that she'd just left.

He asked, was she coming home?

Fiona sighed. 'I don't think so, Dad. Not for a while.'

'I don't know what this is about. I promise I didn't do anything wrong.'

'It's not always one thing though, is it? Sometimes it – it builds up, you know.'

'No, I don't know. I don't know anything.' His voice cracked. 'Is that what she said, that it was building up?'

'If she calls again, I'll tell her to get in touch. It'll be better coming from her.'

'Please.'

There was a pause. 'Have you got food in?'

'We went to Sainsbury's on Saturday.' It seemed a lifetime ago.

All day Tuesday, he wandered through the house, tidying, cleaning. Keeping busy. He dozed in his chair on Tuesday evening. In the early hours, he found himself watching television through misty eyes, voices murmuring in the background, his mind racing through everything that had happened, the signs he'd missed or ignored, until he'd convinced himself that Theobold had a hand in Emily's leaving. The punishment for trying to deliver his confession.

Tyler took the thought to bed with him as the sun came up.

On Wednesday morning, he woke late and put on the same plaid shirt he'd worn for three days. He came downstairs and made tea that was undrinkable. The milk was off, flakes floated around the cup. He walked the short distance to the shop and picked up a carton of semi-skimmed and a newspaper, taking his place in the queue. As he went to pay, the coins slipped through his fingers and rolled across the counter. 'I'm so sorry,' he said.

The newsagent tutted, picking ten-pence pieces from between stacks of papers on the counter. 'It's short.'

'It was all there,' said Tyler.

'It's thirty pence short.'

Tyler went through his pockets, knowing he had no more change. The queue shuffled behind him. An elderly woman touched his elbow. 'I can lend you the extra, lovey.'

'No, thank you. I couldn't.' The newsagent stood poised with one hand out. Tyler said, 'I'll just take the milk then.'

The woman was still rooting through her purse. 'Hang on dear, I'm sure I've got it here.'

He took the milk and left the shop.

On his way back, he dared hope Emmy might be waiting for him at home, but as he turned the corner and the house came into view, a scruffy young man was standing with one foot on the doorstep, hands in pockets, an oversized messenger bag slung over his shoulder. He came to meet Tyler as he walked up the drive, his face as darkly unshaven as Tyler's own. 'Mr Tyler, Michael?'

Tyler ignored the offered handshake. 'Whatever it is, I don't want it.'

'Philip Mercer.'

'Means nothing to me.' Tyler put the key in the lock.

'No reason why it should.' He spoke quickly. 'I'm doing some post-graduate research and someone said you'd be a good person to speak to. I was just in the area, so...'

'They were mistaken.'

As he opened the door, Mercer was at his shoulder. 'I just want to ask a couple of questions. I'm interested in transnational projects, global consortia in public sector procurement, that sort of thing. Multinationals and their lobbying influence on government policy. Ten minutes tops, I promise.'

Tyler took in Mercer's uncombed non-haircut and crumpled flower-print shirt over brown jeans, grubby Dunlop Green Flash trainers. 'I told you, no. It's a bad time.'

'Sure, sorry to have disturbed you. Can I leave you some contact details? You can get in touch when it's convenient.'

'If it's about work, call the Home Office, I'm sure they'll help you.' By now, Tyler had one foot in the hall.

'I doubt they'll answer what I want to ask.' Mercer delved into his bag and produced a scrap of paper. 'Let me give you my number. Have you got a pen?'

Tyler let him stand in the hall while he went in search of a pen. There was usually one by the phone, but now it was needed it was nowhere to be seen. He rooted through kitchen drawers, emptying out appliance instruction booklets for gizmos they no longer owned, bits of wire and broken utensils. He found a biro and Mercer wrote down his number. 'Like I said, just call when you're ready. I'm always available.'

Tyler took the paper. He could feel perspiration glossing his top lip. He wiped it away on his shirt sleeve. He felt weak and sick and had to hold onto the banister.

'Mr Tyler, are you okay? You look pale, if you don't mind me saying. Have you eaten?'

'Not really.'

'Look, I don't have to rush off, will you let me make you a cup of tea? No questions asked – by me that is.'

In that moment, nodding assent seemed easier than arguing. Something he regretted as soon as he'd closed the door. Mercer made tea and fried egg sandwiches. Tyler's went cold on the plate after one bite. Mercer wiped egg yolk from his chin and talked, mainly about himself, for half an hour. He said he was a freelance researcher, postgraduate only inasmuch as he had a degree, but didn't everyone these days? He was thinking about turning his research into a PhD. Sometimes he wrote papers and articles and sometimes they were published, mainly online. He had a blog and occasionally he was invited to give lectures. He knew people who ran websites, other bloggers. People with influence.

'Doesn't that make you an unpaid journalist?' said Tyler.

'Depends on who I'm talking to.' He broke off a piece of crust and mopped HP Sauce from his plate. 'What about you, what do you do?'

'You know what I do. I'm a civil servant.'

'Yeah, but what do you *do*?'

Tyler said, 'I'm a glorified filing clerk. I keep databases. I collate responses to departmental policy enquiries. I compile stats reports for management briefings. Once a quarter I send out an electronic update to our business partners.'

'You do research.'

'Some, yes.'

'The data you collate, where do you source it?'

'I can't tell you that.'

'But internal, from within the Home Office.'

'Mostly.'

'External consultants?'

'Sometimes.'

Mercer stroked his cheek, running against the stubble. 'Can I ask, is Patrick Theobold one of those consultants?'

The name jarred. Tyler was aware he was saying far too much. 'That's it. Enough.'

Mercer continued, 'I just find it interesting that someone like that can be employed on a near-permanent contract and be completely unaccountable. It's not right is it, Michael?'

Tyler cleared the breakfast things and threw away the remains of his sandwich. He filled the kettle. While it came to the boil, he had to support himself against the washing machine. He warmed the pot. As he spooned tea from the caddy, his hand was shaking.

'Two sugars please.' The voice didn't sound as though it came from the table where they'd been sitting. Tyler looked around the door. Mercer was pulling books from the shelf. He picked up the novel Emmy had finished reading at the weekend. *'Beyond Black*. Is this yours?'

'It belongs to my wife. Can you put it back please?'

'What did she think?'

'It terrified her. Please put it back.'

'It's about death in Enfield. Sort of.' Tyler was aware of Mercer watching his reaction. 'Lot of people I know wouldn't touch it after the reviews came out, but when someone's got something to say, you can forgive the medium they choose to say it in – medium being the operative word when channelling the dearly departed.' He put the book back on the table.

'It's not the kind of book I would read, usually. I like history.' Tyler looked at Mercer's jacket on the back of the chair, his yellow notepaper spread across their dining table, the ring where he'd put his cup down without a coaster. The sideboard drawer was slightly open and it hadn't been before. 'You should go now. I don't want to talk anymore.'

'I'm sorry, I didn't mean to be rude, just curious. I'd like to meet your wife.'

'She's away.'

Mercer shrugged. 'Somewhere nice?'

'I don't know.' Suddenly he felt close to tears. He swallowed and had to sit down. 'I think it would be best if you were to ask someone else your questions. I shouldn't be talking to you. I'm very tired and it's not a good time for me right now.'

Mercer sat down at Tyler's side. 'Where's your wife, Michael, where's Emily?'

'I'm not discussing my wife with you; it's none of your business.' Tyler picked up Emmy's book, ran his palm across the pages. There was a faint smell of her perfume in the paper. 'I haven't seen Emily since Monday. I don't know where she is. You should go, I really can't help you.'

Mercer put a hand on his shoulder. 'But you can make the connection with Theobold and Derek Labrosse, can't you?'

In the silence that followed, Tyler tried to collect his thoughts. Mercer was a salesman, keeping him talking, sapping his energy, wearing away at his resolve. But what was he selling? Nothing Tyler wanted. Finally, he spoke. 'Patrick Theobold and Derek Labrosse knew each other. They worked together on the same project and I worked for them both in a very junior capacity. There are lots of other people who can make the connection and I'm sure they'd all be able to tell you more than I can.'

Mercer was stony-faced. 'But they weren't there the day Labrosse died.'

Tyler felt like he was drowning.

'Michael, I want to do a deal with you. I'm interested in what you know about Patrick Theobold. I think it's more than you realise. Give me a chance to use my contacts and I'll find out where Emily's gone. If I do that, afterwards, please will you talk to me about Theobold? Completely anonymous. As off the record as you need it to be.'

Tyler was lost. He was also desperate. He opened the contacts list on his phone and gave it to Mercer. 'Do what you want.' Mercer wrote out their car registration details, then scrolled through until he found a photograph of Emily.

'She looks attractive, Michael, younger than you. I'll need bank details as well – and credit cards.'

'What do you take me for?'

'If I was a fraudster, I'd already have enough information to steal your ID. I can think of infinitely more subtle ways of getting your bank details than *"can I have your bank details?"* I'll get them anyway. It'll just take me longer if not from you.'

Tyler wrote down their joint account sort code and number. He was about to hand them over, but held back. 'How did you get to me?'

Mercer shoved his hands into his jeans pockets. 'I've been doing this for a long time. Monitoring the careers of certain individuals, watching their fields of influence grow. I've built up a network of contacts. I spoke to people close to Derek Labrosse.'

'And you promise Theobold didn't send you.'

Mercer laughed. 'Cross my heart.'

'Then who?'

'Caroline Labrosse told me about you. She wanted me to find you so I found you. It wasn't that difficult.'

He left Tyler a cheap mobile phone, its number sellotaped to the back. 'If you need me, use this. Only this, okay?'

After he'd gone, Tyler sat for a long time. He slept in the chair until the sun's noon glare came between the curtains and fell across his face. He washed the cup and plate Mercer had used, dried them and put them away. He returned Emmy's book to its space on the shelf. As he plumped up and replaced the cushions on the sofa, he heard the postman. There was a letter from the Home Office HR department informing him that he would be required to attend an appointment on Friday morning at which they could *formulate a mutually acceptable solution to the current management issues.* It was accompanied by photocopied pages from the employment manual, highlighted sections on the official warning process, formal reprimands and, in certain circumstances, summary dismissal. The letter said he was entitled to bring a supporter or representative from his trade union but that no formal legal representation would be permitted. Signed Clare Dunstable, Human Resources Team Leader. So now, he had become a 'case', which necessitated him being assigned a Case Officer. Miss Dunstable formed as a caricature in his mind: a smartly bloused young woman with a postgraduate management qualification and unswerving commitment to the corporate cause. She would sit nicely, he thought, with whichever interpretation of the rules Theobold was applying to have him dismissed.

He tossed the letter on the table, then thought better of it and put it away under the good cutlery in the sideboard drawer. He set about tidying Mercer's pages of notes. Among them was a scrawled sheet with a loose arrangement of linked bubbles and jagged shapes. Mercer's ideas popped like small explosions, but in one corner he'd drawn a series of balloons. In each balloon was a name: *Derek Labrosse, Caroline Labrosse, Patrick Theobold, Hannah Rees, James Creedy.* The balloon strings connected at a single point, where Mercer had written and heavily underlined his name, TYLER, as if he was all that was keeping them earthbound.

30

Max

SHORTLY BEFORE 3AM ON Thursday morning, Max received the call that Caroline Labrosse had been found dead. By 4.10am, he was lifting incident tape at the end of the Labrosse driveway, edging past a scenes of crime officer labelling evidence bags under arc lights. Evidently, they'd been there most of the night. In the house, Rothwell's was the first voice he recognised, directing activity in the living room. A forensic officer in full PPE lifted prints from a wine-stained glass. 'Another ten or fifteen minutes, then we're done.'

Rothwell nodded. 'Good.'

Max looked in from the doorway. The place was hot and smelled of piss and disinfectant.

Rothwell acknowledged his presence with a raised hand. 'Wait outside.'

Max had the urge to pick things up, to be left alone to read the scene his own way and in his own time. Rothwell wasn't about to let that happen. The kitchen was the same mess of stacked crockery, empty wine bottles and food-dried plates he'd left on Tuesday night. Caroline's cigarettes were loose on the worktop, the lighter dropped in the empty packet. Death gave the clutter a squalid significance.

'Didn't this woman ever do the dishes?' Rothwell came through, pulling the mask from his face.

'So,' said Max. 'Is this a crime scene or another episode in the Labrosse family tragedy?'

'When we have the evidence we'll make an assessment,' Rothwell said quietly. 'We've found a lot of prescription medication in the bedroom. More than you'd expect. Nothing's ruled out.'

'Because she worked in a hospital?'

Rothwell paused. 'Post-mortem later today, so let's not prejudge anything.'

The forensic officer put his head around the door. 'Finished in the living room, sir. We're just about cleared up.'

'Cheers. Go home, grab a couple of hours, we'll catch up later.' Rothwell waited until the front door clicked shut and they were alone. 'You'd better come through.'

Rothwell led Max into the living room. He indicated the squat lopsided sofa. 'This was where she was found. A neighbour called. The lights were on all day yesterday. They notice things like that around here.'

Max looked around the place. 'Don't be surprised if you find my prints and DNA on those wine glasses. I was here Tuesday night.'

'Why?'

'It's a case I'm working on – you know *why*. I had fresh information.'

'Which you thought you'd share over a few glasses of Shiraz with Mrs Labrosse.'

Max gave a shrug. 'I had a glass.'

'Was she cooperative?'

A nod. 'As best as she could be.'

'What was her state of mind?'

'She was pretty pissed off. Mainly with how she'd been kept in the dark over her husband's death. She was frightened of being alone, had no idea how she was going to pick up her life, but she didn't come across as someone ready to take their own life if that's what you're asking. Far from it.'

'But you gave her a shoulder to cry on, that's nice.'

Max shot him a look. 'You know there's a daughter.'

'She's been contacted.' Rothwell walked to the patio doors and looked into the garden. The sun was coming up. 'Max, is there anything at all you know about this, anything you want to tell me?'

'I don't think she committed suicide.'

'I didn't ask what you *thought*.'

'In that case, why call me and bring me all the way over here? Because you know it links to my case, right? Her husband died in questionable circumstances. Only he didn't get the Detective Chief Superintendent running the show, did he?'

'Interesting use of the work *links* there, Max. Come and listen to this…' He led Max to the hall where the house phone sat in its docking station. The message button flashed. Rothwell pressed it and switched the handset to speaker. A recorded voice: 'You have one saved message. Message received yesterday at 11.32am.' Then Max's voice: *'Caroline, it's me, I just wanted to see if you were ok. I don't know if you'll remember what we talked about last night, but I can help. I will help. You need to know you don't have to deal with this on your own. Just call me. Let me see what I can do.'*

The phone bleeped. *'End of messages.'*

'What did she tell you on Tuesday night that was so important you had to ring up the next morning to offer whatever the fuck that was? What was she dealing with that was in your gift? Come on, Max, you don't do favours and make promises you can't keep to a grieving widow. Or is this you covering your tracks?'

There was a weariness in Max's voice. 'She claimed she was being intimidated – professionally.' He paused. 'It had something to do with money that was being kept from her and criminal allegations threatened against her husband.'

'Did she say who was intimidating her?'

'She was vague. Pissed, as it goes.'

'And you, were you *pissed*?'

Max said nothing.

'I said I'd cover your back, didn't I?'

'Yeah, you did.'

He lowered his voice. 'So, look at this bloody mess, what in Christ's name were you doing here? And why alone? The drink, the phone message. Tell me so that I can understand, why would you compromise yourself like this? I can help, but I need to know what you know, not half a story.' Rothwell watched him intently.

'That's it, there's no more.'

'I don't believe you.' Rothwell walked him to the door. 'Take some advice, Max. Go see Kilby and ask him to reassign you. Put as much distance between you and all *this* as you can. You're out of your depth and Kilby's not about to pick you up a second time.'

They walked out of the front door. Max took a deep breath. 'I told you before that's not an option.'

Rothwell spat into the border. 'In that case, ask your boss why he set this investigation up in the first place. You might learn something, or you could piss him off enough to get kicked off the case, which'd be a result for all of us. Then you can apologise for wasting my time. I can lose this phone message or I can use it.'

As Max made his way down the drive, Rothwell followed. 'And while we're on it, I want you in for a formal statement. Looks like you were the last person to see her alive.'

'Apart from the bastard that killed her.' Max got into his car and cranked up the stereo. *Babylon's Burning* blocked his thoughts.

31

Tyler

MERCER PARKED HIS CAR in the darkest corner of the estate car park. He led Tyler down a dimly lit passage by the side of a block of low-rises. Tyler glanced nervously at every noise and movement, cursing himself for letting Mercer talk him into coming here. He was talking again. 'You worried about the car? Don't be, they can't trace it. Even if they do it won't lead to me. It's registered for scrap. I recycled it. Good for me, good for the planet.'

He'd barely drawn breath since returning earlier that evening in a state of panic to pick up his notes, insisting they leave together. Caroline Labrosse was dead. Mercer claimed she'd been murdered. It stood to reason, if Theobold was 'cleaning up' as he put it, Tyler would be due a visit.

Tyler followed Mercer up the stairs. 'I should have waited. What if Emmy calls home?'

They stopped. Mercer faced him. 'Michael, I've no intention of being on the wrong end of a visit from Theobold. If you had any sense, you'd feel the same. I promise you we'll find her, it's all in hand.'

Inside the flat, Mercer showed him to a room, which he said would be his for as long as he wanted. Not at all came to mind. On the floor was a mattress piled with clothes and magazines and a sleeping bag. What appeared to be Mercer's underwear was in a cardboard box. 'It's temporary,' said Mercer.

'Can I use the toilet?'

'Bathroom's through there.'

The cubicle was impossibly small. Tyler had to turn his knees to sit down. He picked a pubic hair from the soap before washing his hands. Mercer was in the kitchen making toast and coffee. 'That'll sort you out.' The coffee was thick, black, and had sugar in it. He had the feeling Mercer was dosing him up for another round of questions. He got one of his own in first. 'Explain to me how you know Theobold is responsible for Caroline Labrosse's death. Why so certain?'

He opened his laptop and booted up. 'What news outlet do you trust most?'

'I don't know, the BBC, the *Times*, the *Guardian*?'

Mercer set the laptop down and turned the screen towards him. 'Read. And not just what they say; see what they don't say.'

Tyler read the BBC News reports of the death of the widow of a former senior civil servant. The article mentioned the family tragedy, the couple's daughter, Ruth, still at university, and that Caroline had insisted on working throughout her bereavement leave. There was a quote from a senior police officer; they were keeping an open mind. 'So?'

'All very straightforward, you'd think,' said Mercer, 'only they don't say she took her own life and they would if she had, but they're leading you that way. Look at how it's framed, how it's written. It's clever, the seeds are there. You're supposed to think that she killed herself, even though there's not a shred of evidence. I know she didn't. It's impossible.'

Tyler shook his head. 'Nothing is that certain. And it has no bearing on Theobold.'

'Michael, she would not make her daughter an orphan. I swear to you. I know this. Like I know Theobold had a tighter hold on her than he does on you. I spoke to her a lot. She was frightened, like you.' His voice tailed off. 'I liked her, really liked her.'

Tyler took another sip. 'She told you about me.'

Mercer licked butter off his finger. 'You were at the house on the day Derek died.'

'You knew where I lived. She didn't tell you that.'

He buttered another piece of toast. 'I have people who find out these things. Once I've got a name, the rest is easy.' He spat toast crumbs when he spoke. 'It's all online, you just have to know where to look. I can profile you from your shopping, your bank accounts, insurance, Amazon purchases, genealogy subscriptions – see, I know about all that stuff. Same with Theobold, only with him I had to dig a little deeper and there are gaps. What is there is all sorts of shit, like he bought himself out of an army commission, only it wasn't his money. He was headhunted. I think the intelligence services bought him. Until a couple of years ago, he worked solely for them. Then, all of a sudden, they let him go, call him back from a meeting in Strasbourg and kick him out, which means he did something he shouldn't have done. He sets himself up as a security consultant. With his background, his networks, he gets access to some seriously influential people. Pan European, transatlantic, global companies. More importantly for us, he has an ongoing relationship with this company, IDI, that I can trace back to his time in the army. Don't forget, this is before he courted Derek Labrosse and James Creedy and several other very influential associates. Then he pops up again as a government consultant. Ask yourself, how did I find all that out? Because that is what I do. More to the point, I wanted to know why a man like that would give a shit about you.'

'I told you what I do. I'm a glorified filing clerk.'

Mercer ushered him through to the living room. 'Have a seat.' He swept a bundle of newspapers from the sofa. 'Satisfy my curiosity.'

With Mercer prompting, Tyler recalled details of the day

Derek Labrosse died. There was more coffee. Mercer wouldn't let him sleep.

'What bus did you take from Oakwood to the Ridgeway?'

'121.'

'Were there CCTV cameras on the bus? Were there between the bus stop and Labrosse's house?'

'I have no idea. I didn't look. And it was foggy, I remember that.'

'Was Caroline Labrosse expecting you?'

'I think so.'

'You think?'

'She was expecting someone, not me particularly.'

Mercer doubled back, checking specifics. 'You said you were there for the file. Who else was on the distribution list – you know, the front page.'

'I know what a distribution list is. I didn't look.'

Mercer was relentless. *Who were Labrosse's main contacts? Who were the letters and emails addressed to? What had they said? What had Labrosse said? Was Lillico copied in? Was Theobold?*

So much he hadn't noticed or couldn't remember. After a full hour of questions, Mercer tossed his pad on the floor and called a break. He took a call in the kitchen and closed the door behind him. Tyler's head throbbed. He closed his eyes.

Mercer had news about Emmy. After leaving Fiona's house on Tuesday morning, she'd driven to Derbyshire, stopping for petrol at Leicester Forest East Service Station. She'd booked into a hotel near Buxton and, as far as Mercer's contact could make out, she was still there. Tyler wanted to leave immediately.

Mercer said, 'I don't think you should.'

'Why on earth not?'

'She took annual leave from work. Booked three weeks ago. Think about it, she planned this. Now you know she's okay, wait until she calls you.'

'And if she doesn't?'

'She will. Just give her space.'

Tyler was getting used to Mercer's certainties. He laid down on the sofa. On the floor near his head was half a tin of sausages and beans with a plastic fork sticking out. He moved it out of sight. Voices phased in and out of his dreams. Sometimes it was Mercer, low and conspiratorial. Once he thought he heard a woman's voice and he dreamed of Emmy. When he woke, he found he'd been crying. A while later, Mercer came in. 'You back with us then?'

Tyler sat up and took the mug of tea Mercer offered. 'Really, thanks for everything, but I think I need to go home.'

'If that's what you want. I'll drive you, but we need to stop on the way. There's someone I want you to meet.'

'No, thank you. I said I want to go home.'

'My friend can help. Tell her what you've told me. She'll advise you better than I can. In any case, with what you've told me already, you need to know where you stand, legally.'

They walked along a row of shops with their shutters down. Mercer explained that Liz was a colleague and a friend. A solicitor, one of the few people he knew that was totally committed, someone you could trust. 'She's dug me out of the shit more than once.' Tyler noticed he'd shaved and put on a clean shirt.

'It's here.' Mercer buzzed the intercom and they were allowed in.

She met them at the top of the stairs. 'Liz Delaney.' Her handshake was warmly reassuring. 'Come through, we'll go in my office.'

Liz teased Mercer. Why hadn't he needed her services recently? Had he been sitting on his lazy arse, waiting for the hack gods to message him the world was about to change? Mercer defended himself, but she persisted. 'Come on then,

Phil, what nasty little scraps of gossip have fallen into your in-tray in the last month?' She poured them a glass of wine.

'I've been working.'

'Good. Anything to pay the rent on your office?'

He smiled and shook his head.

'More freebies for what's her name with the boobs at *Freemedia*.'

'You mean Becky?' He blushed.

Liz turned to Tyler. 'What about you, Michael? What's got our friend here so excited that he rings me at midnight, insisting we meet?'

Mercer cut in. 'Just say it from the start.'

'Let Michael tell it for Christ's sake. Ignore him, please.' She gestured for him to continue.

For the second time that day, Tyler was saying the words of a story that, with each telling, sounded more like it was happening to someone else. At key points, Liz prompted, coaxing detail, encouraging clarification. She drew him to his confession: a man had died and, in a state of panic, he'd left the scene and failed to informed the police. It was that simple, whatever the mitigating circumstances. She told him he'd done well and topped up her glass. 'Help yourself.' Mercer did.

Mercer rolled a cigarette. 'Want one?'

'No, thank you.' Liz went to work. 'First thing, Michael, I'd like to get in touch with Emily, make sure she's okay and put your mind at rest. If you like, we can do that now. Or I can call her for you tomorrow.' She looked at her watch. 'I suppose it is getting on a bit.'

'I'd like you to do it now, please.'

'Phil, get me the number of that hotel, my laptop's in the main office. It's hooked up, just switch it on.'

'Password?'

'As before.'

Mercer frowned.

'I know, can you just get on with it?'

Mercer left them. Liz said, 'Tomorrow morning, we'll speak with one of my contacts.'

'Do we have to involve someone else? I'm not supposed to tell anyone.'

'Did you sign anything to that effect?'

'I signed to abide by the restrictions of the Official Secrets Act when I joined the Home Office. Same as everyone else.'

'I think you'll find you're within your rights to take legal advice prior to reporting a crime. I know someone qualified to advise us on the best way forward. I'll call him later and set it up.' She reached across the desk for Mercer's lighter and lit a cigarette. 'We need to look after you and my contact will help us do that.'

'Are you sure?'

'I can't protect you from a man like Theobold without help, not if what Phil says is true.'

Mercer slapped a post-it note on the desk. 'All yours.'

Liz made the call to the hotel. The concierge confirmed that Emily Tyler had been staying there. 'May I speak to her… then please ask her to call me when she returns. I have been engaged by Mrs Tyler's husband to verify her wellbeing. Either you call me in an hour or I will drive to you now and question everyone who comes through your reception and bill your head office for my time.' A long pause. She made some notes and put the phone down.

'Emily checked out earlier this evening. She didn't leave a forwarding address.'

'Perhaps she's coming home?' he said.

Liz lit another cigarette. 'Michael, there's something you should know. The concierge said she wasn't staying on her own.'

*

In their absence, Mercer's flat had become unbearably hot. Mercer dumped his bag in the hall and went to use the toilet. Tyler needed time alone. In the bare bulb's light, the walls were grubbily yellow. Wallpaper curled at the seams. The curtains hung like dishcloths. Mercer took a call. The meeting with Liz's contact was confirmed for the following morning. Mercer was full of himself. 'What did I tell you, she's good, isn't she?' He asked, could they talk again as there were things he'd told Liz that he hadn't said the first time around? Tyler knew he'd never stop wanting more. There was no more. He said, 'I want to go home.'

'You shouldn't be on your own.'

Tyler said, 'Please, Phil. I want my own space. I want to go home.'

He shook his head. 'A couple of hours sleep first, then I'll drive you in the morning. D'you want the mattress or the sofa?'

'I had a letter from work,' said Tyler. 'If I don't go in tomorrow, I'll lose my job.'

'Michael, the job is gone.'

'You don't know that. I might be able to clear things up.'

'No chance.'

'Either way, I still have to go. It's important.'

'So is this,' he said bitterly. 'Do you really believe he'll let you go back?' You're a threat to every scheme he's running. Think about it: *Sorry Patrick, I just spoke to a solicitor and a journalist and told them about our little understanding. But I'd like to come back to work now if that's ok?'*

Tyler's head was throbbing. He raised his voice. 'I don't have to tell him.'

'Do you know the first thing he'll ask you? Have you thought about that? How about, why weren't you at home?' Mercer laughed sourly. 'Christ, you're naïve. You won't have a choice. Whatever he can use, he'll use. He'll get to you.'

Tyler gave in. He took himself to bed. The room was so stuffy he could barely breathe. He searched for a key to open the window locks, but there wasn't one. His head ached. He couldn't stand the light. He turned it off and opened the curtains. In the glow of Mercer's mobile, he dialled Fiona's number. Keith picked up and quickly passed the phone to Fiona. Tyler was worried that he'd woken her.

'I'm fine, Dad. I tend not to sleep until late these days. I'm reading a lot more and not just baby books. Takes my mind off things.'

'Good, that's good.'

'You should try it, lose yourself in a book.'

As the darkness closed in around them, it brought an intimacy to their conversation. 'I thought there were some things you should know about mum and me.' He stalled, unsure how to explain.

'It's alright, I know. Mum phoned.'

'When?'

'Earlier this evening.'

'What did she say?'

She paused. Tyler heard Keith whisper something in the background. 'I don't want to talk about it, Dad. If I'm not careful I'll get stuck in the middle and I don't want that.'

'Of course, of course.' From behind the net curtain, he could see Mercer's car parked outside. Some kids were drinking in the playground.

Fiona said, 'Are you still there?'

'Yes.'

'I'm sure it'll be okay, Dad. It's just ups and downs, like everyone has.'

'Is that what she said?'

She sighed.

'Do you know where she's going? You don't have to tell me, but if you... if you needed her?'

'Yes, I know.'

'Good, that's good. Who's she with?'

'Dad –'

'I'm sorry, that's not fair. But, to be honest, none of it feels fair.'

There was another pause and more whispering. She said, 'Shall I come over tomorrow and see you?'

'No, there's no need. Besides, I've got to go into work.'

'Are you sure you're ready?'

'No choice, I'm afraid. There was a letter, they've given me a formal warning. So, I have to go in and plead my case.'

'That's outrageous. Can't you appeal? Tell them you've got domestic problems.'

They discussed what he should do and how he might make his case, as though it all came down to his problems with Emily. It dawned on Tyler that this was the longest conversation he'd had with his daughter in a very long time. He was conscious of keeping her talking. 'I miss you so much,' he said.

'I know, Dad.'

'I suppose I'd better let you get back to your book.'

'There's no rush.'

'Yes, but Keith'll have an early start and I don't want to keep you.'

'Okay. Call me if you need me. Promise.'

'I promise.'

'Night night, Dad.'

'God bless.'

The phone lit up as the call ended, then went dark. As he laid down, he could hear the kids outside throwing bottles at the wall. Tired as he was, he couldn't sleep. From time to time, there were noises from the other flats. He followed every word, tyre screech, and gunshot from a neighbour's late-night film. He longed for his own bed. His t-shirt was soaked with perspiration. He put on his shirt, carried his shoes and socks into the living room. It took a while for his eyes to adjust to the deeper darkness. He made out Mercer's shape, asleep on the sofa, his clothes in a heap on the floor. As he moved towards him, he kicked over a cup. He felt the soggy carpet under his feet. He picked up Phil's trousers, felt in the pocket for money and pulled out a note. Phil stirred. His eyes were open.

'I'll pay you back.'

'Sure.'

'I'm sorry,' he said.

Mercer was silent.

As Tyler came out into the estate, he disturbed a fox foraging in a pile of black sacks. The fox looked up for a moment, weighing threat against reward, then went back to the rubbish. Out in the High Road, a night bus pulled into its stop. Tyler took a seat near the back and fell asleep.

32

Theobold

THEOBOLD RARELY MANAGED MORE than coffee and vitamins for breakfast, but that morning a good mood and the smell from the hotel breakfast bar enticed him. A full English with toast, marmalade and coffee was spread on the table. It was early and he felt a surge of energy, scanning the dining room, where business types were making calls, scrolling phone screens or reading the *Financial Times* over coffee and croissants. If Lillico's perceptions were on the button, negotiations would be finalised later in the day and contracts drawn up for signature the following morning. Theobold spread a napkin across his lap, smoothed the creases and buttered a piece of toast. Hannah Rees came across the dining room towards him. He wiped his hands and stood as she approached the table. 'Good morning, Hannah. Coffee?'

'What the fuck is this?' She handed him three sheets of A4 paper.

He scanned quickly, groping for understanding. The screenshots looked to be from a website, a story headlined *SLEEPWALKING INTO THE AGE OF SURVEILLANCE* that mentioned Derek Labrosse by name, cast doubt on the manner of his death, making a connection with implementation of government security policy by the back door, corporate contracts, kickbacks and shady foreign interference in the Home Office. 'It's speculative. Nothing to concern us.'

'You think so? Read on.'

The second page accused the authorities of complicity in withholding information about Derek Labrosse's death. It highlighted inconsistencies between the official version of events and that of a verified, unnamed witness interviewed by the author of the article. The piece went into detail about Caroline Labrosse's despairing attempts to uncover the truth and her own death in suspicious circumstances earlier that week. The writer concluded, there was no longer any doubt; there had been a cover-up, one that brought police, Home Office, and Government credibility into question. It was now a matter of accountability.

The text blurred. Theobold felt his fury rising. The anonymous witness quoted in the article was Tyler and he knew it.

The colour had drained from Hannah Rees's complexion. 'In case you missed it, it *says* Caroline Labrosse was murdered. It links you, Patrick. It mentions you by name. You said this could not happen. Today, of all fucking days, we cannot afford this kind of a distraction. The only saving grace is that David hasn't seen it yet. When he does, I need to be able to reassure him that it's in-hand. You can deal with it, right?'

'Yes, of course.'

'You're sure about that?'

'Yes, I'm sure.'

'This was posted on a website called *Freemedia* this morning. If they're smart, they'll be looking to syndicate it, have one of the broadsheets pick it up. Our people at home are limiting the damage, taking down any site it shows up on, killing and redirecting the links, blogging up a smokescreen, but if it finds its way to the mainstream media, we are in deep trouble. You need to find the people behind it, nail their sources and shut them down. Now, please.'

He nodded, said nothing.

'You hearing me, Patrick?'

'I'll handle it.'

She walked away. He wiped his mouth, folded the napkin in quarters, slapped it down and pushed the plate aside. A young waitress approached with a coffee pot. 'Would you like a refill, sir?' He ignored her. She waited a few seconds then moved to the next table.

On his way through reception, Theobold grabbed the hotel phone and called Lillico's room. 'Are you up? I need to see you now, it's important. I don't give a fuck if you're with someone, I'm coming up.'

He listened before knocking. There were voices. Finally, he tapped on the door. 'Do your flies up, Gavin, I need to come in?'

Lillico opened the door. 'I think you'd better.'

Sky News rolled by on a silent TV screen in the corner of the room. Hannah Rees sat at a small writing desk by the window, scrolling through phone messages. She didn't acknowledge him. Lillico folded the double cuff of his shirt, fiddled with a gold cufflink. Theobold pictured him offering his sleeve to Sara in the morning to finish dressing, the prince and his consort. The sleeve dropped over his hand. 'Hannah told me.'

'You didn't waste much time.' It was meant flippantly, but landed badly.

She stood up. 'Bittman will want an update, including security issues at our scheduled pre-meeting in…' She checked her watch. 'Fifteen minutes. He may decide to postpone this morning's session, I'd like for that not to be the case. Gavin needs to be kept in the picture. We *all* need to be on the same page.'

Theobold held his hands up. 'My thoughts exactly.'

She addressed Lillico. 'I'll call you if there are any changes.'

'Sure. Reassure David we'll sort this out. There's no need to delay. Just the opposite in fact. And if he wants to call me, I'll be happy to talk through any concerns he might have as soon as I'm done here.'

'He'll appreciate that.' She left.

Theobold took three steps across the room. He took Lillico's wrist and refolded the cuff, threading the link through. He straightened Lillico's tie. 'You've been spending too much time with Americans, Gavin. You're beginning to sound like one. It doesn't suit you. In fact, it grates.'

'I'm doing my job, Patrick. You do yours. Make it go away.' He opened the door for Theobold to leave. *Sky News* burbled in the background.

33

Tyler

TYLER'S DESK HAD BEEN cleared. His in-tray was empty. A rectangle of office dust and sandwich crumbs marked the place where the PC monitor had been. He sat, rereading the letter until it was time to go down for the appointment. His colleagues went about their business with little acknowledgement. Mrs Richards told him it would be more appropriate to wait elsewhere. Where did she suggest? She didn't answer.

The meeting with Miss Dunstable was over inside ten minutes. She wore a smart suit, a cream-coloured silk blouse and emphasised opinions with a click of her pen. She had reviewed his file and agreed with Mrs Richards that poor performance over a period of weeks and recent unauthorised absences constituted a clear case for her involvement. Added to that, the misuse of resources which, she explained, was the use of his PC to write a personal diary on company time, and his managers felt they had no option but to pursue a formal disciplinary process. This meeting was the first stage. She asked, was there anything he wanted to say? He couldn't bring himself to tell her about Emily; he doubted sharing his troubles would cut much ice with Miss Dunstable. She'd been given her instructions and was carrying them out. Tyler was suspended with immediate effect. She confiscated his security swipe card and issued him with a temporary pass. 'You'll need to surrender this on leaving the building.'

He was still shaking when Theobold met him at the lift. 'I need to talk to you,' he whispered. 'Who did you speak to about the file?'

'No one.'

At the ground floor he propelled Tyler through reception, pausing only to return the visitor pass. As they came through the front door, a silver Lexus with darkened rear windows pulled into the kerb. Theobold shoved him into the back seat. The driver looked over his shoulder and edged into the traffic.

No one spoke until they were through the Victoria one-way system. Theobold leaned round from the front passenger seat. 'I knew you'd read the damn thing, I just didn't think you'd be stupid enough to spout off to every shitty little blogger with a grudge to peddle.'

'I didn't tell anyone.'

Theobold looked out of the window. 'Yeah, you did.'

Tyler tried to make a mental note of the roads they drove down, the direction they were taking, thinking that, at some point, he would need to retrace the route to find his way home. But, as they headed out of London, getting back under his own steam seemed unlikely. He put his hand in his pocket. Theobold asked, what was he doing?

'Just seeing if I've got money.'

He caught the driver's smile in the rear-view mirror.

'You won't need it.' Theobold threw him a black hood. 'Put this on.'

He tried to tell himself it was the ordinariness in Theobold's voice and the apparent reasonableness of the request that made him comply. It certainly never occurred to him to refuse. But, as he submitted to the darkness and the musty smell of the fabric, he realised that it was the fear of what Theobold would do if he had said no. The car accelerated, joining a motorway or an A-road, he thought. They drove steadily, at speed, for a long time, perhaps as long as an hour, before taking what felt like a wide left turn and circling back on themselves. After that, the road surface changed, becoming rough and uneven. Tyler fell sideways and clung onto the door handle as they eased to a halt. Theobold lifted him out of his seat, gripped his arm and held it. He heard keys, an unlocking; a metal bar dropped noisily against a heavy door. Theobold ordered the driver ahead. As they walked, he sensed a closing in, dampened acoustics as they turned corners and stopped. Theobold loosened his grip. Tyler heard him fishing for another key. He was taken into a room. They sat him down on a hard-backed chair. As Theobold pulled the hood off, something at ground level scurried into the shadows.

The chair had been planted in the centre of the room. Dots of light came in through a perforated metal window grill. Furniture was stacked by a sink in the corner: a bed frame on its end, a chest of drawers, bedside tables, a lamp with its shade dented and split. Theobold told the driver to wait outside. He secured Tyler to the chair, tugging plastic cable ties tight around his wrists, elbows and ankles. Tyler tried to count the dots of light. Theobold stood in front blocking them out, unbuttoning his shirt collar and loosening his tie. 'Okay, let's get started.' He took a pace back. 'This is a really important week for me, Michael. Years of work come together. A lot of investment of time, trouble and money. So, you can imagine the last thing I wanted shoved in my face at breakfast this morning was this.' He held up a sheet of paper. It shook in his hands. It was impossible to read. Tyler just made out the print heading – *FREEMEDIA*.

'I can't read it. It's shaking.'

Theobold punched him, connecting with his jaw. Tyler's head snapped back against the chair. Theobold screamed. 'It's got my fucking name on it. Shall I tell you what it says? It says, *The UK Government and US-based global security and surveillance systems company, IDI, have joined forces for a multi-billion dollar contract to replace existing security infrastructure – welcome to a privatised police state.* See that?'

Tyler nodded.

Theobold continued. *'Home Office sources have confirmed that the scheme will implement a non-discretionary personal ID monitoring system. The system will hold biometric and DNA data as well as the holder's digital image. Retina scans and facial mapping will replace all existing forms of ID. Citizens will receive their own personalised barcode. Negotiations with IDI are at an advanced stage with contracts due to be signed by the autumn.'* He shrugged. 'That part's wrong, it's this week. *The source has confirmed that personal ID will be linked into revolutionary CCTV software enabling the operator to identify and monitor any individual without their knowledge, as well as gaining access to personal electronic and social media data communications. The Home Office were unavailable for comment.'* Theobold sniffed. 'This part's the killer. *The system ignores warnings given by former Home Office Director, Derek Labrosse, who died in suspicious circumstances in February of this year. Labrosse had argued against the policy of "Soviet style state control and the dangers of contracting such a major UK security contract outside the UK." The deal's main broker, Patrick Theobold, a freelance consultant to the Home Office who, as recently as eighteen months ago, was employed directly by IDI has continued to champion the scheme from his unaccountable position within the department. The man, who has links to UK security services...* I mean was there anything you didn't tell them?'

Tyler didn't say anything. All he could see was the look on Mercer's face when he'd left him on the sofa that morning. He hadn't wasted any time. Theobold paced, then stood with hands on hips. 'I want an answer. Come on, aside from being a deliberate fucking provocation, who is trying to shit all over my career?'

Tyler shook his head. Theobold punched him again. His nose gushed blood. A damp patch spread across his crotch.

'Who else knows what you know?' He looked at his watch. 'I have to get back and explain this, so you've got about five minutes. Who wrote it?'

A dribble of bloody saliva soaked into Tyler's shirt. It felt wet against his chest. 'I did.'

He turned away. 'Bullshit. It's attributed to someone calling themselves *truthhack*. That's a bit on the pithy side for you.'

'I wrote it yesterday morning.'

'Do not waste my time.'

'It was me. I'd had enough of lying. I told you.'

'So, who's your contact?'

Tyler hesitated.

'Come on, Michael, this is you going for broke. Your scoop and you don't know your contact?'

'It's an email address at freemedia.com, I found it online, that's all I know. Anyone can submit posts. That's the whole point, it's anonymous.'

'I know what a fucking website is, Michael. Who else knows?'

Tyler coughed, but said nothing.

Theobold went to the sink and soaked a towel. He moved in close, Tyler felt him twisting the towel around his throat. He felt his head forced back, pressure on his windpipe. 'Have you any idea what'll happen if the papers get hold of this?' The grip tightened. Tyler lost himself in the room, his eyes watering. With his free hand, Theobold covered his nose and mouth, denying breath.

'So that we're clear, I will kill you in this room if you don't tell me who else knows.' Theobold relaxed his grip.

'No one.' His voice cracked like an old man.

'Emily?'

'No.'

Theobold forced his head back again, stood over him, looked into his eyes and twisted the towel. 'Who else?'

Tyler's head swam. Everything went black.

34

Max

MAX DITCHED ANY PRETENCE of city smartness. Back in black jeans, Doc Martens and a polo shirt, he hung his jacket over the back of the chair in Liz's office. Tyler was late and Liz was leaving *where the fuck are you?* messages for Mercer. There was a taut edge to her voice, same as the night before when she'd fallen over herself to tell him Tyler's story. He'd cut her short: let him tell it in person. Now he knew the whole nine yards of Labrosse, Theobold, Caroline, Tyler and the file, and the wellspring of intimidation that came from it.

Liz said, 'Mercer's got four numbers. I've called them all and left messages. What else?'

'Sit down, take it easy.'

'Thanks, Max, always welcome your constructive advice.' She paused, checked herself. 'I'm sorry. Our website was hacked last night. Since about 3am we've been posting links to Eastern European fascist propaganda. I had Jonathon on my case at half-past bloody six. Phil handles all that shit and where is he? Nowhere. Nikki's had a go, God bless her, but it's not her thing.'

'What now?'

'Wait for Phil.'

Max came back to his seat, levered himself back on two chair legs. 'Talk to me. Tell me about Tyler. What's he like?'

She tapped a cigarette on the pad by the phone, shook her head. 'Seems alright. Confused, understandably. Like he's waiting for someone to let him in on the joke.' Her mobile bleeped. A text. 'It's Phil. He says: *Hi Liz, can't talk right now. In the middle of something.*' She thumbed a return message.

'What are you saying?'

'He's got five minutes, or he'll find his shit in the street.'

The phone on the desk rang within a minute. Max picked up the thread, Tyler wasn't coming. He'd left in the night.

'Why?' Liz asked. She held the cigarette in her teeth while she scribbled Max a note. *What next?*

Max wrote *bring Phil in* and turned the pad back.

Liz nodded. 'Not like you to lose a story so easily, Phil.' There was a pause. Liz asked him to repeat what he'd said, then told him to wait. She put the phone down and typed in a web address on her laptop. As she scrolled down, a patch of red appeared on each cheek. Her jaw tightened and she picked up the phone. 'Does Tyler know you did this, Phil? That's not what I asked, did Tyler know this *before* he went into work this morning?' A pause. 'I want you here. Yes, right now.' She hung up and stared into the middle distance. 'So stupid.'

'Tell me, then,' said Max.

'Tyler left Phil Mercer's place in the middle of the night. He was upset, saying he had to get to work this morning, because Home Office HR are threatening him with dismissal. He was adamant he'd make the meeting and plead his case in person.'

'I'll meet him there, then.'

She turned the screen towards him. 'Except Phil spat his dummy at seeing his source walk out the door and published his piece on Derek Labrosse. Everything Tyler had told him. Everything Caroline Labrosse told him. He names Theobold in connection with Caroline Labrosse and her husband, and wraps it up in this global conspiracy. It's all online, all available and very, very public.'

'Print me a copy. And whatever else he's got on Patrick Theobold.' Max called Denny at Carteret Street.

Traffic was slow-moving on the way into Central London. Max was thinking of calling Kilby when Liz called. The *Freemedia* site had crashed. 'Assume they know and are killing the story.'

Kilby could wait.

He met Denny in the Home Office reception area. 'Any news?'

'Tyler's been and gone.'

A uniformed security guard came towards them. 'Have you signed in, sir?'

Max flashed his ID.

'You'll still need a temporary pass.' He ushered Max towards the reception desk.

Denny said, 'The personnel woman, Miss Dunstable, interviewed him just after nine-thirty. The interview lasted twenty minutes at most.'

'What time did he leave here?'

'She doesn't know.'

Max stood in front of the reception camera, keyed in his name and took the picture. The receptionist handed him the printout in a plastic wallet. 'Keep this visible at all times.'

'Do these keep a record of when people come and go?' The receptionist looked blankly. 'These passes. What happens when people leave? Have you got one for Michael Tyler, for this morning?'

'I don't think so.'

'It's here.' A second receptionist handed it across the counter.

'This doesn't tell me anything. What time did you clock him out?' The first receptionist couldn't remember.

The second did. 'It was just after ten o'clock, that's when I came on.'

'Was he alone?'

'He was with Mr Theobold.'

Gavin Lillico's secretary was not expecting visitors. When Max and Denny came through the door of the executive office suite, she was slow to clear her screen.

'Where is he?' Max leaned over, both palms flat down on her desk.

'Mr Lillico is out of the building at the moment. Would you like to leave a message? I can let him know you called.'

'Where is he?' Max turned the PC monitor round. 'Does he know he's paying you to buy shoes on his time?'

Max swept into the reception of the Intercontinental Hotel on Wallace Place, straight to the front of the queue at the desk. 'I'm looking for a guest you have staying here, Gavin Lillico.'

The concierge eyed Max, checked the whereabouts of the security guard. 'I'm sorry, sir, there is a queue.'

Max wrestled his badge and ID from the arse pocket of his jeans. 'I'm a policeman. This is urgent.' Behind him, Denny flashed her ID.

The concierge picked up the phone, dialled, waited. 'He isn't answering his phone.'

'In his room?'

'Yes.'

'He won't be in his fucking room, will he? It's one o'clock in the afternoon.'

'Sir, please, could you keep your voice down.'

'His secretary told me he was here. Could you locate him, please? *Now.*'

Denny called over. 'It's here, the Business Centre, fourth floor. The board says Home Office security seminar.'

They stepped out of the lift on the fourth floor. A security guard in a dark blue suit was on them before the lift doors closed. He positioned himself between Max and Denny and the double-door entrance to the conference room. A buffet was laid out under clingfilm on white clothed tables. It looked expensive and healthy.

'Lunch looks good.'

'May I ask what you're business is here, sir?'

'I need to see Gavin Lillico. I'm told he's in a meeting. I'm told he's in there.'

Dark Suit stepped in closer, his hand on Max's shoulder. 'I'm sorry, sir, I have instructions that no one is to enter the conference centre whilst the meeting is in progress. There are confidential matters being discussed. I am happy for you to leave a message at reception which I will ensure is passed to Mr Lillico as soon as they break for lunch.' He checked his watch. 'Shouldn't be long now.' He pushed the lift button.

Max showed his ID. Dark Suit hesitated just a second. Max slipped past, headed for the doors. Dark Suit caught up, held his wrist. Max swept his arm downwards, shook himself free. 'Maggie, hit the fire alarm.' Denny wavered. 'Now, do it now!' She went for the red box on the wall, Dark Suit went after her.

Fifteen heads turned as Max entered. His eye was drawn to the far end of the room. At the head of the table, sat a tanned, middle-aged man with close-cropped silver hair, wearing the whitest white shirt Max had ever seen. The woman on his right tilted her head, as if waiting to see what he'd do for an encore. Max scanned the delegates for Lillico, making sure his ID was in plain sight. For a billion-dollar contract meeting, you'd expect the principals to have personal security. He didn't want anyone getting the wrong idea. A guy sitting at the far end of the room behind the white shirt was on his feet. Max shook his head. He pointed to Lillico. 'Him. I want him.'

Lillico stood up. 'Ladies and gentlemen, I suggest we break for lunch and reconvene at say, one forty-five. David, is that okay with you?'

The white shirt nodded. 'Sure, Gavin.' He whispered something to the woman. She followed them out, so did the protection officer.

They found a quiet corner. Max said, 'Mr Lillico, I'm looking for a member of your staff, a man named Michael Tyler.'

Lillico prodded Max in the chest. 'I am going to take this as far as it will go.'

'Michael Tyler,' said Max clearly.

'I have no idea who or what you're talking about.'

The woman from the boardroom approached, offered Max her hand. 'Hannah Rees. May I ask what we can do to help?'

Dark Suit hovered behind her, joined by Dark Suit Number Two, whom he recognised from reception. 'Police business,' said Max, 'I'm looking for a member of Mr Lillico's staff. Mr Lillico is helping me.'

Lillico looked to her. 'I've no idea what he's talking about.'

'But you know who he is, right?' said Max.

Hannah Rees said, 'We're at a crucial stage of some very important negotiations here. If Mr Lillico says he doesn't have the answers you need, and he patently does not, you have to go now. Or do we start talking pay grades and I start making phone calls?'

Max ignored her. 'Is Tyler with Patrick Theobold?'

Lillico looked to Hannah Rees.

'She can't help,' said Max. 'Theobold works for you.'

An instant's panic flashed across Lillico's face. 'Genuinely, I don't know where either Michael Tyler or Patrick Theobold are.' Max shoved him in the chest. A second shove and he stumbled against a table corner. A stack of side plates crashed to the floor. Heads turned from the buffet. 'Gavin Lillico, I am arresting you on suspicion of withholding evidence –'

Hannah Rees cut in sharply. 'That's enough, detective. Can we discuss our options here?' She caught Lillico's expression, mouth slightly open. 'It's a business decision, Gavin. There are priorities. I'll handle the consequences.'

Friday afternoon traffic snarled on the way out of town. Max overtook a grey Transit and narrowly missed the bus coming in the opposite direction. Denny sat rigidly in the passenger seat.

'You're not saying much,' said Max.

She stared ahead. 'You're driving like a lunatic.'

There was a hint of open road. Max's foot hit the floor. They moved out to a chorus of blaring car horns. 'You'd better ring Kilby and warn him. Spare him the details as best you can.'

Denny dialled, waited. Janice took the call. Kilby was unavailable. 'Shit. Lillico will screw us for this.'

Max dropped a gear and accelerated. 'Maybe. You'd better read this.' He pulled the *Freemedia* printout from his pocket.

The road opened up before them and they joined the A1, heading north. Hannah Rees had given them the location, a disused motel close to the junction with the A1M at Alconbury. An hour and twenty minutes according to the satnav. Max had them pulling into the car park inside an hour.

35

Tyler

TYLER JUDGED BY THE light it was getting towards evening.
He was alone, his face and neck sticky with dried blood. His
chest wheezed and he couldn't breathe through his nose. His
throat felt raw. He gulped involuntarily. It was like swallowing
a peach stone. He was thirsty, so thirsty. His head throbbed.
Pinpricks of light swayed in front of his eyes. He couldn't have
counted them if he'd wanted to.

The last thing he remembered with any certainty was
overhearing a conversation between Theobold and his driver,
the gist of which was that he should come back soon and they
would *burn it all down*. Tyler expected that Theobold would
end his life later in the day.

He rocked between reconciliation and pure fear. He strained
his wrists against the cable ties until they were sore and
bleeding. He made himself focus on the sounds of traffic
from a nearby main road. After a while, he found you could
distinguish between the rush of cars and rumble of heavier
vehicles. He measured his breathing with the steady rhythms
of traffic. Occupying time until he picked up a different note.
Tyres rolling over gravel.

A car stopped outside.

Doors slammed.

The metallic echo of the outside door.
Footsteps in the hall. Two people.
He prayed it would not be fire.

36

Tyler

THE PLASTIC WATER JUG on the side table had a hairline crack. When the nurse filled it, water seeped onto the table top and soaked into the cardboard kidney bowl. She took his temperature, then his blood pressure; she said he ought to sleep, but the room was too warm and there was too much noise. They all said he should sleep, but when he closed his eyes, a ball of pain rolled between his temples. They gave him something to help him relax, to ease the pain in his throat.

Tyler worried about the cracked jug.

Through the sedative fog, a woman's voice whispered, 'Michael, Emily is here.'

37

Max

DUSK CAME WITH NO drop in temperature. Peterborough City Hospital was oppressive in the heat. Max's eyes felt gritty and sore. He went to the window and watched an elderly woman with a shopping trolley make her way across the car park. A motorbike coming in fast through the gates almost knocked her over. She stood without moving for a long time before crossing the road. She reached the bus stop and stood apart from the rest of the queue. Max realised he'd been holding his breath.

He must have dozed there for a few seconds, leaning on the windowsill. Liz came out of Tyler's room and closed the door behind her.

'How is he?' said Max.

'Still sedated. He hasn't said anything.'

'Does he know his wife's here?'

'I think so. She's holding his hand. Can we go outside, I want a smoke.'

They walked away from the hospital entrance. When Liz lit her cigarette the match flame barely flickered. He lit one for himself, boot-heeling the match into the dust. He wiped sweat from his face on his t-shirt sleeve. 'Thanks for coming, for bringing her.'

'It's the least I could do.' Liz leaned against a low wall, not meeting Max's eyes. 'She had quite a bit to say on the way up. She's been with another bloke, met him a few months back apparently. They've been seeing each other on and off since then and decided to make a go of it. She told me Michael's been a nightmare to live with the last few months, something not right, but he won't tell her what. She says it's like he's taken a vow of silence. They've been on the road since Monday, moving between hotels. I don't think she knows what she wants.'

Max shook his head. 'What's she here for now?'

'Her husband.'

'They would have killed him, you know that?'

'But you got to him.'

'How much did you know?'

She kicked a tiny stone, sent it ricocheting off the kerb. 'Not nearly enough it seems. Phil Mercer's a free agent. He comes and goes. He's got pet projects, things he monitors on a regular basis, so I know what he's into broadly speaking, but not the who, the when, or the how.'

'But you knew he was into Theobold.'

'I had an idea, but not the detail. Certainly not that he was this close to writing what he did.'

'And the rest, the timing of it, was that a coincidence?'

'Once Phil knew you were on Derek Labrosse's case – and for the record it was Caroline who told him, not me – he took that as vindication for everything he'd been doing. He dropped his other work and committed to the story.'

As it grew dark, a helicopter could be heard circling overhead nearby. Max said, 'I have to ask, is the fact that I was working on the Labrosse case the reason we went out?'

'So that I could grill you for information?' She laughed. 'No, that was for your stunning repartee and impressive bank balance.' She dropped the smile and put her hand on his arm. 'Max, honestly, I just wanted to see you. Nothing to do with any of this.'

Max flicked his cigarette butt into the drain. They walked back to the hospital. 'I will have to speak to Mercer. He's at least partly responsible. I need to know what else he knows.' Max expected an argument, but didn't get one. 'And I need him to back off going public with anything else. He'll get himself and a lot of other people into trouble.'

'I can't ask him to drop the story. He wouldn't listen if I did.'

'Just tell him not to publish anything else. The alternative is I pull him in.'

'You'd have to find him first.'

Max swung the door open and held it. 'You know I'd have him banged up inside twenty-four hours.'

Denny was waiting, she looked anxious. 'Assistant Commissioner Kilby wants to see you. Tonight. He says he'll wait until you get there.'

Max looked at his watch. Of course, it would be now. The moment he'd crashed Lillico's meeting he'd overstepped. He told Denny to wait at the hospital, make sure she was there when Tyler was ready to give a statement. He left her the car. Liz would drive him back to London. As he settled in the passenger seat, he felt strangely unconcerned. Kilby would do whatever he had to do. Max had questions of his own.

He was half-asleep, slumped with his forehead against the car window. Liz said they needed to stop for petrol.

He sat up. 'Where are we?'

'Stansted.'

Max rubbed his eyes. The dashboard clock said 8.58, but it felt later. Liz pulled into a sprawling service station complex.

'Can we get a coffee here?' He arched his back, folded his arms and squeezed the kinks out of his spine.

'Sure, if your boss can wait.'

'He'll wait.'

As the glass doors slid open, Max's sleep-fuzzed senses struggled to take in the scene. In a hangar-sized circular dining area, hundreds of people were eating and drinking. Around the periphery were half a dozen fast food concessions. KFC at eleven o'clock, McDonalds at one o'clock, Tex-Mex at four, and a restaurant selling fish and chips and all-day breakfast fry-ups at eight. Each had its own queue of pale, exhausted punters with thousand-yard road stares. Max had to raise his voice to be heard above the noise, 'I just want a coffee.'

Liz took his hand. Tucked in a corner was the Continental Coffee Shop. They found a table easily. Max went to the counter. As he queued, he looked out at the great mass of humanity in transit.

He slid the tray carefully onto the table. 'This place is incredible, not exactly a motorway caff. I got you a Danish.'

'It's like a prison,' said Liz. 'A panopticon, you know? You can observe people without them knowing they're being observed. You never know when you're being watched, or you forget. What's weird is how everyone comes in and moves in the same way. They're all programmed to hit McDonalds.'

Max sipped his coffee. 'Isn't it just the best way to get a few hundred people fed and watered, a few quid lighter and on their way?'

'You could just build troughs.' She broke off the outer ring of the pastry and dunked it in her latte.

Suddenly, there was a commotion at the doors. Uniformed police were preventing people from entering or leaving the complex. Two officers took a post at the exit while a dozen others fanned out across the dining area spot-checking diners' IDs. The senior officer took a position in the centre of the dining area.

'What the fuck is this?' said Liz.

'Spot-checks.' Max turned back to his coffee. 'I doubt anyone minds.'

'I bloody mind. Those girls behind the counter certainly do.'

Over Liz's shoulder, the three girls – he guessed Eastern European – were standing close together as they worked,

NICK TRIPLOW

whispering, glancing with concern at the routes of three officers moving in their direction.

'What happens if you can't produce ID?' said Liz.

People were fussing in bags and jacket pockets to have their IDs ready for inspection. Some of the officers looked to be making light of the inconvenience. Others went grimly, table to table. The noise level dropped. You could pick out individual voices, scraps of conversations.

Max said, 'It's like getting your ticket checked on a train.'

'Is it fuck. That's routine, something you take for granted.' She leaned forward and whispered, 'When did this become routine?'

Two officers entered the Continental Coffee Shop, a lad of about twenty and an older man. People sat upright, waiting in anticipation of the officer's arrival at their table, their gazes drawn to the hardware and handguns on the officers' belts.

One of the waitresses had come out from behind the counter to clear and wipe tables. She moved closer to the younger policeman, checking her movements, trying to hide the fact that she was avoiding him by following behind. Max and Liz had noticed, so had the older policeman.

'What if I refuse to give my details?' said Liz.

'Don't,' said Max.

'Why not?'

'Because it won't help.'

The older officer was heading across the café towards the waitress. Liz pushed herself back in her chair, ready to get up. Max tipped his cup over, spilling the coffee across the table. It dripped onto the floor. He called the waitress. She ignored him at first, but when he beckoned again, she came across. 'I'm so sorry, I've made a mess here. Do you have a cloth or something?'

She began to wipe, moving cups, being overly thorough. The policeman stood behind her. 'Can I see some proof of ID please?'

Max flashed his badge and ID.

'Okay, no problem. Sorry to bother you, sir.' He turned to Liz, who hadn't moved. 'No need to worry if you're with this gentleman.' He waited for the waitress to straighten up.

Max put a ten pound note in the girl's wet hand. 'Please, would you mind bringing me another black coffee? Thank you.' She took the money and hustled back behind the counter. 'So, officer, how many of these have you done?'

He puffed out his cheeks and blew. 'Last fortnight, seven or eight I should say.' He nodded. 'You lose count after a while. Caught a few illegals in transit, not here, another place near Cambridge and one at Peterborough. You'd be surprised what turns up.'

'I bet. Any more tonight?'

'Nah, I'm off after this. Few pints and a curry if I get home in time.'

'Don't let me keep you. Your guvnor looks about ready for the off. Have a good night.'

'Cheers, mate. And you.'

Within seconds of the last policeman leaving, the noise levels had returned to normal. The whole process lasted no longer than fifteen minutes, but the atmosphere had altered. People hurried to finish their drinks and leave. A different waitress brought Max's coffee and gave him back the damp ten pound note. Liz looked at him, shaking her head.

'What?' said Max.

'Nothing.'

'Oh, piss off, it's not about people like her, is it? Some kid from the arse-end of nowhere trying to give herself a chance.'

Liz looked towards the dining area. 'What is it about then? Suicide bombers? Terrorists?'

'Last year was bad enough, what if next time it's dirty or chemical or biological? Here, now. In this place. Everyone dies.'

She raised her hands in mock panic. 'The sky is falling, the sky is falling!'

Heads turned in their direction. Max looked down.

'Max, listen to me. Those ID checks, they didn't happen six months ago and now they do, according to your mate, as routine as his Friday night curry. *Ticket inspection*, you said. Things change. Little erosions and certainties disappearing. It all goes unchallenged and suddenly it's normal. Legal and illegal, according to laws you didn't vote for.'

'That's Jonathon talking.'

'Jonathon knows what we all know, at least anyone with their fucking eyes open. Things don't get this way by accident. One morning you and everyone else will wake up and realise the world isn't the same as it was and you've lost the chance to do anything about it. I don't like it and it makes me angry.'

Liz drove him into Central London. She offered to wait and take him back to her place for supper. Another time would be perfect, but not tonight. He didn't know how long Kilby would keep him and he needed to face the boss without the softening possibility of sharing Liz's bed.

An arc of light shone over the part of the desk where Kilby worked. The nib of his pen crossed and recrossed the pages of a report. Now and then he annotated the text with a shake of his head. Max waited a second, then knocked at the open door.

Kilby didn't look up. 'Have a seat, Max, I'll be with you shortly.' The pen hovered for a few seconds, then he signed off with a flourish. 'I have to brief the Commissioner in the morning.' He came round from behind the desk and closed the door. 'For some reason, he and the Home Secretary and Mr Lillico of the Home Office are pissed off with you.' There was a strange half-smile on his face. Max couldn't tell if he was genuinely amused. 'Apparently, you bulldozed your way into a very important meeting and were rather charmless in how you went about it.'

'I'm sure DC Denny has explained the circumstances, there's no sense in me going over it again.' Max's voice had taken on a post-midnight rasp.

'And the man in hospital is linked to your investigation?'

'Michael Tyler. He was at Derek Labrosse's house on the afternoon he died.'

'Did he kill him?'

'He says it was an accident.' Max looked up. 'He was sent there to pick up a file, which he says contained confidential communications between Derek Labrosse and other members of your steering group. Tyler says there was a misunderstanding. Labrosse thought he was stealing the file, which, effectively, he was, only he didn't know that. He says Labrosse slipped and fell.' He paused. 'Nothing he's told me so far makes it any less of a set up.'

'By?'

'A man called Patrick Theobold. The same man put Tyler in hospital.'

'I know him.' Kilby went to the coffee percolator in the corner of the room, put his palm against the jug and poured himself a cup. He rested his backside against the desk and sipped. 'I also know his background. Army intelligence, Northern Ireland, Iraq, seconded to US Marine Corps. A stint at the Ministry of Defence in Whitehall Main Building, then US liaison for MI5. When he was discharged, he went into business for himself, delivering contracts his former colleagues put his way. Cashing in favours.'

'You didn't think I needed to know that a man like that was involved?'

'I wasn't sure he still was. In any case, you'd have gone after him and that's not what this is about.'

'No?'

'Aside from the fact that he's too well connected here and in the US.'

Max closed his eyes for a second. When he opened them, Kilby nodded towards the coffee pot. Max poured himself a cup of what was, by now, lukewarm, stewed, black and bitter. He dropped in two sachets of sugar and stirred with a biro. 'You know a lot about him.'

'He's a broker. One of those officers that spends his service setting up the corporate career he'll have once he's learned all he needs to make it lucrative. He's a reassuring presence, gives ministers and civil servants the comfort that they've got a specialist on side. James Creedy brought him in to work with Labrosse on the ID scheme, setting up cross-agency connections. Labrosse was suspicious of his motives and methods, so he asked me to have him checked out. He was right to be concerned. I think Theobold picked off members of the senior management group one by one and played them. Persuaded them Labrosse's proposal was too expensive and out of date. Those that couldn't be persuaded, my guess is he bought off or threatened. And, as we know, the Home Office disbanded the group and shut us out. Until now.'

Max pulled out Mercer's article. 'I'm assuming you've seen this.'

Kilby nodded. 'I know IDI. David Bittman was special adviser to the congressional committee on Homeland Security. He's influential, as are his associates.'

Max shrugged. 'That article says that Caroline Labrosse had misgivings about her husband's death, but was prevented from doing anything about it. She thought we were stitching him up. Theobold again.'

'You know who wrote this?'

'Theobold thought Michael Tyler did. He was prepared to kill him for it.'

'But he didn't. Some powerful people will have backed him this far. Don't forget, I couldn't get close. The cash value of the kind of contract he's helping to broker is counted in multiple billions. Its value in terms of influence is infinitely greater. That buys a lot of friends.'

'Doesn't buy him off murder.' There was a long silence.

'No, it doesn't. But you're saying Labrosse wasn't murdered, certainly not by Theobold.'

'I meant Caroline.' Max ran his hands over his forehead and through his hair. 'You should have told me about him, I would have been more careful.'

'I doubt that. And Caroline Labrosse wasn't murdered. Not according to the post-mortem. It was an accident. Excess of anti-depressants combined with alcohol. She suffered a cardiac arrest late on Tuesday night. Chief Superintendent Rothwell called me this afternoon. He says there's no evidence of anyone else being involved, which I understand is good news for you.'

Max caught sight of himself reflected in the darkened window. He thought about his offer of help. Too little, too late. 'Caroline Labrosse was as sick as a dog before I left her, drinking pints of water.' He paused. 'You know Rothwell warned me off this case from the outset. Bailey lashed up the first investigation. Rothwell either missed it or overlooked it for a reason. Unless that was just you setting things up?'

'What you saw in the paperwork was exactly as I found it. An unholy mess.'

Max hadn't the inclination to argue. 'What do you want out of this? You put me here, what do you want me to do now?'

'Get a statement from your man Tyler. If he can implicate Theobold, I'll put some feelers out. We know who we're dealing with and we know they're here and in negotiations. That makes them vulnerable. Given the leverage with you and this man Tyler, they may give us Theobold. I'll speak to Rothwell and see if we can bring him onside.'

There was a briskness in Kilby's tone and a sense of purpose in the way he described their course of action. The penny dropped. This hadn't been about Derek Labrosse, or Caroline, or Tyler any more than it was about keeping Rothwell in his place. This was Kilby working an angle to get back to the table.

Kilby leaned forward. 'I want you to be clear, you do not go anywhere near these people. You've drawn them out and now I need to make representations of my own.' He looked at Max. 'I take it you realise what's at stake here? IDI can undermine us, all of us. Commercially owned, personalised ID systems. Intelligence-gathering without accountability. A privately contracted police service with oversight by their people inside the Home Office. They'll have the resources. If they're successful in making the case that they can do our job more cheaply than we can and there's the political will to make it happen, we must take that seriously. So, I'm telling you to get a statement from Mr Tyler and leave it at that.'

In the street, Max hailed a black cab coming up from Victoria. 'Swiss Cottage, please, mate.' On the way, he asked the driver to stop at an all-night delicatessen in Chalk Farm Road. He bought some rolls and plastic-wrapped smoked ham, but, by the time he got home, he was too tired to eat. He slipped under the duvet, but couldn't stand the noise of the hundred thoughts racing through his head. He put some music on low and prayed that Marvin Gaye might sing him to sleep. Dawn light edged the curtains. Sleep hit him like a black van.

Part Three: July 2006

38

Max

MAX PICKED UP AN order of service and took a seat at the rear of the crematorium. The cover showed a photo of Caroline Labrosse as a young woman, picnicking in the grounds of a stately home, a Laura Ashley summer a long time ago. Ruth Labrosse walked to the pulpit, holding grimly to a sheet of paper. The priest stood at her shoulder. She chose a point of focus at the back of the chapel and took a deep breath before speaking. 'I know we're not here to talk about Dad, but I couldn't help thinking what he'd have said if he was standing here. Probably very little with a few choice expletives.'

A ripple of acknowledgement went through the congregation.

'Actually, that's not quite fair. When it came to it, he always knew the right thing to say. So, I think he would have wanted me to mention what a source of strength and inspiration Mum was to him, how she'd given up such a lot for us both. He might have told you how, on one occasion, after a few too many glasses of wine at Aunt Linda's, she was convinced she could play the piano. She really couldn't. I remember her speaking Italian to a bar full of strangers on holiday in Pesaro – needless to say, she couldn't speak Italian either. It didn't seem to matter. Dad might have said those things. Or he might just have said how much he loved her, how desperately he'd miss her. How it was a terrible thing to lose someone so special, so kind, so loving, so supportive, so positive and vital just when you needed them most.'

She paused and seemed to be searching for someone in the congregation. All Max could see were the backs of heads, black dresses, dark suits and shirt collars. Her gaze settled. 'That's what he would have said. And who am I to argue? My Dad was never wrong and anyone who underestimated him tended to regret it sooner or later. He was our strength. I don't think mum would ever have got over losing him.' And then, almost as an afterthought, she said, 'I hope they're together.'

She stepped down. The priest invited the congregation to stand. He offered his own quiet consolation, but Max wasn't listening. He barely registered the committal, the quiet sobs as the curtains closed and the Mozart, *Laudate Dominum*.

Afterwards, the chapel was slow to clear, emptying from the forward pews. Max hung back and saw Gavin Lillico emerge from the place where Ruth Labrosse's gaze had settled. He stared through Max as he passed.

Sun shone in the courtyard and the mood altered to one of relief. Cigarettes were lit. The undertakers laid out wreaths and they became a focus, an appropriate conversation subject. Max observed Lillico guiding a clutch of Home Office acolytes away from the family. Ruth Labrosse held the arm of a woman who could only have been her mother's sister, he assumed Aunt Linda. Max approached. 'Ruth, I'm very sorry. Mark Lomax, I knew your mother briefly.'

There was a dutiful detachment in the aunt's voice. 'Thank you for coming.' Aunt Linda tried to steer Ruth away.

Max touched Ruth gently on the arm. 'When you're up to it, I'd like to speak with you. Would that be okay?'

She nodded. Close up she seemed a good deal older than the photograph on her mother's bookshelf. 'After the weekend, I'm going back to Uni. You'll have to come there.'

'Do you have a number I could call?'

'I've got mum's mobile, use that.'

They moved away, drawn into the circle of family. They were still there when Max drove past a few minutes later, Aunt Linda bending to collect condolence cards from the flowers and placing them in her handbag, sparing Ruth the formal duties of the bereaved.

The call to set up the meeting a few days later had been perfunctory. Day, time and place. Max found Ruth Labrosse in a wide grassy quadrangle at Royal Holloway College. He'd been directed to the Founder's Building. Green plastic tables and chairs were set out in front of the refectory. Ruth Labrosse sat reading in bright afternoon sunshine, a coffee undrunk on the table. She took off her sunglasses.

Max offered his hand. 'Thanks for seeing me.'

'What do you think?' She waved at the high Victorian buildings with their pillars, arcades, towers and turrets.

'Impressive.'

'I won't give you the grand tour. I'm sure you don't have time and the place is crawling with summer school students. Do you mind if we walk? I want to smoke and you can't do that here.' She stuffed her books in a rucksack. 'There's a gallery. Lots of lovely Pre-Raphaelite paintings, if you like that sort of thing.'

'And do you?'

'Haven't had much time for it recently.'

They followed a path which snaked through well-maintained woodland. She lit a cigarette. Smoking seemed at odds with the little he knew. Max told her he'd seen the photo and had her down as the healthy outdoorsy type.

'Yeah, well things have been a bit stressful.'

Max shoved his hands in his pockets as they sat on the edge of a low wall. 'What are you studying?'

'PPE.'

He smiled. 'You're going into politics?'

'I'm already in it. Or I will be if I ever finish this degree. I must have set the record for the number of extensions and deferments in a single semester. Four at the last count. I could have deferred the whole thing, but there's only my dissertation to finish. *Only*. They've given me until the end of summer to submit.'

'What's it about?'

'*A focused discussion on the critical awareness of surveillance parameters in national security policy making*. A lot of it involves social communication. Weighing the benefits of knowing what private citizens are saying to each other at any given time against the eradication of personal freedoms, the freedom to say what you want, when you want; what free speech actually means. You did ask.'

He nodded. 'It's linked to your dad's work.'

'Some of it. He thought freedom of speech was sacrosanct. I think it's problematic, or at least more complex.' She brushed cigarette ash from her skirt.

'Ruth, I don't know how much your mum told you, but I've been looking into the events surrounding your father's death and information has come to light that the investigation wasn't carried out as thoroughly as it should have been.'

'For which read someone screwed up.'

'Possibly.'

'Mum said you were looking to discredit him, "drag your father's name through the shit" I think were her exact words. You won't find me helping with that.'

'I wouldn't have come if that was the case.'

'Why have you?' She stubbed the cigarette on the wall and tossed it into a bush. 'Tell you what, let me help you. A reasonable question might be: *Why are your mother and father both dead, don't you think that's a bit of a coincidence? Them's the breaks* doesn't quite cover it, does it?'

'Not even close. I have a partial timeline of what happened on the day your father died. Initially, your mum said she was working. The rota at the hospital confirmed she wasn't.'

'She was meant to be, but Dad had arranged a surprise, an early birthday present, high-tea with champagne at the Ritz, then the ENO to see *The Mikado*. Mum liked her G and S. She swapped a weekend shift with someone else. Dad was at work in the morning. He was supposed to join us for tea, but he didn't arrive.'

'You tried calling.'

She nodded. 'We left messages. Mum was late anyway, because of this business with the file and that man Taylor turning up. You know what it's like getting across London, bloody security checks at every station. Anyway, we had tea, hung around the West End, did some shopping and stopped for a drink. We just thought Dad was delayed at work. He had the tickets, not that we'd have gone without him.'

'What did your mum say about the man that came for the file?'

'Not much. She thought he was a bit odd. All anorak and no social skills. I know she was pissed off we were never allowed to see his statement. The police said they'd spoken to him and were satisfied he hadn't been there when my dad got home.'

Max said nothing.

Ruth lit another cigarette. A group of students came past, two wearing Open University sweatshirts. 'They love it, don't they, OU students, they get one week a year to come to a place like this. We're here for three years and take it for granted.'

'Ruth, when you spoke at your mum's funeral, you said something about your dad always being right. It seemed as if you had someone particular in mind.'

'Oh, all of them, the people he worked with. We were upset at how they'd treated him before he died. I never knew the nuts and bolts of it, but mum said he was being marginalised. And then after he died, greasy-arsed Gavin Lillico slid straight in. Mum used to ring me and tell me how bloody distasteful it all was. I was just making a point. Not the most considered piece of public speaking, possibly inappropriate, but there you go. You can get away with anything when you're grieving. What do you think about Dad?'

'I'd go along with that from what I've heard, but I doubt he was taking it lying down. The man who was at your parents' house for the file that afternoon – Tyler not Taylor, by the way – I'm seeing him later.'

'Give him my regards.' Ruth's second cigarette butt joined the first, stubbed out and flicked into the bushes.

They walked back along the wooded path and through the Founder's Building. Briefly cooler in the shade, Ruth asked would he like a cup of tea before driving back? He declined. She walked him to the car.

'You didn't ask which side.'

'Sorry?'

'Politics. You asked if I was going into politics and didn't ask which team.'

'Does it matter?'

'Unless you're a complete cynic. You're not, are you? I think politics is important and, yes, I know there are compromises, but Dad says…' she tailed off, and for a moment was gone from him. 'It's like a fucking wrecking ball. One minute you're here, the next you're rammed sideways. I never see it coming.'

They walked in silence until they reached the car.

'There was one thing. I persuaded Dad to open a Facebook account towards the end of last year, so we could keep in touch. He was always useless on the phone. But, around the time he fell out of favour, his account was hacked. Someone posted pornographic images, not just tits and bums, this was heavier – graphic, S&M, some real filth. I phoned him and he closed the account. When I pushed him on it, he said he thought someone was making a point. *We can get to you, discredit you and destroy your reputation.*'

'Trust me, they failed.'

'Thanks.' Ruth hoisted the bag on her shoulder. 'Look, I realise you can't tell me much, but will you promise me that, if there's anything important, you'll call me?'

'If there's anything conclusive one way or another,' said Max.

'Promise.'

He hesitated.

'I just want to understand, that's all.'

'I'll be in touch.'

39

Max

IT WAS LATE AFTERNOON when Max got to the Tylers. Emily showed him into the living room, sealed and silent until the carriage clock on the mantelpiece chimed five. He watched it mark another fifteen minutes before Tyler appeared. He was pale, the yellowish bruising around his windpipe gave a sickly shadow. 'Thank you for coming.' The voice was hoarse and he had difficulty swallowing. Emily pulled the curtain to ensure he was out of the sunlight and left the room.

Max said, 'I bought you this –'

Tyler took the bottle, studying it for a moment as if he could see through the blue tissue paper, then placed it unopened on the coffee table.

'How are you feeling?'

'I've decided not to give a formal statement.'

'Okay, do you want to tell me why?'

Tyler shook his head. Tears came to his eyes and rolled down his cheeks. 'I didn't used to be a person who cried. Since all this I can't help it. I'm sorry.'

'When we spoke, you said you wanted to help.'

'What can you do to him? Honestly, what would be the worst?'

'Honestly? That depends on the evidence. The Coroner has ruled that Caroline Labrosse's death was accidental, so unless we secure evidence to the contrary, that stands. There was nothing found linking Theobold and I can't see he'll suddenly

236

drop a confession. What we do about him for what he's put you through depends on what you tell us and what we can prove. After that, we put a case together and it's up to the CPS and the courts.'

Tyler looked around the room, anywhere but at Max. 'I'd have to give evidence.'

'Almost certainly. There are people who can support you through that.'

Tyler bit down hard at a hangnail. 'Why is it, after everything this man's done, it comes down to me?'

Max said nothing.

Tyler said, 'You should talk to Philip Mercer.'

'I will.'

'He knows more than I do. He probably won't tell you.'

'He's on my list. I'll speak to him.'

'Ask him why he couldn't give a damn about me, why he lied to me, used me. Ask him why he helped them ruin me.'

Max took a long, deep breath. 'Michael, we need to talk about Patrick Theobold. At the hospital, you told Detective Constable Denny you would be prepared to talk to me, so I'm here.'

Tyler pulled himself forward. 'Think of everything you can't bear the thought of losing, then imagine what it feels like to watch it all get taken bit by bit, day after day after day.' His eyes glistened. 'You can't trust anyone after that. Can you? Once it's gone.'

Max reflected, most of what he couldn't bear losing was long gone. 'You're a straight and honest man, Michael. I firmly believe that. I sympathise with what you've been through. All I can say is that, if you give me enough to act on, I will. But I have nothing without you. If you make a statement, then we have something to work with.'

There were footsteps outside the door. Emmy knocked. Max went to the door and took a tray of iced drinks. 'I thought it might be better for you to get some fresh air.' She unlocked the doors to the patio. Tyler seemed unsure, but Max carried the drinks out and Tyler followed, settling into a deckchair under the striped awning. The heat of the afternoon was steady and intense. Max felt the sweat roll down his back.

Emmy said, 'I'm going over to Fiona's for a few hours, I'll see you later.'

Tyler wiped his eyes on his sleeve. 'What time will you be back?'

'I don't know, ten, ten-thirty, she wants to watch a film. Depends what time it finishes. You've got my mobile if you need me.'

They heard the door slam. Max lowered himself carefully into a wicker seat. 'Is this okay, you need anything?'

'Fiona's our daughter. She's expecting our first grandchild.'

'That's good news. You want to tell me what happened, Michael?'

To begin with, Tyler told his story in slow, painful generalities. Max went after specific details, anything he felt he could build a case on, but the more he pushed, the more Tyler struggled to control his tics and stutters and bit lips. At one point, he broke off abruptly. 'You know Philip Mercer reckons Theobold can't be touched.'

'I don't think anyone's really tried,' said Max. 'If I was you, I wouldn't let Mercer be the sole arbiter of what Theobold can and can't do. He's not the reliable type. But you already know that.'

'Theobold told me he wanted to finish Labrosse. When we were in that place, he said they would have used his correspondence to discredit him. He said there were documents that proved he was working against the country's best interests, revealing secrets that would put our security at risk. He said he'd have ruined him by leaking things in the media and making up the rest. They'd blackmail him and if that didn't stick, they'd brief against him in the press. He said, that's all it would take, just a nudge. He said once Labrosse had dropped out of favour, he'd be forgotten inside a month. But then he died. So, there was no need for any of that.'

'And he wasn't forgotten.'

'I suppose.'

'What happened to the file?'

His hand hovered over the glass of iced water. 'I told you, I gave it back to Theobold.'

Max's phone vibrated, it was Denny. 'Sorry about this.' He strolled across the parched lawn to the shade of a pergola, the sun warming his skin.

There was a weariness in her voice. 'It's your message service speaking. Kilby wants to talk to you urgently. He says there have been developments.'

'What does that mean?' A Red Admiral landed on buddleia and opened its wings, basking. Denny was silent. 'Maggie, what developments?'

'He's cut a deal, Max. He's been with Creedy and Hannah Rees all morning and most of the afternoon. He used what we already have on Theobold to buy a seat at the table with IDI. We can't touch him. He wants to see you when you get back.'

Max ended the call and made his way back to Tyler. 'Michael, I know this is a bit rude, but can we open that bottle I bought you. You don't mind, do you?'

'Is something the matter?'

Max tore away the paper and cracked the Glenfiddich's seal. When he got back to the patio, there were two clean glasses. He poured them a healthy measure.

'Good health.' Tyler sipped gingerly, swallowed and gave a little smile. 'Very nice.'

'Michael, I have to be straight with you. I think, for us to put a formal case together against Theobold, evidence will need to be overwhelming, and even if it is, there's a chance I'll be prevented from pursuing it.'

Tyler held the whisky glass close to his chest. 'Mercer was right, this is a waste of time.'

'I want to find another way.' Max drained the glass and poured a refill. To his surprise, Tyler followed suit.

They sipped in silence. Comfortable enough in each other's company to dispense with conversation. Then Tyler said, 'I have something to show you, wait here.' He disappeared indoors.

Max cleared the tray and glasses from the table as Tyler worked the combination on an old brown briefcase. From a cardboard wallet, he eased out a copy of an email. Holding its clean edge he showed it to Max, careful not to touch the areas stained brown with dry blood. In a neighbour's garden, a lawnmower started up.

'Labrosse?' said Max.

Tyler nodded.

'His notes?'

'Yes.'

'Who else has touched this?'

'Presumably just him.'

'Lay it flat so I can read it.'

CONFIDENTIAL

From: Labrosse, Derek
To: Creedy, James
Sent: 22 December 15:17
Subject: Procurement Strategy – Identity Management

1. This gives every indication of a project being undertaken with undue haste and without realistic assessment of risk. I would argue that whilst external political and current

security considerations make for a unique situation, it does not justify the breakdown in procurement protocols and legislative process proposed by our retained consultant.

If they are intent on rewriting the book, or at least throwing out the one we've got, someone has to say something. Another bloody meeting where we play the emperor's new clothes and I'm the only one telling them they're bollock naked is unacceptable.

2. How are we to proceed without a sustainable business case? IDI's offer of a Private Finance Initiative solution does not meet the initial criteria set – in the long run it is surely in the UK's best interest to 'own' its own surveillance and security apparatus. I also have concerns that the IDI programme for identity management and data interception does not have an acceptable basis in law. It is certainly in contravention of the European Convention on Human Rights. I repeat, from our position as purchasing authority and, therefore, accountable body, there are no checks and balances in place. We have no benchmark from IDI that their proposal for a 'super-database' is deliverable, affordable or proportionate as a response to our needs. Let alone desirable.

3. There is every indication that our retained consultant is feeding confidential data to IDI, his preferred contractor from the outset. This is cause for concern given the sensitivities and the lack of normal processes. Without full cabinet approval, or wider consultation, any decision will rest solely with yourself and Home Office principals. I am willing to inject a note of realism. What is your view?

4. It is my belief IDI intend to resource the system with their own people, possibly those recently returned from tours of

duty in the Middle East and other theatres. This makes the proposal to supplement existing Police Community Support Officers with their people tantamount to a corporately managed paramilitary police force. Have you considered how this will play with the wider public, given that it will make plain an intention to forfeit UK Government autonomy for police, security, and intelligence operations?

Regards

Derek Labrosse
Director of Operations (Home Office Homeland Security, ID and Defence)

Max asked Tyler to turn the page. There was nothing on the reverse other than the same brown bloodstain. 'Theobold is presumably the "retained consultant".'

Tyler nodded.

Max flicked a thunder-fly from the rim of his glass. 'Right. What else?'

The next page carried Creedy's response.

CONFIDENTIAL

From: Creedy, James (Minister for Security – Home Office)
To: Labrosse, Derek
Sent: 22 December 16:23
Subject: RE Procurement Strategy – Identity Management

Derek,

1. I have no argument with most of this. I share your concerns,

however, it's worth bearing in mind that we are working to an agreed strategy and timelines. There are certainly wider implications should protocols and procedures be ditched, but I don't think anyone is seriously suggesting that.

You'd have to be bloody naïve to draw any other conclusion.

2. The forthcoming procurements, IDI included, are necessary to sustain business as usual. They are all sensible and viable contracts in their own right. Their strategic fit and early vetting means less dependence on individual business case approval, etc. PFI was never excluded. You recall our conversation (19/12).

Bullshit. Conversation (19/12) was an aside not a policy decision – he said relax not ditch. No PFI was mentioned because it was (is) inconceivable! Political suicide.

Rest assured, the Justice Department <u>will</u> be part of the consultation process in due course – too soon and we may well find ourselves bogged down. Slippage at this stage may well derail the process completely, to say nothing of the new security legislation. I will consult the AG in due course.

He/they must realise that if we're operating outside of legislation we'll derail later anyway – with greater cost and more mess – and where are the police/ACPO/Met in all this? Attorney General must be consulted now.

3. I will seek reassurances from Patrick. I do not, and neither should you, underestimate the confidence our partners have in him as broker. However, he will be asked to declare an interest if, indeed, this is the case.

Hardly.

4. This is pure speculation, scaremongering. Without ground or evidence, I suggest it appears as sour grapes and goes some way to undermining your other arguments.

Season's greetings to you, Caroline & Ruth
James

James Creedy MP
Minister of State for Home Office (Minister for Security)

'You kept this stuff where?'

'In the cupboard under the stairs. Since February.'

Max shook his head. 'And no one knows?'

'Theobold just wanted the file back. I was trying to tidy it up. As far as he's concerned, he got the file back. There's one more. '

SECRET

From: Creedy, James (Minister for Security)
To: Labrosse, Derek
Sent: 31 January 14:06
Subject: RE Procurement Strategy – Identity Management
cc. Patrick Theobold HO, Gavin Lillico HO, Hannah Rees IDI

Derek,

Re this morning's meeting. I have no intention of pursuing this debate into the spring. Your assertion that we are 'ignoring political reality for commercial expediency and our own private agenda' is inappropriate. I will, however, take that one on the chin if it means the whole thing is out in the open. My position is this: if we are certain that IDI can deliver within timescale and budgetary constraints, we must proceed. I have sought and received grant approval from the Treasury. My decision is predicated on the fact that there will be <u>no further challenge</u> from you or your department. I simply cannot agree with you that we are making bad judgements because of a knee-jerk reaction to Tavistock, 7/7, etc., or indeed that this constitutes an abuse of emergency powers. Our policy is to consider multiple potential providers for all public services and that includes homeland security. I find your attitude provocative and personally offensive. I seek your assurance that you will get behind us now, alternatively I suggest you reconsider your position.

James Creedy MP
Minister of State (Minister for Security

At the bottom of the page, in Labrosse's handwriting, a number: *07892 104222*. This time when Tyler turned the page over there were twenty or more series of names, numbers and letters in the same hand, seemingly in random groups, scanning across the page. Max said, 'You know what these are?'

'I've never really looked. What is it?'

'I don't think they're his lottery numbers.'

At last, the heat in the garden seemed to dissipate and a faint breeze shook the heads of the flowers. The lawnmower had stopped. Tyler said sadly, 'We didn't really do anything with the garden this year. Emmy had plans...'

'Michael, I have to ask, why didn't you call the police?'

He looked up. 'He told me not to. He said he'd dealt with them on my behalf and I believed him. It suited me, I suppose.'

'Does Emily know?'

'Some, I think. But we haven't talked about it. It just hasn't seemed right.' He slid the emails back into the plastic sleeve. 'She doesn't know about these. Nobody does.'

'Can I keep them?'

Tyler looked to the heavens. 'Yes, please. Take them away.'

They went back into the house. Tyler spoke more freely about his work, his family, the birth of a grandchild that he prayed looked like his daughter and not his son-in-law. He managed a joke at his own expense about his obsession with Tyler family genealogy: 'Emmy thinks all I've done is confirm we're the dullest family in England.' When the conversation returned to the subject of Labrosse and Theobold, he was clearer. 'It must look like I gave it to him easily. But when you're conditioned to do as you're told. When you're weak and frightened and as muddled as I was… I made a wrong choice.' He touched the bruises on his face. 'I don't know if she'll stay. Do you think she'll stay?'

40

Max

MAX WAS LOOKING FORWARD to a shower and a change of clothes. Pangs of hunger had come and gone throughout the afternoon and he'd promised himself a takeaway. Tyler's emails were folded in the inside pocket of his jacket. The corner of the envelope dug sharply against his chest as a reminder. As he turned into Goldhurst Terrace, he was met by the sight of marked police units and an ambulance outside the flat. He showed his ID to a uniform at the incident tape perimeter. 'What's the story?'

'Break-in. Second floor flat.'

His flat.

'Who's hurt?'

'A neighbour was assaulted as the intruder came out of the premises.'

'Did he give you a description?'

'He's a bit shaken up. You might want to speak to DS Abbott. She's upstairs.'

The lock on Max's door had been forced, crowbarred and kicked in. The frame was splintered. Not subtle. A fuck-you-very-much from someone not bothered about the noise, who knew the neighbours were out, or should have been. He took a deep breath.

'This is a crime scene, sir, would you mind waiting outside until we've finished?' The officer closed her notebook.

Max showed his ID. 'This is my home.'

'It's still a crime scene.'

He surveyed the room. LPs and 45s and fragments of record sleeves scattered around the floor: dayglo *PisTOLs,* half a Warhol banana; Ray Davies and Mick Avory torn from an old Kinks album. Several books had pages torn out and tossed. The record deck turntable was split, its spindle bent beyond repair. Contents of cupboards had been emptied into the centre of the room with a mess of magazines and papers. He picked up Dexys Midnight Runners' *Dance Stance* single, blew away residual fingerprint powder and slipped it back in its sleeve.

'Did you get a description – the intruder?'

'Not yet, sir. Your neighbour, Mr Dean, is quite confused. They're taking him up to the Royal Free. Suspected concussion.'

'Mind if I have a quick chat first?'

'I'd rather you didn't, not before I do.'

Max found Simon Dean in the back of the ambulance sucking from an oxygen mask. An ugly graze covered half the right side of his face. Evidently, his nose had been bleeding as a bloody gauze plug stuck out from one nostril.

'How you doing?'

He stared at Max, registering the question, but not the person asking it.

'It's Max, from upstairs. The guy who hit you trashed my flat.'

Dean pulled the mask away. 'Trashed my fucking face.'

'I'm really sorry.'

'I'm supposed to be off on tour tomorrow. Can't fucking go now, can I?'

Dean had been a pop star, albeit briefly. He traded with some success on two early eighties ballads, both marginal hits. Since Max had occupied the flat above, Dean had been away as often as he was at home. Singing for cruise ship crowds and seaside summer seasons when the sun was shining and eighties revival tours in the winter. A kitsch peroxide appeal made him an interchangeable face in lineups of barely remembered boy-and-girl acts. Max hadn't seen him for weeks. He'd picked the wrong day to bring his laundry home.

'What did he look like?'

'Fuck knows.' The boy from Gants Hill dropped the mask to take a drag on his plastic fag. 'You got a proper one?'

'Not on me. Was he black? White?'

'White. Bit greasy. Dark hair. Black hoody. Black leather jacket.'

'In this weather?'

'Camo-combats and fuckin' 'orrible shoes. Trainers, skanky white ones. Old style, know what I mean?'

'How tall?'

'Hard to say, I was on the floor.'

'Build?'

He hesitated. 'Biggish, not brick shithouse, but a lump.'

Abbott appeared at the back of the ambulance, 'You take care, Mr Dean. We'll get you to the hospital and have you checked over properly. I'll be along to take a statement later.'

Dean offered Max his hand, a cold clammy shake that slipped through Max's own hand. 'Take it easy, man. We'll go for a beer sometime.'

'Sure,' said Max. The paramedic closed the doors and the ambulance pulled away.

'You can go upstairs now,' said Abbott. 'If you could look through and let me know if anything's missing. You'll need to make a list for insurance purposes.'

Max called Denny. If this was a warning he could be reached, it applied to her as well. One thing was certain, he had been watched.

Max divided his possessions into the non-retrievable and the maybe worth keeping. The first pile grew quickly. To begin with, it seemed nothing had been taken. He rehung the shelves and tentatively lined up a few paperbacks. In the bedroom, among the torn shirts and slashed jackets, he came across the box file usually kept in the wardrobe, its contents – mainly old diaries, notebooks, photographs and letters – all deeply personal, were missing. For a long time, he sat on the edge of the bed trying to remember what was lost and couldn't be replaced.

In the kitchen sink, he came across burned fragments of bank statements. He assumed the intruder had filched his account details. He phoned the bank. Clearing space on the sofa to sit down, he listened to instructions, trying to remember passwords and security question prompts. When they put him on hold, his mind drifted to the stream of lifeless muzak.

Left to his own devices for the rest of the evening, Max would have opened at least one bottle, listened to music and taken a long bath. Somewhere along the line, he would have given time to thinking things through. He might have reconciled himself to the break-in and worked out what its perpetrator had intended to achieve, but shortly before ten, the intercom buzzed. It was Kilby. 'I wanted to see you. Don't mind, do you?'

Max let him in and made coffee.

They sat at the table. Max slipped a magazine under Kilby's coffee cup. 'Sorry, it's the only bit of decent furniture I've got left.'

The boss looked tired, his eyes red-rimmed. He looked around the room. 'It doesn't look good.'

'Better than it did.'

'Did they take anything?'

'There isn't really much to take.'

Kilby nodded. 'You think it's connected to the case?'

'What else?'

'Couldn't just be an opportunist?'

'What, just fancied a browse, kicked the door in and trashed the place?'

Kilby sipped his coffee. 'What do you think they were looking for?'

The letterbox rattled downstairs. Max jumped. 'I'd better see what that is.' He came back and tossed a pizza menu in a drawer with a wad of others.

Kilby ran his gaze along the bookshelves. 'You were at Caroline Labrosse's funeral.'

'Paying respects, seemed the right thing to do.'

'Not the cleverest, though. Given your connection.'

'Maybe. I noticed Theobold didn't show.'

'And you visited their daughter.'

'Somebody needed to make contact. I thought she might give some fresh insight into the circumstances around her father's death, father-to-daughter confidences, that kind of thing. The kid's desperate, wants to know what happened to her mum and dad. She has a right to some sort of understanding.'

There was a long pause. Kilby said, 'Max, I don't know what you think, but it seems to me we've reached the end of the line. I can't see it's in anyone's best interests to pursue this any further.'

'What about the leads we've already got?'

Kilby returned to his seat. 'Did you get Tyler's statement?'

'I spoke to him this afternoon, but he insisted it was off the record. He won't make it official where Theobold is concerned. Says he won't go to court.'

Kilby shrugged. 'There you go. Proves my point.'

'He's badly shaken. I think he could be persuaded if I can give him some reassurance that we'll act on what he tells us.'

Kilby shook his head. 'Max, Theobold isn't our target. Either charge Michael Tyler if you think there's a case or drop it.'

'*Charge him*? Theobold's the man.'

'Tyler left Labrosse for dead in his own home. Let it go.'

Max gestured to the room, the books across the floor, ruined records, busted drawers. His broken record player. 'And what about this? Do I have to let this go as well? You told me you needed Tyler to implicate Theobold. He's done that. Give me time and he'll give us a statement. You've more or less admitted you think he's working as an agent of interest inside the Home Office. If that is the case, who's paying him? He's a security risk.'

Kilby finished his coffee. 'That's up to the Home Secretary to decide, don't you think? Get me a formal statement from Tyler and it will be placed on record. Leave Ruth Labrosse alone, refer her to family liaison if you must, then close this down.'

Max sat at the window and watched Kilby's progress to the end of the street. He admired the smooth choreography as his car arrived to pick him up. The man had an air of quiet certainty that came from thinking three steps ahead. Something about him that night suggested a renewed energy. Whatever transfer of power might be on the cards, Kilby was guaranteeing it rested with him.

Max made a half-hearted attempt to finish sifting through the wrecked books, but found himself distracted, stalling completely when he came across a photo album. There were dozens of landscape snapshots, picturesque but unpeopled. Not much evidence of himself. Then in the last couple of pages he appeared, with or without Liz, but in photos taken during the time they were together on holidays or in meetings. It was late. She would be at home. He took a chance and called. Would it be okay if he came over? She said to bring a bottle – none of his cheap red crap.

He spent well over the odds in Sainsbury's on Australian Merlot.

Late night visits. Like old times, he thought. Liz came to the door still dressed for work, empty glass in hand. 'Fill my glass and you may enter.'

Just like old times.

The flat was different from how he remembered it. The Nepalese throws, scarves and *Marxism* convention posters ditched in favour of blond wood, Miro blue and Scandi-functionality. The sofa had been re-covered. He settled into the end seat cushion he'd occupied many times before. The last time it had been his confessional. He shuddered at the thought. Liz asked, had he seen Tyler?

'This afternoon.'

'How was he?'

'Better when I left him, I think.'

'Good.' She took a drink. 'So, what does the man from the dark side want with me at this time of night?'

'You remember how you said you either had to be part of the conspiracy or conspired against?'

'Was I sober?'

'What would you say, hypothetically speaking, if I told you I'd come across sufficient evidence to warrant further investigation into the deaths of Derek and Caroline Labrosse, Michael Tyler's abduction and intimidation, and maybe more, and that I was being prevented from pursuing those enquiries?'

'Want something to eat?' She rose quickly.

Max followed her into the kitchen. 'Come on, Liz, what would you say?'

She turned on him. 'Don't ask me that, Max. Firstly, it's not hypothetical, so don't say it is. Secondly, don't come here and lay that on me. I'm a lawyer. I have a professional responsibility to my clients. Tyler came to me for help.' She tipped a bag of crisps into a bowl and waved him back to the living room. 'Your side have rules about this sort of thing. Chains of command, official protocols, the Ladybird Book of fucking Policemen. These things are written down. What do *they* say you should do?'

'When one or more links in the chain of command have a conflict of interest and it's as politically charged as this, I don't know. It's not that specific.'

'You want me to help you out and – let me get this right, plot a course around your shitty institution?' She put the glass down. 'After everything.'

Max sensed the past rolling back. It had chosen its moment.

41

Max

HE WAITED FOR AN hour in the rain outside Southgate Station.
When Rothwell picked him up, there was a palpable sense of
urgency. Information from Kilby. An audio clip. It played while
they drove. Eight minutes of Jim McIlroy in conversation with
another man. Eight minutes of incriminating evidence if you
believed a word of it. Max did not. Even as he protested on the
kid's behalf, he knew there was no point. He was powerless, so
was Rothwell. 'I'll keep feeding it back, Max, but they're not
listening.'

Max asked, what did they want him to do?

Instructions from the boss were to stay the course. Rothwell
disagreed. 'Get out now. You've done enough. Walk away.'

'I can't.'

'They will come for him.'

'I'll try and get him out.' Max had expected a counter-
argument: giving grounds for pursuit played into their hands.

Rothwell dropped him off at the far end of Tesco car park.
He walked to Liz's through the rain. Arrived soaked through
and shaking. She dropped the coat off his back and held him,
telling him whatever trouble he was in it would be alright.

'No, it won't,' he said. 'I have to tell you something.'

She broke away.

'They're coming after Jimmy Mac and I need your help –'

'Stop.'

255

He blundered on. 'The security services think he's involved with a known terrorist. My source says they'll come for him, as soon as tonight. They'll have raided his flat, taken any books, pamphlets. His laptop if he doesn't have it with him. If he's lucky, they'll take him to Paddington Green for questioning. It's possible they'll take him out of the country.'

'And you know this how?'

'You know how.' Liz made him say the words. 'I'm working out of an undercover unit set up by the Met and I'm telling you we need to get Jim away. Tonight.'

'Christ, whose fucking side are you on?'

He was lost for an answer.

They fought. He fought to keep her, to convince her he loved her, and when that failed, he fought for her help to get the boy away. She agreed to do that much, driving to find Jim in the campus bar at Trent Park. She brought him back to the flat. They spoke to him together. He swore blind he had no knowledge of anything, no explosives, no terror cell.

Had he bragged about knowing anything?

He shrugged, non-committal until Liz pressed him. He remembered an argument with Andy Grant. Grant had been winding him up. The usual condescending bollocks, telling him he didn't have the guts to take direct action. Jim said, 'I told him I knew people, that I'd talked to people with the means to start a revolution. And when they did, I'd be a part of it.'

'You said that to Grant, those words?'

'Yeah, I lost it a bit. You know what I'm like. Sorry.'

Liz stood and looked out the window. 'Don't apologise, Jim. You've done nothing wrong.'

Max said, 'You remember that lad, Abdi, who came to a few meetings last year? Six weeks ago, you ran into him at college. He told you he'd spent three months at a training camp in the Yemen. You told Grant.'

'It was just something to say.'

'*You told Grant you were involved. That you'd met friends of Abdi's and they'd shown you videos. You said they'd asked you to help them get hold of materials for some kind of explosive device.*'

'*He didn't believe me, though, how could he? Abdi's lot wouldn't touch me with a ten-foot pole. Wrong politics, wrong religion, wrong everything. I saw him once after he came back. That's it, I swear.*'

'*Abdi's name is Moktar Ali Hassan. He's wanted in connection with an Al-Shabaab attack on a UN aid convoy in Somalia in which an American aid worker was held hostage. Three days ago, she was killed by her captors. If Abdi's back in this country, you know what that means? It means any known associate is at risk. The man you and I know as Andy Grant works for the security services. After what you've told him, they will want to interview you. So will the Americans. We need to get you out of sight.*'

'*What difference will that make?*'

'*Twenty-four hours. Forty-eight if we're lucky. Long enough to try and cancel your one-way ticket.*'

Max borrowed Liz's car. They drove north out of London. Windscreen wipers beat an uneven rhythm. Jim's family were in South Yorkshire and would be watched. The best bet was Jim's granddad's place on the coast, north of Scarborough.

A10. M25. M11. A14. Max drove.

Jim said, '*I don't want to be arrested.*'

'*If it happens, you need to come clean. No point in trying to tough it out, so just tell them what you know. Don't be frightened into saying anything that isn't true. We'll get someone to you as quickly as possible. Chances are they'll keep you isolated, but we will be working for you.*'

He gave a half-hearted nod.

'*It'll be okay.*'

'*How come you found all this stuff out?*'

'I have a contact.'

'Yeah, but that shit's classified.'

'Not if you know who to ask.'

Jim turned and looked back.

Max glanced in the rear-view. The road was empty behind them. 'We're fine.'

'Are you one of them?'

He couldn't bring himself to lie. Said nothing.

On the A14, just past the Cambridge St Ives junction, they were overtaken, boxed and stopped by three unmarked cars. Rain pelted through the security lights of a bus garage. Max told Jim to stay put. He got out and walked towards the lead car with an idea of negotiating their being kept together. He kept his hands away from his body and maintained focus on the two armed officers he could see – he sensed others around him. The first officer barked the order for him to get on his knees and place his hands behind his head. Max dropped slowly. He said he was police, undercover, special operations. Told them to call Kilby to confirm. A shout went up behind him. 'Kid's running.'

Max turned to see Jim sprint across the carriageway. He reached the central reservation and climbed over. Max went after him, half-blinded by rain and spray. It was impossible to see clearly, or for Max to make himself heard above the noise of articulated lorries barrelling past. Jim stopped, looking back to see if Max was following. As he turned to make his run for the far side, he didn't see the CityLink delivery van that clipped him. The van broke hard, skidding across the lanes until it collided with the central barrier a hundred metres further on. Its wing mirror swung on a wire.

Jim was still.

Max rolled his coat to lift Jim's head off the tarmac. Blood soaked through his hair. He was unconscious, a swelling above his temple. Colour draining from his face. Max put his fingers

*to Jim's neck and found a pulse. It was weak. He was vaguely
aware of a haze of brake-lights and hazard flashes as traffic
slowed to a standstill. They were alone for what felt like a long
time before he was conscious of paramedics at his side and a
hand under his arm lifting him. A traffic officer escorted him
along the closed carriageway. After that, his memories were
of a procession of faces: the van driver white and shaking at
the roadside; MI5 officers in conversation before they drove
away; the traffic officer who wearily reassured him they would
'do all they could' for his son, and then breathalysed him.*

*Kilby sent Rothwell to pick him up from the hospital. When
he arrived back at Liz's flat shortly before 6am and delivered
the news, her expression did not alter. When he'd said what he
needed to say, she closed the door.*

42

Max

LIZ SET DOWN THE empty bottle.

'What I want is something that feels like peace of mind,' said Max.

'For Jim?'

He thought for a moment. 'For all of it, but yes, for Jim.'

They were, and always would be, bound by that night and all that came afterwards. 'I'm sorry,' he said, 'I shouldn't have come.'

She gave a hint of a smile. 'It's no more screwed up than it ever was. For me it comes in waves. I'll go along for a while right as rain, then the whole lot comes crashing in. Every case I've lost, all those desperate, deluded people, reeling at how unjust the world turned out. Jim was just the first. It was an accident.' She shrugged and raised her glass, but couldn't seem to think of anything worth toasting.

The silence was broken by the click and hiss of Liz's cigarette lighter. 'Sometimes I think it would have been better – for you as much as anyone – if I'd blown you out of the water straightaway. Just held my hands up, told everyone what a job you did on us. Gone public and made it so you could never work in that way again.'

'It suited you not to.'

'Even so, I can't kid myself it was entirely for honourable reasons. When someone you care about makes a fool of you, the fewer people who know the better.'

'Sometimes one person knowing is enough.'

'Perhaps.' She shifted position, supporting herself on a cushion. 'So, in the case of Lomax versus Kilby, if we're bringing the hypothetical into the real world, unjust or not, let me give you a number: three. That's how many successful cases we took to court last year. Know how many clients we accepted? Twenty-six. Not many is it? Know how many enquiries and meetings with potential clients we had?'

Max shook his head.

'I don't either, not without checking. Hundreds probably. Jonathon works on the principle that we don't win many, so we don't take on many. We don't have the resources. But sometimes he or I will take on a case knowing there's not a snowball's chance of winning, because we can open up the system, just force a crack or expose a piece of bad law, or just make someone in a position of authority look bad. It's the same shit they do every day, we just make sure people know about it. Buying column inches, slots on the news, journal articles, earning a reputation. It all chips away. In theory. But that's my world, not yours.' The cigarette end glowed in the low light as she inhaled. 'If you think going after Theobold and antagonising Kilby in the process is worth the consequences, find a way to take it on that makes a difference. Otherwise, why waste your time?'

She unearthed an old duvet and let him sleep on the sofa. He woke after an hour and found himself staring into the darkness, listening to the street. He sat up and put the sidelight on, picked a book off the shelves, a poetry collection which he opened at random and began reading. The phrases passed through him without sticking. Liz came out of her room. 'I'm not sleeping with you if that's what you're thinking.'

'I wasn't.'

She sat beside him on the sofa, pulled the duvet across them both, and held him.

Sometime after she went back to bed, Max worked his way round to a conclusion. If Kilby was refusing to act and he could show there was a case to answer, he'd find someone else who would. He dozed off with that in mind and managed a couple of fitful hours before waking at the sound of Liz's shower.

She came through, towelling her hair. 'Bathroom's free.'

'You're early.'

'I'm in court this morning. Meeting with Counsel at Wood Green.'

Her court clothes were smarter than he remembered. Pinstripe shirt, tailored dark suit. They changed the way she carried herself.

Over toast and coffee, he explained his thinking.

Liz asked, 'Who do you trust?'

'No one, but it's either that or do nothing.'

'That still might be the better option.' She kissed him on the cheek. 'Time to go.'

43

Max

DETECTIVE CHIEF INSPECTOR REDDING was more difficult to track down than Max expected. Still involved with gun and gang-related cases, his promotion had taken him to Harlesden, operating out of Craven Park Police Station. Max was put through at the second attempt. He kept the call light on detail, appealing first to Redding's sense of curiosity – he just wanted to meet. Redding was resistant, what was in it for him? Max dangled the prospect of political traction and it bought him ten minutes.

Back home he pressed his black suit trousers, ironed the only clean shirt he had without a tear or slash, and put on a tie. He sent Denny a text to say he'd meet her later at Carteret Street, adding the postscript: *Personal stuff.* He walked to Kilburn Park, took the Bakerloo to Harlesden and signed in just after ten o'clock. He was shown upstairs to an interview room and told to wait.

Redding was leaner, sharper-suited, that morning dealing with the fall-out from a fatal shooting in a local restaurant. As it turned out, the killing had been a case of mistaken identity – who knew there could be more than one bloke called 'Paul' eating in the *West Coast Café Bar* on a sunny evening? He did not offer Max his hand as he pulled out a chair. 'You're on the clock. What do you want?'

Max began, 'I need to ask that this remain confidential between us.'

He sniffed. 'No guarantees. You haven't earned them.'

'I've been working on a case which has placed me in direct opposition to the views of a senior officer. I believe there has been malpractice within the Home Office. Procurement-related, potentially fraudulent and possibly corrupt.' He had Redding's attention. 'It concerns a commercial contract that's been fast-tracked to evade proper processes. Ministers, civil servants, and now this senior officer, have turned a blind eye. I believe that maintaining deniability has resulted in several criminal acts. Specifically, the silencing of witnesses or opponents to the scheme, by criminal means.'

Redding held up a hand. 'Lomax, I have to ask: why are you telling me this?'

'Because you're the only person I could think of who would be straight with me. You don't like me and you'll tell me to fuck off if I'm wrong. And you have a privileged relationship with the Deputy Commissioner.'

Kilby, along with his colleagues on the senior management team, reported to Deputy Commissioner Ian Best. Best's friendship with Redding was long-established and widely recognised as having played a part in the newly promoted DCI's career development.

Redding blinked and sat back in his chair. 'Thanks. No really, that's just what I was looking forward to when I got out of bed this morning. You dumping your rubbish in my backyard. Let's get this straight, when you say *senior officer*, you're talking about Assistant Commissioner Kilby. You think I want to go over his head on your say-so? You still seeing that counsellor? Might be an idea to book yourself in for a visit.' Redding unscrewed the top of a bottle of flavoured spring water and sipped. 'I take it you have proof.'

'Off the record statements from insiders, who I believe

will go on the record if we press the case. Mainstay piece of evidence is a collection of emails between Derek Labrosse, a senior civil servant who, at the time, was Director of Homeland Security Division at the Home Office and James Creedy, the current minister.'

'Can I see them?'

'I can get you copies.'

'And you can verify their authenticity.'

Max nodded.

'Trustworthy source?'

'But nervous.'

Redding took another sip. 'Okay, so what exactly do you want from me?'

'I need to know how widespread in the chain of command does knowledge of this business extend. If it's all the way, I hope you'll forget this conversation took place. I'll certainly deny it. If not, I would like to meet with Deputy Commissioner Best as a matter of urgency.'

Redding screwed the cap tight on the bottle. 'Wait here.' He left the room. Max badly wanted a cigarette. What price loyalty now? Kilby would string him up by his nuts.

Redding returned some fifteen minutes later, resumed his seat. 'You've got your meeting. In an hour. The DC is expecting you, his office.'

'His office.'

'What did you expect, he'd pop in your place for a cup of tea and a KitKat?'

And that was it. The prick didn't have a clue.

Max boarded the train at Harlesden and found a seat, lost in thought. When he changed at Baker Street, the crowds were thicker. He stood back from the platform edge. The Jubilee Line train came in. He hung onto the rail, looking through the carriage. From a quarter view, he thought he recognised someone he'd seen earlier at Kilburn Park. The way the guy carried himself was familiar. So was the leather jacket. He got off at Westminster and walked. Instead of his usual route to Carteret Street via Birdcage Walk, he headed west on Victoria Street and didn't look back, gave no indication of awareness he was being followed. He cut left into Strutton Ground. Passing trade in the market was light and Max ducked between a coffee stall and a fruit and veg stall. Leather Jacket followed. As he passed, Max shouted, 'Mate, you looking for me?'

He turned and Max took the photo.

It wasn't a great likeness, but Max had a clear enough look at the man's face. Ten minutes on Photoshop cleaned the image sufficiently. He sent it to Denny. 'This is the bloke. If it's who I think it is, I've seen him before outside my flat, certain of it. He might also be the bloke that broke in.'

'You want me to see what I can find out?'

'Yeah, quietly though.' He left her to it. He'd be back later.

Deputy Commissioner Best struck Max as the sort of man who kept regular fortnightly appointments at his barber's. He imagined one of those Mayfair gentlemen's establishments where deference, discretion and light cologne were all part of the service. His bearing was one of neatness and containment as he welcomed Max to his office. It was spacious, divided between a formal meeting area, shelves of labelled files and a pristine workstation. Best invited Max to take a seat at the conference table. He sat opposite with his back to the window. 'You wanted to see me.'

Max set out his reading of the situation, taking care not to be critical of Kilby. Best nodded and occasionally wrote in a hardback notebook. When Max had finished, Best turned his chair side-on and looked out of the window, saying nothing for some time. He turned to Max with a smile. 'To clarify, then, your allegation is that Assistant Commissioner Kilby is engaged in what, by any other name, is a conspiracy – you avoid saying so directly, but we can all read between the lines –

either way, you believe him to be involved with this American company and its representatives, Mr Creedy, Mr Lillico and this man Theobold, whom you say has been heavy-handed, extorting support or buying off opponents of the proposed surveillance contract. Would you say this was a misconduct issue for Mr Kilby?'

The question caught Max off guard. He faltered. 'That's not what I'm suggesting at all. It's broader than that, sir. Theobold is effectively operating as an agent of influence within the Home Office.'

'Surely that's a matter for the Home Office?'

'That's Mr Kilby's view. I thought it would be of concern to you.'

He lifted a finger. 'I'm grateful for you bringing this to my notice. You can leave it with me.' He went to a cupboard door and slipped his uniform tunic from a hanger. 'I'll let you know if we decide to act on your allegations.'

'Is that it?'

'Not quite. I don't know if you are aware -- probably not, it isn't common knowledge as yet -- but in the coming weeks there will be a restructuring of the senior management team; responsibilities, particularly around Special Operations, are to be reallocated. If you want to use that as a reason to tender your resignation, it would be looked on favourably. I'm saying if you want to go, you can.'

Max left him buttoning his tunic. In the street, sun blazed across the rotating grey sign. *Working together for a safer London.* Max didn't go back to Carteret Street. Instead, he walked across Westminster Bridge as far as the London Borough of Lambeth sign, then dropped down the steps near St Thomas's. The handwritten note on Derek Labrosse's email came back to him. *Another bloody meeting where we play the emperor's new clothes.* He could almost hear the man's voice. He shared his sense of frustration.

267

44

Kilby

KILBY WAS SUMMONED FOR what Deputy Commissioner Best described as 'an informal chat' regarding allegations recently brought to his attention. Allegations which, if true, had the potential to develop into an embarrassing situation for the Service and its relations with the Home Office. As such, he'd refer the matter to the Commissioner if unresolved. Christ on a bike, the man couldn't speak plainly if his life depended on it. Without saying so explicitly, Best's precis of the information didn't hide that Max had been the source.

Betraying Max's confidence angered Kilby almost as much as Max going behind his back in the first place, but, for now, he listened and made the right noises. He certainly didn't intend to furnish information that Max had kept back.

It was over in minutes. The smug prick finished by telling Kilby about his planned restructure. He would, of course, be consulted, his views sought.

And ignored, thought Kilby.

Max had given them the excuse they needed.

He went directly to Carteret Street. Max was out and Denny didn't know where.

'Call him,' said Kilby.

She tried. 'His phone's off.'

Kilby dropped into Max's seat. 'I'll wait.'

As it turned out, he wasn't waiting long.

45

Max

THEIR HEADS TURNED AS Max came through the door.

Kilby stood. 'You and you, this case is not to be pursued further. I've asked DC Denny to prepare your files for handover – digital, paper, audio, everything you have. I will deal with the case directly from now on. Do nothing without reference to me. As far as you are concerned, it's finished. Clear?'

'Sir.' Denny looked to Max, who said nothing.

'I want the files with a full report by the end of the day.' He pointed to Max. 'Walk down with me.'

At the foot of the stairs, Kilby stopped, his voice a whisper. 'Have you lost your fucking mind? What were you thinking? Seriously, Max, Ian Best would shit all over me to control this Department. Everything I've worked to build up, to keep people like him at arm's length. You just gave him the ammunition and loaded the gun.'

'These people are taking the piss out of us, Lillico, Creedy.'

'Let them.'

'What?'

'I said let them. They can go so far and no further. You did your job. I told you they'd be vulnerable and they are. With the information you unearthed, I've secured significant concessions.' He paused as a door slam echoed down the stairwell.

'And Theobold's home free, cashing in on both sides and destroying anyone who gets in the way.'

'For the last time, he is *not* your problem. I will deal with him when the opportunity arises. Right now, I have to work out how to limit this. In the meantime, you might want to think about where and when you want your career to end, bearing in mind here and now is an option.'

Kilby marched towards Victoria Street. Max had expected worse, but then the boss had other things on his mind. He sat on the stairs, putting off his return to the office and considering his options. He came up short, reconciling himself to giving up the case. On the slow walk upstairs, his mobile rang. It was Liz. She asked how he was.

'I'm alright. You?'

'Sort of.'

'What's up?'

'We had a visitor at the office while I was in court this morning. Patrick Theobold plus one. He told Nikki he was one of your people and showed some bullshit ID. Said he was here on official business. She let him upstairs. The kid's distraught.'

Max halted on the landing. 'What did he want?'

'He's looking for Phil Mercer. He knows he wrote the *Freemedia* article – he wouldn't have had to look far, the company's registered here, so is the website. Oh, and he made it known he was carrying. Max, he brought a gun into my office.'

'For fuck's sake.'

'Once he'd scared the living daylights out of Nikki, he helped himself to a root through our files, made some lists, names and contacts. He claimed he was looking for information about our sources and our financial backers. He mentioned anonymous donations and money laundering. I called Jonathon. He's reluctant to drag us into making a formal complaint, but he will if I press him. I thought you should know.'

Max didn't know what to say. He settled for a banal, 'Are you okay?'

'Shaken up to be honest.' He heard her light a cigarette. 'Usually, someone has a dig, it's because we're doing our job. It's hardly the first time someone's tried to frighten us, but this time –'

'He's not untouchable. I don't care what Mercer says.'

'He left a note on my desk. He says he'll find Phil Mercer and then come back to see me one-to-one. It's a direct threat, Max. I can't read it any other way.'

'Can I call you later? There's something I need to explain.'

Max punched the combination code into the security door and went back into the office. One more day.

Denny was waiting.

Max said, 'He told you what I did?'

'He did. For someone who wanted nothing to do with the case, you seem bent on letting it screw up your career. And mine. And Kilby's.'

'I can't let it go. More to the point, I can't let *him* go. You know these people. They fuck you up and walk away, then do the same to the next poor sod.'

She took her time thinking it through. 'What do you need me to do?'

'Exactly as Kilby has told us. Pull the files together and start drafting the final report. You know what they want to hear, give it to them.' He pulled out the Labrosse emails. 'And you need to read these. Tyler had them. They're from the original file.'

He pulled his chair up beside her while she read.

'What are these names and numbers on the back?'

'Don't know.'

She read through again, then looked up. 'Has Kilby seen these – of course not, you wouldn't chance it. Do you think you should show him?'

'Maggie, if you give him those, trust me, they will disappear like Keyser fucking Söze. I need you to check that mobile number on the last email? Then we'll back up everything. Duplicates of every item we hand over.'

For the next half hour, Max reread the Labrosse emails. They should have been enough and they still changed everything. The man had been building his case prior to blowing the whistle. Raising his concerns with Creedy had given him nowhere to go. It was there as plain as the blood staining the paper.

Max gathered his thoughts. 'We know Patrick Theobold and James Creedy have undeclared links with IDI. Links that pre-date their appointment to Labrosse's management group, a group set up to look at covert surveillance and intelligence functions at national level. Over a period of weeks, they steer options away from Home Office and Met Police delivery, excluding Kilby along the way. Instead, they pursue a scheme that sets up IDI to receive an initial contract worth billions. Which, by Kilby's reckoning, and now supported by Labrosse's emails, opens the gates to IDI takeover of Met operations. Labrosse makes his objections clear, first to Creedy, but then...'

Denny made a note. 'He'll have reported to someone. Or done what you'd do, gone over their head. Whoever it was, they ignored him or worse.'

'He's run out of options. He's ready to blow the whistle and we know what happens next.'

'That's my understanding, unless there's anything else you haven't told me.'

Max phoned Tyler and had him explain, as best he could, the location of Phil Mercer's flat. As Denny busied herself tidying the case paperwork, Max ran the emails through the scanner, front and reverse, storing the electronic versions on his PC, then emailing them to his phone. He printed a second copy, which he dropped on Denny's desk.

She nodded slowly. 'Let me get this right, we have these and no one else other than Tyler knows we do.'

'Correct.'

She looked down at the Labrosse case file. Bailey's uneven block caps on the cover. Virtually every page was edged with their handwritten post-it notes.

Max made copies of his essential papers, the printer spewing page after page.

'The phone number is for a pay-as-you-go bought with a credit card from a Tesco store in Tottenham on 24 January and registered online to *Freemedia*. Postal address in Turnpike Lane, N8.'

'Phil Mercer.'

'The only calls it received were from two numbers, the first is Derek Labrosse's home number on the 2nd and 7th February and again on the 25th – that last call is just short of ten minutes and the others less than a minute each time – the other number is a mobile, number registered to Caroline Labrosse. Several short calls last December and then one earlier this week. Nothing in between.'

She showed him the printout.

'Have you tried it?'

'Says the number is still live, but it's switched off.'

Max rested his chin on his hand and wondered how desperate Labrosse had to have been to put his faith in Phil Mercer. He thought about Caroline and Ruth Labrosse. He thought about Tyler. Keeping secrets had all but broken him. Theobold had done the rest.

He had cleared his desk and was making ready to leave by the time Denny finished downloading case data onto a memory stick. She handed it over. 'That's everything we have. If this place goes up in smoke, you have the entire case. I'll ring you if I get anything else on Labrosse's management group for the IDI project. See if we can link someone there with the date of those first two emails. I'll have a chat with the woman you spoke to in the Home Office. Kate, right?'

'Be careful. Nothing in writing.'

'What else?'

'I need to talk to Phil Mercer. The rest I don't know yet.'

46

Max

TYLER'S DIRECTIONS BROUGHT MAX to the horseshoe opening of three blocks of maisonettes a stone's throw from Seven Sisters Road. It was late evening, not yet dark and some boys and girls were hanging around a parked BMW, two wheels up on a wedge of sun-scorched grass. Bass bins pounded. Max nodded to a gangly teenaged wannabe in a baggy t-shirt. He slouched forward, trainers scuffing up dust.

'Is one of these Seacole House?' said Max.

The kid cupped his ear, playing to his audience.

'Seacole House.'

'Nah, mate.'

'Are you sure?'

His head jerked back. 'Why d'you wanna know?'

Max half-turned. 'I'm thinking of buying a place.'

The kid smiled. 'You the feds?' The girls giggled.

'Nah, mate.'

The music dropped volume. From inside the BMW a voice said, 'He is.'

Max walked over, looked in. Mo Griffiths, a face from the past. 'Mo, bloody hell.' They shook hands. 'You live round here now?

'They gave us a ground floor place down the way, for my brother.'

'How's he doing?'

'His leg plays him up, y'know. Bad winters 'n that.' When he was a kid, Maurice's brother Kevin had trials for Spurs. He'd been quick, strong for his age and pencilled in for an academy place until a row outside a house party in Edmonton had ended in a shooting match. A stray bullet took Kevin just above the knee. He lost a yard of pace and a world of confidence. When Spurs let him go, he stayed indoors for almost a year. Max had gone after the shooter when others had written off the investigation. It hadn't gone unnoticed.

'You gonna tell me which one of these is Seacole House, or do I have to traipse round every one?'

He looked over his shoulder. 'The end one. Why d'you wanna know?'

'It's just a bloke I'm looking for – white, early thirties, scruffy bastard. Probably scores a bit of blow locally.'

'Drives an old Fiesta, knackered exhaust?'

'Sounds about right.'

'Third floor, last flat, but he's cleared out.' Mo lit a cigarette. He beckoned Max closer. 'Max, what sort of business you into round here, do I need to be somewhere else right now?'

Max leaned in, elbows on the sill, whispered so Mo had to close in. 'I know I shouldn't disclose police business, but you're parked illegally on a grass verge and could be liable to a fifty pound fine according to local by-laws.'

Mo shook his head. 'You're shameful, man. Shameful.'

Max made his way up the stairwell to the third floor. Old style roots reggae, hip hop and some vapid pop tune made for an unholy mix on the top landing. An old guy with a grey cat curled in his lap looked up from his paper and gave Max the once over.

'Nice evening,' said Max.

The guy reached down for a beer, his backside straining the canvas of his deckchair. 'He's not there. Don't matter how many times you people come, he's still not there.'

'Just a job mate, I do what the council tells me.'

'Council, right,' said the old man, not believing a word.

Mercer's flat was last on the landing. Max opened the door. Junk mail littered the mat. None of it addressed to Mercer. Max emptied the bins out. He found a couple of handwritten notes, one a reminder to call Liz, one with Tyler's address. Reluctantly, he shoved a hand down the back of the ratty-arse settee and turned up coins, pens and a couple of till receipts for cash. He tipped it up and tore away the hessian, but found nothing. He worked through the rest of the flat quickly, caring little about adding to the mess, but came up short. Holding his breath, he lifted a yellow-stained mattress in the front bedroom. It stank of cat piss. Silverfish scuttled for the skirting board. As he kicked out at loose papers, magazines and fast food wrappers, his foot caught on the carpet's frayed edge and rucked it back, ripping away a sealed plastic envelope taped to the fused underlay. He rinsed the package under the bathroom tap and wiped it dry on a scrap of yellow towel. Inside was five hundred quid in cash and Phil Mercer's passport.

Mercer would be back. Max pulled up a chair and waited.

By 3am the street was making the kind of sounds a city makes, sleeping with one eye open. Max watched a police patrol car turn into the car park, make a slow circuit and then exit. A minute later two figures moved out from behind the kids' play area and walked towards the block. Max went onto the landing, keeping low. Mo's mates had come inside and were on the stairs, he heard their voices on and off. He lost sight of the two men as they approached the Seacole House entrance. Their footsteps echoed up the stairwell. The kids' voices changed, challenged, intimidated. Max went back inside. He made sure his mobile was off and waited. The men's shadows passed the window and stopped. Their conversation was low, inaudible. The front door clicked open. Max picked up a magazine, rolled it tightly in his fist and bent it in half. He backed into the stinking bedroom and heard the click of the light switch in the hall. The bulbs were out. He'd made sure of it.

'Want me to go get the flashlight?' The accent and intonation were American.

The response came in clipped English. 'For God's sake, just do as I ask and stay put.'

Theobold. It had to be. Max watched through the door jamb as he crossed the living room and snapped on latex gloves, crouching down to leaf through a few sheets of paper, before moving towards the kitchen. Max controlled his breathing in time with a dubstep thud from the flat below. From the hallway the American said, 'I told you, no way was he coming back here.'

No answer.

Max tightened his fist around the magazine.

The same voice, 'You want to wait? You'll be here till fucking Christmas.'

Theobold was talking to himself. 'Mercer, you filthy little shit.'

Max tensed. Theobold took one pace into the bedroom before the stink hit him. 'Oh, Jesus Christ!'

The American came in behind. 'Patrick, this place is disgusting. We're wasting our time. He's gone. Can we do the same? Please.'

'Just wait a minute.'

Max visualised his fist slamming into Theobold's face, the magazine butt driven in hard on the pressure point under the jaw. He'd take him, then take his chances with the American. Unless they were both armed, in which case, he was fucked.

Finally, Theobold took a step back.

'Amen,' said the American. 'Let's go.'

Max gave them a forty second start, then stumbled into the bathroom and heaved into the sink. He ran the tap, swilled and spat. He braced himself, forehead against the cold mirror, until his breathing steadied. He stood up and wiped his mouth.

Saw the dark shape behind him in the mirror. 'Did you find what you came for?'

'Philip Mercer?'

The man's head jerked up. 'Uh huh.'

'Then yes.'

Mercer clutched and unclutched a bunch of keys in his fist. 'I saw them come in so I stayed outside and waited.'

Max perched on the sofa arm. 'You know who that was?'

'Of course.' Mercer took a light bulb from a drawer in the kitchen. 'Theobold and his minder. Like he needs one.' Mercer closed the curtains and turned the light on. It shone dimly, showed a three-day beard and dark ringed eyes. He glanced at the bedroom and the turned carpet. 'So, have you got my money or what?'

'Do you know what he did to Michael Tyler?'

'Can I have my stuff?' He held his hand out.

'He beat the shit out of him, because of what you wrote. Now he's looking for you.'

He paced the room. 'Just give me my stuff.'

'Sit down,' said Max, 'or you can go in there with that cat piss carpet and I'll lock the door.'

Mercer slumped on the sofa.

'Tyler didn't tell Theobold about this place.'

Mercer shook his head. 'It doesn't matter, he's untouchable.'

'But he found you anyway. Tyler took the blame for what you did and Theobold half-killed him for it. When he gets hold of you, mate, you're toast.'

'Un-fucking-touchable.'

There was a noise outside, a door slam and feet skipping along the landing. Max wiped his mouth on his sleeve. 'I think we need to take this conversation somewhere else.'

'There is no conversation. You've got what I want. You give, I go.'

Max breathed heavily. 'Not a chance, son. I go and who keeps Patrick Theobold from putting you in the ground.'

The hotel in Prince's Square, Bayswater, was one Max had used before. It was cheap. He paid in advance from Mercer's money and took a room with a view of the square. Mercer showered for a long time, then sat on the bed, dark rat-tails of wet hair dripping onto the duvet. In a cup smelling faintly of bleach, Max made Mercer a drink that was faintly like tea. Mercer took long slow sips. 'I had to sleep in the car, just driving round in the day keeping out the way, y'know?'

'Because of him?'

'I wasn't trying to drop Michael in it. I just needed to get the story out there. People need to know what they did to Derek, to Caroline. So much information, like there's a wall of news and it's meaningless unless people know how to read it.'

'Tell me what you know about Derek Labrosse.'

'Derek? He was okay, I think he appreciated what I was trying to do.' Mercer shrugged. 'He said he did. I mean he probably didn't, but he said he did. That's worth something coming from a man in his position. It meant something to me.'

'How well did you know him?'

Mercer bent over, examined a callus on one of his toes. 'I've been writing stuff about the surveillance society for years. Two years ago, I wrote a generic piece under my own name on a website called *IDNOWAY*. It's gone now, you won't find it. I took the case apart, why state surveillance systems could never work, the way we give information freely but how, once people knew what it would lead to and how it interfered with their lives, they wouldn't stand for it. There would be so many loopholes that the kind of people they say they want to target – people who'd strap a bomb to their backs and send us all to paradise – they'll always slip through. I built a network of contacts with people preparing to live off the grid. I know how you can do it. Then I made a list of every poxy government IT project that screwed up over the last 20 years. It's not difficult. Child Support Agency, NHS, Immigration Service. Then I added a profile of every minister involved and their personal interests – you know where this is going? You'd have to be insane to think everybody's personal data on one system isn't the biggest disaster just waiting to happen. The piece was name-checked in the *New Statesman*, then in an online piece in the *Guardian*, then it started to get traction, a lot of social media. I got a serious profile.'

'That must have been a result when Labrosse came looking for you?'

'Oh, it wasn't just me.'

'He had your number.'

'There were others. He'd already spoken to people by the time he got to me. People I know.'

'Who?'

'No chance, mate. They're my sources.'

Max opened the window to the sound of raised voices in the street.

Mercer straightened up. 'Do we have to have that open?'

'Fresh air, it's good for you. What did Labrosse want?'

'Same as you, my sources. I turned him down.'

'Now Patrick Theobold wants them. Not so easy to turn down.'

'I can lose him. Give me my passport and my money and I'll go.'

'Can't do it, not yet.'

Mercer rooted through a carrier bag of clothes. He sniffed a t-shirt. 'Smells of fucking cat.' He pulled it on, then a pair of jeans.

'What else did Labrosse say?'

Mercer zipped up his jeans like a man scared of catching his cock. 'Why do you want to know all this stuff, I mean why would you give a shit?'

Max said, 'What did Labrosse tell you about Theobold?'

'That he's too well connected. Things started to happen around him that shouldn't. That he knew things he had no right to know. Confidential details he had no authorisation for. And he knew personal stuff about Derek's family.'

'So, he googled him or picked up office gossip?'

'That's what I said. Derek told me that one time at Caroline's work there'd been a mix-up in some samples they were working on and some patients received wrong diagnoses. All really unpleasant. And Theobold knew the name of one of the complainants. How? And you tell me, how did he get away with Michael Tyler not even being questioned when Derek died? How has he not been in the frame for Caroline?' He tailed off momentarily. 'He killed her and he's still walking around. No one blinks.'

'You seem certain.'

Mercer plumped the pillows, sat with his back to the wall. He spoke slowly. 'Derek adored her. He told her everything. She had a better memory than he did. She could tell you about IDI, how they functioned, where the real money came from, who they bought, who they owned. And she was straight about the political weight they had Derek under. That shit at the Home Office, the minister –'

'Creedy?'

'What is it now, Minister for Security? He's your classic man in waiting. Look for the headline grabber every time, it's him. Wants it all, every last drop. Comes across like a twat, but he's on IDI's payroll, I'm telling you.'

'Phil, so far this is just you ranting in a room. I need evidence.'

Mercer picked a flap of skin from the ball of his foot. 'If

you can't make one man pay, what chance against a global corporation?' He put his foot over the side of the bed, tipped the cup, rattling in its saucer. 'Derek came to me because I knew it had to be fought. I knew how and I wasn't afraid of them.'

'But you are now. Of Theobold.' Max leaned over, picked up the cup.

Mercer was tight-lipped.

Max ran his boot over a burned patch of carpet. 'You bought Derek a phone to set up a contact and gave him a number. The phone was used to call you at Liz Delaney's office on February the 7th, one week before Labrosse died. It received a call from Labrosse's home two weeks after he died. What were you setting up?'

'No chance.'

Max sat on the bed at Mercer's side, close. A patch of missed bristles nestled under his bottom lip. 'Phil, this is your story, but be honest, the piece you wrote for *Freemedia* was online for what, three, four hours before they closed it down? Sure, it got some hits on social media, but it's hardly a decent return for all that work, is it? It'd be a shame for it to end there because you shot your load too soon. And it will end if Theobold gets hold of you. I'll wind up fishing you out of the Thames.'

Mercer laughed unconvincingly.

Max shrugged. 'It's up to you, either you can help or I can wait for Theobold to put you out of my misery.' He peeled off half a dozen notes, dropped them on the bed. 'Use that to keep yourself going, pay for a couple more nights here. Try not to go out too much and don't tell anyone you're here. There's my number, call me when you've made up your mind.' He pointed to the window. 'And I'd close that before you crash out if I were you.'

It was light by the time Max came down the hotel steps. He kept Mercer's room in view as he crossed the square. The window was closed.

Max made a call to an old friend, one of a few that could be counted on. 'Tony, it's me, Max. Look, mate, have you got anything on first thing this morning? No problem, you'll be done by then. Double time if you can get to Bayswater in half an hour.' He gave the address. 'I'll be the bloke looking shifty by the bus stop on the north side of Prince's Square.'

Forty-five minutes later a black Vespa moved smoothly into the square. Its side panels and leg guards bore the dents and scratches of a thousand cross-town runs. The rider's orange hi-vis waistcoat bore the legend *Tony Express*. Max met the scooter as it pulled into the kerb. The rider hoisted it onto its stand, pulled off his gloves and helmet. He gripped Max's hand and clapped him on the shoulder. 'Too long, too, too long.' Tony Jones at five in the morning, still a crooked smile and blue-eyed sparkle, even if the grey had taken over up top. 'So, what are we up to?'

'Waiting for a bloke to bail out of that hotel. I want us to follow when he does.'

'That's a bit high-tech. Is there a back way in?'

Max kept his focus on the hotel entrance. 'There is, but he'll still have to come this way, especially if he wants to pick his car up from the NCP.'

'His car being?'

'A Fiesta. Growls like a V8, drives like a disability scooter.' Max's gaze passed over the Vespa.

'And you can fuck right off, this is faster than any car you ever owned.' He took a spare *Tony Express* waistcoat and a crash helmet from the top box. They waited.

Mercer came down the stairs just after seven. They watched him out of sight, then followed, picking him up as the Fiesta came out of the car park. His first move was east along Euston Road, then north at King's Cross Station. Tony cut across a black cab at the lights. The cab driver's abuse was lost in traffic noise and the Vespa's throaty acceleration.

'What size engine you got in this?'

'Let's just say it's not standard.'

Max leaned into the corner. They were heading towards Stoke Newington. Traffic slowed to a stop at a set of temporary traffic lights. Tony slid the Vespa in behind a blue transit three cars back from Mercer. He turned round. 'Max, any reason why we might have a silver Lexus on our tail?'

'Maybe.'

'Either he's following your bloke or us.'

The lights changed green. The blue transit stalled, its engine turning over, wheezing but not firing. 'Go, go.' Max tapped Tony on the shoulder. They took off as the lights turned red. Mercer was two cars clear. The Lexus lost in a cloud of diesel smoke.

'What d'you want me to do?'

'Overtake, we'll pull him over.'

Tony dropped a gear. Max was grateful for the box at his back. As they accelerated level, he tapped on the window. Mercer nearly took them into a traffic island. They swerved, overtook and pulled him in.

'You off somewhere?' said Max.

'Are you following me?'

'Yes.'

'You've no right –'

Max cut him off. 'For your info, I'm not the only one. Just check out the silver Lexus coming past in three... two... one.'

Mercer adjusted his rear-view and watched the car pass. He said nothing, his knuckles white on the wheel.

'You're looking nervous, Phil. Park up round the corner. I'll wait here.'

Max picked a spot in the café that gave him full view of the door and street. Tony joined them.

'Who the fuck's he?' said Mercer.

'A mate of mine so don't be rude. Where were you running, Phil?'

Mercer looked at Tony.

'Not him, me,' said Max. 'Where?'

'I was going home.'

'You haven't got a home. You're a vagrant.'

Mercer put his fingertips to his temples, studied the stains on the table.

'Now we know they've got you tracked, what's it gonna take, Phil? You're not doing any favours behaving like an arsehole.'

They sat back as the waitress slid a wide tray onto the table. 'Two teas, one coffee, two rounds of toast, bacon sandwich and two eggs on toast.'

'Ta,' said Tony.

'Cheers,' said Max. 'Say thank you, Philip.'

Tony smiled and brown sauced the bacon sandwich. 'Cheers for this, mate.'

'Don't mention it,' said Max, not taking his eyes off Mercer. 'I want to meet your contacts and I want to know what they discussed with Labrosse and all they have on Theobold. Or I'm going to finish my breakfast and me and Tony will walk out of here and leave you to deal with the pissed-off bloke in the silver Lexus who's just come back this way.'

Mercer shrank into his seat.

Tony glanced out of the window, stirring sugar in his tea. 'There he goes, seems keen.'

Mercer looked from one to the other.

Tony looked at his watch. 'Max, if you want dropping somewhere, we need to go now. I've got a regular pick-up at Bishopsgate in twenty minutes.'

Max doubled a slice of toast and picked up his crash helmet.

'Let me set it up first,' said Mercer. 'If they get a sniff of the police, they'll run. I'll set it up. And I'll call you.'

Max fixed on Mercer, sized up the proposition. 'Don't fuck me over.'

Mercer shook his head. 'I won't.'

They swapped jackets. Mercer pulled the crash helmet over his ears and went out behind Tony. Max watched them pull away. He watched for the Lexus. Gave it ten minutes. No show. He tossed himself a catch with Mercer's car keys and ordered another coffee.

47

Max

MAX LEAFED THROUGH A left-behind *Daily Mirror*. The waitress put her coffee on his table and she stood in the open doorway while she lit a cigarette. She was about Max's age, something vaguely bohemian in the vintage dress and leggings with DMs. She smiled. 'You don't mind, do you? I'll blow the smoke out this way.'

Max said he was fine with it.

'First chance I've had. Never stopped this morning. You were miles away then, thinking about your holidays?'

'I was reading this.' The front page showed James Creedy, Home Office Minister emerging from a meeting in Downing Street the previous evening under the headline *PM SPANKING FOR PORN MINISTER*. Max read aloud, '"*Thousands of pornographic images were stored on the computer, which had been seized after a tip-off to the Metropolitan Police. A check revealed that Mr Creedy, personal friend and tennis partner of the Prime Minister, had viewed pornography extensively over a three-month period. Similar material was found on the minister's personal laptop.*"'

The waitress stepped in for a closer look at the picture. 'Oh, him.' Her nose wrinkled with disapproval. 'He is a bit creepy, though. I'd be asking how much his secretary got paid to shop him.'

'You reckon?'

'Or they've had an affair and he's binned her and now she's dropping him in it. She's done herself out of a job, whatever way it goes. He'll bounce back, they always do.'

It was gone nine when Denny called. Max flipped the lid of a biro. 'Go on.'

'James Creedy was on the up. He'd been slotted into the ministerial position at the Home Office three years ago over the heads of others who might have had dibs on the post. Since then he's carved himself a niche on the media circuit, affable, presents well, always on-message. While he was at Oxford, he shared a house with three others, one a producer on the *Today* programme, another an American now working in the US Secretary of State's office. I can't find any detail on the third. He's been cock-up free until the news broke last night.'

'I've seen it.'

'The red tops all have the same story; he's accessing porn sites between answering emails, but I've spoken to a mate of mine who works in his constituency. She says there's a rumour his PA is about to file an indecency complaint. Sexual harassment. Oliver Watts in the *Mail* is leading with Creedy's personal story, the implication being he's a serial fuck monster. Boys and girls working after hours with the boss. Extra hotel rooms paid for by the public purse.'

'Family man, is he?' Max heard a flurry of mouse clicks and keyboard taps. 'What are you doing?'

'Being clever, bear with me a sec.'

She came up with Creedy's London address almost immediately. 'The PA is Miss Hayley Green, no contact details for her as yet and she's lying low. Want me to keep looking?'

Max scribbled Creedy's address in the margins of the paper. 'Sure, do we know the details of this alleged indecent act?' The waitress arched an eyebrow and flicked her cigarette. Max returned the smile. She took her coffee and went back behind the counter.

'Speculation so far,' said Denny. 'She's given no interviews. What doesn't wash is Creedy has to know that all Home Office internet use is monitored. He initiated the policy. Maybe he's got some kind of override on that, but either he forgot –'

'Or he's being shat on.'

'Exactly. If they hacked Labrosse and Tyler, why not pull the same stunt?'

'Anything else?'

'The Home Office-IDI management group reported to a cabinet committee chaired by Sir Gordon Whittingham, now resigned from office. He's since taken up a job as non-exec director for a company called Montrose Holdings. According to Companies House, Montrose is a party funder. Also, you'll like this, Whittingham is on the board of IDI.'

'Since when?'

He heard her flipping pages. 'The document I found was dated December last year and he's listed.'

Max struggled to process the information. His phone gave an intermittent bleep. A low battery warning. 'I have to go.'

'Before you do, I haven't forgotten about your man in the photo. I've got someone coming back to me later today. I'll let you know.'

Max turned the phone off. He was almost out of credit.

The waitress joined him at the table. 'Come on then, give us the smut and leave out the boring bits. You want another coffee?'

48

Max

MAX DROVE MERCER'S FIESTA to a car lot on the edge of an industrial estate in Ponders End, a stone's throw from the North Circular. He dropped the attendant an extra twenty-quid to keep one of the CCTV cameras fixed on it and gave him his mobile number. He caught a cab back into central London and stopped at a call box to ring Creedy. Mrs Creedy tried to put him off. No, her husband would not come to the phone, nor were they 'receiving visitors'. Max told her he had new information and said he'd be there in half an hour.

SW3 was in late-morning sunshine by the time Max walked down the King's Road. He had the beginnings of a toothache. An exploratory finger pushed at something that felt loose and sore. He turned towards the river and, halfway along Chelsea Manor Street, found Grove Cottages. Half a dozen photographers camped on the pavement outside. They paid little attention to Max as he rang the bell. He faced up to the video intercom's black lens. A woman's voice answered. 'Yes?'

'Detective Sergeant Lomax to see James Creedy. I called.' Seconds later the door opened and Max slipped in.

'Sorry if I was a bit short on the phone. I just thought it was them again.' Mrs Creedy's fingers played with the little gold cross at her throat. 'They've been unusually persistent even by their standards this morning. I'll tell James you're here.'

Creedy was on the phone. His voice carried through to the reception where Max waited. He looked up at the all-white walls. Bronze figures occupied each of three arched alcoves. Exposed light wood beams and halogen spots recessed in the high ceiling. He was drawn to his reflection in one of the glass panels set beneath the banister rail. Something tired and beaten about the face looking back spooked him.

'My wife said you had information you felt would be useful to me.' Creedy's hands stayed deep in his chino pockets.

'Possibly.'

'Can I see your identification?'

Max had his badge and warrant card ready. Creedy studied it. 'You work for Assistant Commissioner Kilby, I take it?' His slender fingers ran across the badge. 'Have we met?'

'I'm investigating the circumstances surrounding the death of Derek Labrosse. You knew him quite well.'

Creedy stiffened. 'Andrea said you were here to help with this bloody internet business.'

'There wasn't time to make a formal appointment.'

'Derek's death was a tragic accident. I said all I had to say at the time. I'm sure you've read the obituaries.'

Mrs Creedy squeezed past on her way upstairs. She touched her husband's arm. 'Everything okay, darling?'

'Sergeant Lomax, have you met my gullible wife, Andrea.'

As she skipped up the stairs, Andrea Creedy caught her foot. Her hands slapped down to break the fall. She twisted and hit the stair edge on her backside with some force. Max reacted first. Her cheeks reddened and she waved him away. 'It's fine. I'm a clumsy cow at the best of times.' She made it up the stairs, lingering at the top for a few seconds. Max glanced up and she disappeared into one of the rooms.

Creedy didn't miss a beat. 'I'm fighting these allegations all the way. It's a complete fabrication. You've seen that lot outside. It's bloody impossible.' He pulled his fingers through his hair. 'I could do without any more shit from the police, so if you're not here to help, I have calls to make.'

Max stood his ground, his fingers pressed lightly on Creedy's chest. 'Derek Labrosse had concerns about Patrick Theobold's relationship with IDI and the work you were doing. He confided in you and I can prove it. I think that's worth ten minutes of your time.' He dropped his hand.

Creedy led them through to a study at the back of the house. Patio doors opened onto a walled courtyard populated with healthy-looking container plants. Half sunlit, half in shade. Creedy pulled the doors shut and fiddled with the blinds. They dropped unevenly. He left them. 'My solicitor is one hundred per cent confident that I'll be exonerated with this internet thing. I have the PM's complete backing in spite of what the papers are saying.'

'That must be reassuring.' Max picked up a family photo from the desk, all the elements in place. Creedy in black tie, wife, kids, and champagne on the table. But it looked staged. The same sadness in Andrea Creedy's eyes he'd seen earlier on the stairs.

Creedy sat at his desk and fiddled with his PC until the opening piano chords of some flaccid indie track filled the room. Max moved a ministerial red box off the only other chair and sat at Creedy's side. His voice remained barely above a whisper, 'Mr Creedy, why did Derek Labrosse confide in you when he had fundamental concerns about IDI?'

'I should have thought that was self-evident. I'm the responsible minister. The work was commissioned by my department in response to the policy of the government I represent.' His smile was unconvincing.

'Labrosse had worked with Patrick Theobold before, hadn't he?'

'I believe so.' Creedy pushed back from the desk.

'Did you persuade him to do so again?'

'Theobold has the appropriate experience and he's well-networked. It was his area of expertise. The decision had nothing to do with me needing to persuade Derek. This is all very much water under the bridge. No one is interested.'

'When you made plans to undermine Derek Labrosse, presumably you had a reason. Same as the people screwing you over now.'

Creedy swallowed hard. 'I've reconciled myself to the need to make uncomfortable professional choices. One compromises, end of story. The liberal niceties we're used to are not sustainable at times like these. I believe in a balance between personal freedom and public safety and security. Apparently, Derek stopped seeing it that way.'

Max reached across the desk, moved the mouse to lose the screensaver and scrolled down the ministerial playlist. The man had the worst taste in music he'd ever seen. 'Do you actually like any of this stuff?'

'What are you, the bloody music police, now? Please leave my computer alone.'

'Just like that. One day Labrosse is fine with what you're doing, the next he's going over your head to Sir Gordon Whittingham. A matter of political principle.'

'He made it clear he would prevent the contract from being awarded, whatever it took. He told me about this file of his. He claimed, and I had no reason to disbelieve him, that it held sensitive information, letters, emails – God knows what else. Going to Gordon was a stupid thing to do.'

'Was that why you passed the information to Patrick Theobold?'

'He headed the team brokering the deal. He needed to be made aware.'

'And it shifted the problem.' Creedy's neck reddened. Max cranked it further. 'So, let me get this right, not only is Theobold creaming off both sides with your knowledge, but you believe he's better placed to influence major policy decisions than Labrosse, the civil servant *you* appointed, and who'd expressed grave concerns over the direction your government were taking.' Max's toothache had picked up a little throbbing rhythm.

'Sergeant, you seem to be treating this as if we're some kind of secret faction, one of those insidious little cliques one hears about. I repeat, this is government policy, we have cabinet approval. For God's sake, whose side are you on?'

Max killed the music mid-song. He kept his voice low. 'I don't mind you being what you are. But don't take the piss. It's not about the policy; it never was. Labrosse had valid reasons for going to the wall over what IDI were proposing and he was tearing himself apart about Patrick Theobold's part in it.'

'You know that for certain, do you?'

'Beyond reasonable doubt.'

Creedy unclasped his hands, wiped them on his trousers, leaving sweat marks on his M&S khaki. 'When Derek told me he was going to the press to *explode the whole thing* – his words, I called a meeting.'

'Where and when?'

'In my office, the Wednesday before Derek died. Theobold, Lillico, myself. We considered a range of options.'

'What options?'

'Theobold viewed Derek as a threat, not just to the project, but to the integrity of all our homeland security proposals. He asked us to consider whether he should be removed, which I assumed meant asking Gordon Whittington to promote him sideways or something. We never really took seriously that it might have meant anything else. I know I didn't, though I found out afterwards that Gavin Lillico shit his pants. You see, we didn't know who else Derek might have contacted at that point, so we decided we would get hold of this bloody file and, if needs be, it could be made to look as though he was off the range, so to speak, undermining national security.'

'You'd have gone public?'

'No, no, no.' He shook his head vigorously. 'Patrick felt that, if we controlled the information, we could keep it in-house. Derek might have made a bit of a fuss, but we all felt that he'd be reasonable. I spoke to Sir Gordon and he agreed we should offer Derek an incentive. Patrick felt that, as long as there was something for him to play for personally, we'd overcome any resistance.'

'And you bought that?'

Creedy walked across to a recessed cabinet and came back to the desk with a bottle of Jura malt whisky and a single crystal glass. He poured a couple of fingers, drank it and replenished the glass.

Max leaned across, took the glass and drank the contents. He poured another and pushed the glass towards Creedy. 'Caroline Labrosse told me her husband was out of contact all day on the Saturday he died. I checked the Home Office records. He was with you. I think you wanted to give him one last opportunity to come onside. And I think you knew Theobold had already made up his mind. That file doesn't discredit Labrosse, it discredits all of you.'

The intercom buzzed. Creedy reached across and picked up the handset. On screen, Max could see a man wearing an open neck shirt, loose cream jacket, carrying a briefcase. Creedy let him in. 'Mr Harwood is my solicitor. He's here to discuss the statement for my press conference. You're welcome to stay and discuss your allegations with him, but I have nothing more to add. I think we both know you've pushed your luck as it is.'

Max stood at the door on his way out. 'I hope you get your little problem sorted. Being a wanker's one thing, banging them out on the taxpayer's time, that's something else.'

49

Max

LILLICO SAW MAX COMING as he left the Home Office building. 'Not now, I'm late for a meeting. Get in the queue if you want to harass me.'

As he strode out between the Tothill Street traffic, Max fell in alongside. 'I've just seen James Creedy, he told me you'd be able to verify his whereabouts on the day Derek Labrosse died.'

Lillico looked sick. He was pale and perspiring.

'He says you were together.'

'Tell him to find his own alibi.'

'So, were you with him or not?'

He stopped. His shoulders sagged. 'We had a meeting at the Home Office in the morning.'

'Last chance saloon for Labrosse. Play nicely or get fucked by Patrick Theobold, right?'

Lillico's eyes roamed the street, the traffic, the high windows, the pavement, anywhere but at Max. 'Do you mind if we just get out of this heat a second?'

Max took his arm and guided him into the shadows of St James's Park station. 'It isn't too late. I don't think you wanted this.'

'What I want has got nothing to do with it.'

'Help me to take him down.'

Lillico shook his head.

Max pulled a slightly creased business card from his back pocket. 'You've probably got one of these. Maybe you lost it or gave it to a friend, so take another one and do yourself a favour while you can, because whatever protection you think you've got, or Theobold thinks he's got, I'm past caring.' He patted him on the arm. 'Look after yourself.'

Lillico came after him, 'What would it take for you to stop this?'

Max bit down, turning the toothache into a discernible pain. He backed Lillico against the ticket machine. 'More money than you've got, more balls than Theobold's got, more friends in high places than Hannah Rees and David Bittman and all of you put together.'

He bought a ticket and headed down to the platform. There was a blast of hot air as a train roared out of the tunnel and slowed to a stop. He got on. No one moved for him. No-one spoke. Only the Asian boy with the see-through plastic rucksack offered him a reassuring smile, but then he was doing that to everyone.

50

Max

MAX JOINED THE QUEUE at the cash dispenser on Finchley Road. As he waited, he saw a black Range Rover pass. There was a split-second eye-contact with the passenger before he looked away. Max felt a tap on his shoulder. 'You're next, mate.' The Range Rover indicated, turned left and disappeared.

He took his time, punched in the PIN and waited. The message came up: *refer to bank*. He started south towards Swiss Cottage and made the call to his bank. His current account had been emptied. There was nothing in his savings. The call centre operative put him through to the bank's fraud service. They'd look into it and call him back within the hour. Max doubled back, dropping downhill on Fairfax Road. The Range Rover he'd seen earlier pulled into the kerb some thirty metres ahead. He glanced behind him. One possible about fifteen metres back in grey trousers and a pink short-sleeved shirt. Max kept walking. A swirl of dust picked up on the breeze. He stopped, shielded his eyes. A rust bucket Fiat rattled to a double-parked standstill. The driver, a grungy-looking girl in tie-dye shirt and oversize combats, got out and skipped into Costcutter.

Sunlight flashed off the windscreen of a FedEx van edging past the Range Rover. It raced up and stopped level with the double-parked Fiat. The driver hit the horn hard.

'She won't be long, mate,' said Max. 'Just nipped in the shop.'

He clocked a possible number two coming up on the opposite side of the street. This one was taller, heavy-set, loose blue suit, floppy fringe like a forty-year-old New Romantic, but handy from the way he carried himself. As Max turned and walked purposefully at Pink Shirt, he spotted the man in the leather jacket further up the hill. No mistake this time. It was him, the man he'd seen before outside his flat and whom he'd photographed at Strutton Ground. Max slowed as he approached Pink Shirt, all smiles and open hands. 'Look, if there's something I can do to help you people –' Pink Shirt drew a Taser and glanced towards Blue Suit. Max ran at him, lifted his right leg and kicked out, made a solid contact below Pink Shirt's knee then dragged the side of his boot down his shin, landing full weight with a stamp on the top of his foot. Metatarsals snapped like dry spaghetti. Pink Shirt yelped and crumpled, clutching his foot.

'Sorry, mate.' As Max took off, Pink Shirt ankle-tapped him. He sprawled, hit the pavement hard, got up and ran.

Darting left into Finchley Road station, Max flashed his badge, pushed through the barrier and down the steps. He jumped a Jubilee Line train heading north and moved through the carriages, sweat-soaked and out of breath. He saw Blue Suit jump the bottom half-dozen steps, but fail to make the train as the doors closed.

Max checked himself. He'd grazed the heel of his right hand. There was a rip in his trousers and he'd smacked his knee, but he was in one piece. By the time the train pulled into Kilburn two stops later, he'd got his breath back. He stepped off. Crowds closed in on him and he was carried along down the steps into Kilburn High Road. He took a taxi from Monty's Cabs under the railway bridge.

'Where d'you want to go?'

He said nothing as the cab pulled into the traffic.

'I said, where d'you want –'

'Turnpike Lane.' It was the first place that came to mind.

*

Whatever Max began to feel as he sat at Liz's kitchen table, he knew it had no place. She'd let him in the office, made him coffee, then brought him home to her flat in Hornsey, no questions asked. He'd offered no explanation. 'Thanks for this. I just need somewhere to get a shower and sleep for a couple of hours then I'll be off.'

Her eyes dropped to the rip in his jeans, the skinned knee and grazed hand. 'Why can't you go home?'

'If it's a pain, I'll get a hotel.'

She rattled around in a drawer for a corkscrew. 'You found Phil, then?'

'It wasn't difficult.'

'He called me this morning. He said you and he made some sort of an agreement.' She poured them each a glass of red.

'Does he tell you all his secrets?'

'Not all.' There was a moment's silence. 'I think he quite likes you, in spite of himself. But then he doesn't really know you, doesn't know how dangerous you are to be around.' She put the glass behind her on the worktop. 'This thing you're asking, access to Phil's contacts, it can't happen.'

'It fucking wants to. If I'm pulling the sting out of these people, there'd better be something at the end of it.'

'Like Patrick Theobold?'

'Think what you like, I'm past caring. I just do what they pay me for and I'll find Mercer's contacts like I found Mercer. If he had something to offer Labrosse, I want to know what.' He offered his glass for a refill.

She dumped the bottle on the table. The plates vibrated. 'Pour your own. I'll run you a bath.' Everything said she was pissed off at him for turning up, except she hadn't kicked him out.

He climbed into the bath. Hot water stung his grazed knees. He soaked up to his shoulders in sudsy warm bathwater as the evening sun streamed through the window. He closed his eyes.

Max thought he was still dreaming. He felt the sponge soaping his chest and teasing its way south. When he opened his eyes, the face that came close and smiled at him was real. 'Wake up, Mr Prune,' Liz whispered. She took a towel and dried her arms. 'I didn't want you to drown in my bath. Are you eating first or sleeping?'

'Eating, please.'

'Five minutes then. Should be long enough to down periscope and dry off.' She threw the towel at him and left the bathroom door open behind her.

By the time they'd eaten, finished the second bottle and were well into the third, the candles and their kitchen window reflections were the only light left. Liz wiped her plate with the last scrap of ciabatta and licked her fingers like the naughtiest girl in school. She smiled. 'So, are you allowed to tell me where you're going with this, or are we in need-to-know mode?'

He said nothing.

'Come on, trust me, I'm a solicitor.' She made a Girl Guide salute. 'We take an oath.'

'Really?'

She faked affront. 'Like you wouldn't do whatever it took to get the job done. I've seen that look in your eyes before.'

'What look?'

'The one that says you'll do whatever you have to short of selling your arse to put Theobold away. I don't know if you've crossed the Rubicon, but you're paddling in the shallow end.' She dipped a finger in her glass and drew a Rioja line across the table. 'What swung it?'

'You did. You're my moral muse.'

She laughed, throwing her head back. 'Ah, now that is a first, a moral muse.'

'I tried it the right way and the gates closed, so now I'm trusting my instincts.'

A silence.

'I went to see James Creedy this morning.'

'Disgraced minister and all-round piece of shit. No morals there whatsoever.'

'You know him then?'

'In my line of work? Of course, I know him. If he's involved you won't get close to Theobold. No chance.'

The argument was there to be had and she'd been digging at it all evening, every few minutes another reason why he was chasing a lost cause. The record on the turntable had finished playing. 'Want me to put some music on?'

'No, I'll do it,' said Liz. 'You'll just choose some piece of schmoozy rubbish designed to make me feel sorry for you and then I'll have to take you to bed and that would be a bad thing.' She disappeared into the living room, then reappeared. 'Or you'll do what you used to and put on some piece of crap that John Peel played twice in 1980 and tell me how it's still brilliant, how it's like the first time you heard it.'

He flicked a V.

'Stiff Little Fingers.' She disappeared again and must have changed her mind as the intro to *White Man in Hammersmith Palais* punched through the walls. Max sang softly to himself. *'You think it's funny, turning rebellion into money.'* He wiped the sweat off his lip, stood, with some effort, and raised a glass to his reflection in the window. 'A toast,' he slurred slightly. 'To the memory of Mr Joe Strummer.' He emptied his glass and caught her watching him from the doorway.

The bedroom was dark and the sheets cool on his back. Liz kicked the duvet off.

'Are you sure?'

'Ask me in the morning.'

She backed up as he spooned in behind her and they lay there a while. 'Just hold me,' she said. He could have slept then, but in the blur of tiredness and alcohol fog, his arm came across and he began to softly run his fingertips across her stomach, her hips, feeling his way. She eased his hand down. As he gently stroked, her breath quickened and he felt a layer of inhibition leave him. He kissed her neck, but she wouldn't turn, wouldn't face him. 'Like this,' she said. 'Don't fuck me. Not yet.'

It was 5am when he woke. Liz wasn't there. He rolled into the warmth of the rucked sheets on her side of the bed. He needed a piss and about a gallon of water. He got up, but couldn't find his trousers. He pulled his shirt on and limped across the landing. A light came from around the door of the boxroom she used as an office. He edged it open. She sat at her desk whispering under her breath. Then he realised she was speaking into a digital recorder, a thing the size of a mobile phone. Fresh from bed, her hair winged out on one side. Her cotton dressing gown was loose around her shoulders. His trousers were on the floor. 'I was looking for these.'

She freaked. 'Jesus Christ, Max! I didn't hear you.'

He held his hands up. 'I'm sorry, sorry.'

A flustered look crossed her face. 'I was working,' she said.

'With my trousers?' His eyes were drawn to the PC monitor. On the screen in detail was a section of one of the Labrosse bloodstained pages.

'What are you doing?'

'Giving your case the once over. Is this all of it?'

'On paper, yes. But there's more. Liz, why are you doing this?'

She pulled the gown tight around her. 'Max, if this is it, you don't have a case. You won't even get it to court.'

'That's not really your problem,' he said.

'I'm serious, it's weak.'

He shook his head. 'Liz, it's five in the morning, what are you doing? Tell me now.'

'For Christ's sake, Max, keep your voice down.'

He put his hand on her shoulder. 'I want to know.'

'I'm not going to be interrogated by you.' She pushed past him. He scooped up his trousers and followed her. The kitchen door slammed in his face. He stepped back and kicked it open. The frame splintered.

'Fuck off, just fuck off.' She shook a fag packet, it was empty. She flicked the kettle on, tried to come past, pushed him hard. He didn't move. 'I'm not doing this, Max, it's not me, not anymore. I don't do this *chaos* thing. Just piss off out of my way.' She tried to get past. He stopped her, threw the trousers over the back of the chair. 'I'm going nowhere until you tell me, what have I got that you want?' The kitchen door swung behind him. He pushed it back and walked towards her.

She stepped away, her hands up. The kettle bubbled, boiled, clicked off. 'I was going to tell you.'

Max buttoned his shirt, then had to do it again with a buttonhole missed.

'Your case is circumstantial. There's no hard evidence and none of the main players has made anything like a firm enough statement to justify a prosecution. I assume that is the aim?'

'You didn't steal my memory stick to give me free legal advice.'

She held onto the chair back. 'You won't get Theobold. They'll suppress all you have. Or his friends will get him off. No one will testify.'

'Gavin Lillico will. He's scared.'

'Yeah, of Theobold. Not you.'

'I'll turn him.'

She gave him a look of disbelief. 'Even if you do, they won't let it get to court, there's too much at stake, careers, money, power. We're up against this day in, day out. These people aren't going to be stopped by you, not like this.'

Max knew that he was looking for a single, verifiable truth where probably none existed. Each of these people had arranged a version of events to suit their own skewed interpretation. What remained was worthless. Lies repeated with conviction that would deceive most people if you said them often enough. But if you knew where to look, each lie bore its maker's mark. He would turn them. He would find the liar's weakest point and break them. He started to put his trousers on. 'Liz, last night was the best thing that's happened to me in months, but please don't mug me off.' He went through to the bedroom and picked up the rest of his clothes.

The radio-alarm clicked past 6am. The news filled the room. The *Today* programme's top story: a ministerial announcement that, in the face of a renewed terrorist threat, temporary checkpoints would be installed on routes in and out of all major cities in the UK. The newsreader listed the cities. There had been, she continued, a muted acceptance from the leaders of all the main political parties. The Home Secretary would be interviewed after the 8am news.

Liz switched the radio off. 'I had to do something, Max. What these people are doing frightens me. It should you.'

He found his socks.

She said, 'There's something – you probably shouldn't know this.'

He tried to undo a knot in his bootlaces with his teeth. 'What does that mean?'

'It would compromise you.' She sat on the bed beside him.

'So, don't tell me.' He pulled the boot on and tugged the knot through. The lace snapped.

'If your case fails, which it will, there is another way to undermine IDI and stop Theobold in the process. It's set up and ready to go.'

He went back to his boots, tied the laces a few holes short. 'I'm interested in Patrick Theobold and what he did to Derek and Caroline Labrosse and Michael Tyler. He broke the law. If I can prove he's taking dirty money from IDI or anyone else, I'll screw him for that as well.'

She studied him, biting the tip of her thumb while she weighed the options. 'When Derek came to see Phil Mercer last year, he met with Jonathon and me at the same time. He told us what he was planning and wanted us to act for him, prepare a defence and help to draft a series of statements before he went public.'

'And?'

'Derek offered us all the evidence he'd collected at that point. He told us he had details of bank accounts IDI were paying into and where that money was coming from. We have people that can trace its origin. He also gave us information about their security systems, their PR, their strategy. And he stole a series of codes from Theobold. We have people who can get through IDI's firewall undetected. The account details and codes would have been in the file. You've got part of the file. You've got the emails and if you have the codes… Max, he intended this stuff to come to us, it's what he wanted.'

'Really?'

'We can pull them down. We can fuck with their systems. Make it public. Show the dark money behind it, expose what happens if a system like that isn't secure. We can discredit them, make people see they're sleepwalking into something terrible.'

'Come on Liz, this is England, the twenty-first century. No-one cares.'

'If Theobold thinks you've got this information, he will have you stopped.'

There was a long silence. 'You were right, I shouldn't know and it does compromise me. I've got a case and I'm working it out. Against everybody's better judgement it seems.'

Nothing more was said. She dressed quickly. He heard the front door slam.

On his way out, Max retrieved the memory stick and deleted what little had been downloaded onto Liz's PC. As he came down the stairs, there was a shadow at the door. He opened it to find Denny on the step. 'Good morning.'

'How did you find me?'

'I didn't, he did.' She gestured to a Range Rover waiting at the kerb. Max recognised the floppy-haired, blue-suited driver from the day before. 'DS Martin Lacey. He works for SO15. Kilby thought, if he sent me, you'd be less likely to break my foot.'

51

Max

MAX AND DENNY WAITED in the corridor outside Kilby's office. Janice passed silently between them on her way out. She shot him a look. He was experiencing the beginnings of a headache which worsened when Kilby invited them in and opened the blinds, flooding the room with light. He told them not to sit. Denny stood upright, her hands knotted in front of her. Max moved around so that the full glare of the sunlight was behind him.

Kilby sat down and unfolded a thin blade from a penknife. He unscrewed the battery panel on the bottom of his desk clock. 'In the last forty-eight hours, I've fielded calls from a string of very pissed-off people wanting to know why I'm hounding them.'

'They're involved,' said Max.

The clock's screw dropped between Kilby's thick fingers. 'The Home Secretary was involved in killing Derek Labrosse, is that what you're saying?'

'If he's defending James Creedy, he's involved.'

Kilby's penknife blade stabbed the air. 'Did you not understand that when I said interview Tyler and come back to me, that's what I wanted? That and no more. And that when I told you to finish the case and do nothing without reference to me, that was what I meant?'

'There was a new lead, I followed it.'

'You doorstepped a Minister of the Crown, for Christ's sake. A very influential one.'

'A corrupt one.'

'You can prove that, can you?'

'I have enough to bring Theobold in. I can turn Lillico. The rest will follow.'

Kilby threw the clock down, the batteries pinged out, rolled across the desk, coming to a stop against a fat file. 'Here is what's going to happen: there's a meeting set for nine-thirty this morning; Hannah Rees insists she interviews you personally. Creedy and Lillico will be present. I've given them my assurances that you will back off, but they want to hear it from you. That gives you forty-five minutes to get it straight in your head, make it credible and try not to make me look like a cunt.'

The sun was drawing out Max's headache. A dark shadow formed at the periphery of his vision. 'There are other people involved, people who've stuck their necks out.'

Kilby blinked. 'This isn't the time. Decisions are being made that I must be in a position to influence. This stops now. That's both of you.'

Max was silent. His head fogged, the shadow moved in and his vision blurred then returned, then blurred and stayed that way. He felt a slackness in his bowels. Kilby was mouthing words he couldn't quite hear, hectoring, lecturing. He couldn't formulate a single coherent thought, let alone respond. For twenty, thirty seconds the world went on without him. He was Tommy: deaf, dumb and blind. He dialled the next line into his consciousness: *he sure plays a mean pinball*. And that was it, as long as he kept the little silver ball on the table, as long as he kept flipping, nothing else mattered. Just stay in the game.

His hearing cleared first. No one was speaking. The fog retreated. The need to shit didn't. Kilby came into focus. 'Well?'

'I'll speak to them,' said Max. His head throbbed with the effort of talking.

'Then do it right.'

'I said I'll do it.'

He had no recollection of how they got back to their own office. Denny took his silence as mute rage, but it wasn't. He fell into his chair, one side of his face felt numb and he slurred. 'What do they know, Maggie?'

'I'm not sure.'

'Do they know I've got these?' He pulled Labrosse's emails from his pocket.

Her silence said they did. He looked again at the reverse of the first email, barely able to discern the neat clusters of handwritten black figures, some made almost invisible by the bloodstain. What had it taken for Labrosse to take a risk like this? Max thought he knew.

He lifted himself to his feet. He gently took Denny's shoulders. 'Maggie, he's your superior and he told you to report to him. It doesn't matter. We can talk about it some other time, but right now, please can you go downstairs, get me the strongest painkillers you can find and think about what you told him. I want you to remember everything. No pressure.' He looked at his watch, the numbers waltzed out of focus. 'You've got about fifteen minutes.'

She paused at the door. 'Max, now's probably not the right time, but your photo bloke.'

'Is?'

'Dominik Saski, Croatian passport. Ex-army. Worked for the police in Zagreb until three years ago. Last known address is a halfway house. He did six months in Wandsworth for possession of items with intention to defraud, namely a carrier bag of cloned store account cards and bank cards with a list of names and PIN numbers. Officer in charge suspects he was involved in ID theft, ATM theft. He's a hacker, petty fraudster.

Fraud section reckons he was the end of a chain that makes its way back to central and northern Europe. They say he's been hiring himself out to underworld contacts in the UK, creating false IDs. He's a technical operator.'

'He can do that from anywhere. Why follow me?'

'I've been asking myself that.'

Max's chair was placed apart from the others on one side of the boardroom table. Just out of reach were a carafe of dusty water and four heavy tumblers. He felt a little sick, but the two pink Migraleve tablets had made the fist inside his skull feel less like it might punch its way out. He settled in with an air of detachment as Kilby, Creedy and Lillico exchanged handshakes and avoided eye contact. Hannah Rees entered and gave a curt, 'Good morning, gentlemen.'

Max studied the opposition. Creedy was here expecting a show and could barely keep the smug anticipation off his face. Something to take his mind off the S&M slideshow of his newsfeed. The colour rose to his cheeks as Hannah Rees took her seat next to him and unbuttoned a slim plastic file, touching him on the hand, perhaps accidentally. Lillico, a place apart, looked pale. He twisted a strand of hair at his fringe, caught himself and flipped a page of his papers, but he wasn't reading. Within twenty seconds he was back worrying the same strand of hair. Kilby was at the end, his chair angled at forty-five degrees to the table. He leaned back and unfolded his arms. He might as well have brought popcorn. Max looked up to find Hannah Rees's gaze wired directly into him.

Creedy leaned across to Kilby, 'Before we begin, can we assume your presence here means Detective Sergeant Lomax has been apprised of our views on his behaviour and our requirements?'

Kilby said, 'I've passed on your concerns, the Home

Secretary's and those of our management group to DS Lomax. We're here to offer whatever assurances you require and to agree what our next steps might be.'

Rees hadn't taken her eyes off him. 'You happy with that?'

A smile might have helped sell Max's response, but he couldn't find one. He nodded.

'Let's make a start. Can you tell us exactly what information you're holding on Patrick Theobold?'

Max looked at Kilby, got nothing.

'I think –'

She looked to the ceiling, then back. 'Let's keep to what we know shall we, what do you have evidence to prove?'

'Caroline Labrosse was systematically intimidated by Patrick Theobold for a period of time following her husband's death earlier this year and up to the point of her own death in June.'

'And you have a statement to that effect?'

'Mrs Labrosse died in suspicious circumstances. I didn't have the opportunity to take a statement. I have my own notes and a potential witness.'

'Who is?'

'A journalist, Philip Mercer.'

'The man who slandered my company in a work of internet fiction, who has waged a one-man campaign against us. Our lawyers are looking into it.' This said for the benefit of the panel. 'May we see the notes?'

'I don't have them with me.'

Kilby said, 'I'm having all documentation relating to the case seized. There will be full disclosure and I'll make sure the notes are part of that package.'

'So no formal statement.' She made a note. 'What else?'

The grilling went on, Max giving the truth where possible, a version of it when he thought he'd get away with it. She came to Michael Tyler.

'I met him recently for the first time,' said Max.

'But he came to you before.'

'Detective Constable Denny spoke to him at the Home Office interviews. I didn't.'

'What did you discuss?'

'Tyler alleges he was assaulted by Patrick Theobold. I found him tied to a chair, beaten senseless in a disused motel just south of Peterborough off the A1. He spent a week in hospital and is still not fully recovered from his physical injuries, let alone the effects of the trauma he has been subjected to. I suspect he'll carry that with him a lot longer.'

'But you've got nothing that actually proves Patrick Theobold has any connection with the attack.'

'Mr Tyler didn't do it to himself.'

'But no verifiable link to Patrick Theobold?'

'Other than you telling me where to find him.'

'I told you there was an empty motel that had been used as a meeting point for our covert operatives. I did not make any such connection.'

Kilby's eyes flashed. Something he hadn't known.

Rees gestured to invite comments either side, but neither Creedy nor Lillico had anything to add. Lillico's eyes darted around the room. She continued. 'Did you know Michael Tyler was turned down for a job last year, a promotion he'd been counting on? By all accounts embarrassed himself at first interview. Do you know who chaired the panel and signed off the shortlist? I take it your silence means you did not. It was Derek Labrosse. Would you say that gives Mr Tyler motive to act against Mr Labrosse? Are you planning to arrest Michael Tyler?'

Liz's conviction that he'd never bring the case to court was ringing in his ears. Hannah Rees locking out avenues of enquiry as if playing to a silent judge. At one point, her head tilted slightly. The movement struck him as unnatural.

She touched her hair as if she might put it behind her ear, then seemed to remember herself. 'I'll ask you again, are you planning to arrest Michael Tyler in connection with the death of Derek Labrosse?'

'I've got no evidence to prove he was there.'

'That doesn't mean there isn't any.' She distributed a piece of paper to each of them. 'Chief Superintendent Rothwell has brought to light one or two pieces of evidence, blood samples taken at the scene that aren't Derek Labrosse's. If they can be matched to Michael Tyler, and I believe they can, that's QED, wouldn't you say?' She opened her hands, gave another thin smile.

Max rested his hands flat on the table in front of him. His head was clearing. 'If you want me to back off and leave Theobold alone, I'll do it. If that's what you want.'

Another touch of her hair, this time more pronounced. The penny dropped; she was wired. She asked, what did Tyler do with the file he took from Derek Labrosse's house?

'I don't know anything about that.'

A pause. 'We'll come back to that, if we may.'

As the interview continued, Max kept his tone conciliatory. Creedy didn't press except where the questioning brushed his own involvement. Lillico sweated behind his rimless glasses and asked questions to which he already knew the answers. Kilby's stone cold stare found the middle distance and stayed there. More than anything, he seemed bored. Hannah Rees took the role of inquisitress-in-chief with relish, leading relentlessly through question, reiteration, backtrack, question, backtrack, question. What did he know about Philip Mercer? What was his relationship with Elizabeth Delaney? Why had he sought to undermine IDI? What were his views on advance surveillance technology? Was he still sympathetic towards terrorist causes?

It stopped him dead. 'What the fuck does that mean?'

Creedy butted in, raising his hand to Hannah Rees's glare. 'Just a minute, if I may, I've done my own homework. Sergeant Lomax has gone off the rails before, somewhat spectacularly I'm led to believe.' He held his glasses to his eyes without putting them on and read from his notes. 'Three years ago, when you thwarted an attempt to close down a subversive ecosocialist cell in Wood Green, north London. Then, earlier this year, your rash actions jeopardised a long-term Trident operation on the Broadwater Farm Estate, for which you received a suspension and were ordered to undertake a course of counselling. What can you tell us about that?'

Max took a long time before replying. 'What do you want to know? I'm not bloody perfect, but nothing I've done makes me sympathetic to any cause other than to discharge my duties and obey the rule of law.'

Hannah Rees's questioning had been incisive. Creedy's was blunt, flat and ineffective. Her momentum had been lost. Kilby cut in. 'If there's nothing else, can we draw this to a close?'

Rees raised a hand. 'I don't think so. I want to bring us back for a moment. The file Tyler took from Labrosse's house, you were going to tell us what he did with its contents.'

Max leaned forward, looked at each of them in turn, settled on Hannah Rees. 'I know the man whispering in your ear right now wishes he'd never sent Michael Tyler to get that file. And I know why.' He slid his card across the table. 'If he wants to talk about it, he can call me.'

They waited for Kilby's car in the Home Office lobby. The driver was on his way, but stuck in traffic in South Kensington. Kilby kept his eyes on the street. 'There are likely to be some changes, a restructuring. The Commissioner wants me to pick up some of his workload. He also wants me to be less hands-on in operational matters, management, that sort of thing.' He rocked back on his heels. 'The timing feels right.'

Max was barely listening. A yellow floristry van pulled up outside. A woman in a green tabard delivered a huge bouquet of summer flowers to the desk. Someone's in love, or loved, he thought.

'What I'm saying,' Kilby said testily, 'is that I'm bringing someone in to pick up my operational responsibilities. We interviewed Chief Superintendent Rothwell last week. Very impressive. Obviously, he knows the score.' He turned to look at Max. 'If you can't deal with that, I suggest you jack it in before you're made to.'

'And Denny?'

'She'll move on, or back. They liked her in Dover.'

'I think she should stay, she's an asset.'

'I don't think so.'

Max shook his head. 'Because of me?'

'Look Max, I've spent my life working with people who'd bend the rules until they're meaningless. I'll do whatever I must to be on the inside. There are worse people than Hannah Rees and James Creedy, believe me.' His car pulled into the kerb behind the florist's van. He didn't wait for Max.

Denny had gone when he got back. The office had been stripped, computers seized, every drawer empty, every loose piece of paper vanished. Kilby hadn't wasted any time closing them down. Max took in the bareness of the walls, the clean rectangle where his photograph had been. The frame was in pieces. The photo was on the floor, he leaned over to pick it up, straightened a corner. A green post-it curled up on the desk. He unpeeled it: *It seems we're no longer in business – call me. Maggie.*

He dialled her mobile, Denny answered, 'Hang on.' A largely inaudible station announcement filled his ears. 'I'm going home, Max. I don't want to stay there.' She paused. 'There was nothing I could have done, they just came in. Assistant

Commissioner's instructions, they said. Half a dozen blokes I'd never seen.' Her voice cracked.

'Maggie, listen to me, it'll be okay.'

'If you need me, call me. Otherwise, can I have a couple of days to sort myself out?'

'Sure.'

'I'd have left my leave card for you to sign, but they took it. They took everything, all my work, even the stuff not connected with Labrosse. All my notes and the copies of everything.' She tailed off. He thought she'd finished, then she said, 'Oh yeah, take the photo with you, I had to fight them for that, I thought you'd want it kept. I'm sorry.' She hung up.

'It's not your fault.'

Max flicked through the address book on his phone, hit speed dial and waited. 'Tony? I need a favour. Yes, another one. I'll come to you.'

52

Max

MAX THREADED THE VESPA through the backstreets to Turnpike Lane. He bumped onto the pavement outside Delaney and Coles' green door and chained the front wheel. He buzzed the intercom. 'Got a parcel for Liz Delaney.'

Nikki was uncertain whether to allow him in. The street noise made explanation impossible. He was shouting. 'I have to deliver it to her in person. By hand, it says. I have to get her signature.'

She came down. As the door opened, Max stepped in, pushing her back against the wall. 'Sorry, I'm in a hurry,' he said, and was up the stairs.

She shouted after him. 'You're supposed to sign the book, you arsehole.'

Liz was blowing smoke out of the window when he barged in, Nikki on his tail. 'I'm sorry, he just –'

Max pulled his crash helmet off. 'Close the window, I haven't got long.'

She stared at him.

'Liz, shut the window, please.'

She folded the butt dead on the window ledge and waved Nikki away. Max went close enough to catch a whiff of the perfume he'd woken up with that morning. She took a step back; he held her arm. 'How clean is this place, electronically speaking?'

'Dunno, ask your mates.'

'*Liz.*'

'It's swept for bugs and whatever once a week. It was clean on Tuesday.'

He gave her the padded envelope from his messenger bag. She tore the seal, emptied the contents on the desk: a memory stick and half a dozen sheets of paper. 'That's all of it. All that's left. The memory stick has the case details, names, places and those... you can see.'

She picked up the Labrosse papers. 'Why now?'

'The numbers are on the back of those pages. Everything's scanned onto the stick. You have to make sure these get to Mercer. He'll have to get them to his contacts sharpish. Tell him he can publish under his own name, but –'

'Tell him yourself.' She went to the door. 'Phil, can you come here a minute ?'

Mercer's absent expression hardened the moment he saw Max. He followed Liz's hand gesture towards the pages on the desk. 'Shit.' He rolled his shirt sleeves. The left sleeve dropped immediately. 'Can I?'

'Go ahead,' said Max.

Mercer's mouth twitched as he read the emails. He ran his hand repeatedly through his hair and said 'shit' every time he turned a page. Then a final 'fuck me' when he saw the names and coded numbers on the back of the last page. He looked to Liz. 'What do you think?'

Max said, 'You wanted the numbers, I got you the numbers. If you're not interested, say so. I'll just do what I'm told and hand the whole lot over so they can shred it with the rest of my career.'

Liz said, 'It beats me why you didn't see it coming.'

Max rested the crash helmet on the desk and unzipped his jacket. 'As things stand, this is a better bet than trying to get Theobold into court. You were right. Does it matter?'

'Obviously, it does.'

Max faced her. 'I'm not joining your crusade. I'm just trying to do what looks like the right thing for now.' She turned her back on him. Right then, he was sick of chalking up scores against their past, the backstabbing and bullshit that Liz dealt in. The conviction there was a right way to handle something like this and it was hers. Always.

'And I can use these emails, publish them?' Mercer cut in.

'Do what you want.' Max pulled the bike gloves out of the helmet. 'No caveats, no constraints. Just make good use of them because you won't get another chance. And don't waste them on some poxy fringe website they can bring down in ten minutes. If you've got mainstream media connections, now's the time to use them.'

'And I don't mention you.'

'Or Michael Tyler. Especially not Tyler. In return, I want the names of your contacts. I need to speak to them.'

Mercer glanced at Liz. 'I asked, there's no way.'

Max picked up Liz's phone, offered it to Mercer. 'Ask again.'

Mercer edged towards the door, nodded at Liz. 'Ask her. She'll explain.'

She lit a cigarette, opened the window. 'Sometimes Max, I wonder how you manage.' Mercer could be heard yapping excitedly through the wall. Between calls, his keyboard was taking a hammering.

'Enlighten me,' said Max.

'It's a whole network.'

'You've got a contact of some sort, though, a real person, a name?'

'Maybe Phil has, I don't know and I wouldn't ask, but I doubt they'd trust him face to face.'

'You don't know them?'

'We monitor their output, check their influence. Phil's smart enough to know they're not cranks.'

'Fucking hell, are you insane? How do you know they haven't been infiltrated?'

'These people don't communicate through Gmail. They meet in closed chatrooms, dark corners you wouldn't know existed, let alone access, not without drawing attention to the fact you didn't belong. They invent their own language, their own protection. That's why your lot are always two steps off the pace. You don't know who they are, where they are, what they're saying, who they're saying it to. Everything is encrypted and bounced across continents. Even if you're in the chain, you only get the keys for the information you're meant to see. Then you re-encrypt and give keys to the next in the chain and so on. By the time those IDI codes are used, the originators will be so far in the darkness, you don't stand a chance of tracking them.'

'Do *they* know each other?'

She sighed. 'Each of them has a specific digital signature. Does that mean they'd recognise each other in PC World? Probably not.'

'But they can get into IDI?'

'They'll construct and deliver something, a carrier, what you and I would call a Trojan, though it's infinitely more complex than that.' She closed the window and the smoke cleared. 'It will target specific parts of IDI internal systems and hive off key data, incriminate certain individuals and, given what we already know, embarrass their people and our government. We'll tip off the IRS, IDI's auditors, Serious Fraud Office, and I'll speak to Jonathon and use his media contacts.'

'And it'll get through? '

'Max, most security breaches aren't discovered for days, sometimes weeks. They sleep. We just need a couple of days' access.'

'What about Theobold?'

'What about him?'

'I want him.'

'With this stuff, we will open their firewalls at a precise time and give every hacktivist network within reach the chance to cause havoc, very publicly and with the world's press watching. We'll bring their systems down. If the government still wants to do business with them after that –'

'I want them to target Theobold.'

'You don't tell them what to do. It doesn't work that way. Besides which, I'm not risking this to target one individual. Sorry.'

Mercer stopped him on the way out. 'Max, my car and passport and stuff, I'll need them.'

'Tomorrow afternoon, you around?'

'Think so, yeah.'

'I'll give you a call, let you know where and when.'

'Spot on.' Mercer bounded back to his office.

53

Tyler

TYLER KNEW THEOBOLD WOULD come. It was a matter of when.

Since he'd returned from hospital, his sleep patterns had been erratic, unfolding in episodes of chronic fatigue and dead sleep interrupted by anxiety dreams. That night, when he went to bed, the pillow felt like concrete, but he must have gone deeper because the first thing he was aware of was a pressure on his chest. When he opened his eyes, Patrick Theobold stood over him and there was a faint smell of alcohol. Theobold leaned across and pulled back the duvet. Emmy slept.

Downstairs in the living room, the driver waited. They'd put the main room light on. This time of the morning, its light was cold and cruel. Theobold told the driver to make strong coffee. He pointed to the sofa. Tyler sat.

There was a clattering in the kitchen, a slamming of drawers and cupboard doors. Something dropped and smashed. Tyler wanted to clear up the mess. 'I'll show him where things are.' He made a move to get up.

Theobold pushed him back. 'You got anything to drink?'

The bottle of Glenfiddich Lomax had brought was in the sideboard cupboard, but he didn't want to share it with Theobold. 'We've got some sherry somewhere, I think.'

'Forget it.' He loosened his tie. The driver brought coffee in the cafetiere and three of the good cups. He plunged and poured, took the first cup himself. Theobold waited and eventually poured his own. 'Exactly how much of the file did you keep for a rainy day?'

'I gave it all back to you. You know I did.'

Theobold grimaced, or maybe it was a smile. Tyler couldn't tell; those eyes were staring blackly through him, the pupils dilated. 'You spoke to that hack Mercer, though, then you had a visit from Lomax, right?'

'No,' he said.

Theobold leaned forward, tipped his cup. Hot coffee dripped into Tyler's lap. He cried out and drew back, pinching his pyjama trousers away from his scalded genitals. He tried to stand. Theobold shoved him back down. 'You spoke to Lomax about the file, he acted on something you showed him, what was it?'

Tyler said nothing, his breathing was fast and shallow.

Theobold said to the driver, 'Go wake her up.' He thumbed upstairs.

'Please,' said Tyler. 'She doesn't know anything about it.'

'About what, Michael?' His eyebrows rose. 'What didn't you tell her?'

'Anything about the file. Any of it.'

'Get her anyway.'

Tyler tried to compose himself, put his hands over the warm wet patch. The floorboard creaked as the driver entered the bedroom. There was a heavy silence broken by a scream that stopped as it started. A minute or so later the door opened. Emmy shuffled in first, puffy eyes and messed hair, her lips colourless and her fists clenched at the join of her gown.

'Wakey, wakey, Emily. I think Michael has something he wants to tell you.'

She sat next to her husband on the sofa without a word or look. She pulled the gown so that it covered her knees.

'Tell her how you shoved Derek Labrosse down the stairs and killed him. It's true, isn't it, Michael?'

He said it was.

Emmy trembled.

'Then, rather than returning the highly sensitive file you were meant to pick up as I'd advised, you read it, copied it, and kept part of it here.'

He said it wasn't like that.

'Tell us, what was it like?' Theobold edged forward, put the cup on the table and topped up from the cafetiere.

'There were some pages I wasn't able to put back.'

'Why not?'

'Because they were stained with blood.'

Theobold let out a shallow laugh. 'Show me.'

'I can't.'

'Find them,' he said to the driver.

'They're not here. I gave them to Detective Sergeant Lomax.'

Theobold sat back, nodding as if he'd known all along. 'How many times did I say, Michael, you can't trust those people. How many times? Yet you never listen. What exactly did you give him?'

'Emails, just some emails.'

'And what was in the emails?'

Tyler felt everything inside him shrivel. He said he didn't remember.

The driver's mobile bleeped, a Morse code signal. He checked the display then took the call in the kitchen, his voice too low to make out what was said. He came back in, 'She wants to talk to you.' He jerked his head towards the kitchen. Theobold took the phone. The driver stayed.

He was gone for some time. No one moved or spoke. When Theobold came back, he loosened his tie and threw a look at the driver that suggested the call had not gone well. 'We have to go. That includes you.' He motioned to Tyler. 'Once you've had a chat with Lomax on my behalf, then you and your wife can say goodbye.'

Tyler was convinced it was his time to die. He shrank inside his skin. Emmy, pale and frightened, seemed disgusted by him. In that moment, he stopped caring. He detached himself from the living person he'd once been. He was nothing now, a separate being. He allowed the driver to take his arm and guide him upstairs to get dressed.

'Be quick,' said Theobold.

Tyler stood in the bedroom, naked. Chills crept across his chest and down his arms. The driver went to the wardrobe, opened drawers and pulled out clothes. He encouraged Tyler into underpants and grey jogging trousers, a t-shirt and beige sweater. He moved him back to the bed, sat him down, and knelt in front of him. He rolled socks over his feet, eased them into training shoes, then drew the laces tight and tied them.

'Stand up, Michael.'

As he stood, the wardrobe door swung open, the mirror showed him in passing, neutral colours, white skin. He looked like an old man. The driver put a hand on Tyler's shoulder. Quietly, he said, 'Listen to me, okay. Are you listening?'

He nodded.

'Whatever happens, you have to hang in there, Michael. Understand?'

Tyler thought for a moment. 'Not really.'

54

Max

MAX WAS OUT OF the door in five minutes and through Central London as the sun came up. Streetlights switched off in sequence ahead of him. Tyler's voice had been as thin as old paper, *'He wants me to tell him what I did and I don't know so he's going to take me with him.'* Then the line went dead.

Max dropped a gear, slowed and took the Vespa down a backstreet behind Hatton Garden. He had no intention of being stopped and Blackfriars Bridge was a better bet.

Even with the diversion, he pulled up outside Michael Tyler's house inside forty-five minutes. He pulled off his crash helmet and went round the side of the house. He leaned over the back gate, slipped the bolt and stepped through onto the patio. A light was on behind the curtains, but there was no movement. The patio doors clicked and slid open with a gentle pressure. A cafetiere was overturned on the floor, glass broken, frame bent out of shape. The coffee soaked into the carpet was warm to his fingertips. There was a damp patch on the sofa. Three cups, one unused. Upstairs, a floorboard creaked. Max froze, tuned into the movement, but heard nothing except the blood racing through his ears. As he trod slowly up the stairs, he heard breathing from the room on his right, then a quiet animal whimper. 'Emmy.' His voice filled the stairwell, died flat in the carpet's deep pile. 'It's Max.' The silence unfolded and he took the top three stairs in one.

Emmy Tyler's ankles, wrists and mouth were taped. A cord, tight around her neck, held her against the radiator. Max unlocked his clasp knife and cut her free, first the cord, then the black gaffer-tape. She winced. He let her pull the tape from her face. 'They took Michael,' she said, her voice breaking. 'They took him. He was crying. He didn't want to go with them.' There was a bruise on her arm, another on her cheek, dry blood caked her lips.

'We'll find him.' He helped her to her feet and across to the edge of the bed.

'I bit the man's hand,' she said, and seemed surprised at the sound of her own voice saying the words. She leaned over, grabbed the bin and was sick. She retched again, sat up and wiped her mouth on her sleeve. 'If you have to call people, that's fine, just do whatever you do. If you need fingerprints, there's the cups and the doors and...' Her eyes filled. 'I have to go to the bathroom.'

'I'm going to call an ambulance, Emmy. We'll make sure you're looked after.'

He helped her stand, asked if she needed a hand. She looked at him blankly for a moment. 'No,' she said. 'I can manage.' She put her hand out to balance herself and left a smear of vomit on the wallpaper.

Max called Denny. The local police could wait. Someone needed to be with Emmy when they came and it wasn't going to be him.

Emmy gripped the handrail tightly as she went downstairs. In the kitchen, she poured and drank three glasses of water, one after the other. 'Are they coming?' she said.

'When he called, Michael said Theobold would leave a number I could contact him on.'

'It's here.' She led him back into the living room. On the wallpaper by the light switch was a biro scrawl of eleven overwritten digits. 'That's it, the number. That man's number.'

She stood at his shoulder while he fed the number into his contacts list.

To begin with, she didn't want to talk, then gabbled for five minutes. She didn't want to stay in the living room, then she didn't want to leave it. She moved between the furniture, touching the backs of chairs, picking up photographs and ornaments, then putting them back. She stood at the door, wringing her hands. She said she might as well get ready for work. She wouldn't sit in any of the chairs they'd occupied earlier. Max brought one of the dining chairs into the kitchen and persuaded her to sit. 'Emily, just tell me what they said.'

'I was in bed for some of it, at the beginning when they came in. They must have got in through the back, I can't see any other way, nothing's broken apart from one of the cups and the cafetiere – I ought to clean that up – should I wait until the fingerprints people have been? I suppose I should really, shouldn't I?'

'It can wait,' said Max. 'Can you remember what they were saying?'

'It was about the documents Michael gave you. He wanted to know what Michael told you and Michael couldn't remember the details, not exactly. Then it was the same questions about a journalist who'd been to our house. This house.'

'Philip Mercer.'

'But whatever Michael told them, it wasn't enough.' She closed her eyes a moment. 'I'm really tired now.' A silence. 'I remember there was a phone call while they were here. The American, he kept out of it. He can't have said more than half a dozen words the whole time. His phone went. He answered it, just said, "she wants to speak to you." Then the other one, Theobold, went out.'

Emmy drifted from him. He gave her a moment. 'What happened after that?'

'He made Michael call you, then he took me upstairs... I don't know how to say it, he was *unpleasant*. He hurt me.' Suddenly, she slumped forward. Max caught her. He half-walked, half-carried her into the living room and set her down on the sofa. He covered the wet patch with a loose cushion, swung her legs up and leaned her head back, pulled a throw from one of the armchairs and put it over her. 'He said Michael killed the man he worked for.'

'He didn't. You have to put that out of your mind. It's a game he plays. He lies, makes people feel like they're the ones that did wrong. Whatever he said, it didn't happen.'

She pulled her knees to her chest and the throw over her shoulder. 'That's good.'

Mercer's *Freemedia* site ran a series of stories under the banner headline *'STATE SECURITY AND GOVERNMENT CORRUPTION'* Within two short paragraphs, it named Theobold as a corrupt official, a money-grabbing consultant paid by the government to do a job, at the same time taking hundreds of thousands in backhanders from global security company, ID International. It went on to name Creedy and Lillico as complicit, themselves corrupt and in receipt of sweetener payments. Hannah Rees was singled out as IDI's fixer-in-chief who sanctioned Theobold's violation of UK law in the name of profit.

So far, so good. Max scrolled down. Tyler's only working PC had an ancient mouse that made any kind of cursor movement either pointless or wildly extravagant. He clicked in the text and back-arrowed to the paragraph about Derek Labrosse. It used the lines from the emails verbatim, but then blew it, alternating between unsubstantiated conspiracy theorising and varying shades of hysteria.

Max clicked a link. *SayNo2ID* featured the same story, the more extreme ravings toned down. Better. He spent the next few minutes navigating half a dozen sites, all of which had an angle on the story. As he searched, the loading time of each site slowed. He clicked back to the previous site. It went down as he hit the home page. He searched the mainstream newspaper websites. The first clean hit came from Gwyn Williams in the *Guardian*. A headline on the home page ran *UK PLC GOES BLIND INTO SURVEILLANCE AGE*. They'd bought it, but the angle was of another government IT systems failure. No mention of Theobold or Creedy. Only what they could verify, thought Max. It would take more than Mercer's ravings. He clicked around the other broadsheet news sites, BBC News, Sky News. For now, nothing. He logged off. In the blank screen's reflection, he saw Emmy behind him.

She'd dressed in jeans and a sweatshirt. A little make-up took most of the colour from her swollen lip. 'When are the police coming, the other police?'

'Detective Constable Denny's on her way over, she'll deal with it.'

'Shouldn't you call them – scenes of crime people or something? People who can help look for Michael. I should have thought time is of the essence.'

Max shook his head. 'I'll find him.'

'I want a proper investigation, a proper enquiry.' She pushed her hair behind her ear. 'These people broke into my house. They hurt my husband and they hurt me.' Her voice rose as she came closer, he saw the bruise under her foundation. 'That man made my husband say goodbye to me.'

She looked at him as if there was more to say, but walked out. Her bedroom door closed.

Max went to the window. A steady stream of commuters headed for the station. Denny's car pulled up in the drive. She looked around, then made her way up to the house. Max doubted he'd ever been more pleased to see her.

As they stood talking in the hallway, Emily Tyler appeared at the top of the stairs. She made her way down slowly. Denny stepped forward. 'Mrs Tyler, Maggie Denny, we met before – at the hospital.' She offered her hand. Emily ignored it.

'I want the police, not you people.' She went through to the kitchen.

Max checked his watch. 'I've got a call to make.'

'You think you can persuade him?'

'You ever hear of a debt collector who changed his mind?'

He walked to the end of the garden and made his first call. A sleepy Philip Mercer answered. 'Phil, this is Max. I saw the stuff online this morning. So did Patrick Theobold.'

'That was the point, part of it anyway.'

'Look, Phil, I'm at Michael Tyler's house. There's no easy way to put this, you need to get lost. For your own good. Theobold and his buddy have taken Michael Tyler for a ride. As of now, I don't know what their intentions are, only that they're not good. I want to make sure you get clear. You'll need your car and passport and the cash.'

'Shit.'

'What did you expect, Phil?'

'A bit more time if I'm honest. You want me to come now?'

'I'm busy here. Just get to your office and stay there. I'll drop by later, pick you up and we'll go get the car.'

'Sure, sure, what time?'

'Soon as I can.'

'I'll be waiting.'

Max didn't hang about. The first time he dialled it went to voicemail. He dialled again immediately. Theobold picked up. 'It's me. You left your number.'

'I'm staring at a bloody PR disaster, Lomax. Have you seen what this idiot has done with your assistance? This is years of work. It's a fucking mess and it's likely to get messier. I've got the mother of all clean-ups to deal with, starting now.'

'How do we sort it out?'

'I want the emails from the Labrosse file. Then I want every bit of information you've got, all the shit that wasn't in your case files, all the names you held back. I want names. I want people, anyone who has had access to those emails.'

'I haven't got them.'

'Get them.'

'Then you'll let Michael go?' Theobold's hesitation was enough for Max to know that wasn't part of his plan.

'Bring me all you have. Originals, no copies.'

'What if I bring you Philip Mercer?' Another silence, longer this time. Max rested his boot on a clump of baked earth, it crumbled. He kicked it into the dry bed.

Theobold came back. 'You bring me Mercer and the emails and we're done. Tyler's yours.'

Max gave him time and location and ended the call.

Denny came out. 'Max, we really need to call the locals in. Emily's insisting and she's right. And I think she needs to go to hospital. Has she showered?'

'No.'

'Good. I'll deal with it.'

Max kissed her on the cheek. As he walked through the house, he picked up his jacket and closed the front door behind him.

55

Max

THE CARS IN THE lot at Ponders End were mostly one stop from the breaker's yard. Lines of rusting Fords and crash-dented Corsas, impounded and unclaimed TWOCs picked up from the estates and backstreets of north London whose release fee from the clampers or the bother of collection outweighed their value. They were brought here for a couple of weeks to prevent them being torched on Saturday nights. In time, they would all be broken up for scrap.

Max pulled in through the gates by a paint-damaged Audi. He pulled the Vespa onto its stand. Mercer had just about given up whining. He'd kicked off at the office wanting to wait until Liz got back. 'You want her to hold your fucking hand?' said Max. 'It's your car, so come now or don't bother.' Then he'd whinged about getting back on the scooter. Max tossed him the crash helmet and started the engine.

The morning's hazy sunshine had given way to low cloud and the atmosphere was storm heavy. Max tried to call Denny, but the static charge in the air broke up the signal. He looked around the car lot, then went into the Portakabin, which doubled as a pay kiosk and CCTV hub. Half a dozen screens flicked between views from cameras high above the lot. Max took the keys to Mercer's car and dropped the old watchman a few quid to quit half an hour early. He trotted down the steps. 'This way.'

Mercer ran to catch up. 'Didn't think you'd have left it in a place like this.'

'No one nicks cars from here, this is where the dead cars go.'

'D'you know where it is?' He craned his neck to see over the rows of dusty car roofs.

The Fiesta was a hundred yards from the entrance against the back fence. Max tossed Mercer the keys. 'Your passport's taped under the glove compartment.'

Mercer got in, disappeared under the dashboard.

From the end of the row, a silver Lexus cruised towards them, kicking up a low cloud of dust. As Mercer emerged with the envelope, the Lexus stopped, blocking his exit. 'Hey fuckwit, I'm just leaving.'

Max called across. 'Phil, get in the car, shut the door and stay there. I mean it, you hear me?'

He nodded.

'Do it.'

Max sat on the Fiesta's bonnet. Theobold left the driver in the car. Tyler was in the back seat, head forward against the passenger seat headrest, his mouth moving as if he was chewing. Theobold walked around and offered his hand.

Max ignored it and gestured towards Tyler. 'What did you do to him?'

'Nothing. He's pretty much done it to himself. He's a bit upset, but that's not down to anything I've done.' He shifted, leaned on the car and balanced whilst he lifted a foot to brush off a grey film of dust from his shoes. He looked up. 'Can we get this over and done with, I think it might actually be about to rain.'

Max felt a bead of sweat trickle down his spine. Let it rain, he thought, let the heavens open and wash the shit away. 'You have to let him go.'

'What is this, some kind of cold war theme party? I'm all for nostalgia, but I want what I came for.'

'Mercer's inflicted all the damage he's capable of. Just give us Tyler and we'll go.'

Theobold's jaw tightened. 'I want *him* and I want those fucking emails. It's not open for negotiation. We agreed. This is about national security. There's a contract to deliver and people like him need to understand that there is a price to pay for playing bloody games.'

Max shook his head. 'You know what beats me, how frightened you people are. I don't fear what you fear. And I'm not scared of you.'

'I want what I came for.'

Max glanced at the driver. 'His people don't know, do they? About the codes and the bank accounts. That's sloppy work, mate. When did you realise Labrosse had done you over?'

Mercer came halfway out of the car. Max waved him back, but he kicked off. 'No, no, because it's too late, they've gone. He needs to know how fucked he is. Every website, every paper, every blogger, every fucking TV station's got copies of those emails. Networks you ain't even heard of. You are finished. I screwed you and I screwed your mates and their poxy company.'

'Of course, you did.' Theobold's hand went to his jacket. He drew a gun, levelled and fired in a single smooth movement. One shot. Mercer was thrown back against the car, a hole in his forehead like an old wax seal. The retort echoed across the yard. Mercer dropped. Part of the back of his head had gone. He lay, with one leg still in the car, a dark pool of blood soaking into the dust.

Max went for the gun. He grabbed the barrel and twisted, breaking Theobold's grip. The gun dropped. He swung the crash helmet hard and uppercut Theobold under the chin, then swept his leg around and shifted his bodyweight, throwing Theobold face first to the ground. His knee locked him down. He forced his face into the dirt and tugged his tie round, yanked it tight and held it there. Theobold choked and Max pulled tighter. He glanced up. The driver was out of the car. Behind him, Tyler's face was white against the window. Max heaved harder on the tie. The driver's kick knocked him back, his head hit the Fiesta's radiator and he blacked out.

Max came round on his arse in the dust. There was rain on his face and blood in his mouth. The driver had cut Theobold's tie and he lay gasping and spitting dirt between each shallow breath. 'I'll kill you,' he wheezed.

The driver speed-dialled and turned his back. The conversation was over in seconds. He reached down and picked up the gun, wiped off the dust and checked the magazine. Max looked up as Theobold lifted himself to his hands and knees. It was as far as he got before the driver shot him in the back of the head.

Rain hit the cars hard. It bounced off the metal. A noise like drumming.

The driver opened the Lexus's boot and spread out a plastic sheet. He picked up one of Theobold's feet. 'Help me out here, will you?'

Max pulled himself up and grabbed the other foot. Together, they dragged the body through the mud, his jacket rucked up his back. They rolled him in the plastic and lifted him into the boot. The driver slammed it shut. He opened the rear door. 'You need to get out now, Michael. Sergeant Lomax is taking you home.'

Tyler eased himself out of the car. He had trouble straightening up. In seconds, the rain plastered his hair and his clothes hung limply on his body. His hands shook and he hugged himself. 'What happens now?'

'Come on,' said Max. He took his elbow and steered him down the line of cars towards the entrance. The Lexus passed them slowly, its tyre tracks washed away by the rain.

In the kiosk, Max made a call to the police at Enfield. He told them to find Chief Superintendent Rothwell and tell him Philip Mercer, a freelance journalist, had been shot dead in a car lot in Ponders End. He watched the monitors as the cameras flicked across the lines of parked cars, switching angles at fifteen second intervals. A camera focused on a white Fiesta, with its door half open. Max froze the image, zoomed in on Mercer for a moment. He stared, then switched the camera off. He opened the recorder, pocketed the disk and erased the afternoon's footage from the machine's hard drive. He took a set of keys for a knackered Ford Mondeo and drove Tyler home.

September 2006

56

Max

Covent Garden was nothing like as crowded as it should have been, even for a drizzly Sunday in September. Max downed a scotch in the upstairs bar of the Punch and Judy. He watched a street performer set up her props on the wet cobbles then made his way along Henrietta Street, turning right through the gate into St Paul's churchyard where Liz waited. She pulled her raincoat belt tight. He shoved his hands in his jacket pockets and went to meet her, eyes down.

'Hope you didn't mind coming into town,' she said. 'I had a meeting with Jonathon in Piccadilly and it just seemed best.'

'On a Sunday?'

'Over lunch. That a problem?'

'Yeah, well, I'm not exactly run off my feet at the moment.' She gave a puzzled look.

'Kilby's tossing up what suits him best. The final decision is his. Keep me on and feed me to the review committee or shove me out on the quiet. Until then, I'm on gardening leave.'

He'd been back for a few days to brief Rothwell, newly installed as Commander, Special Operations and Kilby's right hand. He'd pleaded Denny's case, but it was a waste of breath. Rothwell made positive noises then transferred her anyway. Max was instructed to vacate the office a day later, once he'd signed a series of documents binding him to silence. That was three weeks ago.

They walked up to St Paul's church. Max hadn't been inside a church in a long time. He sauntered half a pace behind Liz, reading the inscriptions on memorial stones set into the walls. He ran his finger around a 1914-18 war memorial which listed five names and was dedicated to *The Fallen*.

'Do you want to talk then?' He took a pew near the back.

Liz squeezed past. She sat down and undid a couple of buttons on her raincoat. 'I was at Phil Mercer's funeral last week. His family don't accept the official version of what happened. They've asked Jonathon to press for an inquiry.'

'They're wasting their time.'

'Are you saying that because you set him up?'

Max leaned forward. 'I didn't plan for him to get shot.'

'But you knew he might.' She shook her head.

'No, I didn't. Phil wouldn't keep his mouth shut. Theobold worked himself into a state and lost it. Is this why you asked me here?'

'His mum calls every day, asking what I'm doing about it. She's lost her son, so you tell me, what do I tell her?'

'Tell her he died doing something he believed in, that usually goes down well.'

'Fuck off.'

'I don't know, tell her straight. Say he died because you and Jonathon filled him with unrealistic expectations of what one bloke, a laptop and a network of nobodies can do. Or that he died because he'd lived in a virtual world so long that he didn't know what a real lunatic with a real gun was capable of.'

She stood up and edged past, shoving him back in his pew. 'You set him up. You're responsible. Don't lay it on me.'

Max sat in silence, staring ahead, trying to find the thoughts and words for a prayer. He wasn't surprised when nothing came.

He found Liz at the back of the church. 'Mercer was your initial link to Labrosse, wasn't he? Ruth told me. Her dissertation even references articles Mercer wrote. He went to

341

the college and delivered a seminar last year. I'm guessing that was Jonathon's doing, drumming up business with the next generation of eager politicos. Ruth says she sought him out and they spent time together afterwards. When Derek Labrosse realised the full extent of Creedy and IDI's intentions, Ruth acted as a conduit between you and Jonathon and her dad, with Mercer on a promise of publishing the outcome. You fed him, and you and Jonathon funded his work. But, of course, you're not accountable.'

He followed her out into the courtyard. She lit two cigarettes and gave one to Max. The wind gusted between the buildings and, as the rain came down harder, Liz opened a red and white polka dot umbrella, offered it to him to hold and took his arm – a matter of convenience. They walked. Liz said, 'James Creedy released a statement announcing a moratorium on any further investment in new surveillance technology. Last Thursday. They've been forced to accept that no system is ever one hundred per cent secure and there were inconsistencies in the scheme they'd put forward.'

'I heard.'

'Superficially, a redrafted proposal is out for consultation. In reality, you can hear the sound of a plug being pulled.' She steered him into a doorway. 'The virus that Phil's network created was delivered into IDI's system two weeks ago. People know, those who need to know. There's a steady stream of classified information beginning to find its way online. It's given the government all they need to call a breach of contract. IDI claimed they were one step ahead, secure systems, impregnable firewalls and the rest of it. Guarantees that were worth nothing. It suited Creedy and his cabal to believe it, but we exposed them, Max. Now we'll bury them.'

Something about her sense of triumph, the total conviction she was right, jarred with him. Even if she had it spot on, IDI would come back. If not now, soon, another way, and for as long as it was in the best interests of people like them to control information. If not Hannah Rees and David Bittman, there would be others. 'Liz, tell me, do you still believe in the rule of law?'

She dropped her arm. 'I thought you'd want to know the outcome. I thought it might make things better for you.'

'Better?' He felt like a dick holding the umbrella.

'This is coming out wrong,' said Liz. 'Can we get a drink and I can explain it properly. Please?'

In silence, they made their way down to the Strand against the heads-up tourist crowds. As they entered the Coal Hole's panelled surroundings, her mobile rang. 'It's Jonathon, I have to take this. Back in a minute.'

Max rested both hands on the bar and waited for the barmaid to work her way along. 'What can I get you?' she said.

He hesitated.

'What do you want?' The smile fell from her face.

'I don't know,' he said. 'Forget it.' There was nothing to be reconciled here, nothing he wanted. The pub door rocked on its hinges and swung back as he left.

Max turned towards the Strand, instinctively throwing a glance behind him as a dark leather-jacketed figure moved sharply before disappearing down the Savoy steps. An instant's recognition: a man glimpsed in the shadows at the end of his street. The same man who invaded his flat, tore up his books and trashed his records. The man in a blurred photo in Strutton Ground. Max took the wet steps two at a time and slipped on the last. The man Denny had identified as Saski was maybe thirty metres ahead, the gap opening. He glanced back once then broke into a trot and crossed to the river side. Max followed, jogging first then running hard. Embankment traffic fumes hit him full on and he struggled to keep up. His toes crushed in his shoes. Each pace sent concrete shocks through his knees.

He shouted, 'Dominik.'

Heads turned. But not Dominik's.

Max found another gear, closing the distance. Saski looked back. Thrown off balance, he stepped into the road. His rucksack skidded across the pavement. Cab brakes screeched. Max dragged him back by the collar. 'No roadkill, not today, mate.' He held Saski's arm and forced him, gasping for breath, against the river wall. He picked up the bag. 'This is important, right? This and whatever's in it?'

He nodded.

Max hung it over the wall, the river churning underneath. 'It goes in unless you tell me why you're following me.'

'Technically, you followed me.'

Max made to drop the rucksack, but held the strap. Saski held up a conciliatory hand. 'Okay, no problem.' He bent over, hands on his knees. 'Can we go sit?'

Max walked them to a bench. Saski pulled a pack of cigarettes from his jacket pocket and offered one to Max. They lit up. Max opened Saski's rucksack. There were mobile phones, connecting cables. A tablet. And, of all things, a written alphabetised, indexed notebook. He opened it and flicked through.

'Under M,' said Saski, 'I know they call you Max.'

There in fine black print were his credit card numbers, bank details, car insurance, licence number, NHS medical number, police service number, movements, contacts, friends, relations, social media links, what he ate, what he drank, every connection he'd made for the last six months. 'If I tear this out and sling it in the river –'

'I have a backup.'

'You know it's over, right? Whatever IDI didn't get, it's out of my hands. They'll fire me anyway.'

A look of bewilderment came over Saski's face. 'IDI?'

'Your employer.'

'I don't know these people.'

'Bollocks. Who was it? Theobold? Hannah Rees? He's dead and she's gone back to the States.'

He shook his head, 'I never heard of these people. I work for Andre.'

'Who the fuck is Andre?'

'Andre Connor. He's a big guy. In prison, they call him Bird.'

From the dim past Max remembered a proverb: *A coin dropped in a wishing well is a lifetime touching water.* 'Bloody hell, shoot me now.' He bundled Saski's bag and shoved it in his lap. 'You're working for Andre Connor?'

Saski explained with a shrug. 'In prison, you need friends or money. I have no friends, no money. So fucked, right? I cut a deal with Andre. He looks after me inside. Outside, I show him how to do credit cards, store cards, IDs, ways to make easy money, low risk. I owed a favour. After you wreck his car, he says you're his favour.'

'It's about his *car*? What does he want?'

Saski shrugged, 'He wants you fucked up. I take it easy, though. Nothing personal.'

'You broke into my flat and destroyed my record collection. That *is* personal.'

'I know a guy, in Kentish Town. He can get records.' He reached in the bag, unzipped a pocket. 'Your diary and letters. I kept them.'

Max took the diary. 'You emptied my bank account.'

'You want it back? I can sort this. Soon as I get home.'

Max nodded. 'Too right you will. What does he actually want? I mean how do we stop this?'

Saski offered Max another cigarette. 'We never talked about it.'

They sat for a long time, saying nothing. Max barely noticed Saski move away, losing himself in the crowds. He had an idea about going home and made his way towards Parliament Square, counted CCTV cameras on traffic signals, on

Hungerford Bridge, on the Ministry of Defence Main Building, on Portcullis House. He was stopped outside Westminster Tube Station. Armed uniforms checked the ID of everyone going in, searching bags and asking questions. He tried to pass and was taken to one side. He showed his warrant card and badge. When they let him go, he walked back the way he came.

He found himself leaning on the parapet of Waterloo Bridge, watching river traffic. If there was anywhere he'd find the words for a prayer it was here. The rain had stopped and the sky was a grey shade lighter. Too many times when his heart hadn't been in it, his feet had gone stumbling on, but not this time. A half-empty pleasure boat cast off from Westminster Pier and made its way downriver. Max saw it under the bridge, watched its wake settle. He was aware of someone standing next to him.

'You ever been on one of those boat trips?'

Max didn't look up. 'Yeah,' he said. 'My dad used to take me from Greenwich up to Tower Pier on Sunday mornings.'

'Lotta history on the river. Great way to see the city.'

Max turned to face him. 'I clocked you down at the station checkpoint. What do you want?'

'I was asked to find you. She wants you to have this.' Theobold's former driver held a business card between his first and second fingers. 'She wants you to contact her.'

'Why?'

He shrugged. 'It's what she wants.'

'And if I don't?'

'Just take the card, Mr Lomax. Call her.'

'I'll think about it.' Max ran his thumb over the raised black lettering then slipped the card into his back pocket. He turned and walked across the bridge, south of the river.

* * *

Acknowledgements

I'd like to thank my agent, Philip Patterson, whose backing made a world of difference at a time when it mattered most. Thanks to Ion Mills, Steven Mair, Ellie Lavender and the team at No Exit Press; Carolyn Mays, Polly Halsey, Laura Fletcher, and all at Bedford Square Publishers, for your encouragement, advice and expertise. To my friends and readers, Tina Jackson, who never stopped believing and made damn sure I didn't either; Cathi Unsworth and Rachel Malik, thank you for your wisdom and insight. Thanks to my Hull Noir partner in crime, Nick Quantrill. To Angela Hunter for permission to use the James Varda quote and to Leigh, much missed and never far from my thoughts.

To my wife, Beverlea, with love.

About the Author

Photo credit: Neil Holmes Photography

Nick Triplow is the writer of crime thriller *Never Walk Away* and south London noir, *Frank's Wild Years*. His acclaimed biography of crime fiction pioneer, Ted Lewis, *Getting Carter: Ted Lewis and the Birth of Brit Noir*, was longlisted for the CWA Gold Dagger for Non-Fiction and HRF Keating Award. Originally from London, Nick lives in Barton-upon-Humber and is co-director of Hull Noir Crime Fiction Festival.

@nicktriplow

GETTING
CARTER
TED LEWIS AND THE BIRTH OF BRIT NOIR
N I C K   T R I P L O W

Getting Carter is a meticulously researched and riveting
account of the career of the doomed genius, Ted Lewis.
Long-time admirer Nick Triplow has fashioned a thorough,
sympathetic and unsparing narrative. Required reading for
noirists, this book will enthral and move anyone who finds
irresistible the old cocktail of rags to riches to rags.

9780857303417 £19.99

www.noexit.co.uk

Bedford Square Publishers

Bedford Square Publishers is an independent publisher of fiction and non-fiction, founded in 2022 in the historic streets of Bedford Square London and the sea mist shrouded green of Bedford Square Brighton.

Our goal is to discover irresistible stories and voices that illuminate our world.

We are passionate about connecting our authors to readers across the globe and our independence allows us to do this in original and nimble ways.

The team at Bedford Square Publishers has years of experience and we aim to use that knowledge and creative insight, alongside evolving technology, to reach the right readers for our books. From the ones who read a lot, to the ones who don't consider themselves readers, we aim to find those who will love our books and talk about them as much as we do.

We are hunting for vital new voices from all backgrounds – with books that take the reader to new places and transform perceptions of the world we live in.

Follow us on social media for the latest Bedford Square Publishers news.

𝕏 @bedsqpublishers
facebook.com/bedfordsq.publishers/
@bedfordsq.publishers

https://bedfordsquarepublishers.co.uk/